LOST Treasure

DeDe Ramey

PRAISE

De Ramey's books are so authentic and beautifully written! The characters seem like real people you'd find right next door. - Shannon Miracle

Dede Ramey has brought an amazing world to her readers -Jen

Publishing Coordinator – Sharon Kizziah-Holmes
Book Design – Monica Holcomb

Paperback-Press
an imprint of A & S Publishing
Paperback Press, LLC
Springfield, Missouri

ISBN -13: 978-1-964559-33-9

DEDICATION

National Center for PTSD - https://www.ptsd.va.gov/gethelp/
K9s for Warriors - https://apply.k9sforwarriors.org/
Support for those who have been bullied -
https://www.nationalsafeplace.org/bullying

ALSO BY DEDE RAMEY

Dalton Skies Series

24 to Life
A Life Unknown
Life in the Limelight
Flashes of Life
Bring Me Back to Life

Coming Soon
A Life of Illusions-Dalton Skies book 6
Elena Shores series

ACKNOWLEDGMENTS

I would like to thank some very special people who took time to help me bring Lost Treasure to life
My editor- Michelle Fewer
My Proofreader-Karri Roden
My Sensitivity reader-Cookie McJingles
My Cover Artist- Tracie Fread
My Formatter and Publisher- Paperback Press
My Mentor- Tierney James
Author Kelly Seibold who is always willing to listen to my crazy ideas and read anything I put on a page.
And my family for supporting and encouraging me to follow my passion

EXCERPT

"In my darkest days, I thought about trying to contact you at least a thousand times. Sometimes several times a day. Because I felt like you were, honestly, the only person on earth who knew and understood the real me.

"You never once made fun of me or questioned my crazy ideas. No one, and I mean no one, ever made me feel seen the way you did. People made me question who I was, while you, you always made me feel like I had superpowers. Our bond was special. I never forgot that. Never. And I never forgot you."

CHAPTER 1

Owen Cramer listened to the sound of shuffling footsteps on the green Astroturf behind him as he stood at attention. In front of him, rows of white headstones dotted the landscape. A sight that sent chills up his spine. The smell of fresh dirt filled the air as he breathed in, trying to forget why he was there, his eyes drifting upward to the clouds filling the sky, beckoning the first drops of rain to fall.

"Fire."

He flinched as shots rang out. Once. Click, click. Twice. Click, click. Three times.

The sound of the discharge and the smell of the gunpowder filling the air brought him back to a dark place he would just as soon forget. Tears welled in his eyes. He fought to contain them, but the memories were relentless. With the first strains of the bugle's cry, they fell.

His mind replayed the events of the past few weeks. The phone calls, the arrangements, the packing, the drive. Owen had to come to grips with the fact his dad had vanished from his life like a brief gust of wind. He knew in their line of work, it was always a possibility. But it wasn't supposed to happen. He was supposed to be coming home. His time was over. The moment he received the news, Owen realized he wasn't remotely close to being prepared.

His dad was too young to die. The military had consumed him. So many memories of the man he held in the highest regard raced through Owen's mind. The loss was as powerful and as painful as a direct hit to his chest.

The flag that draped his father's casket was carefully folded and presented to his mom before the men in uniform shook her hand, then moved to his siblings, and finally to him. He saluted.

As the music ended, his mom's soft sobs were the lone sound filling the cemetery. He didn't dare look at her for fear he would break completely.

His brother Beau and sister Trish stood stone-faced with their hands clasped in front of them. It took a funeral to bring them together for the first time in more than two years. They had never been close. Both had been out of his life for a while, too busy building lives for themselves with their own families.

"Everyone, please be seated," the minister instructed as he stood. He began to talk about the bravery of Phillip Cramer, his many tours of duty, and the admirable legacy he left behind. "This was a man after God's own heart."

Owen tuned him out, his mind drifting back to his childhood. Days he would spend working with his dad in the garage he'd converted into his workshop. Whether he was building a birdhouse, fixing a carburetor, or working on perfecting some piece of electronic equipment, Owen enjoyed being with him, learning at his side. Those moments he would cherish forever, but never be able to create again.

Echoes of the minister's voice filled his head, and he briefly returned to the present. "Please bow your heads." As the minister offered a prayer, Owen's thoughts led him back in time once again. Back to the house with the yard of dark green grass and trees that were bent every which way. Back to the time when he had his sanctuary in those trees. Back to the best time of his life.

After the minister finished, he made his way to Owen's mom and shook her hand, sidestepping down the line and finally shaking Owen's hand. Behind him, more people began to line up.

Owen tried to be cordial, but he couldn't stop staring at the casket, now topped with bundles of fresh flowers. Memories of the man who'd been his hero flooded his brain, flashing like an eight-millimeter film. He wanted to make more memories with him, help him with one of his inventions, take another hike in the mountains, go deep sea fishing, or just listen to another one of his stories that always ended with a nugget of some great advice. But it wasn't meant to be.

Owen didn't just feel the loss, he felt lost.

He had always been the cautious one. Always reserved. Always quiet. He spent most of his life with massive walls erected around him to protect him from his older brother's incessant picking. His mom loved him, he knew that, but she had her hands full with three kids, and he hadn't connected with her like he had with his dad.

He was the only one who'd seemed to be able to break down the walls and give him the guidance and the reassurance he needed. They'd shared something innate in their passion for technology and their desire for order. No one else understood him.

The only other person he'd ever experienced that level of kindred spirits with was Bahn. She was his alter ego; his childhood friend. For three years they were practically inseparable.

Then, in the blink of an eye, she was gone.

She was never far from his thoughts though. He'd gotten a glimpse of her only once since she'd disappeared from his life. It was an unexpected encounter, and she didn't even know he was there, but it left him feeling confused and disillusioned.

Today he needed her. Needed to hear her snarky comebacks. Needed to know there was someone out there for him.

When the last few people filed out from underneath the white awning, the family slowly dispersed, heading to their cars. Glancing back, he watched Beau prop his baby daughter, Sadie, up on his shoulder, while Trish wrapped her arm around his mom. He wanted to be a part of their world. But he wasn't.

While people streamed by as they approached their cars, Owen continued to think back to the days when he was young. When he could crawl up in his treehouse and escape. He needed it now, when it seemed like a fog had blanketed everything around him.

He could hear his young nephew jabbering behind him and felt his warm touch as his tiny hand slid into his palm. Moments later, Beau asked him to hold Sadie as he buckled the carrier in place for the drive.

Owen carefully cradled the baby in his arm and stared down at her as she cooed. The little boy's hand suddenly jerked free, and

Owen's eyes darted to make sure he was safely back with his dad before returning his attention back to the baby he held. Out of all the sadness, he couldn't help but smile as he took in all of her cherubic features. Her chubby fingers latched on to one of his and she tried to drag it to her mouth. Beau turned, gently gathering her into his arms to lock her into her seat for the ride home, and Owen felt a strange loss from the short connection they'd made.

He rubbed the back of his neck as he shuffled to his car, his throat tightening from the emptiness consuming him and the envy it evoked toward the life his brother had.

Approaching his old blue Honda, he plunged his hand in his pocket in search of his keys. The door groaned as he wrenched it open, the heat baking the insides spilling out. Already feeling beads of sweat on his neck, he decided to shed his heavy military jacket. As he unbuttoned it, he scanned the people getting into their cars— very few of whom he recognized—stopping when his eyes found someone in the distance who appeared to be staring back at him. She was too far away to see clearly, but something about her seemed familiar. The way she had her hair pulled back, and its deep honey color, pricked his memory.

His fingers paused on the last button as he tried to get a better view, his heartbeat ticking up as he narrowed his gaze, peering into the distance.

"Nah. It couldn't be."

Shaking his head, he popped open the last button and shrugged out of his jacket, leaning into his car to lay it on the passenger seat. When he glanced up again. She was gone.

When her mom called with the news of his father's passing, something deep inside told Bahn Jackson she needed to be there for Owen. And come hell or high water, she was going to make it happen.

It was May. School had ended for the year, and she had a few days before she had to be back to clear out her classroom. The only problem she faced was figuring out where the money for the flight would come from. It wouldn't be cheap. She'd saved some money over the past few months, but using it would wipe her out, cutting into the funds she needed to attend a conference at the end of June she'd already signed up for.

Giving herself a moment to weigh her options, she ultimately decided to follow her heart over her bank account and pulled out her laptop. Scanning the flights between Eugene, Oregon and Gulfport, Mississippi, she booked her flight and hotel, then sat back on the sofa with her head against the cushion.

Thoughts of her childhood had a smile tugging at the corners of her mouth. She could still see his bright blue eyes with those long dark eyelashes and that crooked smile he sometimes wore. As a wave of excitement filled her chest, she grabbed a notepad to make a list of things she needed to do before she left.

Multiple layovers had made for a long flight, but it wasn't horrible. She spent a portion of her trip talking about the upcoming basketball season with a wonderful older gentleman who was flying home from a work trip. The rest she spent reading a Tierney James novel. Luckily, she got a window seat, so she didn't have anyone reading over her shoulder.

After stopping to pick up her rental car, she headed to Biloxi. It was late when she arrived, and she was exhausted, but she couldn't help but smile as she passed some of the places that were part of her childhood. Her school where she played basketball. The little burger place with the best burgers.

She pulled into a spot on the edge of the beach and got out. The sound of the waves collapsing against the shore immediately sent a calming rhythm to her heart. Closing her eyes, she pictured her and Owen walking along the beach searching for shells and treasures. The memory was so vivid, she could almost hear their voices. Her heart became heavy as she remembered what she was there for, and she quickly made her way back to her car.

Arriving at the church she'd attended as a child, she watched the line of people streaming in as she exited her car. Memories of the little boy with dark wavy hair and wire rimmed glasses flooded her mind once again. A lump clogged her throat, and she paused her steps as she felt a tear slide down her cheek. Wiping her eyes, she lifted them once again to the opened doors. He was in there. He needed her, but not like this. She had to be strong for him.

Tugging at the car door, she decided it would be better if she just attended the graveside service. Hopefully, she could get her emotions under control by then. That was wishful thinking.

Owen was visiting with a few people under the awning when she caught her first sight of him, and she let out an audible gasp seeing him in military dress blues. She stared in disbelief. Was that really him? Her stomach swarmed with butterflies, taking in his guarded movements.

As people gathered, spilling out around the large white tent, Bahn took her place in the back. She'd attended military funerals before. She knew what to expect. But as the gunfire rang out, her heart plummeted at the finality. At the loss of the man she knew and the devastation she knew Owen felt. Closing her eyes, she took several deep breaths hoping to stave off the tears, but it was useless. *Why is this so hard?*

As the service ended, she stepped in line to offer her condolences. Her mind played through what she wanted to say, but the minute she saw Owen up close—standing with his hands clasped in front of him, tears glistening in his eyes—all thoughts escaped along with every ounce of air in her lungs. Panic flooded in. Her eyes darted to the people around her, and she stepped away. She couldn't bring herself to talk to him.

Wandering across the cemetery on the way to her car, her eyes caught the names on a few of the headstones as she swiped at the tears still falling. She stopped and let her attention drift back to the gravesite where everyone was dispersing. Scanning the faces, she found Owen holding the hand of a little boy, a baby cradled in his other arm. *Wait, is he married? Did I miss seeing his wife?*

She watched as the little boy ran to another man and Owen handed the baby off to a man, who had to have been his brother, before walking away. As he shed his jacket next to an old, beat-up, blue sedan, it was like he sensed her watching him. His eyes lifted and fixed on her, and he stopped. She was frozen in his gaze. Her body tingled, and suddenly fear gripped her again. A thousand thoughts ripped through her mind. *What if he wants to talk to me? I can't let him see me crying.*

He dipped his head to place his jacket in his car, and she quickly stepped behind a tree, waiting for him to drive away before continuing to her car.

Geez, what is wrong with me? Her head tipped back, pressing against the headrest of the car as she continued to wipe the tears from her cheeks. Finally, pulling out in line with some of the other cars continuing to slowly exit the cemetery, she headed for her hotel.

She wanted to offer her condolences to his family, but the moment she laid eyes on Owen, her heart broke, and she couldn't bring herself to confront him. He looked so handsome in his uniform, something she never dreamed she would see him dressed in. His eyes were still the prettiest shade of blue, even from a distance. But the haunted look he carried in them split her heart in two. She knew how close he was to his father and couldn't imagine what he was going through.

Her mind battled with her desire to see him and her fear. Fear. Something she was never known to have. She'd always considered herself fearless. Why it had crept into her psyche now was a mystery.

Driving into the hotel parking lot, she found a spot. Lingering with the engine running, she tried to decide if she should stay or pack up and head to the airport. Staring off at the waves in the distance, she wondered what was causing her to be so scared. *I'm here to give him moral support. What's the worst thing that could happen? What if he's married? Mom would have told me if he'd gotten married. Wouldn't she? I know she's talked to his mom. It would have come up.*

Her mind made up, she threw her car in reverse, took a deep breath, and pulled out.

CHAPTER 2

Driving to his parents' house, Owen barely recognized the town where he spent several years of his life. Though his family had moved a few times, this place always felt like home. Newer buildings lined the streets, along with vacant lots left behind by a vicious storm that had brought the town to its knees.

Occasionally, he saw places that took his mind back. The skating rink where his sister broke her arm while attending a friend's birthday party. The baseball field where his brother used to play his games. Memories of afternoons sitting on hard metal bleachers in the scorching sun, slathered in sunscreen, eating salty soft pretzels with mustard, flashed through his thoughts.

He'd been back to the town a few times since his mom and dad had moved back, but this time was different. This time the old places stood out. Each one he passed held meaning, and he could recall the memories vividly. Burger Hill Drive-in was still there. They had the best hickory burgers in town. The patty was perfectly seasoned and had crisp edges. The buns were buttered and toasted. And the secret hickory sauce, on top of a layer of sweet onion, made it perfect. *I wonder if they still make them.*

He slowed as his parents' place came into view. Cars lined both sides of the street and people stood out on the front porch, talking. Parking his car up the street, he took the steps by two, nodding as he entered the modest house into a sea of strangers. He heard a multitude of conversations, catching only a snippet of each, mainly memories people had of his dad. He shook hands with several men clad in their dress blue uniforms—coworkers of his dad who were there paying their respects—and he briefly listened as they shared their stories.

His mind raced from the roar of the voices. Searching the crowd for a familiar face, he finally caught a glimpse of his mom. She was visiting with a woman he didn't recognize.

Weaving through the throngs of people, he drew closer to her and noticed how she'd aged in just the past few days. He could see the dark circles under her eyes from lack of sleep and tears shed. Though she smiled as she spoke, he knew she was in pain.

Closing the distance, he caught her attention. She motioned for him to come closer. He dodged guests to finally get to her, and she turned and introduced him to a plump, gray-haired lady, who smelled like she had taken a bath in some flowery perfume. She was his aunt, but he couldn't remember meeting her before and, honestly, couldn't have cared less who she was. Falling back on his manners, he gave her a light hug and thanked her for coming.

He leaned into his mom so she could hear him over the din of the voices. "How are you doing?"

"I'm okay."

He knew that would be her response. It was the same one she'd given him every time he'd asked since he'd arrived.

Another woman tapped her on the arm, dragging her attention away. He didn't want to wait around to find out how he was kin to her, so he waved his hand and waited for his mom to make eye contact.

"I'll be back in a little bit. I need to get some air."

Her brows dipped in concern, but she nodded.

As he stepped away, he asked, "Do you need anything?"

She smiled, glanced quickly at the trays of food and drinks sitting on the table and countertops, and replied, "No. I think we have enough to last us for a good while."

Nodding, he made his way through the crowd, pouring himself out the door and sucking in a deep breath of fresh air once he was outside. Dark clouds continued to gather. Rain wasn't far away. Nothing new for Biloxi. Storms would roll in off the ocean, drench the area, and within twenty minutes the skies would be blue again.

He reached for his keys as he walked toward his car, wondering where he would go. He had no specific place in mind, he just needed to get away from the noise. From the people. From everything. He wished he could get away from the reason he was there.

As he cranked the key in the ignition, the car spit and sputtered, then finally started with a little coaxing. The music skipped while he flipped through the stations until he found a song he liked. With his window rolled down, he let the sea breeze fill the car.

The scent of the ocean as he headed up Beach Boulevard was one of his favorite smells. A familiar guitar lick from an old southern rock hit played. He boosted the volume and started drumming on his steering wheel.

Gazing at the scenery, he spied an old apartment complex, and the recognition of where he was caused a grin to spread across his face. Suddenly, he found himself heading up a street he knew all too well from his childhood.

The white house on Magnolia Street sat at the top of a hill on a corner lot. Leaning over the passenger seat to get a better view, he thought it seemed smaller than when he'd lived there. The house was now trimmed in navy paint, and shutters had been added to the front to dress it up. The big magnolia tree still stood in the corner of the front yard, white blooms dotting it like big clumps of snow. He always loved their smell. The pink and white azalea bushes were overgrown and about done blooming, but still added color to the front along with the two blue hydrangea bushes that flanked the stairs.

Giving in to his curiosity, he got out of the car and strolled up the driveway. As he did, he spied a sign on the corner that had been almost hidden by a couple of well-placed bushes. For sale. Since there were no cars in front of the house, and the one car garage was closed, he wondered if someone still lived there. He hesitantly walked up the steps and peered through the narrow window by the door. A smile tugged at his lips. Empty.

The hardwoods in the living room and dining area looked the same as they had when he'd lived there. Off to the right was the hallway to his, his brother's, and sister's bedrooms. To the left, a small hallway went to his parents' room.

He took off around the corner of the house where an old, rickety, cedar fence stood… barely. The latch was rusty and hard to move. He pressed down on the lever with some force, gave the fence a good tug, and it released, dragging the ground as he wrenched it open. The thick grass filling the yard needed mowing. The shrubs and rose bushes were overgrown and his mom's flower bed was filled with weeds, but it still held some faded tulips and daffodils she'd planted all those years ago.

Peeking through the sliding glass door, he noticed that the walls in the kitchen had gone from a stark white to a smoky gray, with white cabinets and trim. It looked nice. The counters were still covered with a faux marble Formica and were showing wear, but the Terrazzo floors had a nice glossy finish and looked almost new. *They weren't there before, were they?*

His eyes scanned the back of the house as he traipsed through the tall grass, his focus falling on the window on the end. His room.

He peered in. The walls were painted the same gray color as the rest of the house, except for one wall, which was a midnight blue. As he took in the empty room, his mind journeyed back, and he pictured how it used to be decorated.

Thunder rolled and his eyes jerked to the sky, gauging how much time he had before the rains came. Then, he saw it. There, at the back corner of the yard, nearly hidden by the overgrown brush and dead tree branches, a structure was tucked in the corner like a secret refuge.

He hiked out to the ladder at the base of the structure. Some boards appeared weathered, but still felt sturdy. Rung by rung, he tested each as he climbed, taking it slow in case one gave way. Pushing the trapdoor open, he lifted himself inside and looked around. The door shut with a thump, and a puff of dust filled the air as a filthy rug fell back into place.

The rug took up most of the floor space and was so dirty he couldn't make out the faded design. Rolled up underneath the window on the far side, a rope ladder lay covered in dirt and a scattering of sticks and leaves.

It had been his oasis. His sanctuary. They'd hung white Christmas lights all around the top, tacked pictures on the walls, and there was once an oversized red bean bag chair off in the corner. Funny how many memories he had, and how much the treehouse meant to him.

He could remember when they first moved there. The worry he'd harbored that his brother would claim it and not let him use it. But Beau had gotten so involved with sports, that he quickly lost interest. And Trish didn't want anything to do with it, insisting it was too dirty, and probably infested with bugs. So, it was his, and his alone.

Although that wasn't exactly true either. It was his and Bahn's. And they'd worked on fixing it up together.

Glancing out the window, the back of the house she'd lived in came into view. The rope swing still hung from the tree in the yard, but the house looked dark, just like the day she left. His chest tightened from the thought. The treehouse wasn't the same after that. There was no laughter. No treasure hunting. No games of checkers. Her energy was gone. And the treehouse became just a space for him to escape to when life got to be too much. Like today.

He leaned his head against the wall, closed his eyes, and exhaled. Thunder echoed in the distance, and as the memories came, so did the crushing pain of the current events. He longed for the days he had back then, and the people who meant so much to him. His dad had been such a rock, the one person he could always count on when life got too hard, and now he was gone. He would have to stand on his own.

The dust kicked up, scattering like glitter through the beams of sunlight coming through the window as he slid down the wall until his butt hit the floor.

Just like when he was nine, he felt the comfort of the treehouse, and he let the tears he'd been holding back since he got into town fall. His chest heaved as he began to sob and released the pain of his loss, of his uncertainty, of his loneliness.

"God," he cried out, "if you're really up there, what have I done to deserve this? Why did you take him away? He was..." Tears spilled out of his eyes. "He was the only one who understood me. The only one," he yelled. "I'm trying so hard, but I don't know if I can take much more of this. Please. I really need some help. I need things to turn around. I need things to get better. Is that too much to ask?"

CHAPTER 3

A noise from below startled him and Owen quickly dried his face with his hands, trying to regain his composure. *Maybe it's the wind.* He sat silently, hoping it was nothing, but then heard another noise and felt the treehouse shudder.

Someone was coming up.

His mind raced. *Great. Let's just add humiliation to my agenda for the day.*

He remained quiet as the heavy rug moved and the trapdoor opened. His heart raced, panic setting in. A glimpse of thick, caramel curls peeking through the opening rocketed him back to his childhood.

No way!

The wild curls were a shade darker, but as he caught sight of her golden skin, chills erupted all over his body. *It can't be.* Had he conjured her up just by thinking about her?

When she lifted her gaze to him, his eyes narrowed, and a knot lodged in his throat as he took in her features. There they were. Those amazing gold and green eyes. It was her. But how?

"Bahn?" he questioned, his voice barely audible as his mind continued to process whether she was actually there.

She wore a long, loose-knit, gray sweater with oversized sleeves and a pair of black fitted pants with black flats. Her hair was secured by a pastel multi-colored scarf, tied at the nape of her neck. She was so beautiful, he found himself breathless.

Gazing directly at him, she lifted the corner of her rose-colored lips. "Yeah. Hey," she said nonchalantly, letting the door drop and waving the dust away. "I was just in the neighborhood. Thought I would stop by." A piece of her hair dropped to the side of her face. She noticed it and let out a puff of air, trying to move it away, but shrugged when it refused.

He chuckled and shook his head. Feeling the burn behind his eyes, he leaned his head against the wall and turned his gaze away, back out the window, still trying to reconcile that she was there.

She scooted over next to him, pulled her knees to her chest, and dusted her pants off. He peeked at her, and she caught him, giving him a playful nudge, obviously trying to lighten the mood. "So," she drew out the word, "how ya doin?"

The feeling of her next to him somehow simultaneously excited and calmed him. Closing his eyes, he took a breath and said, "Not great, actually," then turned his gaze to her before dropping it to the floor and marking the dust with his shoe.

A slight smile crept over his lips. "But things are looking up." He let his eyes settle on her. "I can't believe you...you're here. I was just thinking about you today. I feel like I'm in some kind of crazy dream. Good crazy," he added after a minute.

Her eyes widened and she took in a deep breath and smiled. "Whew. For a moment there, I thought I'd made a huge mistake coming here."

He chuckled quietly. It felt like the clouds were starting to part.

"But seriously," her voice softened, and she put her hand on his leg. "I'm so sorry about your dad, Owen. I know how much you loved him."

The comment stung, but the touch of her hand somehow eased the pain. "Yeah. It was just so unexpected. He was done with the job. They were waiting for their flight out."

"How's your mom doing?"

"About as good as expected. She's got a house full of people right now."

Bahn leaned in and peered over him to the yard below, just as she had a thousand times before when they were young. Owen's breath stalled in his lungs. The fresh smell of her soap and the view of her curves, currently splayed across his midsection, awakened his body, and he quickly sat back.

Gazing back at him, she smiled and chirped, "My swing! It's still there!" Her eyes darted below again. "I wonder if it could hold me now."

His eyes focused on her, and a wry grin spread across his face. "Pay ya a dollar to sneak down there and try it." It was like they were nine years old again.

"Looks like the place is empty." She shook his hand. "So, game on!"

He unfurled the homemade rope ladder and let it drop into the yard next door, clamping the hooks on the window frame. Bahn backed out of the window and carefully made her way down.

Looking through the sliding glass door of the house from a distance, she yelled back, "Yep. Empty." She dusted the seat of the dirty white disk, but the embedded grime didn't budge. The seat jiggled as she lowered herself down, and when she gently pushed off with her feet, the tree branch above swayed and the swing went with it.

Tufts of her hair moved in the breeze. Owen couldn't take his eyes off her. It was like she was moving in slow motion. He chewed on the corner of his lip while he watched her. *Damn she's gorgeous.* With her legs crossed tight, she balanced herself, and slowly let go with her hands. Letting out a high-pitched squeal of excitement, she quickly grabbed the rope again and leaned back to gain speed. A chuckle bubbled up in his chest and it felt good...really good.

She closed her eyes, and he pictured the fearless little girl he once knew. One more push, then she let the swing come to a stop. Her leg swung over as she moved off the disk and dusted her bottom. Staring up at the window, she grinned, and he locked his gaze on her.

Her eyes narrowed, and she pointed up at him. "You owe me a dollar."

He smiled, because he knew she would hold him to it. He was good for it. Letting out a breath, he realized it was the first time he had felt genuinely happy in a long time.

She made her way back up the rope ladder and into the treehouse again. "You know, I swear that window used to be bigger." As she sat down beside him, she continued to dust herself off. "That is one very well-built swing... And one very sturdy tree." They both laughed. "Now, that is what I've been waiting to hear," she said as she slapped him on his leg.

The touch of her hand sent a jolt of electricity through him, and he swallowed hard.

"Geez, you're still a nut. You still aren't scared of anything, are you?"

"Nope, not much. And I bet you still are!"

"Not as much." He paused. "I think I've gotten better." Pausing again, he added, "Maybe. Eh, who am I kidding?" His gaze drifted off. "You should have seen me when I heard you coming up the ladder," he said, his voice rising with embarrassment. "I was mortified. I just knew it was some kid whose parents were looking at the house. I had the whole scenario worked out in my mind." He motioned with his hands. "I could see the cops cuffing me and taking me away."

Bahn busted out laughing. "You always did jump to the most insane scenarios."

"Well, who would have ever thought it would be you? I mean, you were the last person I thought would be coming through the hatch."

"I guess you got me there."

He studied her for a moment, shook his head again, and turned away. "I still can't believe you're here." He turned back to her. "We're here. How did you know?"

"Know what?"

"Know where I was."

Bahn paused for a moment. "Well, my dad heard about your dad. Your dad is kind of a big deal, you know. Word travels fast. Plus, our moms have stayed in touch some, I guess. Mom told me he'd passed away. I wanted to call so many times when I found out, but honestly, I didn't know what to say. When I got the information about the funeral, I decided to come. I got in yesterday."

"I didn't see you at the funeral."

"I just went to the graveside service." She turned to him. "Let me just say, for the record, I was completely shocked to see you in uniform. I mean, I seriously had to talk myself into believing it was you. Anyway, I wanted to come and give you a hug, but there were so many people, and I thought it would be better if I just stopped by your parents' house."

Owen peered at her under his lashes. "I thought I saw you, but I talked myself out of it. After all these years, I didn't believe you'd come."

"Thanks for the vote of confidence, buddy."

"No. I meant—"

She bumped his shoulder. "I was just picking on you." She rubbed her pants legs, and Owen noticed she suddenly seemed nervous. "I saw you walking back to your car holding a baby with a toddler in tow. It was very sweet.

He chuckled. "That's Beau's little girl Sadie, and Trish's son Preston, I—" He stopped and cocked his head. "Wait. I get how you knew to go to the cemetery, but how did you know I came here?"

"That was honestly a complete coincidence. On my way to your parents' house, I decided I would swing by our old neighborhood. When I passed your house, I saw the blue car out front and remembered seeing you with it at the graveside service, so I stopped. I thought you might be looking around. When I didn't find you around the house, and saw the treehouse still here, I had to check it out."

"Pretty much the same thing I did. I was at Mom and Dad's house, and there were so many people I just couldn't deal with it. When I left, I headed to the beach. Passed those old apartments we rode our bikes to. The memories hit, and I just had to come by.

"I've never had a chance to see the place since Mom and Dad have been back. I would have never thought the treehouse would still be standing." He leaned forward and stood up. "I can remember the first day we got here." He dusted his pants and walked to the door. Pushing it open, he stepped out on the balcony, and, testing the sturdiness, carefully leaned up against the railing. "It was about this same time of year, because we moved right after we got out of school."

Bahn followed suit and joined him on the balcony.

"I hated moving," he said emphatically. "Not that I liked living in Texas, it's the fact that I had just gotten used to living there, and we moved again. But when I saw the treehouse from the back door, the minute I stepped foot in here, I knew I never wanted to leave."

He looked back at Bahn. "The first time I saw you, you came out that door," he pointed, "and started swinging on the swing. I can remember everything about that day."

CHAPTER 4

❖

Seventeen years earlier

The sun hit directly at eye level as the bulky U-Haul carefully maneuvered past cars in front of cookie cutter houses. Owen's father pulled the visor down, but to no avail. The sun still blinded him, and he sat up straighter, trying desperately to find relief.

Owen sat quietly in the passenger seat, staring out the dirty side window so he wouldn't be blinded like his dad. His dark, wavy hair framed his pink cheeks, currently dotted with droplets of sweat. Wire-rimmed glasses framed his crystal blue eyes, accented even further by the dozen or so amber freckles scattered across his nose.

Leaning over, he glanced into the large rearview mirror to check on his family's old van following behind them, then returned his gaze to the window, watching house after house, each one like the other, pass by. It was an all too familiar sight. They had moved two times in the past six years. He'd hoped it would at least be better than the last place they lived, but from the looks of the houses, figured it was going to be more of the same. His dad said he'd found a great place that Owen would love, but he didn't hold out much hope. At least school was out for the summer, and this place sat close to the beach.

The brakes screeched against the weight of the truck as it came to a stop before turning down Magnolia Street. Crepe myrtles canopied the road and scattered their pink blooms along the asphalt. They swirled like a kaleidoscope of butterflies as the U-Haul rolled by. Owen had to admit, this street seemed nice.

The truck began to slow. "Owen." Hearing his name had his eyes shifting to his dad who spoke for the first time since they'd driven into the neighborhood. "Look for twenty-nine hundred. If I remember correctly, it'll be on your side."

Staring intently at the house numbers, he began reciting the number in his head. *Twenty-nine hundred. Twenty-nine hundred. Twenty-nine—*

"There it is." His dad pointed. "It's on the corner."

Owen was underwhelmed. Another white, nondescript house.

His dad pulled the truck around the corner, stopped, and turned the engine off. Hopping down from his lofty seat, he stretched for a moment before making his way to the passenger side of the truck to make sure Owen got out okay.

Standing slightly above six feet, Owen's dad towered over him. Like Owen, he had a lean frame and dark brown wavy hair, his with a sprinkle of gray at the temples, and glasses.

Owen and his dad rounded the corner to the front yard of the house just as the rest of the family was exiting the van. Patting his pants then plunging his hand deep into the right front pocket, his dad pulled out two keys on a small key ring and held up his prize.

As his dad turned the knob to their new home, Owen wondered what his new life would be like. The anticipation of something different, something exciting, was doused when he saw the same plain white walls and wood floors, this house closely resembling his house before. Second verse, same as the first.

Beau chose a bedroom in the far back corner of the house, and his sister Trish chose the one next to it. That left Owen with the room across from them. A room of his own. At least that was a happy surprise. In the previous house, he and his brother had shared a bedroom, which gave his brother ample opportunity to pick on him.

He was the polar opposite of his brother. Where Owen had dark hair, blue eyes, and was on the lanky side, Beau was stocky, with dirty blond hair and brown eyes. And while Beau was always involved in sports, and Trish was into art and had recently started cheerleading, Owen—like his dad—was more interested in technology. He had never felt like he was part of his sibling's world.

He made his way to the sliding glass door that opened to the backyard and spied something peeking out of the trees. There, in the back corner of the yard, perched in the branches of a massive tree, was a large structure. He hollered for Beau and Trish a few times, then gave up and darted across the deep green grass.

Reaching for the first rung, he quickly climbed the ladder and pushed open the trapdoor into his home in the trees. Except for where it wrapped around the tree, securing it tightly to its pedestal, the massive loft was completely enclosed. Wooden closures with braces created pop-up windows in four spots. A door on one side opened to a balcony that spanned three sides of the structure. A few empty soda bottles still littered the floor, along with an old, broken, plastic chair left by the previous occupants. In the center of the room, a single bulb with a push button hung from the ceiling.

Owen walked around the room, looking out every window, then ventured out to the balcony. He smiled. He could already imagine the time he would spend in his new place. The wind picked up, making the treehouse creak, and he returned inside to gaze around the room, visualizing what he needed to make the place perfect.

As his thoughts drifted, he heard a thump, and then felt a shimmy that drew his attention back to the room. The trapdoor flew open, and Beau shoved his way in. Owen's heart sank because he knew he would again be pushed aside, and probably never allowed in the treehouse again.

Checking the view out one of the windows, Beau commented, "Wow, you can see right into that house over there."

Owen hadn't even noticed earlier, so it made him curious. He turned his attention back to the window and dropped his gaze to the house below.

The sliding door opened, and a girl about his age bolted over to a tree swing. Her hair was shiny caramel curls, pulled back with a brightly colored band that barely held it into place. She wore cut-off denim shorts with a neon floral tank top and flip-flops.

Grabbing hold of the rope attached to the tree, she plopped down on the disk seat and began to swing. Owen couldn't quit staring. He'd never seen anyone like her.

Beau's voice carried, and with a tilt of her head, her eyes captured

Owen's. Her feet hit the ground as she tried to stop the swing, and Owen ducked behind the wall of the treehouse. After a moment, he crept closer to the window to see if she was still looking. She stood in the yard with her hands on her hips, staring straight up at the treehouse, and she locked eyes on him again.

"Beau, Owen, let's go," their mom yelled from the house, rallying the troops. Owen and Beau glanced out the opening, realizing their fun had ended. Their mom stood on the back porch with her hands on her hips. Her sandy blonde hair, that had at one time been pulled up in a slick ponytail, had fallen, the strands blowing in the breeze.

Owen peeked in the neighbor's yard once more, but the girl was gone. As they climbed down the ladder, Beau began rattling off items he needed to furnish the treehouse, but Owen barely heard him. His mind still held the visual of the girl.

Their mom met them at the door. "You guys need to help your dad get some of the stuff unloaded so we can at least make camp tonight. There should be some sleeping bags and pillows in one of the storage tubs."

Right on cue, their dad came through the living room with an armload of boxes. "What'd you think of the surprise?" he asked, smiling as he dropped the boxes in the corner.

"It's huge," Beau stated, motioning with his hands. "Can I sleep there tonight?"

Owen followed his family as they exited the house to grab more items out of the truck that was now backed partially up the driveway.

"Let's focus on getting stuff unloaded for right now. We can discuss where we're going to sleep later, once we find something to sleep on," their dad stated as he climbed the ramp into the rear of the truck to retrieve boxes to hand off.

He leaned down to give Owen a nondescript tub just as a tall, Black man rounded the corner of the house. Behind him was a woman with long, white-blonde hair and an ivory complexion. Owen saw them walk up, and as he turned toward the house, the girl from before came around the corner. They again made eye contact, and he froze.

His dad hopped down from the back of the truck to greet the guests.

"Hey, do you need some help?" the man asked as he approached.

"I'm Alex Jackson. I live in the house behind you."

"We'll take any help we can get. We'd planned on getting here earlier, but I've learned the hard way to never make plans when you're moving, they're bound to change."

Owen's mom, sister, and brother exited the house. "Phillip Cramer, by the way." His dad extended his hand and Alex obliged. "This is my wife Carissa, our boys, Beau and Owen, and our daughter Patricia." He pointed at each as he introduced them.

"This is my wife Vanessa," Alex returned, "and our daughter Siobahn." He put his hand gently on his daughter's head. "She said she saw someone up in the treehouse, so we decided to come investigate. The Clarks moved away a few months ago. They had a daughter named Joanie that Bahn was friends with." He made eye contact with his daughter—like a silent acknowledgement that he knew how she felt about her friend moving away—before looking back up. "It's good to have you guys in the neighborhood."

While the adults got acquainted and Beau disappeared into the house with boxes, Owen and the little girl—who he'd now learned liked to be called Bahn—remained silent, shyly catching glances. He couldn't help himself. He was completely enamored by her appearance. And now that he saw her up close, he was held captive by her green and gold flecked eyes. She fascinated him.

"Owen," he heard a voice say from inside the truck.

Turning, he quickly ran up the ramp, taking a stack of boxes from his dad. He headed down the ramp, trying to balance the boxes blindly. Just as he hit the bottom, he swayed, and the top box began to fall. He wobbled back and forth, trying desperately to regain the balance, to no avail. The box tumbled, and Owen watched as Bahn dove in for the save. Placing the box back on top of the pile, she did a victory dance like she'd just saved the football game. Owen gave her a sheepish smirk.

The sun began to set and dressed the sky in vibrant purple and orange as Owen's dad loaded him down with a few more boxes. Carissa emerged from the house. "Phillip, it's nearly seven, and the kids are getting hungry. Do you want me to run to the store and grab some sandwich stuff?"

Vanessa piped up, "Oh, there's a great burger place right up the street. Why don't I go get some, and you guys can come over and have dinner with us. The last thing you want to do is get on the road again." She turned to get an agreeing nod from her husband.

Phillip wiped his brow with his sleeve. "We don't want to impose on you guys. You've been such a huge help already."

Alex waived a dismissive hand. "No. It's done. It's no trouble."

"Okay then," Phillip agreed. "We'll meet you in, say, twenty minutes?"

"Sounds great. See you then."

"Make sure you dust yourself off before you go in," Carissa instructed as the kids started into the Jackson's house. They took a step back and wiped at their pants a couple of times. Beau and Trish checked their hands and then entered the house.

Vanessa pointed. "The bathroom is down the hallway on the left."

The Jackson's house was nicely decorated in a beachy theme. The walls were a pale blue with white trim. The terrazzo floors in the kitchen were a myriad of blues and greens, with flecks of quartz that glittered when the light hit it. Owen thought it looked like confetti. On the table, Vanessa had laid out paper plates and napkins.

Taking a detour to wash his hands, Owen looked around and saw the door open to Bahn's room. There was no pink or frills. The walls were a blue-green color. Her bed was a mess, and the floor was littered with clothes and shoes. Tucked in the corner was some sort of aquarium, but he couldn't make out what might be in it.

In a flash, Bahn ran past him and shut the door, then turned with a sly smile and walked off.

Owen finished washing up and entered the dining room just in time to see everyone getting ready to sit down.

There were piles of fries on one paper plate and burgers on another. Alex walked up to the table. "There are regular burgers on the right"—he pointed—"and cheeseburgers on the left."

Bahn and Owen both grabbed for the same cheeseburger, and both backed away at the same time. She looked at him and motioned with her head, and he went ahead and reached for the burger again.

After dinner, Carissa helped Vanessa gather the plates and cups while the men stood and talked, and the kids snuck out the sliding door to play on the swing. As Owen exited the house, he looked up into the tree to admire his treehouse. He felt a warmth next to him and darted his eyes to see Bahn standing there. He still hadn't said a word to her.

When Carissa hollered from the doorway, "Guys, we need to get back to the house. Tomorrow is going to be a busy day," Owen turned and ran.

CHAPTER 5

Present Day

Laughter echoed from within the treehouse. "How long was it before you actually spoke to me?" Bahn questioned, still giggling.

Owen ran his finger through the dust on the floor. "Oh, it had to have been a couple of weeks. I was absolutely terrified of you."

"Why?"

He looked at her from the corner of his eye. "You were a girl."

"Yeah, but you had to have been around girls at school."

His eyes widened. "And I was terrified of them too. And you were living next to me. I'd never lived next to a girl." He paused. "I'm still afraid of girls. It's never gone away."

Bahn let out a bark of laughter. "Oh, no you're not."

He looked right at her, chewing on the corner of his lip, and nodded.

A flash lit up the treehouse, and they both jumped as the thunder boomed.

"Oh crap! We're fixing to get soaked," Bahn said, a bit of humor lacing her voice.

"I probably need to get back to the house anyway."

"Do you mind if I come too? I mean, I would like to stop by and see your mom."

"That would be great. And at least then I'll have someone to talk to."

"But aren't you scared to talk to me?"

Backing away, he tilted his head, feigning fear, and Bahn snickered.

As the first patter of rain hit the roof, Owen opened the trapdoor and crawled down the ladder. He reached up to make sure Bahn made it down safely, and when her foot slipped, he caught her.

"You okay?"

"Yeah, I think that rung was wet."

The sky opened up as they headed for the gate. Fat drops poured down and they both began to run. Bahn reached her car, and Owen hollered "Follow me."

She nodded and yanked open her door.

Owen jumped in his car and ran his hand through his hair, trying to get rid of the excess water as he eased away from the curb. Pinching his shirt that was plastered to his chest, he tried to peel it away, but it was no use. He watched Bahn in his rearview mirror and felt the heat rush to his face. *Dear Lord, I'm in so much trouble.* He couldn't deny he was attracted to her, but he knew there was no reason to act on it. Nothing would happen between them. He just hoped he would be able to rekindle their friendship.

By the time they both arrived at the house, the rain had diminished some. There were still several cars lining the street, so they were forced to park farther away. Owen grabbed his jacket from the seat, ran to her car, and threw it over both of their heads while they hurried to the house.

Shaking off the moisture as they entered, he immediately searched for his mom so he could introduce Bahn. Noticing her talking to a woman he didn't know, he absentmindedly took Bahn's hand and weaved through the remaining guests. Bahn squeezed his fingers and Owen realized what he'd done. He tried to loosen his grip, but she squeezed tighter, and a jolt of nerves shot through him.

As they maneuvered through the crowd, he locked eyes with his mom who smiled when she saw him. "Oh, Shirley, this is Owen." She wrapped her hand around his arm as she introduced him.

He gently released Bahn's hand and held his hand out to shake Shirley's, waiting for his mom to explain that Shirley was his long-lost grandma's sister's cousin's daughter, or something, but she never did. So, it was simply Shirley, from who knows where.

"Pleasure to meet you, Shirley." She stared at his outstretched hand with a strange expression. It was then he noticed he was still a bit wet and wiped his hand off on his pants, but it didn't do any good. "Sorry. It's raining pretty hard out there." He held his hand out once more, and when he didn't get a response, he let it drop, stepped back, and turned to see Bahn standing behind him. His mom didn't see her, so he gently placed his hand on her back to move her closer.

"Mom, do you know who this is?"

She looked at Bahn with a blank stare, then back at Owen for an answer.

"It's Bahn," he said with a smile.

She still seemed lost.

"Siobahn. Jackson?" He paused, noticing his mom still stared blankly. "From when we lived on Magnolia Street?"

Recognition bloomed on her face. "Oh my gosh, Siobahn! I can't believe you came." She reached over to embrace her.

Bahn gave her a distant hug. "I'm still a bit damp." She backed away, but Carissa continued to hold her hands. "How are you doing? I'm so sorry for your loss."

"Thank you. I'm okay." She paused. "Your mom and I exchange letters occasionally. She said you're somewhere in Oregon?"

"Yes. I've been there for a while now. It's beautiful."

"What took you all the way out there?"

"Well, Mom and Dad got transferred to Vandenburg, in California, and when I finished high school, I got a scholarship to a small college in Oregon. I finished my degree there, and now I'm a high school girls' basketball coach, and I teach Art."

After listening to their conversation, Owen realized he knew nothing about her. From the time they reconnected in the treehouse, he never once asked her about herself.

As she and his mom made small talk, he walked into the kitchen, poured some tea for them, and continued to listen to their conversation. Returning with the tea, he handed his mom and Bahn theirs as another unknown gentleman in uniform came up and introduced himself.

"I'm Colonel Tom Blaisdale. I understand you'll be joining our staff soon."

Owen set his tea down and stood tall at the man's introduction. He rubbed his palms together, making sure they weren't still wet, and held out his hand. "Yes, sir."

A smile spread across the colonel's face as he grasped Owen's hand firmly. "Great. I worked with your dad. He was a brilliant man and spoke very highly of you. I look forward to having you working with us."

Owen pulled his hand back but didn't relax. "Thank you, sir."

"Why don't you stop by later this week, if you have time, and I can show you around."

"Yes, sir. Thank you, sir."

Owen turned to notice Bahn looking at him, while Colonel Blaisdale reached over to grab Carissa's hand.

"Tom, thank you for stopping by," she said warmly.

Owen tipped his head, signaling he was headed outside, and Bahn gave his mom a hug before following him to the back porch.

They sat down in a pair of rocking chairs under the awning to watch the rain. Bahn turned to him as she set her tea on the table next to her. "I'm impressed."

Owen lifted an eyebrow. "At what?"

"You. You were so confident and dignified," she said wistfully, her eyes skimming him up and down. "Sorry. Just still a little thrown by the whole military thing."

"Psh..." He shook his head, brushing her comment away. "So...you flew from Oregon to be here? How long did it take you?"

"About eight hours. I had a layover in Dallas, so I grabbed some food. It wasn't bad."

"Seriously? That's... that's..." He searched for the right words, but they weren't there. "That's just so incredibly nice of you."

"Why wouldn't I? We were best friends."

Owen turned, and he studied her. "When we were like twelve. I'm sure you've made many friends since then."

"Well, yeah. I've had a few." Her delay in answering surprised him. "But honestly, I never forgot you. You were one of a kind."

He'd sometimes wondered if he was an annoyance. Their childhood friendship consisted of him constantly questioning her when she came up with crazy adventures for them to go on. But the corner of his mouth lifted as her words made a beeline for his heart. He felt the same way about her.

"We had some great times, didn't we?" He focused his eyes on the rain and lifted his tea to his lips.

Bahn perked up. "Do you remember when we found the crawdad in the drainage ditch after the rain?"

A smile slowly spread across his face. "Maybe."

"You didn't know what to think of me. I don't think you'd said a single word to me yet."

"Again, I was scared to death of you."

"I believe it." She stared out at the steady drizzle. "It had been raining off and on for days. Mom suggested I invite you over, I think to get me out of her hair. On our way back to my house, you slipped in the mud and slid down the hill into the ditch. And when I tried to help you, I slipped too."

"You lie!" he immediately responded, chuckling. "You didn't slip. You thought it was funny when I fell, so you slid down the hill."

"Slipped. Slid. It's semantics."

Owen continued to chuckle. "I remember I had mud down my pants, all in my hair, and you were caked in it. We must have *slipped* down that hill ten times before your mom came out to find us. I was so scared we were going to get in trouble. We were trying to wash the mud off with the water in the ditch, and you yelled and pulled up this, this... creature."

Bahn's mouth gaped open. "He was cute."

Owen snickered. "I don't think cute is the word I would use. He kept waving that claw at you." He leaned his head against the chair and continued to play the memory in his mind. "Your mom was always so calm about all of our adventures."

"Yeah, that woman had the patience of Job. It's a wonder we didn't give her a nervous breakdown with some of the things we did."

"We got into everything. And to think, I was such a good kid until I met you."

Bahn turned and glared at Owen and then grinned.

He checked his glass and tilted it for the last little bit of ice. "Do you want some more tea?"

"Sure, that would be great."

He reached for the glass after she took the last sip, and his hand brushed against hers. His breath caught as their eyes connected. He could tell by the shocked look on her face that she felt the same prickle of electricity that shot up his arm. He was held captive in her gaze, and something within it made his whole body ignite. Was he imagining it?

He turned and quickly disappeared inside, letting out a long breath and rubbing his forehead, trying to get the feelings he was having to go away. The ice clinked in the glasses, setting his already frazzled nerves on edge.

She's off limits.

He figured his body would get the memo at some point. So far, it hadn't.

He glanced at her through the window and caught her staring back at him with that same fire in her eyes.

Why is she looking at me that way? What kind of game is she playing?

He filled the glasses with tea and headed back out to the danger zone.

CHAPTER 6

Bahn watched as the sky continued to release large droplets of rain that splattered against the concrete like water balloons. The sound, along with the cool breeze against her damp skin, should have soothed her restless soul, but she still felt like she was on the edge of a cliff about to go over.

She had never thought of herself as being an emotional person. She was always pretty good at controlling her feelings, or at least hiding them well. Although her parents had called her a drama queen a time or two, it was usually because of angry outbursts on the court from bad basketball calls by the ref. But something about Owen had brought out feelings so strong she had a hard time containing them, even when they were kids.

Seeing Owen for the first time at the cemetery had sent a storm of emotions through her so powerful she could barely breathe. Questions fired off. Would he remember her? How would he react? The doubt and panic that had taken over, along with the profound sadness, had her running from him and rethinking her decision to see him. But hearing the pain and anguish in his voice as she'd stood under the treehouse filled her with the same desperation she had when she booked her flight. She'd needed to get to him. There was no urge to run, to escape like she had at the church and the cemetery. She needed to be with him, to hold him. And not just for him, but for her too. Because when he hurt, so did she. It was so strange. And so confusing.

Her heart and mind were in emotional turmoil as she'd tried to quickly formulate a plan while climbing the rungs. But the moment she'd pushed open the door and laid eyes on his tear streaked face, her heart had shattered into a million tiny pieces, the pain almost unbearable, and all the thoughts she'd had of the things she'd say vanished. Visions of the little boy she'd left had melded with the man sitting before her, and she froze.

Confusion had filled his face, and she'd remained silent, panic making her heartbeat thump so hard she could feel it deep in her bones. What do you say to someone you haven't seen in over a decade but still feel so connected to, someone who might not even recognize you?

But when he'd breathed her name, with so much emotion wrapped around it, all the worry and concern disappeared. In its place was a comfort and easiness she'd always felt around him. She never had to pretend with him, never had to be anyone other than herself.

It was like they picked up right where they'd left off when they were kids. Like all the years that had separated them were inconsequential. The conversation flowed, and so did the laughter. In the midst of profound sadness, she'd felt a joy she hadn't experienced in a very long time. It was genuine, effortless.

She sighed as she watched a bird splashing in a puddle at the edge of the porch and realized she missed the laidback life she'd had as a kid. Her life hadn't been as easy as she'd hoped. Goals hadn't been reached. Bucket list items hadn't been achieved. She wasn't complaining, because all in all she'd done fine, it just wasn't exactly what she'd hoped for.

Mesmerized by the steady downpour, a smile pulled at her lips as her mind wandered, recalling more moments from the past and the little boy who'd quickly become her constant companion. Moments like eating hot dogs and watermelon until their stomachs hurt then shooting off fireworks on the beach on the fourth of July. And falling asleep in the treehouse after spending hours trying to figure out their math homework.

Turning, she watched Owen through the picture window talking to another man in uniform. The sad truth was, he wasn't the same little boy she knew all those years ago, and she wasn't the same little girl. She couldn't assume he felt the same strange connection that she felt for him. They were virtually strangers. She had so much she wanted to tell him and so many questions she wanted to ask.

God, he'd changed so much. That confident swagger he now had, and the tenor of his voice that threatened to suck the air right out of her. But there were moments she could still see that sweet, timid little boy who'd been her best friend, partner in crime, and confidante for so long.

His comment about being scared of her made her shake her head and smile. She remembered how shy and quiet he was. For the longest time he'd only communicated with a nod of his head or a shrug, and she'd wondered if he'd ever actually speak to her. She'd made it her secret mission to make him talk, and when he did, it was a sweet victory. But when she made him laugh for the first time, she felt like her heart was going to explode. Much like it felt when she got him to laugh in the treehouse after she found him in tears only a few hours ago.

She loved to make him laugh. Now though, his laugh did things to her. It had a rasp to it and sat right in the middle of the register, so it wasn't too deep or too high, just right to be perfectly sexy. Which was bad.

She hadn't expected him to be so damn gorgeous. She didn't exactly know what she expected, but definitely not that. There was no question he was handsome when she saw him at the cemetery, but she was stunned when she saw him up close for the first time in the treehouse. It was a weird feeling because she saw the features of the little boy she knew—the blue eyes, the dark wavy hair, and the sprinkle of freckles—but then she noticed the defined jaw that held just a light five o'clock shadow and full kissable lips and God did he smell good. She scolded herself when her thoughts and her body betrayed her when she was supposed to be there to comfort him.

The murmuring from inside the house became louder as the storm door opened. Owen set two full glasses on the table between them before he returned to his chair, and they sat in comfortable silence sipping their tea.

Bahn leaned her head back on the rocking chair and breathed deep. "The rain smells different here."

"Oh yeah?" Owen said with a chuckle.

"Yeah, it does. It smells like sea mist. Almost salty."

"And how does the rain smell in Oregon?"

"It's hard to describe. It's like it takes tiny pieces of the leaves and pine needles as it falls and then blends it with the rocks and dirt as it hits the ground. At least that's what it smells like up in the mountains."

"I can almost smell it."

Bahn paused as the thought of it brought up a memory. "Someone got the bright idea to do a camping trip in the mountains as a team building exercise for the coaching staff. It wasn't a bad idea for those who enjoy the outdoors, and the campground we stayed at had nice bathrooms and a ranger's station just up the road that provided kayaks and supplies. It was a pretty decent weekend actually, but the planners overlooked how much it rains in the mountains in Oregon. We'd been there a couple of days before it started raining, and then rained some more. When people get cold and wet, their true personalities come out. Let's just say we had a few coaches on our staff who weren't fond of being wet."

"I'm guessing you weren't one of those people."

Bahn narrowed her eyes toward Owen. "Do you even remember me? How many times did I drag you out of your house to play in the rain?"

"Too many times to count. And it sounds like you still enjoy playing in it."

"Well, I don't make it a habit to play in the rain anymore. Mainly because it rains so much in Oregon, I wouldn't be doing much else. But being in the mountains, with nature wrapped around me, I did take a moment to just enjoy having the rain beat down on me. I'm still getting some strange looks from some of the other coaches."

"And look at us, barely reunited for more than an hour and you got me out playing in the rain again."

"Hey. I believe you have that backward. This one is on you. But you gotta take advantage of it when you can."

Owen nodded and tugged at his still damp shirt then let his eyes rest on her again. "So, you're a coach."

"Yeah."

"I guess I could ask what made you choose that career, but I remember how obsessed you were with basketball."

"Yeah. It was one of those things where you go to the college that pays you to go, in hopes of doing that thing you've always dreamed of, only to find out the WNBA doesn't think you're as good as you think you are and doesn't sign you to a lifelong contract. So, you wind up doing the next best thing."

"What made you choose Oregon?"

"It kind of chose me. The college held a career recruiting event for public and private schools from around Oregon, and my roommate and I went. We were both getting ready to graduate so we both needed jobs. We both interviewed with Cabin Creek, and they hired us on the spot. She was hired as their volleyball coach and world history teacher, and I was basketball and art."

"Yeah, I'd say that was the perfect job for you if you didn't get your dream job with the WNBA. Basketball and art. That's a combination. You always loved doodling. Do you remember the comic strip we did?"

"The Adventures of Gully and Toot? Of course. I still have some somewhere."

"You do?"

"Yeah. I remember finding a couple of the books my mom made for us in my stuff when I moved. I think she put them in there. I gotta say, they weren't too shabby."

"No. You always had skills."

"They were as much your creation as mine."

"Yeah, but you had the art skills. You brought them to life."

"They wouldn't have come to life at all if you hadn't made up the stories. Still can't believe you named the turtle Toot. Such a guy thing to do."

"Hey that's what he said his name was. I wasn't going to argue." Owen chewed on his lip, as he stared in the distance, obviously playing through the memories in his head. "Do you remember when we wrote the first one?"

"Yep. Well, sort of. I remember taking our bikes to the beach and finding the little green sea turtle that had been washed into a hole in the rocks. There was a seagull that was standing guard, and he wouldn't let any of the other seagulls near him. And then you came up with the story of how he helped him get back to the ocean and they became best friends. Now that I look back on it, he was probably just protecting his lunch."

"Don't say that. Gully would never eat Toot for lunch."

Bahn chuckled and shook her head. "Just keeping it real."

Owen laughed along with her. "Good times. I remember going back to the beach trying to find Toot and Gully. And you swore you found Toot when you and your parents went to the beach one weekend. You said he had some weird design on his shell."

"He did. He was different. He had a sunburst on his shell. He was pretty."

"I don't know if he was different or not. He was the only one I ever saw on the beach, so I had nothing to compare him to." Owen paused. "Do you have any up in Oregon?"

"I don't know. The few times I've been to the coast, I've never seen any turtles. I figure we probably do though."

"So, where in Oregon do you live?"

"Cabin Creek is about thirty minutes southeast of Eugene."

"Is it nice?"

Mulling over the answer, she finally responded, "Yeah, it's nice. Quaint. Has some cool historical buildings. The town is pretty small, so we don't have all the chain restaurants and stores. It dates back a couple hundred years, so it has that old town charm."

She wondered what else she could say about it. It was pretty and all, but after years of living there, it still didn't feel like home. "It sits in a really scenic area with rolling hills. And again, since we get quite a bit of rain, and fog, it's very green." She continued to struggle and finally said, "It's not as hot as it is here."

"Okay," Owen said, drawing out the word and raising a brow. "Do you like it there?"

She paused again as an uneasiness stirred. Oregon was beautiful. There were mountains and streams, canopied country roads and beautiful waterfalls. She'd gone to its famous beach, hiked along trails with some of the most beautiful sceneries she'd ever encountered and taken in its beautiful cities, but still, it hadn't wrapped around her heart and held her prisoner like Biloxi had. "I do. It's just... different. Nothing like here."

"This place is special, isn't it. It's grown a lot since we lived here. I was driving around earlier, and there are so many new businesses it was hard to get my bearings."

"Yeah. It seems like a lot of the old places are gone. I figure the hurricane took them out. But there's something about it that still feels like home, you know? I guess it's just..." She giggled and leaned back in her chair. "I had so many great memories here."

"Me too. I thought about that this morning when I drove past that apartment complex we used to ride our bikes to. Even that place has changed. Whoever bought it after the hurricane fixed it up. And it's not Ocean Shores anymore. It's Beachside... Beachview?" Owen looked away. "No matter what it's called now, it'll always be Ocean Shores to me."

"Me too."

His gaze drifted, a smile spreading across his face, and Bahn wondered if he was remembering the same thing she was.

CHAPTER 7

17 years earlier

Barely a month had passed since the move, and Owen had been in an all-day war with his brother that ended with their mom sending them to their rooms just to separate them. Owen had had enough of his brother's constant picking. He'd lashed out. He knew it was useless—he was no match for Beau—but it was all just too much already.

Boredom set in, so he quietly slipped out the sliding glass door hoping his brother didn't get the same idea. He climbed through the trapdoor of the treehouse and stared at the bare walls. Plopping down on the floor, he picked up a rubber ball he'd found in the corner and bounced it against the wall. This had become almost an everyday occurrence for him.

He was so excited to have a treehouse at first, but after merely a few short weeks, it had lost its luster. Sure, it got him away from his brother's taunting, but it had become boring. There was nothing to do.

He heard the rustling of leaves below the window and knew Bahn was swinging. He dropped his arms on the windowsill and sat, silently watching her. She pushed off and began to spin. As she twirled around, her eyes met his and she smiled. When the swing began to slow, she slid her feet in the dirt and came to a stop.

Her head tipped up. "Wanna come swing?"

"Sure, I guess," Owen responded with a shrug.

"You can come over by climbing out the window and down onto the fence. Joanie and I used to do it all the time."

Owen was never a daredevil. In everything he did, he erred on the side of caution. But something about how confidently Bahn spoke to him gave him a new sense of courage.

He carefully climbed out onto the window ledge and put his foot down on the fence rail. Reaching his hand down, he grabbed for the picket and slowly lowered himself to the ground. Bahn stood up from the swing and let Owen have a turn. He pushed off and began to spin, and Bahn gave him a little shove to help him spin faster.

"So, what were you doing up there?" Her eyes glanced back to the treehouse while she continued to push Owen.

"Nothing really. There isn't anything up there."

"Yeah, we really need to go treasure hunting," she stated.

Owen continued spinning, slowly straightening his legs and arms. "Do what?"

"Go hunt for treasures." She backed away and let the swing slow.

"Treasure hunting? Where? How?"

"You've never been treasure hunting before? Really?" She stopped the swing mid spin. "Do you want to go?"

He shrugged. The idea of going anywhere away from his brother excited him, but going with Bahn still had him in a bit of a panic. He just didn't want her to know that.

"Do you have a bike?"

"Yeah," he said sarcastically. "Why?"

A smirk spread across Bahn's face. "Go grab it and meet me back over here. We're hitting the road."

Owen rushed home, opened the storage door in the back of the garage, and grabbed his bike, setting it just outside the door. His body was vibrating with a newfound emotion. It wasn't fear exactly, more excitement and a bit of curiosity. Exactly what would the treasure hunt hold? Should he be worried about what he'd just agreed to? Sure, he was wondering what he was getting himself into, but fear wouldn't have put the smile he was currently wearing on his face.

He raced through the backyard, opened the door, and yelled to his mom, "I'm riding bikes with Bahn."

Carissa appeared from the kitchen. "Don't go too far, just a couple of blocks. And stay together."

He nodded, let the storm door slam shut, then hopped on his bike and pedaled around the corner. Laying his bike against the curb in front of Bahn's house, he ran up the sidewalk just as Bahn was coming out of her house. She went over to her bike sitting in her driveway and walked it down to where Owen's sat. As she buckled her helmet, she looked straight at him. "Where's your helmet?"

He pushed his glasses up his nose. "Don't have one."

Rolling her eyes, she marched back to the house, returning moments later with a gray helmet. "Here, put this on. It's my dad's, so it might be a little big, but it'll have to do for now."

He grabbed the helmet, perched it on his head, and snapped the buckle. Sitting nearly over his eyes, it was obvious the helmet was way too big. Bahn wrinkled her nose and held out her hand. Owen returned the helmet, and she began to work in silence, making adjustments. After a few minutes, she held it out once more. This time when he settled it on his head, it fit like a glove.

Still silent, but with a spark in her eyes, she ran back up the driveway and returned moments later dragging her wagon. A long piece of rope bounced behind her like a tail. She positioned her bike in front of the wagon and attached the handle to her seat with the rope. After tightening the knots securely, she tested the handle to make sure it didn't rub the tire.

Motioning to Owen to do the same, she hopped on her bike and took off. "Whoever heard of not wearing a helmet when you ride. Don't you know how dangerous that is?"

Owen was astonished. With all the things he'd witnessed her doing, things that made his whole-body clench with fear, he was perplexed at why she took this cause on.

"I will be sure to let my mom know." Owen glanced at Bahn, who remained silent as she pedaled like she was on a mission. "Oh shoot. I forgot to get money!"

Bahn rolled her eyes again. "You really haven't been treasure hunting, have you? You don't need money."

"I don't? I just figured we were going to some garage sales or something."

Bahn shook her head. "No. No way. That's not treasure hunting.

It's not a treasure if you have to pay for it."

"Whoa, we aren't stealing anything, are we?"

"Nope. Stealing is not treasure hunting either."

Owen checked the wagon as it bumped along over rocks and sticks that dotted the street and wondered what they would fill it with. Bahn paid no attention, just kept pedaling. They made a right, then a left, and another right. Before he knew it, Owen was lost.

Bahn smirked and turned into a narrow alley with a privacy fence on both sides. As they rode up the path, a distinct smell filled the air, and Owen couldn't believe what he was seeing. Dumpsters lined both sides of the path. This is what Bahn called treasure hunting? His eyes made their way around the area. Dumpster after dumpster was overflowing with garbage bags, but more importantly, furniture. As Owen's eyes zeroed in the different pieces, he started imagining what the treehouse would look like fully furnished, and he finally understood what Bahn meant by treasure hunting.

They hopped off their bikes and he looked around. "Wow, this place is amazing! How'd you know this was here?"

"I found it one day when I was riding my bike. It's the dumpsters for the Ocean Shores Apartments. I've been out here a few times looking for treasures. This is the best time to come."

"Why?"

"It's the end of the month. People are moving out and they leave all kinds of stuff behind." Bahn took off her helmet, heading for the first dumpster, and Owen followed suit. "I'll take this side; you get the other."

As he started to look around the items that had been discarded, he remembered when he was moving, and his mom made him sort through his toys. She said if he didn't play with it, it wasn't going with them. Staring at an old, blue, plastic toy box covered in stickers, he now wished he hadn't gotten rid of all his cars and the train set his aunt gave him. He frowned as he imagined them sitting by some dumpster, waiting for the truck to haul it all away.

Bahn's shouts drew him out of his depressing thoughts. "I found something!"

Owen turned and saw her holding up a wooden folding chair. He walked over to examine it closer.

"There are two." She opened it up, tested it out, then ran and grabbed the other one. Bahn raised her brows, questioning. Owen nodded. She folded them, and carefully placed them into the wagon, and they continued their search.

Now that they had found one treasure, Owen's heart was racing. He carefully stepped up on the arm of a beat-up sofa and scanned the inside of the second dumpster, but all he saw were bags of garbage. Moving on to the third, he'd nearly given up, when he saw a wooden leg peeking out from under some bags. He quickly began moving them and pulled up a wooden side table. The legs were bowed in a crescent shape, and the top of the table had squares of slate covering it. Underneath, there was a narrow drawer. He set it down and put his hand on it to see if it wobbled. It was a little scratched, but otherwise it seemed sturdy.

"What do you think about this?" he asked.

Bahn's head poked out of a dumpster. "Oh...perfect."

He brought it over and set it in the wagon, then continued the search. Bahn dug through another dumpster, and within a short time her voice echoed. "Whoa. What is this?" She climbed out, then reached over and pulled out some loosely rolled fabric. Once she had it out, she unrolled the huge print of the continents. "How cool!"

Owen stepped out of his pile and walked over. "Oh, that's awesome. But how are we going to get it back to the treehouse? It's too big to fit in the wagon."

"Leave it to me. I'm a good packer." They brought it back to the wagon and set it next to it.

Comparing the size of the wagon to the size of the rolled-up fabric, Owen doubted Bahn would be able to come up with a good way to cart the piece back to the house, but he figured he'd let her try. Kicking an old pizza box out of the way, he returned to his treasure hunting.

Under a pile of venetian blinds next to one of the dumpsters, they found an old rug that took them both to get it to the wagon.

Continuing to dig through the piles of treasures, they found a checkers set, two framed wall hangings of flamingos, a cork bulletin board—to which Bahn exclaimed, "We can put pictures of our adventures on this,"—a massive ball of Christmas lights, a bowl with a starfish on it, and an oversized vinyl bean bag chair.

Once they got it all back to the wagon, Bahn stood silently for a couple of minutes, surveying their scavenged goods. Removing the chairs and table from the wagon, she unfurled the rug and placed all the finds strategically inside it. She wandered back over to the blinds and pulled several of the cords out, tied them together, wrapped them around the rug, and the wagon, then attached them to her bike.

Dusting her hands on her shorts, she admired her skills for a moment, then grabbed her helmet. Owen took the cue and put his on. Bahn leaned forward, putting her weight on the pedals, but the bike didn't move. The weight of the wagon was too much.

Owen's heart plummeted. He stared at the rolled up rug containing all their treasures and hated the thought that they might have to leave it behind. There was no way his parents would come back to get it if he told them about treasure hunting. In fact, he might get grounded once they knew how far they'd ridden.

No. He was smart. There had to be a way. Bahn continued to try to get the pedals to move but just didn't have enough strength. Then a thought hit him.

"Feet on the pedals," he said. Holding onto the seat, Owen pushed while Bahn stood up and pedaled.

Once she got going, he ran to his bike to catch up. His heart was racing, and a smile filled his face. He'd never felt so energized in his life. "I can't believe we found all this stuff!" he said as he pulled up next to Bahn. "This is so cool!"

Bahn glanced at him and smiled. "I know! I'm so excited."

As they rounded the corner by Owen's house, he saw his mom in the front yard getting the mail. Her eyes widened, and Owen immediately began to worry.

Studying the contraption Bahn was pulling behind her bike, Carissa asked, "What in the world have you guys been up to?" Confusion, with a little bit of added humor, laced her voice.

"We've been treasure hunting," Bahn said proudly. "We're going to decorate the treehouse."

Owen held his breath as his mom stepped closer.

Carissa examined the dusty, rolled-up rug. "Oh really? What do you have? And where did you get it?"

Bahn untied the chords to release their treasures from the wagon. Owen joined her, helping drag the bundle off the wagon and onto the grass where they unrolled it to display their booty. Owen's mom stood gaping at their finds, and Owen studied her face trying to gauge her reaction.

"We found it in the dumpsters behind the Ocean Shores

Apartments."

Owen stiffened, knowing the apartments were a far cry from the two blocks his mom had given him permission to go. He elbowed Bahn hoping she would take the hint and shut up, but she was too excited about their haul.

"It was going to get taken to the dump anyway, so we saved it," Bahn responded confidently.

Carissa's expression soured, and Owen steeled himself for the reprimand. "You were digging through dumpsters?" She stepped closer to them, turned her head away, and waved her hand in front of her face. "You guys both go get bathed. I'll wipe the stuff down and clean it up, then you can take it to the treehouse." Bahn and Owen both sniffed their shirts. "Trust me. Go."

Owen didn't wait around to see if his mom was going to tack on a reprimand. Maybe she didn't hear the part of where they got the stuff. He felt fortunate that she was too disgusted with their smell to think about where the complex was, and how far they'd actually traveled for their treasures.

By the time Owen ran out the front door after his bath, smelling fresh as a daisy, his mom had finished disinfecting everything in the front yard. Bahn came around the corner a few minutes later, just as Mr. Cramer pulled up. Owen ran up to his dad's car and retold the story of his and Bahn's adventures. He figured if his mom didn't get mad at him, his dad wouldn't either since he had a completely different view than his mom when it came to him riding his bike.

Carissa pointed out the rug they found. "If I didn't know they pulled it out of the dumpster, I might have considered stealing it."

Owen's dad chuckled, telling them he remembered going on treasure hunts when he was a kid. "I'll change and then help move the stuff."

"You went on treasure hunts?" Owen questioned, astonished by the fact that his father never said anything about it.

"Yep. We never were fortunate enough to find treasures like this, but there was an old man who lived up the road from us that was always collecting junk. One day, when we were riding our bikes, the old man was outside setting this painted flamingo statue in his yard. Uncle Brad stopped to look at an old bike wheel that had pieces of colored glass filling the spokes and the old man invited us to look around his yard. He had a bunch of stuff that he'd recycled into his 'art.' He said we could take anything we wanted as long as we asked. So, we made a haul that day. Grandma and Grandpa weren't too excited about our 'art' pieces though."

Owen's dad examined all the items again. "I hope all this fits up there. Why don't you figure out where you want everything while I get changed?"

Bahn and Owen stood in the middle of the empty treehouse planning their design, when the creak of the trapdoor opening caught their attention. Owen's dad shoved one of the flamingo paintings onto the floor and chuckled. Owen practically vibrated with excitement as he placed it against the wall it would be hanging on. It was happening. He'd been worried his mom would take one look at the stuff they found and throw it out. But to his surprise, that hadn't happened. He was going to have his refuge in the trees, and it was going to be amazing.

Once the rest of the items had been dropped off, they climbed down and helped move each item. Owen's mom even crawled up into the treehouse and helped Owen and Bahn tug the canvas wall hanging and heavy rug through the hatch while his dad pushed from below.

When everything was in place, Bahn began untangling the strings of Christmas lights. Owen was crossing his fingers that they would work. He wasn't holding out much hope since they dug them out of the dumpster, but the energy in the growing expectation was palpable. When his dad plugged the strings of connected bulbs in, a thousand glittering white lights lay neatly on the floor and Bahn and Owen both simultaneously screamed, "Yes!" and high fived each other.

They strung the lights from the center of the ceiling to the corners of the treehouse, and Owen stood in the middle of the room speechless. It had come together just as he and Bahn had planned. His eyes darted to her, and he thought he saw a glisten in her eyes. Was she crying? Her gaze made it to his, and she reached out and grabbed his arms. "We did it," she squealed as a wide grin spread across her face.

Owen's dad sat in the bean bag chair while his mom took a seat at the table, each eyeing the other with conspiratorial grins on their faces.

The glow from the string of lights reminded Owen that the day was nearly over, and what a day it was. It had started out craptaculous but was ending as one of the best days of his life.

Bahn looked at the table and immediately disappeared down the ladder. Owen watched through the window as she vanished into her house. A few minutes later she returned to the treehouse with a bag of M&Ms and poured them into the bowl that was sitting on the table. They all grabbed a handful, then continued to admire their work.

Owen's heart hadn't stopped pounding in his chest, and he was hard pressed to wipe the grin from his face as he stared at the finished product. He knew he would be spending all his time there. He never wanted to leave.

CHAPTER 8

Present day

Turning in her chair, Bahn brushed a curl from her face and tucked one foot under her. "Did you notice that rug was still there? You could barely see the design anymore because it was so dirty, but that was the same rug."

"That was a good quality find, my friend." He held up his glass and Bahn clinked hers against it. Bringing his glass to his lips, Owen locked his gaze on her and she felt the surge of heat scorch her skin until he finally tore his focus away.

Her heart thumped wildly, and she wondered what he was thinking. That wasn't the first time she thought she saw something in his eyes.

Following his focus, she stared into the distance, trying to find what he was looking at before turning back to him. His jaw ticked, and he remained silent. He'd grown into such a handsome man. Sitting in his dress blue military pants, his white shirt with the tie loosened and the sleeves cuffed, he held very little resemblance to the little boy she remembered.

His piercing blue eyes, though, were unmistakable, and they currently held a storm.

Her attention returned to the gentle rain, and she debated whether to find out how severe his storm was. But she'd crossed the country to be there for him. For whatever he needed.

"Whatcha thinking about?" she finally asked, her voice barely above a whisper.

"My dad. He had so much fun helping us get that treehouse set up," he said with a sigh. "You could see it in his eyes, and I'll never forget his smile when we finally walked back to the house. I think he might have been as excited as we were." His eyes drifted to hers. "I remember every moment of that day."

Silence fell between them again. Then, barely above a whisper, he confessed, "God, I'm going to miss him. I would much rather remember those days than these last few weeks."

Bahn wasn't sure she should broach the question, but Owen seemed like he wanted to talk. "How did it happen? I mean, I kind of know some of the story. After mom told me, I saw something on the news about it."

Owen took a deep breath and scratched at something on his pants. "He was planning on retiring a few years back, but he'd been such a valued asset to the military, they offered him the training position to stay on. That's when they transferred back to Mississippi. He was basically teaching others his skills and doing some research and development for new equipment.

"The military had purchased a new design of his that was hypersensitive on detecting enemy weapons. Not common knowledge, but we used to talk about the stuff he was working on because I kind of followed in his footsteps.

"Anyway, they were itching to get it activated, but they didn't feel comfortable having anyone else put it together and get it calibrated. So, they asked him to go on one more mission. It was supposed to be an in and out thing. About eight weeks. He was only there to get the equipment up and running, then he was done. Once it was completed, they would move to another location to await the flight home. During the transfer, their vehicle was ambushed. No one survived."

Bahn took his hand, because she had no words. Nothing felt right.

"It's the single hardest thing I have ever had to go through. I mean, I knew one day I would have to say goodbye to my parents, but I thought it would be when they were old. He wasn't old. To know that one moment he was alive and healthy, and the next he wasn't, knowing I wasn't there to protect him, and there was nothing I could do…" his voice trailed off.

Bahn felt the burn in her chest hearing the emotion in his voice. "I can't even imagine."

"What's weird is, we talked one night a few months ago, and he told me how much he truly felt blessed with the life he'd been given. He confided he was a bit scared of dying but was ready for what awaited him."

Bahn rubbed her thumb against the back of his hand as her eyes welled with tears. "I think, in some ways, it's harder for the family when someone is in the military. Those serving come to terms with their mortality when they get called up, but the family is left at home wondering if they'll return."

"I just keep thinking of all the things we did together. I was his sidekick." He paused. "Don't get me wrong, he loved my brother and sister, and he went to all their games and concerts and plays. He supported everything we did." He wiped away tears and put on a brave smile. "But I was his favorite."

Bahn laughed at the comment, picked up her glass to take another swig of tea and found it empty.

"Need some more?" He pointed to the glass still in her hand.

"Nah. As much as I hate to, I really think I should be going so you can spend some time with your family." They both turned and noticed that the crowd inside had dwindled.

Owen tipped his head as his eyes fixed on her. "Yeah, I guess I need to get in there."

Walking back inside, Owen gently put his hand on Bahn's back. The unassuming move made her body buzz. Goosebumps prickled her skin, and she sucked in a deep breath. It was such an innocent touch, but her body was not reacting so innocently. The longer she was around him, the more confused she became by the way he made her feel. She needed to focus on why she was there—to comfort him. But he was making it awfully hard when he touched her like that.

Owen's mom stopped them to reintroduce Bahn to Beau and Trish. They chatted for a short time, and then Owen escorted her to her car. The rain had stopped, and the air had become thick and warm.

"Thanks for coming. You made this day so much better by being here."

"Oh, you're welcome." She paused, then asked shyly, "What do you have going on tomorrow?"

Owen shoved his hands in his front pockets. "We have to meet with the lawyer sometime after lunch. Why?"

"Do you want to grab some breakfast?" she asked, opening her car door.

Owen propped himself up against the car, crossing his arms, then his ankles. "Sure. When's your flight back?"

"I leave Sunday."

"Oh. You're here for a few days then." Owen chewed on his bottom lip, but the slight smile didn't get past her. "Okay. That would be great. Where are you staying?"

"The Surfside Inn on Beach Boulevard. Give me your number and I'll send you a text."

He stood and waited for her to grab her phone from the multicolored crocheted bag sitting on the passenger seat and type in her passcode. Once she'd unlocked her phone, he took it from her.

"What are you doing?"

"Giving you my number," he said with a playful whine. She watched as his fingers flew across the keypad. When his phone dinged, he handed it back.

Glancing at the screen, she snorted and then fell into fits of laughter when she read *'Don't be scared.'* "Wait, are you telling me not to be scared, or you?"

Owen opened his eyes wide and scooted back a step.

"It's only breakfast. Do you know how many times we ate Pop-tarts together as kids?" She continued to laugh. "God. You're still such a dork." She dropped her phone back into her bag. "I'll text you, and we can figure out where to go."

Owen gave her a crooked smile. "Sounds good."

Bahn hesitated, then reached up and gave him a hug. His arms wrapped around her and squeezed her tight. She wondered if he could feel how fast her heart was beating.

"Thank you so much for coming. You don't know how much this means to me," Owen whispered into her shoulder, then lifted his head. Their eyes held each other captive for a long minute, then Bahn raised up on her tiptoes and kissed his cheek.

A smile crossed his face, and hers felt like it had been set on fire. She pulled back and brushed the stray strands of hair from her face.

Her eyes didn't leave his until she hopped into her car. Glancing in her rearview mirror, she watched him wave as she drove away.

Breathing would have been nice, but her body seemed to have forgotten how. *What just happened?* It seemed so surreal.

Nothing had prepared her for the news that sent her first few days of summer on this wayward trajectory. And although she hadn't seen Owen in over a dozen years, she had thought about him. But she never thought seeing him would cause her to feel this way. Her mind flashed through the events of the day. Something had brought her to Biloxi in search of him, and when she saw him, her world stopped.

A lump filled her throat when she pictured the first time they made eye contact. The pain in his eyes gutted her. And the first time she heard him laugh, it sent a charge through her that nearly lifted her off the ground. She was not prepared for how her entire body reacted to him.

And she wasn't ready to consider how handsome he'd become. Or why she suddenly thought of him that way.

His hair was a short fade on the sides, longer on the top, and finger swept to one side. His jaw was defined and the dimples when he smiled were deep and irresistible. Long, dark lashes framed his sky-blue eyes that were no longer hidden by the oversized glasses. And he still had a few dots of freckles across his nose and cheeks.

Her senses were in overdrive, and her mind raced with thoughts of the day, flipping through snapshots like she was thumbing through one of her photo albums. Sitting next to him in the treehouse. Making bets on the swing. Running in the rain, and then reminiscing about their childhood while drinking sweet tea. She laughed out loud thinking about how comfortable it felt. Just like when they were kids.

CHAPTER 9

O wen sat at the dinner table, an empty container that held a random casserole in the middle of it, and pushed his plate aside to begin going over legal papers, and the lists of things he needed to do with his mom.

Since his brother and sister both lived out of town, had families and job responsibilities, and needed to return home the next day, he'd agreed to handle his father's affairs. His dad had already gotten pretty much everything in order—it was something the military required—but still, all of the accounts needed to be transferred into his mom's name, and businesses needed to be notified.

His mom was in and out of the room and had dropped off some photo albums for everyone to go through. Beau sat with Sadie, who was asleep on his shoulder, and Preston sat next to Trish, playing with his Hot Wheels. Their spouses were sitting in the living room, watching something on TV. Owen took in the scene. This was the first time he could remember that they all seemed to be on the same page. The conversation came easy. He was finally a part of Beau and Trish's world. Although, as they shared memories, some seemed to be far different than he recalled.

He dug his phone from his pocket, checked the ringer, then bumped up the volume a little. Scrolling through his messages, he hoped he might find an unread text from Bahn he'd missed, but there was none, so he returned his phone to his pocket and continued to study the old photos and reminisce.

As he stared at a photo of his dad holding him as a toddler, his mom set three yellow notepads in the middle of the table. "Write down the things of your dad's that meant something to you, that you would like to have. You can take them home with you when you leave, or over the next few weeks. I'll gather them up and send them to you if need be. If there's anything more than one of you wants, we can discuss it. Feel free to go through the clothes and shoes. I can't handle going through anything right now. Eventually, I'll pack everything up that I don't want to keep and take it to the thrift store up the street."

Owen felt waves of sadness wash over him again. It was all over. His dad was gone, and now it was time to divvy up his stuff. It all seemed so cold. He knew his mom didn't mean it that way. She wanted them to have something to remember him by. But at that moment, it felt wrong.

He glanced across the table and noticed Beau and Trish had already grabbed notepads. Unable to bring himself to pick his up, Owen stood from his chair and walked to the kitchen to get a glass of tea. As he reached for the pitcher, his phone buzzed. Dragging it from his pocket, he noticed it was an unknown number with the message. The message he'd sent earlier still made his mouth twitch.

Unknown: **Don't be scared.**

Then he saw her message.

Unknown: **Hi. It's me.**

His smile turned into a wide grin. Setting the pitcher on the counter, he grabbed a glass from the cabinet and tried to think of something witty to say in response.

Owen: **Hi, Me.**

Unknown: **You dork. I'm sitting in the hotel lobby, and you just made me snort-laugh in front of who knows how many people. Where do you want to go tomorrow? What do you think about High Tide out on Bayview? I think they have a little bit of everything.**

Owen: **Sounds perfect. What time?**

Unknown: **I am not a morning person...at all. So, how about 9:30?**

He leaned up against the counter chuckling as he poured himself some tea and typed.

Owen: **I am so surprised...not! 9:30 sounds good. Do you want to just meet there?**

Unknown: **Where did this sarcastic attitude come from? I don't remember this. And by the way, if you haven't noticed, it's summer. I am on vacation, and I am going to take advantage of sleeping. And seriously, have you slept in these beds? They're like sleeping on clouds. What did you ask me? Oh. Yeah, we can meet there.**

Owen: **Who's sarcastic? All right. See you tomorrow.**

He continued to smile as he programmed her name into his phone then returned it to his pocket. Walking back to the dining room, he stopped abruptly, trying to remember why he'd walked into the kitchen before he was so rudely interrupted. He chuckled again, then noticed his glass and the pitcher sitting on the counter. Returning the pitcher to the refrigerator, he grabbed his tea from the counter and sat back down.

Trish and Beau had disappeared with their kids. He grabbed a pen and, with a sigh, reluctantly slid the yellow notepad in front of him. Twirling the pen in his fingers, he lowered it, tapping it on the pad, but his brain just couldn't engage. He took a long swig of his tea and stared off into space, but still nothing came. He couldn't make himself think about the situation. It made his chest ache. The paper remained blank.

Sitting back in his chair, he chucked his pen on the table and crossed his arms. The text from Bahn captured his thoughts. What was it about her? She just seemed to give him a confidence, a feeling of freedom, that he normally didn't have. Even after all these years, he still felt he could say anything to her.

Beau walked up behind him. "What's the deal, man? You don't have anything on your pad."

His comment pulled Owen back to reality. "What?"

He tapped Owen's pad of paper.

"Eh, I just can't think of anything right now that I can't live without. I'm not settled anywhere, and it makes it hard."

"Well, this," he paused, "is hard."

Owen tipped back in his chair. "Yeah. It is. I just expect him to come through the door any minute."

Beau sat back down across from him. "I know. Me too."

"What did you write down?"

"Remember when dad was so adamant about teaching us golf? He was never able to get any of us interested, but I've gone out a few times recently with my friends, and I had a pretty good time. Didn't play well, but it was fun. So, I wanted to take Dad's clubs. I just think he would be happy that one of us has them."

"I agree."

Trish, Carissa, and Preston reappeared from the hallway. Preston was wearing Phillip's fishing hat, and Trish was carrying several of his fishing poles in one hand and his tackle box in the other. "If it's okay with you guys, we'd like to take this stuff so we can take Preston fishing."

Both Beau and Owen nodded in approval and Trish set the items in her hands next to the front door, but Preston refused to give her his hat. Owen had to smile at how big the floppy hat was on Preston, even though his throat felt like it was closing up. It had been a required part of his dad's fishing attire for as long as Owen could remember.

Coming back over to the table, Trish tapped Beau on the shoulder and jerked her head, motioning for him to follow. Beau positioned the baby more securely on his shoulder, scooted the chair back, and followed Trish and Carissa up the hallway. Owen was confused and glanced at their spouses, who both held similar, confused expressions. He could hear their voices but couldn't make out the conversation. He just shrugged. His life was full of those moments.

Taking another long swig of his tea, he got up and headed for the back door. Stepping out onto the porch, he set his drink down and slowly took a seat. The rain had left the air with a fresh scent and the temperature a bit cooler. Picking up his glass, he took a sip and let his mind drift back through the day, revisiting the conversation with Bahn while they were watching the rain. He set his tea on the little table between the two chairs, locked his fingers behind his head, leaned back and closed his eyes. What a strange turn of events.

He felt sad that his dad was gone, but the day had also brought some great surprises. He was blown away from seeing Bahn again. His brother and sister were including him in their lives, to some degree. Dare he imagine what was next?

The bang of the storm door made him jump and he peeled one eye open to see Preston wandering toward him. His grandpa's fishing hat sat so low on his head he had to lift his chin to see, and he carried something in his tiny hand.

"Hey, little buddy." Owen lifted Preston into his lap, tilted his hat back so he could see his face, and got a glimpse of a set of keys. "Whose keys do you have," he asked, thinking he probably stole them from his mom's purse.

"Unca Beau told me to bring you dees."

"He did?" Owen took the keys and examined the worn leather keychain. Something about it looked familiar. Engraved in the leather was a simple cross, and attached to the ring were two keys and a fob.

Preston hopped down and ran back to the door. He tugged on the handle but couldn't get the door open. Owen decided the mystery of the keys needed to be solved before they got lost, so he got up to let Preston in.

As he helped Preston back into the house, he said, "Hey, little guy brought me—" His eyes lifted to see his family all staring at him, and a pang of unease shot through him. "What's going on? Preston brought me these." He held out the keys, dangling them from the leather keychain.

"You don't recognize them?" Beau asked.

"They look like Dad's keys. But why did Preston give them to me?"

"Well, we're tired of you embarrassing us driving around in that heap of junk you call a car. Mom said she didn't need Dad's truck, and since it's paid for, we decided you should have it."

Owen took a step back, processing what Beau said. "I'm sorry, what?" His eyes went from Trish to Beau to his mom, seeking clarification, but no one spoke. They all just smiled at him. His eyes and nose began to burn, and he pressed his fist to his mouth, trying to stifle the tears.

"Sweetheart, the truck is just going to sit there. It's too big for me to drive," Carissa explained.

He took a deep breath as a tear trickled down his cheek. "You guys are, are kidding, right? The truck is practically brand new."

Beau popped off, "Yeah, and your car is vintage. You've had it since high school. I'm surprised pieces don't fall off when you drive it."

"Beau and Dan already have trucks," Trish pointed out. "Mom has a nice car. Your car is on its last leg, and we thought this would keep Dad's truck in the family a little longer. Or a lot longer, the way you hold onto cars."

Owen dabbed at the tears, but they continued to fall. He pinched his nose to try to keep it from running and stared at the keys. "You're serious?" he choked out quietly. They all nodded again.

Wiping his mouth, he stared at the keys again, then chuckled. "Wanna hear something funny?" He looked up through his lashes. "I swear when I was driving up here, I heard a noise and saw something flying off in my rearview mirror. No joke."

His brother let out a hardy laugh and his sister shook her head.

"But seriously, I don't know what to say." He smiled and chuckled again, continuing to fight back tears.

"You're going to need it when you move," Carissa commented.

"That's a true statement. It will come in very handy, although I really don't have that much. Most of the furniture was there when I moved in."

Beau's eyes fixed on him. "Move? I thought you were just on leave." He crossed his arms over his chest.

"When Mom called with the news about Dad, I wasn't sure how long it would take to get all of his affairs taken care of, so I talked to my CO who knew dad well. Since I only had a few weeks left to complete my commitment to the Air Force I didn't know how the leave would work.

"While we were talking, he asked if I was planning on re-enlisting or finishing out my commitment and told me there was a civilian job in technology at Keesler that I could transfer into. It's tied to what I was already doing at Patrick, so I would still be working with the same people I was before, just long distance. He said I might have to travel some, but that wasn't a deal breaker.

"After the cluster that happened in Afghanistan, I really wasn't ready to sign on the dotted line again. And the job would allow me to be close to Mom, so I told him I'd gladly take the civilian job."

"That worked out great!"

"Yeah. It did. A whole lot better than I thought it would. The three weeks' leave they gave me ends at the end of next week. I'll report to Keesler sometime this week and sign some papers. When I get back to Patrick, I will finish out my commitment, sign some paperwork there, then pack up, and head back here."

"In your new truck," Trish added enthusiastically.

"Yeah. Damn, you guys. This is so…" Studying the keys in his hand, he took a deep breath and shook his head. "This is so overwhelming." He lifted his eyes to them. "Thank you."

Beau gently passed his sleeping daughter to her momma's arms, then slapped Owen on the back. "Let's go take a look."

Opening the door to the garage to let the light in, Owen got his first glimpse at his new ride. There, on the far side, sat the deep blue metallic, crew cab truck. He stood in the doorway, taking a moment to let it sink in. It was his. He'd only seen his dad drive it a couple of times, and he kept it in pristine condition.

Stepping around his mom's car, he looked at it closely, then opened the door and climbed inside. The interior still smelled of new leather. He studied all the gadgets on the dash and tried to figure out where everything was on the steering wheel.

As his hand skimmed the seats, he noticed something in the back. Reaching over, he realized it was his dad's Bible. He picked it up and let it fall open. Plenty of scriptures were underlined in it, and several pieces of paper marked locations. His dad had told him that he would go out to the pier and sit, listening to the waves come in, and read. He said it gave him comfort.

Beau appeared in his line of sight. "Don't you want to take it for a drive?"

"I think I'll wait until tomorrow. It's getting late." He slid out of the seat and shut the door.

They returned to the house, and Carissa caught him as he walked past the dining room table where she was sitting. She stood and hugged him. "You deserve it, sweetheart." Backing away, she brushed her fingers through his short hair.

"Thank you."

"We can transfer the title while we're out this week getting all the paperwork taken care of."

Owen nodded, and his mom's eyes dropped to the item in his hand. "It's Dad's Bible." He held it out for her to have.

"You can hold on to it if you'd like?"

"I think I will for a little bit, if that's okay?"

She nodded, and he strolled up the hall to the room he was staying in, dropped off the keys and the Bible, then returned to the living room. His mom was leaning against the wall that separated the living room and dining room. He wrapped his arm around her. "Thanks again."

She turned and snaked her arms around him and kissed his cheek. "He would be happy knowing you have his truck."

"I'll take care of it. I promise."

"I have no doubt. You're just like your dad."

Beau stood up and grabbed the diaper bag. "We need to get back to the hotel. Tomorrow is going to be a long day. What time do we meet with the lawyer?"

"Not until one. We can meet here for lunch and head over. There's plenty of food."

"Sounds like a good plan. Sandra and Dan are taking Preston and Sadie to the park."

Dan stood and gently picked up Preston from where he'd fallen asleep on the sofa. He rested his head on his shoulder, and as he walked out the door, he grabbed the fishing poles. Trish trailed behind them. The sun was just about gone, and the air had gotten a bit of a bite to it. He sat the poles against the car and opened the door to put Preston in his car seat for the ride. Beau was doing the same with Sadie.

Owen watched carefully. His siblings, who had either ignored him or picked on him as a kid, were now parents, and good ones at that. He could tell how much they loved their kids. His dad was a great example, and he hoped to live up to that standard one day.

Beau went back to the house and disappeared inside. Within a minute, he returned with the clubs slung over his shoulder. Owen caught his eye and commented, "Maybe one day we can go out and play together."

"Start practicing now, little brother," Beau said with a smile, and patted Owen on the back.

Owen smiled back, hoping that day would come. As he watched the cars disappear up the street, he felt his mom's hand on his back. They turned to go back in the house. Things were changing.

CHAPTER 10

◆

The smell of fresh brewed coffee as it wafted through the house brought Owen back to consciousness. His eyes slowly opened, and he rolled over to grab his phone. Rubbing the sleep away, he blinked, trying to focus. Seven thirty. He didn't even remember going to bed. Was yesterday a dream?

He sat on the side of the bed, reached for his jeans at the foot, and slid into them. Snatching his T-shirt from the chair, he tugged it over his head while opening the bedroom door and stumbled up the hall to the kitchen.

His mom was seated at the table staring at a newspaper. His focus settled on the pot of black gold. Pouring himself a cup of coffee, he sat down across from her and grabbed the comics from the pile she had already discarded.

Her eyes lifted to him as she lowered the paper. "Did you sleep well?" Those had been her first words to him every morning since he could remember.

"Yes. I slept like a rock."

"I'm glad. I did too. The stress of the day must have worn me out. But everything went well, I think. I got to see some people I haven't seen in a long time, and that was nice." She sighed. "I can't believe Siobahn flew in. Her whole family was so sweet."

The mention of her name had him revisiting the events of the previous day. "Yeah, I was surprised. She said her mom and dad would have come if they didn't already have a trip planned. We're having breakfast later to catch up some more."

"Oh? That's wonderful. So, did you just run into each other here and recognize each other?"

He took a sip of his coffee. "Weird story," he said, putting the paper down. "I thought I saw her at the graveside service when we were leaving, but there was no way I could convince myself it was her. But later, I drove by our old house. It's for sale, so I decided to look around and see what's changed. I was there, looking around, when Bahn showed up."

"You always were kindred spirits. I'm not surprised you both wound up at the house."

"It looks good, by the way. They've painted it and added shutters." He took another sip of coffee. "The treehouse is still there too. We crawled up into it, sat there talking and reminiscing about some of the crazy things we did as kids."

"Yes. You two were definitely adventurous. It never seemed to phase Vanessa, but I wondered sometimes how you guys survived. I figured Beau would give me gray hairs. You, on the other hand, were a surprise. You were more like your dad, very cautious and careful. But Bahn seemed to bring out more of your adventurous side."

"Those were some of the best memories I have growing up."

Getting up to retrieve more coffee, he glanced at the clock on the oven. It was after eight. "You need a little more?" he asked, holding the coffee pot up to his mom. She nodded, and he added some to her cup before replacing the pot on its stand. "I'm going to grab a shower and get ready." He took one last gulp from his cup then put it in the sink.

"Wow, you look nice," his mom commented when he came through the dining room in a pair of khaki shorts and an untucked, pearl snap, printed shirt.

"Thanks. Do you think this will be okay to wear to the lawyer later?"

"Yeah. It's an old military buddy of your dad's. I think he's just going to go over the will and the stuff we need to take care of this week. I don't think it'll take that long."

"Okay good." Dropping a pair of leather deck shoes on the floor by the chair, he traipsed into the kitchen, picked up his cup from the sink, and added a splash of coffee.

"You smell nice too." His eyes landed on his mom as he returned to the dining room, and his stomach tightened from her words. He lowered his chin to his chest and sniffed, wondering if he overdid it. He was just a little bit nervous about his breakfast date.

Setting his cup on the table, he sat down in the chair to put on his shoes. "What time are we meeting for lunch?"

"I'd say just be back around noon. I'll have something ready, and we can head over there around twelve forty-five. It won't take five minutes to get there."

"Got it." He stood, grabbed his cup, and took the last swallow before returning it to the sink. The clock on the oven read nine fifteen. "I gotta get rolling."

As he stepped into his room to retrieve the keys, his gaze shifted to his dad's Bible that sat on the nightstand. Grazing his fingers across the worn leather, he studied the tattered pages and bookmarks that protruded from countless locations, indicating how much the book was used. With little thought, he picked it up, tucked it under his arm, and hurried up the hallway.

After giving his mom a quick hug, he headed to the garage. A lump caught in his throat as he climbed into the truck. He was still in disbelief that his family decided to give it to him. Placing the Bible on the passenger seat, he examined the buttons and knobs and tried to get comfortable behind the wheel. Then he backed out and slowly pulled onto the street.

The sky was awash with pinks and purples and blues, coloring the few remaining clouds that hadn't burned off as the morning sunlight peek through, glinting off the windshield. He looked around at the scenery. Streets were lined with an array of colorful buildings and hotels to accommodate the tourist season. There were a few historical buildings mixed in here and there that gave a glimpse of an earlier era of the town's southern roots.

As he rounded the corner onto a quieter street, he could see the sign for his destination. He immediately felt excited, but also conflicted. There was no doubt he and Bahn still felt comfortable with each other, but he wasn't prepared for how stunning she was, and the intense connection he felt to her. He knew nothing would ever happen between them but wondered why she seemed to enjoy flirting with him. Could he have just misread her?

Pulling into the parking lot, he looked for the burgundy car she was driving the day before, but didn't see it. Deciding to wait for her inside, he got out just as she pulled in.

"Fancy meeting you here," she said with a wide smile when she exited her car. Her face glowed from the sun, and his heart thrummed as she walked toward him. He couldn't help but smile.

She was dressed in a plain white V-neck T-shirt that played against her bronze skin and revealed just a hint of her cleavage. Her cut off jean shorts weren't booty shorts, but where they hit on her toned thighs had him sucking in a deep breath as his eyes traveled all the way down her mile-long legs to her tie-dyed flip-flops. Her hair was down, and the sun reflected off the caramel-colored ringlets making them sparkle. The only thing keeping the curls out of her face was her bright red sunglasses. He couldn't take his eyes off her, and hoped she didn't notice him staring as he committed every inch of her to memory.

A groan escaped his throat. *Why does she have to be off-limits?*

"What?" She looked around at her outfit. "I told you, I am on vacation, so this is what you get."

"No. You look great!" was all he could manage to say.

Her eyes quickly glanced up and down, giving him a once-over and an approving nod. "I have to say you look much more comfortable today." Her focus traveled over his shoulder. "And what's with the new ride?"

He turned around to glance at his truck again, still feeling weird calling it his. "Well, that is a very interesting story." He pointed to the entrance of the restaurant and pulled open the door.

The young lady at the front escorted them to a booth in the corner and an older woman with scrawny arms and dyed black hair, dusted with gray at the roots, delivered the menus along with glasses of water. They both began to peruse the offerings.

Bahn scanned the surroundings. "I can't believe this place is still here. I would've thought it'd been destroyed by the hurricane."

"I'm thinking some of it's been rebuilt, but they did a good job matching its original design." As Owen surveyed the area, Bahn's eyes met his, and a slow smile crept across her face.

He quickly dropped his gaze to the menu, suddenly feeling like his shy, awkward, teenage self. She was so beautiful she was almost hard to look at. It was still hard to believe she was sitting across from him.

They both remained silent until Bahn closed her menu and pulled his down. "Okay. So where did the truck come from?"

And like she had some kind of mystical powers, his nerves settled, and he smiled. "After you left last night, my mom sat us down and told us to pick out things of my dad's that we would like to have. Something of sentimental value. I was wracking my brain, trying to figure out what items of my dad's meant the most to me, and I couldn't decide on anything. Everything of his meant something to me. Then, Beau, Trish, and mom decided I needed my dad's truck, because my car is literally falling apart. They surprised me with the keys."

"Wow! That's cool. And I have to say, I agree with them. Your poor car has seen better days."

Owen feigned offense. "That car has taken me across the country more than once, with very little complaint."

"You're damn lucky then."

She wasn't wrong. He'd wondered many times when he would wind up stranded on the side of the road. "Yeah. This is the first time I've driven the truck, and I admit, it is a much smoother ride. I nearly wrecked it right off the bat. Had to try out all the buttons."

"You're going to have to take me for a ride in it when we get done here."

"All right."

"What are you going to do with your old car?"

"I don't know. I guess I'll try to sell it. It's not worth much. What I can get out of it, though, will help with my moving expenses."

"Moving expenses?"

"Yeah. I'm moving back here to help my mom out."

"That's awesome!"

The waitress came by to fill their coffee cups and take their order. Having completely forgotten about ordering, Owen lifted his brow to Bahn. "What are you going to have?"

"I haven't decided." She picked up the menu again. "How about you?"

"I don't know. There are so many choices. I may just stick with the usual bacon and eggs."

"Oh geez. All these choices"—she thumbed through the pages—"and you're going to choose bacon and eggs? At least add some French toast or something." Flipping the menu around, she pointed. "Look. Brioche. It's made from homemade fancy bread!"

She glanced at the waitress, standing there with a scowl and her arms crossed. "Do you mind coming back in a minute?" The waitress turned and walked away without saying a word.

Bahn leaned into the table, staring at Owen with one brow raised, and Owen smirked, realizing she was patiently waiting for an answer. "Okay. You're right. I'm beginning a new chapter in my life. Might as well start with breakfast."

"Yay." She clapped her hands softly. "At least that's a good place to start. Breakfast is the most important meal of the day, you know."

"So I've heard. Have you decided?" He glanced at her, then returned to the menu to find something different than his standard bacon and eggs. She was doing it again, taking him out of his comfort zone, just like old times.

"I don't know, there are so many choices. I might just stick with bacon and eggs," she mocked.

His eyes tipped up above his menu and he growled. She wrinkled her nose and blew him a kiss. His body immediately felt that kiss like a bottle rocket hitting him directly in the chest and exploding. *Geez, this woman.* He wasn't mistaken about her flirting. *Could I have been wrong about her?*

The waitress approached the table with her pen and pad ready, offering them a fake smile that looked more like she smelled something foul. "Are you ready to order now?"

"I'll have the sausage egg and cheese frit, frita, frittata? And a side of French toast and coffee." He glanced at Bahn from the corner of his eye, waiting for approval.

"Not bad. Not bad." She slowly bobbed her head and turned to the waitress. "I'll have the California omelet, no onions, add avocado, and a toasted English muffin with cream cheese and strawberry jelly."

The waitress grabbed the menus and turned to leave. They both stared at her as she walked away. Bahn leaned in and put her arms on the table. "She could use a happy meal," she said a little louder than necessary, and Owen's eyes darted to the woman, hoping she didn't hear.

"Geez, woman."

"Well? Am I right?"

Owen shook his head and chuckled. Some things never changed.

CHAPTER 11

"So, spill the beans. You're moving back and"—she motioned with her hand in a frantic manner— "what else is going on? How have you been all these years? What's happened? Where have you lived? Where do you live now? What are your plans? Spill it." She tapped the table with her index finger as she finished her rapid-fire interrogation, then grinned.

From the number of questions she was throwing at him, Owen felt like he was being pummeled with snowballs. How much had she learned from her mom? "Hasn't your mom kept you updated?" He was hoping to avoid having to share too much.

"Has yours?"

No such luck. His body tensed with the rapid rise of anxiety just thinking about where his life had taken him. Places he didn't like revisiting. He needed to shut her curiosity down somehow. "Ummm, sorry to burst your bubble, but it's pretty boring."

She motioned with her hands to continue. He should have known it wouldn't be that easy.

He rolled his eyes and began. "Okay, so let's see, we were in Biloxi five years. Dad got transferred to Andrews, in Maryland, after that. It was cold and rainy. I spent part of high school there and then he got transferred to Maxwell in Alabama."

"So, you were still here when Donella hit?"

"Yeah. We got a little water in the house, lost some shingles, and a bunch of limbs from the trees, but that was it. As funny as it sounds, I think we were protected by all the trees around us. We lost power for a while, but we were kind of prepared for that. Under the circumstances, we fared pretty well.

"There were houses all up and down the street that got demolished. Your old house lost a portion of its roof over the garage. There was massive damage all over town. This place was, for all intents and purposes, shut down for quite a while. Of course, Dad was called in to help. He got orders for Maryland in the middle of the cleanup but was granted permission to stay until they had things back up and running.

"Let me tell you, I don't ever want to go through that again. Dad drove us inland before the storm, but he stayed behind on the base. Even though we drove all the way up to Hattiesburg, we still got some high winds and heavy rain. I've been through some storms since Donella, but nothing compares.

"The city was obliterated. It had wide-spread damage from the storm surge, and from an outbreak of tornadoes it produced."

"Yeah, I can remember seeing the news with all the people left homeless in the shelters and all the destruction."

"Highway 90 was hit hard. Even when we moved, the area still really hadn't recovered. Many of the buildings that were just rubble hadn't been touched. You can still see slabs of concrete in different areas where homes and buildings stood that were never rebuilt."

"So sad. Especially losing some of the old buildings." She paused and he thought maybe she might move on to a different subject. But then she continued, "So then you moved to Maryland?"

"Yeah."

"Did you like it?"

"It was okay. School was fine, I guess. I didn't do a whole lot." His brows raised. "But you would have been proud of me. I did try out for the basketball team."

Her face brightened while she took a sip of her coffee, obviously surprised.

"I'm sorry to say, all the hours you spent trying to turn me into a basketball player? Totally wasted."

She snickered. "Hey, at least you tried."

"Yes, I did." He shook his head with a grin. "And I failed

miserably. But I can't imagine what I would have been like without your training." He chuckled.

"Anyway, let's see, after that we moved to Alabama," he paused, trying to remember, "my junior year. I was glad to get back to a warmer climate. I guess I am just a beach bum at heart. That move was better, but I still wasn't involved in much. Got out of high school, went to MIT, and then joined the Air Force. Boom! Done."

She shook her head as she digested his story, then stopped abruptly.

"Wait, you went to MIT? …Hold on." She leaned forward, grabbed his chin and moved his head.

Confused, he jerked his face from her hand. "What?"

"Just checking to see if you had brains oozing out of your ears." Owen rolled his eyes. "What did you study?"

"What do you think? Computer engineering and information security." He leaned back. "Dad worked on several projects while I was growing up, and when he realized I had taken an interest in what he was doing, he started teaching me. I took the ACT, scored pretty high, and got accepted with a decent scholarship. When I went into the Air Force, Dad and I actually worked on a couple of projects together."

Bahn took a sip of her coffee. "And you said the job he had here was teaching?"

"Partially, yeah. It was research and development and training commander. He always liked teaching, and he was excited when he got the position. I think this felt like home to them too.

"My grandparents had passed, and my brother and sister had married and settled down, so I think this is where they'd planned to retire once he decided to leave the military behind. I came home over the summer…no, I think it was spring break actually…"

He stopped mid-sentence, recalling the move and the events surrounding it, and quickly got lost in thought. A familiar ache pierced his chest.

"So, you came home for spring break?"

"Oh, yeah." His voice was quieter than he had expected. "I helped them move, then wound up enlisting. After I finished my degree, I went in."

"What made you enlist? I'm just curious. You were always so shy. That would be the last thing I would figure you would want to do."

Owen let out a deep breath and stared into his cup of coffee for a moment. "I always thought once I got out of high school, I would know exactly what I wanted to do with my life. Then when that didn't happen, I just figured it would be college. But, when I came home that spring break, I realized I was still no closer than I was in high school. My siblings had both gotten married, had good jobs, and seemed to be heading down great paths, and here I was.

"My only somewhat serious relationship fell apart, and I didn't have a job. Not even a prospect. I was just mindlessly wandering through life. I always respected my dad. He was the epitome of everything I wanted to be. I figured the military made him who he was, so it was the logical next step for me."

"Did you do any overseas tours?"

His stomach tightened with the question. This was exactly where he didn't want the conversation to go. He didn't want to remember. He couldn't. He didn't want to lie to her, but he needed to somehow shut down the topic.

Glancing out the window for a moment, he then turned his gaze back to her, hoping the direct approach would work. "I did. But I don't...." he said slowly.

The waitress returned with a pot of coffee and refilled their cups. He grabbed the sugar packet and sprinkled some sugar in his coffee as his thoughts played her words over in his head. *Did you do any tours overseas?* Memories of his time in the military flashed through his mind. He could still call up the smells and tastes. He could still hear the sounds of war and feel the pain. His eyes closed. He wasn't ready to travel down that road with her yet.

"Really? You're just going to leave it right there, with me twisting in the wind?"

He took a sip, grabbed another packet, and sprinkled more sugar. Then he picked the cup up, took another sip, and saw her glaring over the edge of the cup.

"I just don't want the coffee to get co—"

"Owen," she interrupted, waving her spoon at him.

He took a deep breath and felt his jaw clench as he mulled over the idea of letting her peek at some of his darkest moments. But one glance in her direction somehow steadied his erratic pulse. Her face held an expression he couldn't identify but was also familiar. She'd used it on him many times when they were younger. Without words, he knew she was right there with him, through the good and the bad.

"Okay, Okay. Yes. I did a couple of tours in Afghanistan with a special ops technological unit. The first tour was eight months. It went like clockwork. In fact, it went so well, we completed the assignment early and headed home. I got back, spent another six months training, and did a second tour over there for thirteen months. It was supposed to be pretty much a second chorus to the first. Only it didn't turn out that way."

The waitress returned with her arms loaded down with plates. She set everything down, and Owen was relieved, hoping it provided a reprieve he could use to change the subject before things got too deep. "Can I get you anything else?" They looked over their food and both shook their heads, and she was gone in an instant.

"I think she's still waiting on that happy meal," he said while he drizzled syrup over his French toast then took a bite.

Bahn continued to stare at him, her chin perched on the palm of her hand. Owen tried not to glance at her, because he knew if he did, he would have to finish his story. She didn't budge. Her food sat in front of her, untouched, as her eyes bored holes in him until he couldn't take it anymore.

He swallowed hard. "What? You really like making me drink cold coffee and eat cold food, don't you?"

The look of irritation on her face made him smile. She was fixated on him, drumming her fingertips on the table, patiently waiting to hear more of his story.

She rolled her wrist. "Continue."

"Continue what? I did two tours. End of story."

She peeked at him through her lashes and shook her head. "No. Not end of story. You know you don't get a pass with me. Something happened. I need to know. I want to hear everything. Tell me."

CHAPTER 12

She was relentless. Always had been. When she knew he was struggling with something, she made him talk. Whether she was able to help or not, she wanted to know. She wanted to be there with him to at least lighten the load. And it never failed. He felt better once he had.

He stared at his plate, slowly cutting another slice of French toast, trying to figure out how to formulate the story. Was he really going to do this? He'd never told anyone exactly what had happened, not even his therapist. But somehow, he felt a strange sense of security telling her.

"First tour was okay. Like I said, we were able to accomplish everything we were assigned to do while we were over there." He stared out the window next to him, recalling the circumstances. "It was such a different way of life. Being that it was my first tour, I was pretty psyched. And honestly, there were so many new experiences, it went by quickly. Our location was considered safe. I mean, the heat and everything was unbearable, but all in all, we were as safe as we could be.

"We had a mission. Worked long days. Fell into our bunks at night. Woke up early. Lather, rinse, repeat, until we got the mission done and got out."

"What were you doing?"

"I could tell you, but then I would have to kill you." His eyes darted to her, and he gave a sly smile.

"Oooh, sounds intriguing." She leaned forward a little more.

He shoved some egg into his mouth and noticed she still hadn't touched her food. *Damn, is she going to eat or just stare at me the whole time?* "Wow, this is a good frittata."

She raised her eyebrows then squinted her eyes. "Continue," she said with a bit of a growl.

His attempts to stall were lost on her. She knew exactly what he was trying to do. His body began to shake as the memories came closer to the surface, and his eyes scanned the area for people eavesdropping. He had no clue how reliving what happened would affect him.

"Seriously, you don't want to hear this," he fought back, giving her a humorless chuckle. She nodded her head.

She has no idea what she's asking.

He inhaled a deep breath and let out a heavy sigh. A knot stuck in his throat. He contemplated whether he should continue, but in a weird way, he wanted her to know. Ultimately, he decided it might be good for him.

He leveled his eyes at Bahn and her features softened. She must have seen something in his expression.

"It's me, Owen." She paused. "You know—"

"I know. It's okay." It wasn't. It was so not okay, what happened. He took a sip of his coffee then chewed on the corner of his lip as he stared down at the table, letting the memories seep in. "Second tour didn't go quite as we'd hoped." He picked up his fork and stabbed at his French toast trying to keep his emotions under control. "It was supposed to be a longer stint, eighteen months, which I wasn't excited about, but it wasn't like I could argue about it.

"My training was more intricate. I knew the mission was going to be a little more in depth, and could possibly be more dangerous, but I figured, since we were special ops and basically involved in technological stuff, we would be fine. I mean, the last tour was.

"I should have known better. From the beginning, the whole mission was a cluster. Our flight out got messed up. Our supplies were delayed.

"We were supposed to be there to put together some receivers for satellite equipment. Our first location was in an area similar to our prior mission. It was outside of the heaviest fighting. The equipment would come in. We would put it together, get it up and running, then we'd move to another location.

"The operation went smoothly, and I was counting down the days until we were done. It had been a little over a year, and we had gotten most of the equipment together at the different locations. We were on the downhill slope of the mission when we got a call that a couple of our trucks, carrying the last of our supplies and equipment, had been rerouted. The convoy had hit an IED in the middle of an area that had not been secured, and we were going to have to go recover it. We had no idea if the equipment was damaged, or if we could salvage anything.

"We loaded up three trucks to go pick up the stuff. My buddies Robbie Cooper—this crazy redheaded guy who never met a stranger—and Skip Reynolds—who we found out was related to some movie star—were in the truck ahead of us. I was driving the second truck with another buddy, Rowdy McCall, riding shotgun, and there was a third truck behind us with four more guys from our unit.

"Rob, Rowdy, Skip, and I had been deployed together before. We were tight. We knew if anything were to happen, we had each other's back. Not gonna lie, I was scared. They trained us well, but I had a bad feeling from the moment we found out about the mission.

"When we got to the location and found the equipment, it seemed to be in decent shape. The truck with the supplies was toast. We salvaged what we could, loaded the equipment, and we were turning around to head back, when the first truck hit another IED. The force of the explosion flipped our truck over and blew shrapnel through it, all the way into truck three. It happened all at once. I remember seeing dust fly, then this jarring sensation when we went airborne. My ears began to ring and my whole body felt like it had been stung by a thousand bees. And then nothing.

"When I came to, I was being airlifted to the hospital. They had me strapped down and were working on me. I couldn't breathe. My ears were still ringing, so I couldn't hear anything. Then the helicopter was fired on and one of the medics working on me got hit in the leg. There was blood everywhere. They bandaged him up and continued to work on me. I found out later, he nearly bled out by the time we reached the hospital."

Bahn latched onto his hand. Her watery eyes gazed into his, and he considered how much more he should share. He could feel his throat tightening. Then she nodded. It was barely noticeable, but that infinitesimal motion told him she was with him.

A tear slowly slid down his cheek and his voice was barely above a whisper when he spoke again. "I had pieces of shrapnel all over me." He flipped his left arm over to show her a couple of scars. "I got one in my chest that punctured one of my lungs and came dangerously close to my heart." Leaning his head, he ran his finger down the left side of his neck. "And one right next to my carotid.

"Rowdy was hurt too, but I found out later, he saved our lives. He killed some enemy combatants when they began firing on us after the explosion."

His gaze drifted out the window as he tried to steady his voice that had begun to shake. "I spent some time in the hospital in Germany. I will never forget the looks on my parents' faces the first time they saw me. Mom couldn't stop crying.

"Once I was out of the woods, I was flown home for more treatment. I started back to work last December."

"Are you okay now?"

He took a sip of his coffee that had grown cold and thought about how to answer. "I'm better." He knew it would be a while before he would be able to slay all his demons. "We lost Rob and Skip, and another guy who was in the truck with them. We nearly lost Rowdy. Some shrapnel slashed his liver. I think he finally got to come home the last part of March. He had a really hard time. I haven't gotten to talk to him since he got back.

"When I first came home, it was kind of tricky. My senses were off the charts. Any noise, any smell, any quick movement, even a strange place would set me off, but I've been seeing a therapist, and things have gotten better."

He took another bite of his food. "When I talked to my commanding officer about needing to take leave, he asked me about re-upping. I was getting close to completing my commitment, but after that last tour I'd had enough. I think he knew it because that's when he told me about the civilian job here."

"When are you done?"

"I'm on leave until the end of next week. I'll head back to Patrick, where I'm stationed now. Mid-June I complete my commitment, finish up a few things I'm working on, sign some papers, grab my stuff, then head back here, then I officially start the new job as a civilian."

CHAPTER 13

Bahn sat spellbound by Owen's story. Tears wet her lashes, but only a few escaped. She never thought he would join the military. And now, knowing the ordeal he went through, and that he came so close to dying, she felt sick to her stomach and wondered how he would react when she didn't eat her breakfast. Her entire body hurt for him.

She couldn't break down though. It wasn't what he needed. He couldn't see what his story did to her. He needed to know she was strong enough to handle it. So, she sucked in a breath and smiled.

"So, you're moving back here for good?" Her tone brightened.

"Yes, for the foreseeable future at least. Basically, I'll be doing what I'm doing at Patrick, but as a civilian at Keesler. It works out great because I can be close to mom if she needs me. I'm seriously wondering if some strings were pulled to make it happen."

"However, it happened, it's a good thing. I know it'll be a big help to her right now, having you close."

"Actually, I'm going to be very close for a while, at least until I find a place to live. I love my mom, don't get me wrong, but I'd rather not be living under the same roof with her for too long."

"Oh. Well, if you want, we can look for places this afternoon. Or maybe tomorrow?"

"Nah, I wouldn't do that to you. I know you would much rather be digging your toes in the sand instead of checking out musty apartments. And anyway, I gotta go see the lawyer this afternoon."

"I don't mind. It'll be fun. I'm not doing anything tomorrow."

"I'll think about it. I just don't want to interfere with your vacation." He cut another bite of French toast and dipped it in the syrup.

Bahn suddenly jumped up. "I can't believe I haven't done this yet." She dug into the side of her bag and pulled out her phone. After moving her plate over to Owen's side of the table, she slid into his seat and held the phone up to take a photo. Owen rolled his eyes, but smiled and leaned in.

Bahn's body immediately prickled like there was a kinetic charge between them. Her eyes met Owen's. Did he feel it? It seemed every time they touched, her body tingled.

She reached over, gave him a hug and a kiss on the cheek as she snapped another photo, then shoved her plate back, moved back to her seat, and stowed her phone.

"I am so mad I didn't get a photo of you in your uniform."

Owen chuckled and shook his head. "It's probably better. If you remember, we spent most of the day soaking wet."

"True. But you still looked so dignified in it."

And he did. Seeing him in his dress blues for the first time blew her away. When she'd left town, he was still a scrawny kid. Since then, he'd grown into a ruggedly good-looking man with broad shoulders and muscular arms. From the way his clothes fit, she could tell the rest of him was muscular as well.

He stared at her through his lashes and a smirk crossed his lips, making her wonder what he was thinking. Could he read her thoughts? She took a bite of her eggs and studied him. How was he doing really? She couldn't imagine the shy little boy she knew carrying a gun and fighting enemy insurgents. He seemed to be different now. But there was something about him that still made her think that shy little boy was still in there.

The waitress returned to check their cups and Bahn fixed her gaze out the window, lost in her thoughts.

"So now you know all about me, how about you? What have you been up to since you left?

She turned back to Owen and grabbed a bite of food. "Nothing much." She grinned.

"No, no, no." He wiped his mouth and leaned back in the booth. "You don't get a pass. I had to pour my soul out. It's your turn. Spill it, Jackson."

She stuck her lip out. "But mine isn't even remotely as interesting as yours."

"Doesn't matter," Owen chided and leaned in. "Tit for tat."

"Fine." She rolled her eyes. "We lived in Virginia for four years. It was okay. Yeah, the weather wasn't the greatest, but it was another coastal area."

"Wait. You were at Langley when we were at Andrews. Why didn't our families get together? The bases aren't that far apart, maybe a couple of hours."

She shrugged. "Don't know. The life of military families. Never get too attached, ya know?" The ache in her chest made her highly aware of the truth she'd shared.

"I know that's right," he agreed with a nod, then leaned in again. "Sorry. Please continue."

She let out a deep sigh. "It took me a while to get comfortable there. Dad encouraged me to try out for the basketball team. Said it would help me make friends. I made the team."

"Shocker," he broke in as he took a bite of his food.

She squinted and smirked, still surprised at his newfound playful, sarcastic attitude. It sent an odd tingle through her.

"After that, we moved to California. Dad got transferred to Vandenburg when I was a sophomore. I remember I was so excited about the move. It just seemed like such a cool place to live. I was enamored with all the Hollywood hype, and the stars living there. Unfortunately, it wasn't anything like I had imagined."

She moved her eggs around then looked up at him. After hearing his story, her problems seemed trivial even though they left scars too, just not visible ones. "You really don't want..." her eyes drifted away from his. "I feel like I'm complaining about nothing."

A groove formed between his brows. "Tell me. I want to know."

Her fork stabbed at her food but the thought of taking a bite suddenly nauseated her, so she went on, "Don't get me wrong, where we lived was nice, other than the traffic. It was near the beach again." Her eyes returned to her eggs as a familiar feeling hit her gut, souring it even more. She pushed her plate away as a deep hurt stole her breath. Her teeth clenched and her tone hardened. "But the people were horrible."

Owen stopped mid bite and lifted his gaze to hers.

Her focus drifted to the cars going by outside their window. She could feel Owen's eyes on her, but she didn't want him to see the pain just thinking about those years caused.

The warmth of his large hand wrapping around hers had her attention jerking back to him for a second. But the thickness in her throat hit and, too scared of what his eyes might hold, she turned away again as she started to relive her experiences.

"You would think California would be pretty laid back and accepting. I mean that's how it's kind of been portrayed through the years, and maybe there are areas where that's the case, but not where we lived. I immediately noticed the cliques when I started school. If you were new, you basically had a target on your back. You didn't stand a chance. Unless, of course, you put out. It was established early on that I didn't. The first semester I had no less than a dozen offers, but since I wasn't interested, I got a new label, and the bullying started."

She finally glanced at him, hoping she'd gotten control of her emotions. His gaze was intense, but it wasn't filled with pity, more concern than anything. Why she even thought he'd judge her had her irritated at how insecure she'd become.

"My somewhat saving grace was the fact that I made the basketball team, and I did pretty well. But when I became the target of the popular clique, most of the team didn't want anything to do with me unless we were out on the court. That's the only place I got any respect."

"I can't imagine anyone not liking you, Bahn. What were they doing?" Owen's voice was quiet, his tone soothing the ache that had lodged in her chest.

"Everybody was very much into themselves, and *so* fake. I didn't fit their mold. I was too fair-complected for some and too dark for others, so that was an immediate strike against me. My race was a constant topic of contention. And I wasn't the typical girly-girl because I didn't wear short skirts or revealing tops. Strike two. And finally, since I wasn't totally boy crazy, and I was good at sports, that was my third strike. They loved questioning my sexuality. Like it was any of their business.".

"I got teased some in Virginia too, but it was nothing I couldn't handle. California was on a totally different level. It wasn't just teasing. I got bullied mercilessly. They were ruthless. If they weren't talking about me behind my back, and sometimes straight to my face, they were shoving crap—literally—in my locker. Or *accidentally* tripping me, or spilling things on me.

"They would steal assignments out of my backpack. One time, after lunch, they put banana pudding in my backpack, ruining everything in it.

"I got threatened several times, and one girl jumped me after school. When I went to the principal, they had their loyal followers lie, insisting I'd started it.

"Mom nearly removed me from school. I wouldn't let her, though. I was doing well on the basketball team and knew I could possibly get a college scholarship from it. Plus, I didn't want to let the team down, even if one of the bullies was on the team. I didn't want to leave. I didn't want them to think I was weak, and they'd won. "

Bahn had always been confident in herself, but as the faces of her tormentors filled her memories, it left her feeling wounded. And based on Owen's expression, he knew.

"I'm so sorry that happened to you."

She stared out the window again, watching a bird grab a crumb off the patio table.

"They were jealous, Bahn."

Bahn turned back to him and scoffed. "Of what?"

"You. You're absolutely stunning. You don't need any makeup or to wear skimpy clothes. You have a natural uniqueness about you that catches peoples' eye. The guys noticed you. And the girls, with the short skirts and the pound of makeup, weren't getting the attention they were used to, so they blamed you. Couple that with the fact you stood out on the court with your skills, and I'm sure those girls felt like you pissed in their playground. They were out for blood, but regardless, there's no excuse for bullying."

Her eyes moved from the window and found him staring at her.

"Their loss that they were too jealous to get to know you and how awesome you are."

She let out a long breath and gave him a half-hearted laugh. "It's trivial compared to what you went through."

"No it's not, Bahn." Owen's voice had dropped, and there was a hard edge to it. "Whether you have external scars or not, you still were hurt. Don't ever play it off as trivial. What you went through was traumatic."

Bahn had no idea how to respond to him. She didn't figure he was actually mad at her, but she could tell by the way his nostrils flared that he was upset. So she tried to change the subject.

"Anyway, I got through it. Then I blew out my knee at the end of my senior year, during the championship game, so I didn't get the athletic scholarship I was hoping for from Oregon State. But I got a full ride from Bexler College in southern Oregon. So, guess where I went?"

"Hey, you got your college paid for just because you got mad skills. That's saying something."

"And I got player of the year my freshman year."

"See. That might not have happened at Oregon State."

"That absolutely wouldn't have happened at Oregon State." She paused as she thought back to those first few months, and the year that followed. "Freshman year was crazy. You would think I would get used to moving to new places after a while. My first year of college was a whole new way of life, again. I realized I was pretty sheltered."

"Oh, I know exactly what you're talking about. My first year of college was so bizarre."

"Well, I would think MIT would still be fairly conservative."

"Yeah. And you'd be wrong."

"Bexler was a huge party school. My freshman year, I wasn't too bad as far as partying. I studied and played basketball, but that was about it. Sophomore year I kind of had the routine down, so I was getting into my groove and loosening up. I had a great roommate that I became close with. Her name was Sarah. The end of our sophomore year, we got caught up in the party life, so part of my sophomore and my junior year were a bit of a blur.

"Like you, I was trying to figure myself out, and basically gave up for a while. I think all the negative juju in high school caught up with me." She drifted off for a moment, continuing to put her memories together. "Anyway, I had some crazy stuff happen my junior year. Partied way too much."

Her expression brightened suddenly. "Did you say you were here during spring break your junior year?" Owen nodded. "Oh my gosh.

So was I! I wonder if we were here at the same time?"

Owen's brows shot up. "Maybe."

"That would have been crazy if we'd run into each other."

A quiet laugh fell from Owen's lips, and he looked away again. "Yep. Pretty crazy."

CHAPTER 14

◆

A strange expression passed over Owen's face, but as quickly as it came, it was gone. Bahn wondered what it was about, but finally refocused and flipped her hand, waving away the thought. "Anyway, I finally got my life somewhat straightened out, finished college, got hired as a coach, and now here I am. Tada!"

Bahn gave a half-hearted grin as the waitress came by to refill their coffee cups. Adding some cream and swirling the spoon around once, she laid it down without saying anything else. She lifted the cup to her lips and took a sip, still not able to confront whatever expression he was sending her way as he processed whatever he was also thinking about.

"Do you like being a coach?" Owen finally asked.

Her eyes met Owen's, but she couldn't quite work up a smile, and that bugged her. "Yeah. I do," she said as she sat back. "It's great to start at the beginning of the year and watch the team grow together and learn. We got to state semifinals this year. Not that anyone came to the games. Girls' sports just don't draw the crowds like the boys do."

"That's still impressive."

"You would think, yeah. I just wish the school saw it that way."

She became lost in thought again, wondering why thinking about her life right now suddenly made her feel so depressed. Things had worked out fine, even better than fine. Owen was right, her job was perfect for her. She was happy, wasn't she?

Picking up her cup, she took another drink, pinching her lips together as the hot liquid slid down her throat. Her eyes met Owen's. "Do you ever think about when we were kids? I mean, I know the past few days you have, but like before that?"

He answered without even batting an eye. "All the time. I don't think you know how much you traumatized me. You were relentless with your quests for adventure."

She tilted her head and dropped her jaw in mock astonishment. "Like when?"

"Let's see, there was the time I nearly drowned when you thought it would be fun to let the water suck us through the dam gates at the low water crossing. What did you call that? You had a name for it."

Bahn's face lit up. "Popcorn? Oh my gosh, I remember that," she said with a soft giggle in her voice. "That wasn't dangerous, it was fun. The water was like three feet deep. You could easily stand in it."

"Don't care. I've never been a huge fan of water, and that was terrifying."

She held her coffee cup up, smirking at him. "You had fun, and you know it. And if you haven't noticed, you live with water all around you. You better get used to it."

Owen bobbed his head back and forth then pointed his finger at her. "Oh, and then there was that time you nearly got us killed crossing the highway."

"Okay, okay." She put her hands up, giving in. "I admit, I was... wait, when did I nearly get us killed?"

He paused trying to remember. "I think it was like the beginning of sixth grade. We missed our bus, and you got the bright idea to test the traffic on the highway."

"Oh yeah. We got a ride home with that girl. What was her name?"

"I have no idea. You said she lived near us, so I bought into catching a ride."

"Well, technically, she did," she said, flipping her hand. "Anyway, it worked out. We got across the highway in one piece, and then the bus picked us up right after that and dropped us off at our stop."

"I was petrified. You, on the other hand, took it all in stride."

"I was scared out of my mind."

Owen glared at Bahn. "Scared? You said you had crossed the highway tons of times."

Bahn winced. "Yeah, I might have lied about that just a little." She wrinkled her nose and held up her thumb and finger slightly apart.

"You lied?" Owen teased.

"Just a little," she chirped back, then a smile slowly spread across her face. "Maybe I was a bit of a daredevil, but you have to admit, we had some amazing adventures!"

Owen narrowed his eyes, studying her, then sat forward. "What other adventures, that you risked my life on, did you happen to lie about?"

Bahn snickered. "You don't want to know."

"No, I do. I really do." He sat back and crossed his arms.

"No, trust me, you don't."

"Okay. The look on your face right now tells me I definitely need to know."

"What look?" She tried to keep her expression impassive, but she was barely holding back her laughter.

"That one right there that tells me you are definitely hiding something."

Bahn stared out the window as she mentally prepared her confession. "Well, you know all those times I talked about me and Joanie going on the same kind of adventures?" She lowered her chin, pinched her lips together, and dared to peek at Owen through her lashes.

Owen's eyes widened. "None of them?"

She shook her head slowly. "Owen. She liked dolls and Barbies. She wasn't much into the dirt and mud and dumpster diving stuff."

"But why'd you lie?"

"You wouldn't have done half the stuff if I had told you I hadn't done it either. And I knew it was going to be fun."

"So, the time we were walking along the railroad tracks when the train came by, and we climbed on?"

Bahn shook her head. "Nope."

"Good thing he didn't go very far when he took off, or we may never have been seen again."

Bahn giggled then confessed, "Honestly, I was terrified."

"Yeah, especially when the engineer came and yelled at us. How about the old haunted house on the hill?"

"Haunted house? I don't remember a haunted house."

"The one out by the big cemetery."

Bahn continued to think. "Cemetery? Oh! the big white colonial?"

"Yeah. You dragged me out there to go explore. I was scared out of my mind. That place was so creepy."

Bahn laughed. "I remember. I about peed myself when we heard that noise in the attic. We were tripping over each other trying to get out of there."

"You told me you and Joanie went out there at night and there were candles shining in the window."

"You believed me?"

Owen just sat and scowled. "What about when we went—"

"Owen, can I share a secret?"

"Oh, please do."

"Joanie barely rode bikes with me anywhere. Heck, we barely made it out of the yard. She was nice, don't get me wrong, but she didn't have an adventurous bone in her body. I played with her because she was the only kid in the neighborhood my age. It was sad because I can count on one hand the number of times we went up in the tree house. She was scared of it."

Owen sat back and began to grin. "So, you're basically saying all of the adventures were... our adventures alone."

Bahn could see the satisfaction sparking in Owen's eyes as she nodded.

"We must have ridden our bikes a thousand miles."

"And we were always only two blocks from the house," Bahn added with a giggle.

Owen busted out laughing. "It's surprising our parents never questioned where we had gone."

"They had to have known. We were gone for hours." Bahn smiled and turned up her cup to polish off the last little bit of coffee. "So, what else do you have planned for the day?"

Owen shook his head. "I'm not sure. I don't know how long the lawyer will take, and what we'll need to do afterward. I know Trish and Beau are leaving sometime this afternoon. They both have to be back at work Monday."

"Well, if you don't have anything going on later this afternoon, let me know. You can meet me at the beach, or we can go grab a bite to eat or something. I don't have any plans."

The waitress came by with the checks and dropped them off to each of them. Bahn reached over and grabbed Owen's.

"No, absolutely not. I should be paying for yours."

"Why? Because you're the man?" she questioned sarcastically.

Owen's expression hardened slightly, and she felt a twinge of guilt. "Well, no," he said slowly. "That's not it at all. I'm grateful that you came so far to be with me and my family. It's the least I could do to repay you."

"Repay me? Why in the world would you feel like you had to repay me? This wasn't something you asked me to do as a favor. I came here as much for me as I did for you. I wanted to see you. I wanted to be here for you."

"Really?"

"Yeah." She shrugged. "So, we could catch up. And I want to pay for breakfast because I invited you." She opened her wallet, pulled out some cash, and put it on the tray with the tickets. The waitress picked it up as she walked by. "I don't need change," she said to her back and wondered if the woman heard her.

Owen's eyes met hers. "Wow. I don't know what to say."

"Thank you for letting me do that." A satisfied smile spread across Bahn's face. "This has been fun." She glanced down at her watch. "Oh, geez. It's nearly noon. When is your appointment?"

"It's at one, but I told my mom I would be back for lunch at noon. I don't know how I'm going to eat anything else though."

They slid out of the booth and Owen's hand gently caressed the center of her back. She turned at his touch, and... *did he just check out my butt?*

Her eyes slowly made their way to his. He dropped his hand, and his cheeks filled with color. His guilty expression was all she needed to know she was right, and a grin spread across her face.

He walked her to her car and stood, silently studying her. Her mind raced as she stayed locked in his gaze. The past two days had been so much more than what she'd expected. She'd hoped the trip would rekindle their friendship, but the minute she saw him, her emotions took over.

She couldn't even approach him at the funeral because she was too emotional. Too scared. Scared? She had never been scared to approach anyone in her life, but she was afraid he wouldn't want to see her. They were just kids when they parted, and she'd worried he wouldn't care about her anymore, or even remember her.

When she saw his car in front of his old house, she nearly drove away. But the minute she saw him in the treehouse, she felt like she was twelve again. The tears he couldn't hide, his anguish, brought back memories of when she moved. All she wanted to do was wrap him in a hug and tell him—.

"I'm so glad you're here," Owen said, a grin spreading across his face.

She snaked her arms around him and squeezed tight. The thump of his heart vibrated against her chest, sending chills coursing through her. She could feel his heart racing. Was she imagining him flirting with her? Those little looks he was giving her. His gentle nudges and touches. Or was he just trying to be nice, and she was reading it all wrong? All she wanted right now was for him to kiss her and put all her questions to rest, and it kind of freaked her out.

She lifted her head, and her heart sped up when he leaned down. But he held back, placing a gentle kiss on her forehead.

A pang of disappointment filled her chest. *What am I thinking? We haven't seen each other in years. He just lost his dad. He isn't looking for a girlfriend, you idiot.*

She gave him a couple of gentle pats on his sides, then backed away. "Well, like I said earlier, I don't have any plans. So, if you get bored this evening, you have my number. We can go find something to do."

"The question is, will it be safe?"

"I'm not making any promises, but you know it will be fun."

"I don't want to impose—"

"I just said I don't have anything else going on." Her voice rose. "How many times do I have to tell you, I'm on vacation."

Owen matched her tone. "Okay, okay, I got it! You're on vacation."

She slid into her seat, and he shut the door and walked to his truck.

She sucked in a deep breath as she watched him walk away from her, feeling oddly lonely. Jumping out, she yelled to him, "Don't forget, you owe me a ride in your fancy truck."

He turned back to her, chuckling, "Yes ma'am," then opened his door and hopped in.

As they pulled away, she watched him in the rearview mirror, still chuckling and shaking his head. He followed her down the road for a while, and she giggled thinking about the memories they'd shared. The way he acted around her continued to invade her thoughts. She wondered if it was just his personality now, or if it was for her. Was she imagining it? He was always so timid and shy as a kid. Although, she did manage to drag him out of his shell occasionally. Was that it? That she was able to bring something out in him no one else could? She let out a long sigh and watched his truck disappear.

CHAPTER 15

Owen walked through the front door and was immediately hit with a wonderful smell. An aluminum pan rested in the center of the dining room table; one bite left of the nondescript casserole in it. Just as well, he wasn't even remotely hungry. Glancing out the window, he noticed everyone sitting on the back porch, so he walked to the door.

"Did you have a good time with Bahn?" His mom questioned with a smile as he opened the storm door.

He remained standing with his hands in his pockets, his focus resting on his mom. "Yeah. We had fun catching up." A smirk pulled at his cheek thinking about her catching him checking out her butt.

"We were just about to start loading up. Are you ready to go?"

"Ready as I'll ever be." He turned, opening the door for everyone, and felt his phone buzz within his pocket. His breath caught when Bahn's name showed up. It was the photo from that morning. His grin was accompanied by a silent laugh. Then a second photo appeared of her holding a beautiful brown and beige lace murex seashell. Seeing it took him back to when they would wander up and down the beach from early morning until dusk, combing the washed-up seagrass for that one special shell.

Another buzz. "Geez! Hold on a second."

Bahn: **Found one!**

He nodded, realizing she was having the same memory.

Owen: **That looks like a spectacular find.**

Within minutes, there was another buzz. This time there was a video of waves crashing on the beach.

Bahn: **You need to be here.**

A smile crossed his face. "Yeah, I do." He wanted to be. Watching the video made him wonder where she was. There were several areas they would frequent, but one spot was kind of hidden and it had the best shells.

Along the main beach, there was a large horseshoe shaped dune on one end. Rocks and cement chunks were dumped there years ago to protect the area from hurricanes. The horseshoe barrier jutted out to a point at the water, and the sand that covered it was dotted with native wild grasses and shrubs. It was their favorite place to go.

Most people wouldn't take the time to trek over the dunes to the other side; it was a bit of a climb. But that was the only way to get to the beach. It was by far the prettiest in the area, protected on all sides by the tall dune. Large rocks could be seen in certain areas, while other areas were completely transformed by the sand and grass. He flashed on the memory of the day they found it and gave it its name.

Owen: **Are you at Dune Canyon?**

Bahn: **No, I haven't been over there yet. This one is up the street from my hotel. Oh my gosh, we have to go there before I leave.**

"It's twelve forty-five. We need to get going," Owen heard his mom say from the kitchen.

He slid his phone back in his pocket and turned to his family. "Do you guys want to ride with me in Dad's truck? I think we have plenty of room. Dan and Sandra are going to the park, aren't they?"

"Yeah. That works for me," Beau responded.

"Let me grab the stuff we need to bring." Carissa jetted off up the hallway.

Owen slid into his truck. Finding the Bible in the passenger seat, he picked it up and thumbed through it for a moment remembering he needed to find time to take a look at some of the stuff his dad had marked. He set it on the console, leaving the seat free.

Beau and Trish got the kids buckled into their car seats and kissed their spouses goodbye, then they joined him in the truck.

"I haven't ridden in the truck before. It's nice," Trish said as she climbed in.

"Yeah. I drove it this morning and it's going to take me a little bit to figure out all the equipment."

His mom climbed in and gave him the directions as she shut the door. She was right. In no time, they were pulling into the parking lot.

When they arrived, they were introduced to Bill Sherman. Carissa reminded them he was an old military buddy of their dad's. He ushered them into a room with a large conference table. After sliding out papers from a folder he had sitting on the table, he took the folder Carissa brought. Everyone found their seats and Owen let his eyes drift around the room.

Bill spoke of his friendship with Phillip, and how they met. He handed out a few papers to each family member, then cleared his throat. "Your dad was well prepared. He had no debt, all funeral expenses were covered, and that's just the beginning. You each have a copy of his will in your papers. He left everything, of course, to your mom, except some savings accounts he had set up for each one of you. On the second sheet of paper, you'll see the balance in the accounts. You can leave it there, cash it out, or do whatever you would like."

They each slowly lifted the top sheet of paper to reveal a nice sum of money listed on a summary statement from the Federal Credit Union. Owen felt a mix of emotions. He was relieved—the money would help with his move and finding a place to live—but he just couldn't be happy, because it came at the expense of his dad's life.

"The life insurance is currently being processed and should be dispensed within the next sixty days."

As Bill spoke, Owen's mind drifted off to the text Bahn had sent him from the beach. He imagined her walking along the shoreline looking for seashells and letting the surf lap at her toes. Oh, how he wanted to be there instead of here.

He began to recall their chat over breakfast, and the looks she would give him as he spoke. She had such a free and easy spirit and had a way of making him feel the same when he was with her. He wished he felt that way more often. A smile began to cross his face, and then his mind clicked back to the present as a brown packet slid in front of him.

"We have been in contact with all of his income sources, and have given them the information, so your mom will continue to receive benefits." Bill's eyes bounced between Owen and Carissa. "You will need to go to each location on the list in the packet and drop off a death certificate. Also, you will need to go by the banks and savings and loans and get everything put into your name. Anyone who will need access to the account will need to sign a signature card."

She turned to Owen, who nodded in acknowledgment, not really knowing what he was agreeing to.

"Now, let me see what you have in your envelope." He opened the packet she'd given to him. "Oh, okay. These are his patents on the equipment and programs he designed." He turned to Owen and his siblings. "We've been talking to a few companies your dad was working with, to negotiate a purchase of his designs." He turned back to Carissa. "You hang on to that until we've come to an agreement. It looks like we have some very promising deals in the works. I'll let you know just as soon as I hear something." He sat back in his chair. "Do you have any questions?"

The room fell silent. Owen finally gathered his courage. "I just want to know that she's taken care of, or if there's anything we need to do to make sure she is." He grabbed his mom's hand and Carissa glanced at him and leaned her head on his shoulder.

"Oh, yes. Again, your dad was very smart with his money. He made very good financial decisions. Your mom is going to be well cared for. She might even want to take some trips and see the world.

"Your dad had several patents that he sold for a very nice sum of money, and the ones your mom has will probably do the same." He took one last look around the table. "Well, if that's it, we are done. Like I said, if you have any questions, let me know." He tucked the rest of the papers back into his folder as the family stood, each retrieving their packet of papers. "I'm certainly glad to finally meet you all. Your dad talked about you all the time," he said as he escorted them to the door.

The mid-afternoon sun started to heat the day as Owen helped Beau and Trish load their cars for their trips home. Carissa leaned over Sophie's carrier and gently pressed a kiss to her forehead, then picked up Preston and gave him a big hug and kiss before Trish put him in his car seat. With the babies loaded, Carissa gave her son and daughter-in-law hugs, then turned to Trish.

As Owen watched her kiss Trish on the cheek, Beau snuck up, grabbed him from behind, and gave him a big bear hug, lifting him off the ground. Trish decided to join in, and Owen was suddenly in the middle of a sibling sandwiched. Beau gave him a couple of hearty slaps on the back. "Take care, baby brother. And thanks for taking care of mom."

Owen nodded but there was no way he would be able to utter a single word with the knot that was currently blocking his throat.

Watching the cars pull away, Owen turned to his mom, who was wiping away tears. He wrapped his arm around her shoulder, tugging her into his chest, and set his chin on top of her head, trying desperately to swallow away the tears. When her arms tightened around him, he realized he'd definitely made the right decision.

As they walked back to the house, his thoughts returned to Bahn. Checking his phone, he asked his mom, "What do you need me to do this afternoon?"

"I have nothing. Do you have plans?"

"I was thinking about going down to the beach for a little while. Would you like to come?"

"Not right now. I think I'm going to lay down for a little bit. It's been a busy couple of days."

"Are you okay? Do you need me to stay here?" Concern laced his words.

"Oh no. I'm fine. I just want to relax for a little bit."

"Okay." He headed to the kitchen for some iced tea, and his phone buzzed. Sliding it from his pocket, he snickered at the text. It was like she'd read his mind.

Bahn: **Are you done? If you are, come to the beach.**

He couldn't stop himself from being a little mischievous. She brought that out in him.

Owen: **Bahn. I told you, we're in a very important meeting.**

Bahn: **I am so so sorry! I thought you would be done. Text me when you're home.**

Another snicker wheezed in his throat. "Got her," he said under his breath, and he texted back.

Owen: **Just kidding. We're done.**

Bahn: **Damn it, Owen. I'm going to murder you. Do you know how guilty you made me feel?**

Owen: **Murder? Is there something you haven't told me? Maybe I should rethink my plans of joining you.**

Bahn: **No. No. Come. Please.**

Owen: Wh**ere are you?**

Bahn: **Just go up ninety-four until you see the Redfish bait and tackle shop. Past that on the right is Beachside. Take that down to the beach and park there. I'll keep an eye out for your truck.**

Owen: **Alright. Give me about twenty minutes. I'll text you when I pull in.**

CHAPTER 16

His wheels crunched in the sand as he entered the beach area, and he slowed his pace looking for a place to park. The shores were crowded with people, RVs, umbrellas, and tents. He finally parked in a vacant spot and scanned the beach for Bahn, but didn't see her. With the hundreds of people, he wondered if he would find her.

A loud rapping on his passenger side window startled him. He jerked his head, and there she was, rolling with laughter. His eyes narrowed, and she gave him an impish grin. "You scared the life out of me," he said as he hopped out of the truck, shutting the door.

Bahn sauntered over. "Just returning the favor. I really thought I pissed you off."

Owen immediately realized what she was talking about and flashed her a playful smile.

"So how was your meeting?"

"It was okay. The lawyer went over the will and what needed to be done. But for the most part, other than dropping some paperwork off and transferring some accounts, everything is basically taken care of."

Owen followed Bahn to the edge of the water and removed his shoes. The icy water washed up on his feet, melting away the sand beneath them. Tipping a squinted eye to Bahn, a smile curled on the edge of his lips. "This never gets old."

"I know. I think I could stand here for hours just watching the waves and listening to them crash."

"You said your town isn't that close to the coast?"

"Not really. It's about ninety miles away."

"That's not too bad. Do you go much?"

"I've been out there a few times, but it's not like living here with the beach down the street. It just doesn't feel the same. Here, it feels like it's my beach. There, I feel like a visitor. It's not familiar and feels like it never will be."

The sun, now orange in the sky, struck Bahn in a way that made her hair shimmer as it caught the sea breeze. Her eyes seemed translucent, and her face glowed as the sea mist dotted her cheeks. Still wearing the denim shorts from that morning, Bahn had removed the top and was now sporting a brightly colored, vintage, crocheted, bikini top that showed off how fit she was. Owen's pulse ticked up, appreciating how the purple and pink colors played off her bronze skin.

It struck him how one look at her made his heart race. He kept telling himself he couldn't have her, but that mantra was getting harder and harder to accept. He had no idea how this was going to play out, but he never wanted to be without his friend again. She made him feel alive.

He turned, and began to walk up the beach, letting the breeze pull at his shirt. Bahn followed suit, walking in silence for a short time. Owen reached down and picked up a shell but tossed it back when he noticed it still had an owner.

"So, what did you do this afternoon?"

Bahn smiled and motioned him to follow her. They strolled over to a large beach towel held down by a small collapsible cooler on one end, and a large beach bag on the other. She sat down and motioned for him to join her.

Leaning into the beach bag, she pulled out several beautiful shells, sand dollars, sea glass, and other trinkets she found on the beach. "Look at this one. It has this beautiful iridescent color." She delicately placed the shell in his hand. "And look at this sea glass." She held it up so the sun could reflect in it. "Look at the colors in it. Isn't that cool?"

"Wow. That's awesome. That's a big piece too. You don't find them that big very often."

Bahn finished digging out her treasures and looked at Owen. "Do you want something to drink? I have water and beer."

"Beer."

She pulled two cans from the ice and popped the tops, handing him one. Owen tilted his head back and took a long swig. "Looks like you have quite a treasure trove here. What are you going to do with them for your trip home?"

"Not sure yet. I might have to leave them with you. They probably wouldn't make it back in one piece if I put them in my luggage."

"Yeah. That, and your clothes would smell like seawater by the time you got home."

"Ewww. Yeah, that too. But maybe you could use them when you're decorating your new place."

"Ha. You said decorate. Like I would even understand that concept."

"We did pretty well decorating the treehouse."

"Yeah, but the key word there is 'we.' Take 'you' out of the equation, and my decorating skills are slim to none. You're right though. We did do pretty well decorating the place."

He paused, recalling every nuance of the treehouse. "Do you remember the green metal box we found that we put all the seashells and stuff we gathered on the beach in? It sat over in the corner."

She tipped her can back and nodded. "Yes. Do you remember what we did with it?" she asked with a gleam in her eyes, knowing the answer.

Owen looked straight at her. "Of course. Do you think I would ever forget that? We hid it in the rocks at Dune Canyon."

"Yes," she said, her eyes sparkling with excitement. "You know what I'm thinking?"

He knew. Because he was thinking it too. "I doubt it would be there. I'm sure Hurricane Donella washed it away a long time ago."

"Maybe so. Maybe no. We will never know unless we check it out. Are you up for an adventure?"

"Sure." He chuckled and shook his head as he stood, because he knew there was no responding 'no' to her. Especially when she had that look in her eyes.

She grinned and picked up the seashells, carefully putting them back in the bag, then folded the beach towel and added it on top. Owen grabbed the cooler and shoes and followed Bahn back to his truck. They loaded his pickup without saying a word. A slight smile crossed his face, because it felt so normal having her back in his life, and them going on an adventure.

As Bahn climbed up in the cab, she picked up the Bible that was sitting in the passenger seat. "That was my dad's." Owen took it from her and set it in the back seat.

She looked back at it. "It looks like it was well used."

"You know, your dad was the one who got him started reading it." He glanced back at it. "Told me he would go out to the pier quite a bit and read, and it gave him comfort. Right after I got back from my tour, we went out there and talked for hours. That's when he told me that if anything were to happen to him, he was happy with how his life turned out. I don't know if he was relieved I didn't die, and I still had my life to live, or he somehow knew his end was near."

The sun was bright in the cloudless sky as they headed to Dune Canyon. Owen squinted through the glare on the windshield. "Man, I would pay good money for a pair of sunglasses right now."

Bahn reached behind his seat to grab the beach bag. After a moment, she sat back up and handed him a pair bedazzled with rhinestones in the upper corners of the frames.

Raising one eyebrow to her, he grabbed them and put them on, then puckered his lips for the full 'Zoolander' effect. "What do you think? Could I pull it off?"

She cackled with laughter, and he started to yank them off.

"No, no, wait." She reached in the bag again and retrieved her phone for a quick photo. Owen felt his face flush but played along.

He checked the console and pulled out a pair of his dad's reading glasses. For a brief moment he became melancholy, then he returned them and kept searching.

Bahn reached up to the flip-down glasses holder above the rearview mirror and found a pair of Aviators. She held them up like a prize.

"Well, who would have thought there would be some there?" Owen traded the bedazzled sunglasses for the aviators.

"Those definitely fit your style better. You look hot in them."

A twinge pulsed in his chest and heat flooded his cheeks as they eased into the beach parking area a short distance from their destination. Both grabbed items from the back of the truck and set off on their journey.

The beach was filled with families sitting under umbrellas, flying kites, playing in the surf, and setting up picnics. Owen's thoughts drifted back to the days when his family did the same. He remembered many weekends they would come to the beach and his dad would barbeque or grill hot dogs while he built giant sandcastles and watched the waves wash them out to sea.

They walked along the wet sand letting the waves wash up on their feet. The number of people dwindled as they got closer to their destination. The dune loomed before them, and he glanced at the cooler he was pulling behind him, realizing he should have left it in the truck. The climb through the shifting sand would completely wear him out as a kid. But the beach on the other side was worth it.

They began their climb up the soft sand, putting their hands down occasionally to keep their balance. Plants dotting the area offered no help until they got farther up the berm and the grass and plants thickened, the sand becoming more packed and easier to navigate. When they reached the ridge, they stopped to take in the view. Both noticed the other breathing hard and laughed.

"Why did this seem easier before?" Bahn asked between gasps, her hands resting soundly on her knees.

"I claim adolescent energy. It definitely has nothing to do with being out of shape."

She pointed her finger at him, gasping out, "Yeah, that's it," as she continued to lean over trying to catch her breath. "The problem is, I'm supposed to be in shape, so this is rather humiliating."

"Nah. I'm used to working out and I'm still winded."

Dead seagrass and seashells littered the higher elevation of sand, but the beach seemed untouched. It was like no one had been there since they'd claimed it all those years ago.

They slowly made their way down the side and took in their surroundings. Chunks of exposed cement, granite, and large rocks meant to break up the waves jutted out from the berm. Deep crevices formed around some of the structures. One area was washed out between two piles of cement and rock, making the sand hard, and creating a small cave.

"I can't believe more people haven't found this place. It is such a perfect spot."

"I'm sure most people think it's too much work to get here," he said as he continued to try and catch his breath. "Do you even remember where we stuck the box, because I have absolutely no clue."

She looked around for a little bit. "Give me a minute, I have to get my bearings." They set the cooler and bag on a large rock and looked around. "I want to say it's somewhere over on this side"— she motioned to her left—"because this is the side we always came in on. Oh, and there was this great big, red, glittery looking rock. Remember?"

"Sure." Owen's brows pinched together, not remembering any of her description, but she seemed confident in her memory, so he went with it.

"I think it might have been a piece of granite. I just remember we found a hole somewhere around it."

They searched each of the rock formations, dusting sand, dried seaweed, and debris from different structures, hoping to find the glittery red rock Bahn remembered. Owen moved to a stack of rocks piled with sand and noticed a glint in the sunlight. As he dusted the dirt from one of the pieces of cement, a dark rectangular chunk of rock underneath it came into view. Wiping the sand from it revealed the shimmering surface and his breath stuttered as he dared to hope.

"Bahn, I think I found something."

She turned quickly and met his eyes. A smile spread across her lips, and she jogged up beside him, sand blowing from beneath her feet. They wiped more sand from the rock, and realized it was definitely a large chunk of red granite.

Bahn's hair began blowing across her face, and she kept moving it away, finally pulling a band from around her wrist and securing it in a loose bun at the nape of her neck. Owen couldn't keep from staring. His body flooded with goosebumps, and Bahn didn't even seem to notice. *Does she even know how beautiful she is?*

Years of surf and storms butting up against the berms had driven sand and dirt deep into every crevice. They scraped away the sand, revealing more of the large chunk of granite sitting at an angle amongst the other rocks. Bahn dug her fingers into the packed sand. "You take that end, and I'll work on this one. We can work our way toward each other."

Owen scraped away big handfuls of sand and debris from around the rocks, slowly creeping deeper and deeper into the formation. As he dug, he opened a hole between the two sides, and he could barely see Bahn on the other side.

"Owen! Oh my gosh! I think I felt something."

"Seriously?"

"Yes. Come here."

He dusted his hands and headed to the other side while she continued to dig. She backed out, trying to see where it was, and then continued digging. The excited expression she gave Owen immediately ramped up his heartbeat and put a smile on his face. He reached into his pocket and held up his phone to snap a photo of her, then flipped on the flashlight.

Leaning in close to her, he held up the light. "Be careful."

"I swear I can feel it, but I can't quite grab onto it." She took his phone and shined it into the hole, squinting to see. A grin captured her face, and she turned to Owen with wide, sparkling eyes. "I think we found it!" she squealed.

Handing the phone back to him, she lifted his hand to position the light where she needed it. Prickles surged up his arm at her touch.

"Shine it right there."

Owen stepped closer to Bahn again and leaned over her shoulder, trying to get a good line on the hole. He smelled her coconut tanning lotion and felt the heat radiating from her skin.

"Do you see it?"

He squinted, trying to see what she was talking about, then leaned back out of the hole. "All I see is some plastic."

"That's it!"

Owen's gut soured thinking about how disappointed Bahn would be if it was just some washed up trash, but he didn't want to dim the twinkle in her eyes, so he kept his mouth shut.

She stepped back in front of the hole, wiggling around, trying to catch a glimpse, then grimaced as she reached inside with her entire arm, trying to snag it.

"Do you want me to try?" Owen asked, seeing the frustration on her face.

Her eyes widened suddenly, and she bit down on her lip. "I think... I got it." Tugging a couple of times, she finally dragged her prize out, letting it fall to the sand with a metallic thud.

They both dropped to their knees over the large, muddy, plastic bag. Bahn rubbed the sand and muck from it, and through the smear of brown sludge, Owen could see a tinge of green and his heart soared.

The smile on Bahn's face spread to an awestruck grin. "Oh my gosh, Owen. We found it!" Dusting her hands on the back of her shorts, she carefully opened the bag.

Bahn reached in and an old, rusty, metal box emerged from the bag. Owen worked on the latch, finally prying it open to reveal another plastic bag.

Bahn retrieved the second bag and started to open it when Owen suggested, "Let's spread out the towel, so we don't lose anything in the sand."

"Oh, yeah. Great idea."

He ran over to her bag, dug the towel out, and laid it on the sand, securing it with the cooler and Bahn's tote bag. She brought the bag of treasures and metal box over and dusted herself off before sitting. With the bag between them, their eyes met. Owen couldn't help but chuckle seeing Bahn practically vibrating with excitement. He had to admit, he was excited too.

Opening the bag, she pulled out the first treasure of their past.

CHAPTER 17

14 years ago

A crispness filled the mid-March air. Spring had arrived, and with it came farmers markets, art festivals, and celebrations. Owen was up early. His dad had come in late the night before and asked Owen to help him get something special out of his car. When Phillip opened the trunk, Owen had excitedly stared down at the large white metal box.

"What is it?"

"It's a mini fridge."

Owen was a bit confused until Phillip told him a friend had given it to him for the treehouse. The thought of what a mini fridge would mean in the treehouse brought a grin to his face. And although his dad was also smiling, he seemed preoccupied. They'd carried the fridge into the house, and then his dad had disappeared into the bedroom.

Sleep had eluded Owen, and he was eating his second bowl of cereal when his dad came out of the bedroom for his first cup of coffee. Still dressed in his pajama pants and T-shirt, he poured a cup and sat down at the table, eyeing Owen's shoe covered feet.

"Where do you think you're going this early in the morning?"

"I was going to head out to the treehouse to figure out where we can put the fridge."

Phillip chuckled and shook his head. "So, I'm guessing you want me to get dressed so I can help you get it up there."

"You don't have to right this minute."

"Well, it looks like you're ready to go."

"I can wait."

"Let me finish my coffee, then I'll help you get it up there."

Within a few minutes, they were carrying the small white fridge across the backyard. Phillip tied a rope around each side of the appliance and crawled up into the treehouse to pull it up while Owen pushed from below. Once the fridge was in place, Phillip ran a cord to the power strip where the lights were attached. The fridge began to hum, and Owen's whole body lit up with excitement.

"Can I get some stuff to put in it?"

"Sure. I think we have some Cokes in the house."

Back in the house, Phillip found a small box for Owen to put the drinks in. As they were loading the cans, Carissa came into the kitchen. Although she wasn't the most talkative person anyway, she seemed unusually quiet, barely saying a word when she got Owen's cereal earlier that morning. Pouring herself another cup of coffee, she sat at the table with several papers in front of her.

Phillip immediately turned quiet as well. He shut the fridge after putting the last item in Owen's box, continuing to keep his eyes locked on Carissa. "Go ahead and take these out there for now. We'll have to stop at the store and get some more later."

Owen turned and happily carried the box out the door. When he returned, his mom and dad were huddled up in the living room. And by the tone of their voices, the discussion was serious.

"When are you going to tell them?" Carissa asked in a barely audible voice as she studied the papers in her hand.

"I'll sit them down later and talk to them. It's not like they didn't know it was coming. We've been talking about it for a while. This is how the military works. You get stationed, you get deployed."

"I know. It's just that we've been here for a while, and you were busy doing your work here, and I guess I got used to it. I know you've been deployed before, but the kids were younger. They didn't really understand. Plus, your deployments have always been in locations that were low engagement. You're going into a combat zone."

"I know, I know. It's not like I asked for this. I would rather not be going at all. But I'll be fine."

Owen stopped in his tracks, unable to keep the question from escaping. "Where are you going this time, and when?"

Phillip looked at Owen then back at Carissa, knowing he would have to answer. "I'll be heading to Afghanistan in about a month or so."

Owen looked away for a moment, realizing he had no idea where Afghanistan was. "How far away is that? Will you be able to call home?"

"It's pretty far. I probably will get to call occasionally."

A wave of panic washed over him. "Mom said it's a combat zone. How long will you be there?" His dad reached out and pulled him into a hug. Owen leaned in, feeling the sting of tears in his eyes.

"Around eight months, maybe a little longer. Yes, there is some unrest there, but I'm sure I'll be fine."

"What will you be doing over there?"

"Just military stuff. Working with technology."

"Will you have to carry a gun?"

"Probably sometimes."

Owen could feel his throat tighten up as he continued to process the information. He tried hard to show his dad he was strong and could handle the information, but he felt like he was beginning to lose the battle. He stepped out of his dad's embrace, swiped his eyes quickly, mustered up an "okay," and then rushed from the room, out the door, and across the yard to his safe haven.

His mind raced through the conversation with his dad as he plopped down in the bean bag chair. He could hear his mom saying 'it's a combat zone' over and over in his head. Picking up a twig that had blown onto the floor, he began to break it into tiny pieces.

The familiar creaking of the tree outside the window shifted his attention to the swing. To Bahn.

He called her name, but she didn't turn, so he shouted. She still kept her back to him.

Chucking the ladder through the window, he crawled down into her yard, but as he approached her, she stopped her swing and kept turning her back on him. He knew something was up. She had never ignored him.

"How come you won't talk to me?"

She continued to turn away from him and kept her head lowered. He tried to grab the rope on the swing, but she quickly moved away.

Throwing his hands in the air, he barked, "Fine," and walked away, climbing the ladder back to the treehouse.

Just before he climbed through the window, he heard her faintly say, "We're moving."

Owen stopped in his tracks and swallowed hard. Surely he hadn't heard her right. His gut tightened and he climbed back down the ladder.

"You're what?" he questioned, hoping he'd heard wrong. She was the only way he would survive his dad's deployment.

She continued to look away. "We're moving…to Virginia."

It was the final blow. In a matter of minutes, his whole world had caved in, and he couldn't breathe.

"Why? When?"

"My dad got reassigned there to head up some project." She looked directly at him, and he saw that her face was wet with tears. "We leave in May."

Panic returned. His face flushed as he sat down on the ground in front of her and tried to stifle the tears. Bahn just sat on the swing pushing it back and forth. Neither said a word.

After several minutes, Owen wiped the tears from his face. "I'm going back to the treehouse. Wanna come?" She scooted off the disk and they both slowly climbed the ladder to the window.

Once inside, she spotted the new addition. "What's that?"

When Owen didn't respond, she walked over to the fridge and opened it, turned to Owen with her mouth gaping wide, and gestured for a drink.

"They might not be very cold."

She retrieved a can, popped it open, then fell into the bean bag chair. Owen grabbed one for himself and motioned with his hand for Bahn to make room, then he joined her in the chair.

"So, when did you get the fridge?" she asked with no enthusiasm.

"Dad brought it home last night. One of his buddies gave it to him. We got it set up this morning. Then everything fell apart."

"How so?"

"Really? You really have to ask that?"

"I'm just asking what all has happened. Maybe I'm missing something."

"First, I found out my dad is going to Afghanistan in a few weeks, then your wonderful news."

"Yeah, I think yesterday was the day of notices. You either got orders to deploy or a change of station."

"It sucks!"

"Your dad's left before. You know what it's like."

"He's never been to Afghanistan. He's going into a war zone."

"Yeah, it's not the same."

"And you're leaving Bahn. Who am I going to hang out with? It's not like I have a thousand friends, or my brother even pretends I'm alive." He took a quick glance around. "And we finally got this place like we want it."

Bahn stood, her eyes darting from place to place.

"What are you doing?"

"I want to remember everything."

Owen stood and closed the space between them. Following her line of sight, he noticed the checkerboard that they had many a heated game on and he had to wonder if they'd ever get a chance again. In the opposite corner, was the big red bean bag. Next to it was a wicker basket that held a blanket. He remembered snuggling up next to her with the fuzzy blanket tucked around them as they played on their handheld gaming devices. A fake plant they'd picked up from the side of the road during one of their treasure hunts sat next to the fridge. Bahn had said it looked sad and needed a home. Everywhere his eyes landed held a memory, a piece of their souls, and when she left, he knew it would never be the same.

Her eyes moved to the bulletin board covered in photos from their different outings and adventures, the many hours that they'd spent together. And Owen's chest burned knowing that soon those adventures would end.

Below the photos, on a small, narrow, side table with a green ceramic inlay, sat their treasure box.

Bahn whipped around and grabbed Owen's arm. "I know what we need to do." She ran over to the window and climbed down the ladder without saying another word. Owen wasn't far behind. They entered her house through the sliding door, and Bahn raced to her room and grabbed a box from her closet.

"What are you doing?" Owen asked, as she ran back up the hallway and out to the laundry room, gathering up a piece of art paper and an old soda bottle. From there, she ran into the kitchen, climbed on the counter to reach above the cabinet into a jar of corks, and pulled one out. Then she set it all on the dining room table.

Once she stopped, and didn't look like she was going to take off again, Owen repeated his question. "What are you doing? What is all this stuff?"

"We're going to bury a treasure!" she said emphatically. She dumped out the box to reveal several items, including a set of tickets, a few seashells and sea glass, and a newspaper article about her playing basketball. She picked up the tickets first. "These are from when we went to the Ole Miss football game." Reaching in and picking up the sea glass, she reminded him, "And we found these on the beach after that big storm. This"—she picked up the newspaper article—"was when I made that long shot that won the game last year."

She laid it all out, then went into the kitchen and came back with a felt tip marker. "I think that's everything. Oh, no, wait." She ran to the closet in the living room, flung open the door, grabbed a small black bag and a lightweight nylon backpack, and shut the door.

As she walked back to the table, Owen looked at the small black object she had in her hand. "What is that?"

"It's my camera. We need to document this."

"Ooooh, got it. Good idea."

"You ready?" She stuffed all the items into the nylon backpack.

"I think I might have a few things I can put in there too."

They raced out the front door and around the corner. When they burst into the house, Phillip and Carissa were sitting at the table, joined now by Owen's brother and sister. They all stopped talking and stared at Owen and Bahn as they ran down the hall into Owen's room.

He jerked open the bottom drawer of his dresser to reveal a shoebox filled with trinkets. Dumping it onto his bed, they started to rummage through it. To their treasure, they added purple, green, and gold beads and doubloons from a Mardi Gras parade, a small rubber mouse Owen had won at the local fair last fall, and a keychain with a rocket ship that had a flashlight for its thrusters. Bahn had found and given it to him on their first beach treasure hunt.

After gathering all the objects, they finished their trek where it started—back in the treehouse.

Bahn grabbed the metal box from the table and opened it up. Inside were treasures they had found on the beach—several coins, a few more seashells, an old rusty key, and a small chain. Then she stopped and stared at the photos on the bulletin board. "We need a few of these, so when someone finds the treasure, they know who buried it." She pulled several photos down and stuffed them in the box, along with the other items they had brought.

"Maybe we should get some plastic bags," Owen said, "because this isn't very airtight. We don't want everything to get ruined."

"Good idea."

Owen scampered down the ladder and into the house. Within minutes, he returned with two plastic bags. "We can put all of the stuff inside one of the bags, and then the whole treasure box in the other."

"We need to figure out where we want to bury it before we draw the treasure map."

"Well, we could bury it under the treehouse."

"Nah, that would be too hard to get to if someone found the map."

"Yeah, they would have to walk into our backyard."

They both fell silent for a moment.

"Why don't we bury it at the beach? I mean, isn't that where most treasures are buried?"

"Yeah. Good idea." They bolted out of the treehouse and ran through the gate. Owen grabbed his bike and leaned it against the carport before running to the front door and pushing it open.

"Can I ride my bike down to the beach with Bahn, please?"

He could hear his parents mumbling but couldn't make out the words.

Finally, Carissa spoke up. "Yes. But only to Central Beach, and don't get on the busy roads. Be careful."

"I will." He slammed the door shut.

Bahn grabbed her bike and ran to get permission, and within minutes, they were peddling up the street, their treasure in tow.

Once they arrived at the water's edge, they stopped and looked around for a good burial place. There was nothing but beach and water.

Riding a short distance along the hard sand, Owen finally stopped. "What about there?" He pointed to the large dune covered in seagrass that extended out into the water. It had been one of their favorite spots for finding treasures.

They hopped on their bikes and rode up the coastline to the edge of the dune. After traveling as far as they could in the sand, they left their bikes at the bottom of the dune, Bahn slung the bag that contained the treasure over her shoulder, and they started to climb. The sand loosened and spilled through their hands and feet as they slowly made their way to the top.

A pristine beach lay below them, a large horseshoe barrier of rocks and large chunks of cement making up a seawall. Several spoke legs were also contained within the secret beach to ensure the seawall was protected. They climbed down the jagged barrier and stood on the desolate beach, littered with seashells.

Owen stood silent, until something caught his eye. He ran over to the edge of a deep fissure created in the sand, and knelt, returning to Bahn moments later with his hands gently cupped together.

"What did you find?"

Opening his hands, he revealed a starfish.

Bahn's eyes lit up, and a grin captured her face. She ran to her bag and dug out her camera to take a picture.

Owen let the little creature move within his hands for a few minutes, then returned it to the edge of the water.

Bahn turned and glanced back at the rocks. "We need to find the perfect spot to bury the treasure."

As they wandered through the barriers, Bahn began running her hand along the edge of a rock dotted with glints of sparkling quartz. Above it sat several jagged chunks of cement, creating crevices where they joined. "I think this is the perfect spot!"

Owen inspected the small triangular hole and nodded.

Bahn sat down in the sand with the treasure box in her lap, making sure the items within it were sealed tight, while Owen took her picture. They slid the box in the bag and placed it in the crevice. Once the treasure was hidden, Bahn found a flat surface on one of the barriers. She quickly drew a map to the location of the treasure and then flipped the paper over and began to write. When she was done, she read it to Owen.

"To the person who finds this map, I am Captain Bahn! I have traveled from a faraway place with my first mate, Owen. We have gathered great riches, and if you follow the map carefully, you may find them. Great treasures await you!"

She began to roll the paper up, but Owen grabbed it out of her hands. He studied the map and then flipped the paper over. "This doesn't rhyme. Isn't it supposed to rhyme?

"Uh, no, it's not a song."

"And why are you the captain? You're a girl! Shouldn't I be the captain?"

She ripped the paper out of Owen's hands and rolled it up. "Again, No. So what if I'm a girl? I could take you in a heartbeat." She stood and lunged at him, and he immediately flinched. A grin spread across her face, and she let out a giggle. "Anyway, I came up with the idea, so I should be the captain!"

"True," Owen huffed.

She grabbed the soda bottle, stuffed the note inside, and squeezed the cork into the mouth. They ventured to the top of the tallest berm closest to the water, and Bahn turned to Owen. "Do you want to do the honors?" She held the bottle out to him and motioned for him to pose as she took another photo. He took the bottle by the neck, reared back like he was going to throw a baseball across home plate, and hurled it into the surf. "Nice. That went way out there," Bahn cheered.

The roar of the surf overtook them, and they watched the bottle bob in the waves. Owen looked down from where they were standing and saw their bicycles.

"Do you think we should head back?"

Bahn turned to Owen with the sunlight causing her to squint her eyes. "No." She slowly descended the rocky structure to the beach below. "Why would I want to go home? I don't like it there right now and look at this place. It's perfect. With the rocks and dunes and seashells, it's our own little secret canyon on the beach."

For the rest of the afternoon, they played at the beach, and explored their secret treasure that Bahn aptly named Dune Canyon.

CHAPTER 18

Present day

Everything is perfect, like we put it in there yesterday," Bahn said excitedly as she continued to carefully examine the different treasures in the bag. Mardi Gras beads, seashells, and sea glass, she held up each item then handed them off to Owen. There was her newspaper article, still neatly folded. She reached in and pulled out a handful of photographs. Looking through the different scenes from their life together, a knot formed in her throat. It felt like yesterday.

Owen grabbed his phone and moved beside her. She held up one of the photos of them together, and he snapped the photo.

In photo after photo, their cheesy grins flooded her with memories. When she dropped the photos and took a deep breath, Owen tilted his head, a puzzled expression on his face.

Bahn stood and walked to the water's edge without saying a word. She let the surf splash onto her calves, her arms crossed at her chest as she looked out over the endless expanse of blue.

Owen slowly rose and walked to her, remaining quiet for a moment. "Are you okay?" he asked finally.

Wiping tears from her cheek, she glanced back at him. "Yeah. It just suddenly hit me. This all seems surreal." She looked back at the dunes. "Being back here…and finding the treasure. It brought back all the memories."

Her gaze drifted to the waves. "That day we buried the treasure box was easily one of the worst days, and one of the best days, of my life. I remember every detail of it—where I was, what I was wearing, even my dad's voice when he told me we were moving. It felt like I was having the life sucked out of me."

Tears began to pool against her lashes and stream down her cheeks. Owen slowly put his arm around her, and she rested her head on his shoulder. It felt so natural to be in his arms. The way he held her made her feel safe from the outside world.

"I remember sitting on the swing thinking about how I was going to run away so I wouldn't have to go." She turned to him and squinted her eyes against the sun. "Then you showed up. Next thing I know, we're off on another adventure. You always knew how to cheer me up."

"Wait. What? I didn't do anything. Burying the treasure was your idea…remember?"

"Yeah, but you were always my willing accomplice. You never questioned or made fun of my crazy ideas."

"Well, honestly, they were great ideas. Scary as hell sometimes, but I knew when we went on one of your adventures, we were going to have fun."

The breeze from the ocean brought a wet chill with each gust. Bahn shivered and Owen drew her tighter against his body and rubbed her shoulders. She turned into him and breathed deeply. The mix of his soap and natural scent was comforting, and she melted against him as he wrapped both arms around her and gently rubbed her back. Her mind played out the scene of him slowly leaning down to steal a kiss, caressing her cheek, running his fingers through her hair. Her heart pounded and he snuggled her closer.

It was a bit surprising how strong her feelings were for him even though they'd just reunited, and there were signs that he might have the same feelings. But something about him nagged at her. There were times when she felt like he wanted to kiss her, only to withdraw, like something was stopping him.

He spoke of a girlfriend that he broke up with, so maybe that had something to do with it. Or maybe there was someone else she didn't know about. The scenarios started to spin out of control, and just when she was about to ask, he backed away but kept his hands on her arms.

"If you're getting cold, maybe,"—his eyes lifted to the berm—"maybe we should head in."

Confusion filled her, and she slowly stepped back. "Oh…no, not before we finish searching through the treasure."

"Okay, but only if you're sure."

They made their way back up to the beach towel. This time Owen took control of the bag. He reached in and retrieved the key and silver chain, the tickets to the game, and the doubloons from the Mardi Gras parade. After a few more seashells and some sea glass, he reached in for the last item. It was the spaceship flashlight keychain Bahn had given him.

"Oh my gosh!" A grin filled his face. "I forgot about this!" He wiped his hands on the towel to remove any sand, and when he pushed the button, it lit up. "It works! I think I need to add this to my new keychain. Everybody should have a rocket ship flashlight. You know, in case of emergencies." He sat back, reached into his pocket, and pulled out his keys.

"Hold on." Bahn dug into her bag and pulled out her phone. Owen proceeded to attach the rocket then held it up with a satisfied grin. Bahn rolled her eyes and smiled then snapped a photo.

After checking for items, they may have missed in the folds of the bag, Owen returned the bag to the box and shut it. "I think that's everything."

"I am *so* glad we found it!" Bahn lifted one of the photos. "These photos"— her breath hitched, and tears welled in her eyes as she pressed the pictures to her chest— "I'm glad we have them back." She never knew how much they meant to her until they were back in her possession. "We gotta get a picture of us with all of it." Bahn motioned.

"How?"

"Here, lay down with your head facing this way." She motioned and he followed her directions. Then she laid down next to him and held the phone up. He grasped her hand, sending sparks up her arm, and she turned and kissed him on the cheek as she snapped the photo. Tapping her phone once she sat up, she said, "I sent you the photos," just as Owen's phone chimed.

The sky began to gather with familiar gray clouds, and within a few minutes they heard the first rumble of thunder. "We might want to make our way to the truck before we get caught in a storm again. I'm sure it's getting close to dinner, so I should check on my mom as well."

"That's probably a good idea. I hate leaving though."

They gathered up all the treasures and supplies and quickly climbed the berm and headed to the truck. Bahn placed the beach bag in the backseat and hopped in. Just as Owen shut the door, the clouds opened.

Bahn's eyes widened as the windshield filled with drops of rain. "Woohoo! Perfect timing!" She turned and they instinctively gave each other a high five. "I haven't had this much fun in a very long time. Probably fourteen or so years."

"That might have rivaled some of our old adventures."

"I think you may be right. So, what are we going to do tomorrow to top this?"

"I don't know that we could top today's adventure. But what are you thinking?"

Bahn sat back and tipped her head back and forth. "Well, not that it would top today's adventure, but we need to find you a place to live. That could be an adventure in itself."

Owen let out a heavy sigh. "I don't even want to think about that. Way to put a damper on a great day."

"Well, don't you think it would be better looking at places with me than alone?"

Owen bobbed his head, debating her question. "I guess…maybe," he said sarcastically.

Bahn playfully backhanded him in the gut. "I'll do some searches on my computer tonight and send you some places I think you should look at. You don't have to do anything except say yes or no. Does that sound good?"

"You know you don't have to do this. I mean you *are* on vacation."

"I know, but this is fun for me. I love looking at places and figuring out how they should be decorated."

They pulled up under the awning of the hotel and Owen hopped out and ran around to the passenger side of the truck to open the door for Bahn.

"Well, aren't you the gentleman?"

Reaching in the back, he grabbed the beach bag and handed it to her. "Is that everything? Do you need me to carry anything?"

"Yeah, I believe so. I think I can handle it." Setting the bag on the pavement, she removed the towel and found the bag of treasures. "You should keep this safe for us."

Owen gingerly took the bag. "Are you sure?"

"Yeah. As much as I would love to take it home with me, it probably wouldn't end well. The shells would get broken."

As she handed the bag to Owen, she wrapped her fingers in his hand, and tugged him down, lifting on her toes to kiss his cheek. "Thanks for coming to hang out with me today." His smile reached his eyes, and she couldn't pull her gaze away. "I had a great time." She continued to hold his gaze as she said, "I'll text you later, okay?"

Bahn dropped her bag on the yellow vinyl chair in her hotel room and kicked her shoes off. The visions of the day had completely taken over her thoughts. The fire in his eyes when she kissed his cheek was unmistakable. There were feelings there. And it was exciting and scary all at the same time.

She picked up her phone and stared at the photo of them together, and a smile captured her lips.

Bahn: **Okay. I know it's not later, but I just wanted to thank you again for such an awesome day.**

Owen: **Are you trying to kill me? I'm not supposed to text and drive.**

Bahn: **Well, if you aren't home by now, you obviously drive at the speed of a turtle. And we both know that's not true. Not falling for it this time, Cramer.**

Shedding her clothes, she wandered into the small bathroom to wash away the sand and lotion from her day at the beach. A smile remained on her lips, and she giggled at their easy banter. But there was still something niggling at the back of her mind.

As she let the warm water wash over her sun-soaked skin, she could feel the familiar tingles from time in the sun and sand. Grabbing the soap, she lathered a washcloth and slowly rubbed it against her arms and down her stomach. She let her memories take hold and recalled the feeling of her body against his, his arms wrapped around her. Nothing felt more right. Gently running the cloth over her face and mouth, she could still feel his five o'clock shadow against her lips. But the uncertainty remained—there was something in his expression and body language occasionally that had her unsure of how he felt about her.

Her instant attraction to him caught her off guard, yes, but even more, she wondered why she felt so compelled to be there for him. She had thought about him many times through the years, but although she didn't feel that way when they were together, fourteen years apart meant they were practically strangers.

Was she imagining the lust she saw in his eyes? There was no doubt in her mind he'd checked out her butt. He'd basically confessed with the sheepish expression on his face. But everyone has their moments, and she knew those shorts did wonders for her butt and legs. There was a reason she wore them. Maybe he was feeling guilty because he only saw them as friends. Or was there something else standing in the way?

Was he just overwhelmed with what he'd been dealing with the past couple of weeks? Or maybe he was in a relationship he didn't want to tell her about. There was so much she still didn't know about him.

After she toweled off and threw some clean clothes on, she pulled her hair up in a loose, messy bun, snagged a small notepad and pen out of her backpack, and propped herself up on the bed to search her laptop for apartments and rentals. Her focus wasn't there though. It kept circling back to earlier in the day.

She chewed on the corner of her lip and a smile bloomed. Her fingers tapped out a text and hovered over the send button for just a second before she committed.

Bahn: **Hey, I just wanted to check with you to see if you had any plans for tomorrow evening. Since it's my last day in town I thought maybe we could do something special.**

Owen: **I got nothin.**

Bahn: **Great! I'll take care of dinner. Okay?**

Owen: **Are you going to cook?**

Bahn: **Maybe.**

Owen: **Are you holding out on me? Are you staying in a fancy suite or something?**

Bahn: **You're just going to have to wait and see.**

Owen: **Should I be worried?**

Bahn: **Um… well I haven't killed anyone… yet.**

Owen: **Somehow that doesn't really ease my mind, since you said you wanted to murder me earlier.**

Bahn: **True. But I think I got my revenge for that little stunt, so we're even.**

Owen: **Are you sure?**

Bahn: **Have some faith.**

Owen: **I just have one request.**

Bahn: **Oh. Now we're making demands.**

Owen: **No. It's a request.**

Bahn: **I don't know if my cooking skills can handle requests, but fire away.**

Owen: **Please, for the love of God, don't make a casserole.**

She threw her head back in a belly laugh at his 'request.'

Bahn: **I think I can honor that request. I'll text you later and we can make plans.**

Owen: **Copy that.**

She looked at the text, confused, and then giggled, realizing his military training was showing.

Searching for her notepad and pen that had gotten hidden in the covers, she found them and started to jot down a list, then ripped the paper from its bindings. Her mind quickly flipped through what she needed to do as she checked the list, then she scooted off the bed, threw on some flip-flops, grabbed her keys, and was out the door within a few minutes.

CHAPTER 19

Owen was kicked back in his dad's old recliner, staring at the TV but not really paying attention. He was too busy wondering what Bahn was up to. His phone buzzed.

Bahn: **Here are a few apartments and houses I found. I wasn't quite sure what your budget would be, so I kept the price kind of in the middle. Let me know what you think. Do you want to get together around ten?**

Even though she seemed excited, he really didn't relish the idea of making Bahn spend her vacation looking at places with him. He scrolled through the listings she sent and picked out four places he thought might be worth looking at. One house seemed okay, a little outdated, but appeared to be in good shape. The more he thought about finding a place of his own, the more he liked the idea. It would be great to have something locked down before he moved his stuff from Florida.

Owen: **Yeah, ten would be good. I'll swing by the hotel and pick you up.**

Bahn: **Okay. I'll be in the lobby.**

Owen: **Not going to show me your fancy suite?**

Bahn: **I'm not that kind of girl.**

Owen stared at the comment as panic seized his lungs.

Owen: **I'm sorry. I was just playing.**

His phone rang. Bahn.

"Hello?"

"That's called a comeback," Bahn giggled. "You toss a zinger to me; I toss one back."

"I just didn't want you to think—"

"I know what you meant. If you're going to be wielding this new cocky attitude like a sword, you must learn how to use it, Grasshopper. I'm here to teach you."

The melodic meditative tone she used, meant to be funny, sounded more sensual to him and sent sparks through his body. He took a deep breath and cleared his throat. "Thank you, Sensei."

"So, what are you doing?"

He tried to think of a clever comeback, and blurted, "I'm playing with my sword, waiting..." Bahn burst into laughter. Heat flooded his face as he played the words over in his head. "Oh...shit...I didn't mean it like that..."

She always had a great laugh, and it never failed to make him smile, even if it was at his expense. And now it was enhanced with a deep, velvety tone. The heat continued its path throughout his body, feeling like he'd taken a drink of good rum. But he wasn't sure if it was from the embarrassment, or the sound of her laughter. *Geez, this is so unfair.*

He chuckled and rubbed his scruff as he shook his head, hearing Bahn in fits of hysterics. The minute she tried to calm down, the giggles would ramp back up, torturing him even more.

"Oh, god..." she said through giggles, "I would pay good money to see your face right now."

He couldn't help but laugh along with her.

"I bet you're as red as a beet."

She would have won that bet.

"Oh god, I can't breathe."

If she says that one more time...

As they settled down, Owen could still hear Bahn trying to keep the giggles at bay when she said, "Okay. Lobby. Ten. Be here."

"Yes, ma'am."

"Goodnight, Owen."

"Goodnight, Bahn."

His eyes were becoming heavy, and he realized how exhausted he was. Grabbing a drink of water from the kitchen, he gave his mom a hug while she sat reading through a few cards that had come in the mail, before traipsing up the hall to his room. He clicked on the lamp and removed his shorts and shirt before crawling under the covers.

As he reached over to turn the lamp off, he spotted his dad's Bible. Since finding it in the truck, he'd kept it close. It gave him an unexplainable comfort similar to how he'd felt any time he was with his dad.

Seeing all the bookmarks sticking out, curiosity took over, and he picked it up. He hadn't thought of his dad as a spiritual man, but after moving to Mississippi, they'd attended church with the Jacksons many times. And when Bahn was hit by a car while chasing after one of his wayward basketballs, they'd all gathered and prayed at his dad's suggestion. Owen could remember thinking that was the first time he heard his dad pray, and it might have been the first time he genuinely sought God's help.

There were a few times when he saw his dad pick up the Bible, looking for something within it, although he never spoke much about what he read, or believed. He was more private, though his kindness and willingness to help spoke volumes.

Owen held the book in his hands and felt its weight. The binding was tattered and torn, and there were places where the cover was coming apart. Pages were yellowed from age and brown from the many times they'd been read. As he flipped to the pages marked by different pieces of paper, Owen found many verses had been underlined or marked with highlighter. Some complete chapters had been marked.

Page after page, words had been written at the top or on the sides. Verses had been marked in red and circled, all showing that his dad didn't just read the Bible, he studied it.

He turned to one spot marked with a dark green bookmark that said, 'Your love is a treasure.' A verse was highlighted and underlined. 'She is more precious than rubies, nothing you desire can compare to her.' He remembered how his dad always treated his mom, like she meant everything to him, and how he'd scolded him and his siblings on several occasions when they'd talked back to her.

His mind flashed to Bahn, a vision of her laughing, and he smiled. How had she completely taken over his psyche in just a couple of days?

Thumbing through different places that had been marked, he'd barely scratched the surface when the Bible fell open. Marking the spot, were several pieces of folded white paper that he moved out of the way and his eyes were drawn to the scripture underlined in red ink that said, 'This is a gift from God.' As he continued reading over the words, he eyed the pieces of paper that were used to mark the page.

Laying the Bible on the bed, he opened the papers. Equations and intricate designs filled the plain white sheets. It was obviously something his dad had been working on. He separated the pages and began to study the designs. The second page had an app with a username and password.

Owen hopped out of bed, threw on his shorts, and darted up the hallway. His mom was still sitting in the living room. "Mom, do you have Dad's computer?"

She leaned her head back. "I thought you'd gone to bed. Yeah, It's on top of his chest of drawers."

"Do you mind if I get it? I need to find something."

"Not at all."

"You wouldn't by chance have his login and password, would you?"

"I do." She stood and went to the kitchen. Reaching into the cabinet, she handed Owen a spiral bound book that said, 'Old Family Recipes.' His brow lifted with confusion, but he continued his journey, figuring he would understand when he opened it.

After retrieving the computer, he headed back to his bedroom and opened the laptop and the book. Every login and password, for every account they had, was hidden in the cookbook.

Typing the one for the computer into the required space, he scanned the icons when the page loaded. Nothing matched what was on the paper. He dug deeper, searching through folders, and it finally paid off. After entering the username and password, he began clicking through the tabs, diving deeper into the information the program held then scanning the material on the paper.

As he worked his way through his father's designs, comparing it to what he had within the program, he realized his dad hadn't gotten to see the project to completion. It seemed to be associated with a satellite project he'd discussed with him before, and if he could figure the design out, it could be a massive boost to the security of the military satellites.

The puzzle before him immediately piqued his desire to solve it, but he knew he wouldn't be able to do much good before he ran out of steam and fell asleep on the keyboard. This would take time.

He moved the Bible back to the nightstand, set the computer and papers on the floor, and turned off the lamp.

CHAPTER 20

T he morning light broke through the sheers on the window, and Owen felt like he had never gone to sleep. His mind kept going over the information he'd found the night before.

He slipped on his shorts and a T-shirt and plodded up the hall, carrying the laptop and papers he'd found. After pouring a cup of coffee, he sat down at the table and began to scroll through the design again.

"What are you looking at?" Carissa asked as she poured herself a cup.

"I found some papers Dad had in his Bible, and it looks like a project he was working on. I'm trying to figure out what exactly needs to be done."

"Are you sure it's not one of those we submitted to the lawyer?"

"I don't think so. It looks like he was still working through some of it. Do you have that packet of Dad's patents?"

"Yes, I do." She headed to the bedroom and returned with the large, brown envelope and handed it to him.

He riffled through the papers, studying each one closely. When he got to the bottom, he returned them to their folder and pushed it aside.

"I didn't see it in there." Returning to the computer, he scrolled through the information, trying to follow his dad's thought process.

With each calculation or scribbled design on the paper, he could see his dad was onto something, and Owen was determined to solve the mystery. "If I can figure this out, it'll be one more patent you might be able to sell and get some good return on."

"Do you want some breakfast?" Carissa broke in, halting his thoughts.

"Sure, if you're making you some," he commented without looking up from the screen.

"Owen, if you're able to complete that project of your dad's, it's yours. He always talked about how much he enjoyed those projects you both worked on."

His eyes lifted from the screen. "But it—"

"How about some eggs and bacon? Waffles, too?"

He knew, with her avoiding the subject, she was done talking about it. She'd made up her mind and there was no changing it. He let her words sink in about completing the project with his dad. They'd discussed some ideas on different projects but hadn't gotten to work on one to completion. It stung that his dad couldn't be there to see this one finished. If he was able to finish it. That was still up for debate.

"Owen?" Her voice called him back from his thoughts.

"What? Oh. Are you sure that isn't too much trouble?" he questioned, letting his focus fall back to the information on the screen.

She looked over the screen and caught his eye. "No. No trouble at all."

He smiled. "That sounds delicious then."

She turned toward the kitchen, and his eyes went back to the computer for a moment before lifting to her again. She had a smile on her face. Yeah, he was definitely happy with his decision to move to Biloxi.

Setting a couple of pans on the cooktop, his mom dug all the ingredients she needed from the refrigerator and got to work. Her eyes met his. "I got a phone call from the funeral home. I need to run by and pick up some of the flowers, and then I'm going to the grocery store. Do you need anything?"

Trying to split his focus from the computer and what she asked, he responded, "Nothing I can think of. Do you want me to go?"

"Honestly, I just want to get out, maybe stop by a few stores. I think it'll do me some good."

He knew that was his mom's way of saying she needed some time alone. Although he knew she appreciated having him there, it had to be hard dealing with grief and having a houseguest. Even if it's your kid.

Lifting his gaze above the computer screen, he responded, "Okay. I think Bahn and I are going to go check out some places for rent, and apparently, she has plans for us this evening."

A soft, knowing smile filled her face and Owen blushed. "That sounds fun and works out perfectly for me, because one of my friends asked me to dinner tonight. I'll call her back and let her know I'm free." She set another bowl on the counter and started mixing some ingredients as she continued talking. "It was so nice that Bahn came down. I'm glad you've been able to reconnect. It sounds like she's doing well."

His mom's words resonated in his head and made him curious exactly how much she knew about Bahn. He stopped what he was doing and closed the laptop. "How often do you and Mrs. Jackson talk?"

"Not much. We usually send cards during the holidays. I think Alex stayed in contact with your dad more. Why?"

He rose from the table and walked into the kitchen with his cup. Pouring some more coffee, he leaned against the counter. The smell of the waffles cooking, and the bacon frying, had his stomach rumbling. "I was just thinking. We were talking about everything that's happened in the years we've been apart, and I was wondering if she ever talked about Bahn, or if you told her what had happened to me."

"I know I told her when you enlisted, but we kind of put life on hold when you got hurt."

"I understand. I was more curious to know if she shared anything about Bahn." He'd hoped his mom might be able to shed some light on the mixed signals he was getting.

"Well, like I said, we sent each other updates over Christmas, and we exchanged graduation announcements. She let me know about Bahn's job. But that's about it. Why?"

"Bahn talked about having some difficult times in school. She said Mrs. Jackson nearly took her out when they were in California. Told me she had a couple of years in college that were a bit crazy, too."

Carissa dumped the eggs in the hot pan as Owen spoke. "Oh. No. No, she never talked about that. She always said Bahn was doing great with her sports and stuff. She did tell me when Bahn got injured, but never said anything about her having trouble. She's doing okay now though, right?"

Owen realized his investigative work had brought him no more information than he already had, and now he was feeling like he probably should have kept his mouth shut. "Yeah, she's fine."

Carissa scooped up some eggs and handed Owen the plate, motioning to a pile of bacon and waffles on the counter. He grabbed what he needed and sat down at the table to dig in. Carissa filled her plate and joined him.

"You said you and Bahn are going to look at some places to live?"

"Yeah. I don't want to put you out too long."

"You know you can stay here as long as you like. It's kind of nice having you here. I like the company."

"I know, Mom, but since I got a job, and it looks like I'm going to be staying around for a while, I figured I needed to find my own place. It was actually Bahn's suggestion. She said she loves doing stuff like this, so I might as well take her up on her offer while she's available. Anyway, I'm sure it'll take some time to find something. You may be tired of me by the time I leave."

"I doubt that. Having you here has helped me. You are so much like your dad. It's comforting." She paused. "Just don't ever think you would be a bother to me living here, Owen. You're my baby. You're welcome to stay as long as you need to."

"I know." A shard of guilt pierced him, thinking about leaving his mom. He knew she still had some hard days ahead of her adjusting to being alone. But he couldn't help being a little excited about finally taking the first step to a life on his own, free to make his own decisions. And doing it with Bahn at his side was just icing on the cake.

Owen pulled up to the front of the hotel to find Bahn waiting in the lobby, just as she'd said. When he laid eyes on her, she was sitting at a table, totally enthralled by a recap of a basketball game from last night playing on one of the televisions across the room. She had on a pair of seersucker shorts and a white, sleeveless, buttoned-down shirt. Her hair was pulled completely up in a multicolored scarf, and a pair of silver dangly earrings brushed her collar. He couldn't help but stare. Even as a kid he was intrigued by her appearance, with her riot of honey-colored curls, her tawny-colored skin, and her light green eyes. She was captivating then, and now, she was breathtaking.

"Of course it's sports," he said as he quietly snuck up on her.

Jumping at the sound of his voice, she sent him a glare and pointed her finger. "Well, yeah. Of course. But actually, I was more interested in the weather that was just on. They said it's supposed to be windy and warm, with a chance of afternoon showers. I'm hoping that chance will be more like slim to none, otherwise my plans might be ruined." She stood up, slid the papers from the table along with a small backpack, and they headed out of the hotel.

"Oh. What plans?"

"For dinner."

"Where are you taking me?"

"It's a secret."

Owen gave her a pout and she grinned. "See what sneaking up on people can do? I may have told you if you'd been nicer."

"No, you wouldn't have, and you know it."

"Nah, probably not." She laughed as he opened the door to the truck, and she hopped in.

Bahn's list of places was much longer than the four he'd sent back to her that he liked. He thought those would be the only ones they'd look at, but obviously she had other ideas. The first few, Owen thought, were okay, but they were nondescript. They had no special qualities. The first townhouse they looked at was nice, and Bahn started describing different ideas for decorating it. Owen liked her suggestions, but the living area was on the second floor, with the garage beneath it, and the thought of climbing the stairs with furniture really didn't appeal to him.

A second townhouse was very modern, built within the past few years. The price was a little much, but doable. The only problem was its proximity to the beach. It was in a location where other buildings once stood that were destroyed by Donnella, conjuring up images of losing everything with one bad hurricane.

The next location, a two-bedroom house, was in their old neighborhood. As they drove by his old house, he slowed, noticing a car in the driveway and another on the street out front. An unexplainable sadness stabbed at his heart.

"Do you think someone bought it?" Bahn questioned, reading his thoughts.

"I don't know. The sign is still in the yard."

"I hope they have kids."

Owen nodded, although he was hoping their observation was wrong, and drove on.

The house they stopped at was nice and would definitely meet his needs. It had a big backyard and a large deck for parties, but he still wasn't completely sold. And although he couldn't put his finger on why exactly, it was the same feeling he got for every other place they looked at.

When they stopped for lunch, they talked about the different places, but the look in Bahn's eyes told him she knew his mind was somewhere else.

"You okay?"

Owen shifted his gaze to her. "What?"

"You just seemed lost in La-la land somewhere."

"I don't know. It's just hard to decide. I don't know what I want. I mean all the places seem fine, but…."

"None of them jumped out at you?"

"Not really."

"Well, keep looking then. It's not like you need a place tomorrow."

"True."

"So…" She drummed her fingers on the table. "I need you to take me back to the hotel and then meet me—" Owen leaned in with a smile, waiting for her to finish, "—at Dune Canyon."

"Yeah?" The thought of meeting her back there definitely piqued his interest, but then it hit him. "Wait, you're going to cook at Dune Canyon?"

"Maybe. You leave that part up to me and just show up at five."

"I can do that."

"Oh, and wear your bathing suit."

They made their way back to the hotel and Owen dropped Bahn off. Heading back to his mom's house, he decided to make another pass by his old place to see if the cars were still there. When they weren't, he pulled into the carport. Just as he had a couple of days before, he made his way around the house, looking through the windows. Testing the sliding glass door, he was surprised when it opened.

The house smelled of old wood and some lemony dusting spray. Although the paint, tile, and appliances looked fairly new, the Formica countertop was cracked in a few places. He opened the doors of the cabinets and peeked inside. They seemed to still be in decent shape, needing nothing more than a good scrubbing and maybe a fresh coat of paint. The hardwood creaked as he ventured down the hallway, but also appeared to be okay.

In the guest bath, there were a few places where the tile around the tub was cracked, and the sink had some rust stains, but he could live with that. The bedrooms had all been painted a light gray with different accent walls, and the wood trim was a bright white. He walked past the kitchen and dining room to the main bedroom. The walls were also light gray, with a deep purple accent wall. He liked that. The ensuite bathroom had been updated with a nice walk-in shower and double vanity. "I don't remember this room being this big."

A smile tugged at his lips as he walked out to the living room. Noticing the realtor's card sitting on the windowsill, his heart began to race. He picked it up, took a deep breath, and dialed the number.

CHAPTER 21

His feet sunk into the sand as he made the long trek over the berm. When he reached the crest, he noticed the glow of a campfire. As he drew closer to the bottom, he could see Bahn had set up a wonderful picnic, complete with plates of fruits and cheeses, and a bottle of wine chilling in an insulated cooler. She was still wearing the same outfit she had on earlier, but her hair was down and loose. The wind captured the tendrils, and they were blowing softly against her cheek. A grin filled her face when she saw him, and she clapped her hands.

Owen smiled. "Wow, this is nice. How long have you been out here?"

"Not too long," she said with a mischievous grin.

"It looks great." He sat down on the large, tie-dyed beach blanket and grabbed a grape from the plate, popping it into his mouth. After a moment he chuckled. "So… is this all there is to eat?"

She narrowed her eyes. "Could be for you if you keep talking like that."

He gave her a devilish smirk. "Hey, I'm a growing boy. I gotta eat."

She inhaled deeply in mock frustration. "Are you hungry or do you want to swim?"

His face fell. "Swim? I don't remember anyone mentioning

swimming."

"Uh…I did tell you to put on your swimsuit." Her eyes raked over his body, and she pointed. "And it looks like you followed the instructions. What did you think was going to happen here…on the beach… next to that big, beautiful, body of water?" She motioned with her hand to display the scene.

"I don't know. Build some sandcastles? Hunt for seashells? Maybe climb the rocks?"

"None of those require a swimsuit. Swimming on the other hand—"

"No," he whined. "Please don't make me go swimming. I told you, I am not a fan of water. And the surf is freaking frigid this time of year."

Bahn snickered at his boyish tantrum. "This is my last day here. Don't spoil it for me." She stopped for a moment, pursing her lips. "How about this? I'll feed you first, and in return, you will at least get in the water."

Owen pouted but agreed. "Okay, fine. If it means I get to eat, I'll do it. But only because it's your last day, and I'm starving."

Her face lit up. "Perfect."

Although he wasn't happy about what he'd agreed to, seeing that look on her face, with her eyes sparkling, had him smiling in response.

She dug out container after container and sat it on the blanket, then produced plates, plastic utensils, and plastic wine glasses from the bottom of her bag. Opening the containers, she revealed steaks, baked potatoes, glazed carrots, and crusty bread.

"Wow! I must say, I'm impressed. I didn't think those hotel rooms had stoves."

"They don't. I ordered everything from Frank's Steakhouse. I initially thought about getting a little hibachi grill to bring out here so I could grill the steaks and everything. But honestly, I didn't want to lug everything over the hill, and I had no idea what to do with it after we were done. So, I figured this would be just as good."

"Ah. Great idea, but yeah, that is an awful lot of trouble. Not that this isn't. This is amazing."

"Dig in before it gets cold."

He grabbed a steak and potato while she opened the wine and poured them each a glass.

"So, when is your flight tomorrow?" Owen asked, still loading his plate.

"It's at one thirty. I get into Eugene around nine thirty, and then it's another half hour to get home."

His mouth dropped open, and his eyes lifted to hers. "That really makes for a long day. Do you have to go to work Monday?"

"Yeah. We have in service this coming week. It's nothing but cleaning out the classroom, meeting with the principal, going over test results, and my performance evaluation. Yay," she said with no enthusiasm.

"What do you have going on the rest of the summer?"

"I have a coaches' conference at the end of June in Mobile, Alabama, and another teachers' conference in Eugene at the beginning of July. Sarah and I are trying to plan a trip to California to see my folks and go to Big Sur, but that's about it."

"Sarah?"

"Oh, yeah. Do you remember me telling you about my college roommate, Sarah? You would love her. We pretty much were inseparable, and we're living together now. We both got coaching jobs in the same town."

And there it was. The confirmation he'd been looking for. His mind drifted back, remembering that night during spring break when he stumbled onto a party at Dune Canyon and talked to a guy who mentioned a girl named Bahn who'd brought them there, with her girlfriend Sarah. He'd wondered if it was his childhood friend, and all doubt was erased when he saw her.

His chest burned, picturing the moment, and a disappointed sigh escaped as his hopes that he might have been wrong were dashed. Now he knew. It hurt, but he was relieved that he didn't have to question her confusing actions toward him. Why didn't she say anything though? And why did he get the feeling she was flirting with him.

He brushed it off, figuring she was just comfortable with him. He was happy to have her back in his life, even if she would only be a friend. It was time to move on.

Bahn snapped her fingers. "Earth to Owen. Are you in there?"

Owen blinked and sucked in a deep breath. He couldn't ignore the increasing pain in his chest, but he was bound and determined to have a good time with her on their last day, so he forced himself to smile. "Oh, sorry. You were just talking about where you lived, and it made me think. I may have found a place."

Her face brightened. "Really? Where?"

"It's over in that same neighborhood where the other house was."

"Is it nice?" Her voice was filled with enthusiasm.

"Yeah. I think you would like it. I haven't gotten everything finalized yet. I'm waiting for them to call me back."

"Yay! Can we go see it?"

"What? Now? No. You put together this great spread of food, and then we *have to swim*, remember?" She smiled as he shoved another chunk of meat in his mouth. "Anyway, I don't know if I can get it, so I really don't want to get my hopes up."

"What's it look like?"

"It's four bedrooms, two baths. Nice backyard with lots of trees. It's a little older, needs some work, but it's really perfect."

"And it's in your price range?"

"Yeah. Like I said, it needs some work, But really, it's not in bad shape."

"Yay! It sounds perfect. When do you think they'll let you know?"

"I'm hoping before I leave."

"I'm excited for you. Things seem to really be falling into place."

He nodded and finished his last bite of steak, setting his plate aside.

The fire crackled and popped. Owen stood and walked closer, grabbing some wood along the way to stoke it. He was hypnotized by the blowing embers from the wind coming off the surf but noticed the wind shifting. "Do you think we should put this out? It looks like the wind is picking up."

"Yeah, it might be a good idea. The embers and smoke are blowing right at us. I brought a lantern just in case."

While Owen separated the burning pieces with the stick he had picked up, rolling them in the sand to put the fire out, she dug in her bag, set the lantern on the blanket and flipped it on. Dusting his hands off, he turned to head back to the blanket.

"Get in the water!" Bahn shouted with laughter in her voice. Glancing back at the water, he responded, "I don't know if that's a good idea. The wind is really beginning to whip up the waves." He was only half joking, noticing the surf beginning to get choppy as the clouds rolled in.

"Oh my gosh, don't make excuses."

He turned with narrowed eyes and huffed before walking over, removing his shirt, and throwing it at her. Bahn's eyes popped open, and she whistled. His heart slammed against his chest with the mixed signals she was sending, but he felt more assured now that it was just playful banter between friends.

Wading into the water up to his knees, the chilly temperature caught him off guard and goosebumps coated his body. "Damn. It's freezing. You're crazy if you want to swim in this." His voice trembled with each word.

Bahn giggled and pulled out her phone. "Smile."

Owen looked up at her. "Aw, hell. If you're going to make me do this, I might as well go all in." He spread his arms wide and fell backward into the surf. The frigid water wrapped around him and took his breath away and his hands skimmed his face and hair as he surfaced. "Shit, that's cold."

Bahn threw the phone back in her bag and immediately removed her shirt and shorts, revealing the multicolored crocheted bikini top and boy-shorts bottoms. Owen watched as she strolled up to the water's edge. The suit was modest, and he loved that about her. She didn't try to be sexy, she just was, and Owen tried desperately not to stare at the way she filled out the suit. He could feel himself holding his breath, and quickly looked away.

She stood beside him with her legs in the water. "It's not cold, you big baby."

"It is too. My goosebumps have goosebumps." He gave her a little shove, and with the aid of a perfectly timed wave, knocked her off balance, plunging her into the water.

That was all the encouragement Bahn needed. Cupping her hands, she popped a splash right into his face. He returned the favor, and within seconds, water rained between them. Owen started moving toward Bahn, and she quickly swam away. He swam after her, but she went under, so he stopped and waited for her to surface, only to have her surface for a split second, then go under again.

He chuckled. "I'm done. You win," he called out. But when she didn't surface again, a wave of panic swarmed in his belly. "Bahn?"

She surfaced once again, panic filling her face as she stuttered, "Owen, help," and then disappeared in the surf.

"Shit."

The water swallowed him as he dove forward and began swimming with everything he had. He reached out, felt a brush of her hand and latched on. Wrapping his arm around her body, he began to swim back to shore. The weight of her body, and the force of the riptide, caused him to struggle to stay afloat. He could hear her gasping for air and coughing, and it ramped up the panic coursing through his veins, prompting him to step up his efforts.

When they got close enough to shore where they could stand, he swept her up in his arms and headed for the blanket. Gently setting her down, he dropped to his butt then fell backward, breathing heavily. Bahn leaned over, coughing, water spewing from her mouth.

Owen sat up and patted her back gently. Tears streamed down her face as she shivered uncontrollably. Grabbing the beach towel from the bag, he wrapped it around her, then cradled her in his lap, letting her head rest against his chest. The pain he had felt in his chest earlier had nothing on the crushing thought of nearly losing her.

A knot formed in his throat as he admitted, "I am not a fan of water."

Bahn looked up at him and gave a halfhearted laugh then coughed again.

Owen sat quietly and gently tugged her closer to him. "Maybe we should go to the hospital?"

"No." Her voice was tight and shaky. He didn't know if it was from the cold, or if she was scared. Bahn and fear were two things that never coexisted in his mind.

"I think I'll be okay."

"Geez, Bahn, you scared the shit out of me."

She continued to shiver uncontrollably. "Me too. I couldn't get my footing. The riptide was so strong. I could feel it sucking me under." She wiped the water from her face with the towel, but the tears continued to stream down her cheeks.

Owen could count on one hand the number of times he'd seen

Bahn cry, and it unnerved him. He tightened his arms around her and continued to hold her.

Moving a tassel of hair stuck to her face, he leaned his cheek on her head and rocked her. "I'm just glad you're okay. I thought you were joking at first. Then, when I realized you weren't, I was scared I wasn't going to get to you in time. You went under so fast, and I thought I lost you." His voice cracked with the tightening of his throat, and he felt the sting of tears in his eyes. He was surprised by how much of an effect she already had on him, especially after not seeing her for so many years.

Bahn looked up at him, fear still gleaming in her eyes. He glanced out at the surf, trying to hold back the tears, but with everything that had happened in the past few days, he was just too raw. His lips pinched and he could feel his chin quiver.

Bahn put her hand on his cheek and pulled him to face her. He looked down at her, knowing she saw the tears on his cheeks, but he tried to smile anyway. When he met her gaze, he could see her studying him.

She didn't move for several moments. They sat silently, their focus unwavering, until Bahn finally raised up. Her fingers slowly inched from his cheek to his neck, pulling him down until their lips met, and he was immediately lost in her. The coolness of her skin, the moisture on her lips. She was more than he could ever imagine, and he wanted to commit every nuance to memory.

His eyes closed and the smell of her coconut tanning lotion lit up his senses. Sand grated against his fingers as his hand slowly wrapped around the back of her neck. He shifted his head, deepening the kiss, tasting her for the first time—sweet and spicy and rich, like champagne and chocolate.

Tightening his arm around her, he brought her closer while their tongues lazily danced against each other. This was what he'd wanted, dreamed about, since she'd appeared through the trap door of the treehouse the day of the funeral. But a sudden flash in his memory made him jerk away, the confusion reemerging.

Bahn's brows furrowed, her eyes searching his, then she quickly pulled back. "Owen, I'm—" she swallowed hard as the color drained from her face, "—so sorry. I shouldn't have—"

"No. I'm just—"

"No. You don't have to say anything. This is on me. I just got caught up in the moment." Realizing she was still curled up in his arms, she jumped up.

"Bahn, wait. I'm, I'm sorry, I—"

She began dusting the sand away with the towel and continued to talk without making eye contact. "I just thought, maybe, you were a little scared to... Oh my gosh—" she looked back at him, "—I'm so sorry."

Owen slowly stood, still shaken from his water rescue and fighting the flood of confusion wracking his brain. What the hell was he supposed to say?

Pink bloomed in Bahn's cheeks as she hurriedly started putting on her clothes and gathered her stuff together.

Owen grabbed her arm and stopped her. "Listen to me."

She turned to face him, but her eyes quickly darted away. "I just can't believe I..." Tears spilled down her cheeks and she pulled away from his grip to grab her bag. "Owen... I'm—"

"Bahn, will you stop." He moved her bag out of her reach and sat her down. "It's not that I'm not attracted to you. I'm just a bit confused."

"Confused? I think I made myself pretty clear."

"Yes, but I kind of..." Now it was his turn to be lost for words. He was feeling more and more confused and unsure of what to say.

"You...kind of what?" Bahn's expression suddenly hardened.

His heart and mind battled, but he knew he needed to be honest. "I thought you were gay."

CHAPTER 22

Bahn's uneasiness turned into an immediate sucking pain, leaving her struggling to breathe. Her body began to shake uncontrollably, but it had nothing to do with the chill of the water that remained on her skin, because there was a fire erupting within her.

Tears stung as they poured from her eyes, and she tried to force words from her lips, but they wouldn't come. She stared into Owen's eyes, questioning where his assumption came from. A chorus of voices from the worst years of her life now screamed at her over and over again. She begged for the universe to tell her she'd heard him wrong. He wasn't like them.

Pursing her lips, she shook her head then stood, accepting the fact that she'd heard him quite clearly. She just didn't want to believe it. "You too?" she gritted out. "The one person in the world who I thought understood me." She wiped her nose and continued packing the containers. "But, oh boy, was I wrong. You're just like them. Putting me into some damn box. Thinking that because I'm a little more athletic and adventurous, I'm gay. That because I'm more comfortable wearing pants instead of dresses short enough to show off my ass, or because I don't cake on the makeup and get my nails done once a week, I'm gay."

"It's not—"

"Oh, I beg to differ. It's exactly that."

She stood up, looking around at what else needed to be packed. "No, Bahn. It has nothing to do with that."

Again, she looked him in the eyes. "It has everything to do with it, Owen." Her tone lowered to a growl as she spoke through her gritted teeth. "I fought this constantly in high school. People mocking me, judging me by my appearance or my athletic ability, making assumptions and conclusions, when, quite frankly, it was none of their damn business who I chose to date. But they sure as hell made it their business. After high school, I thought it was over. Just high school drama. But, oh no, it continued on into college."

Her eyes focused on the water, and, as she relived the evening, she finally understood his confusing behavior. But it only made the moment more awkward. "Why didn't you just say something instead of letting me…"

Her chin quivered. Geez, she hated angry crying. And Owen being the reason for it only made it worse.

Grabbing up the remaining items, she chucked them into the bag, rolled the blanket up, and threw it over the beach bag. The tears came hard and fast, causing her to cough, which made her gag from the sea water all over again. The whole evening made her sick to her stomach.

"I thought you were better than them," she yelled. "Whether I was gay or not, do you not realize how making assumptions like that hurts?" Bahn grabbed her bag and ran to the edge of the berm.

Owen followed her. "Please, Bahn, wait. Let me explain."

"You don't need to. I heard you loud and clear. Just stay away from me."

Fighting exhaustion and the searing pain in her lungs, she dug into the sand and climbed as fast as she could over the berm.

"Bahn, please, just listen."

She turned and glared back at him, then began to walk quickly to her car.

Owen jogged to catch up to her. "You don't understand. I saw you—"

"You saw me?" She tilted her head. "At one time, I thought you were the only one who truly did. But I was obviously mistaken."

"Would you just listen for a second? I saw you—"

She dropped her bag, planted her hand on her hip, and glared at him. Her gaze locked on his, and she was taken aback by the desperation marring his chiseled features. "I, I just can't believe…"

For a moment she thought about giving in. Then his voice resonated in her head and the voices of the past chimed in behind his. "You know what? Never mind. I'm done caring what other people think of me." Tears streamed down her face as she dug in the bag for her keys, quickly retrieving them and unlocking the door.

"Bahn, stop. If you'd just listen—" Owen pleaded, reaching for her.

Bahn jerked away from him, threw her bag in the car, slammed the door and turned to Owen. "No. You listen. Do you know why I really wanted to come down here?"

Owen hesitantly shook his head.

"Because time and time again, throughout those horrible years, when I was being bullied and called names, and people were shoving me into their freaking box of who they thought I was, one person would come to mind who would keep me from going off the deep end. You. You, Owen. In my darkest days, I thought about trying to contact you at least a thousand times. Sometimes several times a day. Because I felt like you were, honestly, the only person on earth who knew and understood the real me.

"You never once made fun of me or questioned my crazy ideas. No one, and I mean *no one,* ever made me feel seen the way you did. People made me question who I was, while you, you always made me feel like I had superpowers. Our bond was special. I never forgot that. Never. And I never forgot you."

Owen stood in silence.

"When my mom told me your dad had passed away, I wanted to be there for you, but I also thought this was my chance to reconnect with you and tell you how much your friendship meant to me, without it being weird.

"That first chat in the treehouse felt like old times, and I knew I was right, we had something special. Or at least I thought we did, until now." Her voice broke, and she paused. "God, I was so wrong about you."

She turned away, opened the door and crawled in, slamming the door in his face.

Owen banged on the window as she started the car. "Bahn. Wait. You don't understand."

She understood. The fairytale fantasy she'd concocted in her brain about him, about this trip, was just that, a fairy tale.

Turning up her music so she wouldn't have to hear his voice, she glanced at him one last time and backed away. As she pulled down the road, rain began to pelt her windshield, and she looked in the rearview mirror and saw him still standing there with his hands on his hips. Tears streamed down her face as she looked forward. She couldn't breathe.

The silence was deafening as Owen slid into his truck. He knew every word she spoke was true, because he felt the same way. He never felt as comfortable with anyone as he did with Bahn. She was with him in school when he felt out of place. She was with him on the battlefield when he'd lie awake at night hearing the distant explosions. She was with him when he was recovering. And when he heard the news about his dad, she was with him then too. The minute he saw her come through that trapdoor in the treehouse, he wanted to wrap his arms around her and never let go. She was his lifeline.

There was no doubt he was drawn to her, and not just physically. Their connection ran much deeper. She knew every nuance of him. How could he have been so wrong about her, though?

He knew what he'd seen that night. He heard what she said on the beach. There was no mistake. How could he not have come to that conclusion? The confusion caused a deep growl to burst from his throat.

"Damn it!" He banged his hands against the steering wheel, trying to clear his head.

Throwing his truck in reverse, his tires spewed sand behind him as he sped from the beach. When he arrived home, he found the house dark and empty. Removing his wet clothes, he turned the shower to hot and stood under the water, letting the searing jets coat his body.

Thoughts clouded his mind as he replayed the evening events over and over. The pain in her eyes as she confessed her feelings filled his head. If she would have just let him explain, things might have been different, but she just kept cutting him off.

Walking back into the bedroom, he put on his sweatpants, propped himself up on the bed, and reached for his phone. When he opened it, he noticed he had a message from her. The hope that she wanted to talk filled him, but instead it was just a video of him falling spread eagle in the water.

His thumb tapped the screen to call her, but it went to voicemail. He figured his text would go unread, so he tried calling directly to her room, but still no answer.

Setting his phone on the nightstand, he again noticed his dad's Bible and picked it up. Adjusting the pillow, he leaned back and let it fall open to the scripture with the green bookmark. 'Your love is a treasure.' Then he found the scripture, 'She is more precious than rubies. Nothing you desire can compare to her.'

He knew he was in love with her. From the minute she'd appeared in the treehouse, he'd felt it, and maybe even when they were kids. Theirs was a connection that transcended time.

Bahn kept her composure through the lobby of the hotel and in the elevator, but once she was in the room, she felt her throat tighten and the sting return to her eyes. She dropped her bag and blanket at the door, yanked her sunglasses off, throwing them on the credenza, then shucked her clothes onto the floor and headed to the bathroom.

Steam curled above the curtain as she stepped into the shower and laid down in the tub, letting the beads of water pound her body. She sobbed as her mind flipped back and forth from the fear she felt being pulled under, to the passion of their kiss, to the pain of his words.

She had heard those words so many times before, that at one time she'd questioned it herself.

But why did he think she was gay? She was obviously attracted to him. Couldn't he see it? He should have known.

The tears wouldn't stop. She recalled the previous days, and how comfortable she felt with him. It felt so safe to be in his arms. Why did it have to turn out this way? Why did he have to ruin everything?

He did. Right?

But then why did he look so confused? He said he was attracted to her. Was she too hard on him? What did he mean by 'he saw her'? Should she have let him talk?

She played the scene over and over in her head until her cell chimed, and then the room phone rang, and she knew it was him.

CHAPTER 23

O wen woke early the next morning. Technically, he'd just decided to get out of bed. He hadn't slept. But that wasn't new. He was worn out from the past few days. His mind wouldn't allow him to sleep. He needed to talk to Bahn, and the sooner, the better. Her flight wasn't until the afternoon, so if he made it to the hotel by ten, he should be able to catch her. He had to make things right. He had to explain.

Pouring a cup of coffee, he wiped his hand across his face and yawned.

"You feeling okay?" his mom asked, coming into the kitchen. "I saw your truck in the driveway last night when I got home, but your door was already shut, so I figured you'd gone to bed."

"I'm fine. Bahn and I got into a fight, so I came home early." He played with his cup, moving the handle from one hand to the other, continuing to replay everything for the millionth time.

"What happened?" Carissa sat down at the table, concern creasing her brow.

"I hurt her with something stupid I said. I didn't mean to. It was a misunderstanding, but she wouldn't let me explain."

"What did you say?"

"I made an assumption I shouldn't have, and…"—he took a breath— "it might have cost me the best thing that's happened in my life in a long, long time. I never would have thought seeing her, being with her, especially after all these years, would affect my life the way it has."

"Sometimes you just know things are right from the beginning. Your dad said the first time he met me, he told his roommate he'd just met the girl he was going to marry."

"Well, last night might have ruined anything we might have had, in her eyes at least. I'm going to try to catch her before she leaves, and pray she's calmed down enough to listen."

"Then I suggest you go now, that way you have more time to talk."

His mom had a point. Owen looked at his watch. It was eight thirty. He jumped up, grabbed a nice button down and his khaki shorts, then ran to the bathroom, smoothed his hair as much as possible, and brushed his teeth. Slipping his shoes on, he grabbed his keys off the nightstand, hugged his mom, and gave her a quick, "Thank you," and headed out the door.

Somehow, the thought of seeing her again made him feel encouraged that things were going to work out. He would show up at her door, she would let him explain, forgive him, and everything would be set right.

Easing onto the highway, he continued to construct a plan, and got so lost in thought, he barely remembered when to exit.

He stopped at a local grocery store, grabbed a colorful bundle of roses from the display, and a smile broke out across his face as he sped up the road, picturing her face when he gave her the flowers. Flowers probably weren't her thing, but she would appreciate the gesture.

Pulling into the parking lot of the hotel, he found a spot and sat for a minute to collect his thoughts. Lifting the flowers from the seat, he checked the mirror and ran his fingers through his hair one last time before exiting the truck. As he entered the hotel, he realized he had no clue what room she was in. His eyes locked on an older woman with salt and pepper colored hair at the front desk. She noticed the flowers in his hand and smiled as he approached.

"May I help you?"

"Could you tell me what room Bahn Jackson is in?"

"I'm sorry sir, we can't give out our guests' room numbers."

"Oh, yeah, of course. I should have known that. Well, can you call her room for me?"

"Sure, I would be happy to." She pushed her glasses up her nose. "What was the name again?"

"Bahn Jackson."

Her brows furrowed as she studied the computer. "I'm sorry, I don't see that name listed. Could they be under any other name?"

"Oh." He stopped for a moment. "Siobahn Jackson."

A smile reappeared on her face as her gaze returned to her computer but disappeared quickly as she lifted her eyes to Owen. "I'm sorry sir, she's already checked out."

Her words rang in his ears, stabbing at his heart. He was too late. The flowers he was holding dropped to his side. His body suddenly felt too heavy. He let out an audible sigh as he rubbed his hand across his mouth.

Dropping the flowers on the counter, he slogged out to his truck, completely broken. She was gone, and it was all his fault. He couldn't imagine not having her in his life now that they'd been reunited. It couldn't end like this. He had to do something to make it right.

Throwing his truck into drive, he sped out of the parking lot. His mom was still sitting at the table when he got home. Without saying a word, he stormed up the hallway to his room, grabbed his duffle from the closet, tossed a few pieces of clothing inside, then headed for the bathroom and gathered his toiletries.

His eyes scanned the room for other items, landing on his dad's Bible. After placing it on top of the clothes, he zipped the bag shut. Tucking his dad's computer under his arm, he strolled into the dining room and opened it up.

"I take it Bahn didn't want to see you?"

"She'd already left for the airport. Would it be alright if I helped you with Dad's stuff on Wednesday, instead of tomorrow?"

A smile crossed her face, and she reached over and patted his arm. "I think that would be fine. I have a few other things I can do in the meantime."

Scanning the flights, he found one with layovers in Atlanta and Seattle leaving in three hours. It gave him just enough time to get to the airport. His finger hovered over the button for a second before booking the flight, then he found a rental car.

His mind wandered, going through his trip, planning out one

moment to the next. The layovers sucked, but he didn't care as long as he was able to get to her.

How could he have developed such strong feelings for her so fast? The familiarity, the comfortable conversation had always been there, though. He'd never forgotten her. He just couldn't stop thinking about her now that she'd returned.

Summer travelers crowded the airport. Once he'd cleared security and found his gate, he pulled out the laptop and studied the project his dad had been working on, comparing the information on the pieces of paper with what was on the computer. He welcomed the distraction from the what-ifs surrounding his and Bahn's relationship, and was fully engrossed in the project, when the announcement came over the PA system for boarding.

The flight to Atlanta would only take an hour, and the lack of sleep was catching up to him, so once he was settled, he leaned his head against the seat and closed his eyes.

"Please return your seats and tray tables to their upright positions." Owen jumped hearing the flight attendant's voice over the intercom. Within minutes, the plane was on the ground and passengers were filing out.

Spying a deli in the concourse area, he stopped and grabbed a sub then found his gate. He'd set his plan in motion and hoped everything went smoothly but he had to admit, his nerves were a bit frazzled. The announcement for his next flight came as he shoved the last bit of his sandwich in his mouth, so he dusted his hands, disposed of his trash, and headed for his gate.

The second leg would be the longest. For a moment, he wondered if he was making the right decision. His mind tormented him with different scenarios. *What if I can't find her? What if she refuses to talk to me? What if I make things worse?*

He tended to think the worst, and this was no exception. It was a good thing he was already too far into the trip to turn back. He had to let this play out.

Boarding the plane, he was greeted by a flight attendant with a bright smile. He smiled back and squeezed up the aisle to find his seat. The plane lifted off, and as it settled into its cruising altitude, Owen dug the laptop out of the bag and opened it. He studied the intricate design and information within the program and began to see the pieces that were missing. "What goes there?" he said under his breath. The person in the seat next to him briefly glanced at him and smiled.

Hours went by, and he continued to search for the connection until his brain became foggy. The nap he'd had earlier wasn't near enough to offset the sheer exhaustion he felt. He placed the computer back in the bag, slid it under his seat, and sat back in his chair. His eyes closed, his mind drifted, and within moments he was asleep.

The jolt of the plane touching down on the tarmac startled him awake. People gathered their belongings, ready to explore their new destination. As everyone deplaned, Owen followed suit, plodding off the plane, his body still feeling the results of sleeping in the cramped seat. He rolled his shoulders, trying to relieve the pain as he made his way up the concourse.

When he found his final gate, he took a seat, putting his head in his hands, physically and emotionally exhausted. His mind drifted to the explosive conversation that he and Bahn had. The pain in her eyes still haunted him. He had to make it right. He had to make her listen.

Rubbing his hands down his face, he tried to collect his thoughts and somehow pull himself together enough to create a plan of action. The past three days had been such a whirlwind. He desperately wanted—needed—everything to work out.

The boarding announcement came over the intercom and he stood, waiting to get in line. This was it. Within a couple hours, he would be in Cabin Creek.

Bahn woke to the ungodly buzz of her alarm clock. No matter how many times she heard it, it shook her to her core, instantly making her angry. But now, with everything that had happened, she wanted to chuck it against the wall. No one better cross her today.

She rolled over, turned it off, and slowly opened her eyes, taking in the familiar surroundings. She was back in her own bed, back in her real life, and back to the grind. Frustration set in.

Throwing the covers off, she sat up and put on her fuzzy robe, then shuffled to the kitchen to start the coffee. As the dark magic potion began to brew, she curled up on the sofa, slid her phone off the table, and checked the messages. Nothing.

Even though she kept telling herself that was what she wanted, she couldn't get the pain in her chest to go away. Owen had destroyed her with one comment, but it was better that way. It would have never worked if anything did develop between them. They lived on opposite coasts.

She needed to move on. The problem was, she couldn't. Her mind was at war with her emotions. She could still feel his arms around her, taste his lips as they pressed against hers, hear his voice as the words, 'I thought you were gay,' and 'I saw you,' played over and over. And she could still see the haunted look in his eyes as she drove away. It all lingered in her head and wreaked havoc with her emotions.

The coffee pot sputtered, and she jumped up to steal a cup, hoping to relieve the exhaustion she felt.

After showering, she felt more awake but still was only willing to put in minimal effort, so she threw her hair up in a messy ponytail and added a smudge of mascara to her lashes. She spied her suitcase sitting on the chair in the corner of her room, and a jolt of pain hit her as her memories of Owen skipped through her mind.

Ripping her eyes away, she went to her dresser and threw on a pair of overalls and a T-shirt, then checked herself in the mirror. It would do. Since she was going to be cleaning, she wasn't going for professional.

Sarah joined her as she ran back to the kitchen to fill her large travel mug with coffee.

"Need a little coffee today?" Sarah quipped after seeing her fill the mug to the brim.

"I am going to need every bit of this."

"What time did you get in last night?"

"Around ten thirty."

"Did you have a good time? I mean, after the funeral and all?"

She knew Sarah would want to know everything. They'd talked about what the trip meant before she left, but then Sarah had left for a weekend getaway with her girlfriend, Jean, so they didn't get to touch base while she was gone.

As the memories clicked through her brain, her nose began to sting. It was time to face reality. She knew she could let her guard down with Sarah, and knew she would understand whether she shared or not, she just wasn't ready to go into detail.

Releasing a sigh she said, "It was fine. It just didn't go exactly as I had hoped. I mean, I don't know what I was expecting. We hadn't seen each other in so long. Maybe I set my expectations too high." The stabbing pain returned to her chest. "Oh well, life goes on. Right?"

Sarah stared at her, concern flowing into her eyes. "Aw, babe, I'm sorry. It was hard enough having to go to the funeral, but then to have your hopes dashed. That's got to be painful." She pulled her into a hug and rubbed her back.

"It is what it is. I'll be fine," she lied as she backed out of the hug, retrieved her phone, and chucked it into her backpack. Turning, she opened the refrigerator and gathered the fixings for sandwiches. "Ham or turkey?"

"Turkey."

Quickly assembling two sandwiches, she slid them into plastic bags and found two bags of chips in the cabinet. Handing one off to Sarah, she put the other in her bag. Then, finding her sunglasses, she propped them on her head and asked, "What's your schedule today?"

"I think I'll be done around two-ish, but I made plans with Jean, so I'm going to leave from school. I'll probably be out late. Is that okay? I can cancel if you need me to."

The idea of being alone with her thoughts was definitely not appealing, but neither was rehashing it, and she knew Sarah would want the whole story if she asked her to stay. "No. Go. Have fun. I'll be fine."

Sarah gave her a wary glance. "Are you sure you're okay, Bahn? Seriously. You seem upset. I can stay home."

She obviously wasn't putting on the brave front she thought she was. "Yeah, I'm just exhausted. It was a long flight."

"Okay. I'll text you if my plans change." Sarah picked up a large tote bag, slung it over her shoulder, and they walked out the door together.

As Bahn drove up the road, she flipped on the radio, hoping to clear her thoughts. The glare of the morning sun was too much, so she pulled her sunglasses from her head, and giggled thinking about Owen wearing them. Then swallowed the lump that immediately formed.

Shoving the glasses on her face, she tried to focus on what she needed to get done. It seemed futile. Her thoughts kept playing scenes from the past few days. She cranked the music louder even though she knew it wouldn't help.

As the old brick building came into view, she saw teachers carrying boxes and pulling wagons full of supplies, preparing to clean and box up the books and supplies from their classrooms. She stared at the scene and heard Owen's voice. "Do you like it there? Do you like your job?" The unsettled feeling returned. She did, didn't she?

Meandering through the maze of hallways, carrying a couple of boxes filled with cleaning supplies, she passed classroom after classroom until she came to the one with her name above the door. Her eyes scanned the room as she tried to relieve the uncomfortable feeling. A surge of anger hit. Owen had caused her to question everything.

Letting out a sigh, she turned on some music and tried to figure out what would be a good starting point.

CHAPTER 24

Owen's flight landed right on time in Eugene, and his drive to Cabin Creek was shorter than what he'd anticipated. With the sun cresting the horizon, he entered the quiet little town with ornate, historical buildings lining the main street. Lamp posts dotted the brick sidewalks, adding a bit of charm to the downtown. Most of the buildings looked like they had been restored, some with amazing artwork painted on the side.

He stopped at a small gas station and checked his trip app for hotels in the area, then set his directions for the Cottage Grove Inn. Dawn had brightened the sky enough for him to see the rolling hills popping up on the other end of town.

Within a couple of blocks, his destination came into view. The stately Victorian house had potted plants lining the walkway and rocking chairs on the wraparound porch, welcoming the guests. A gray-haired, heavy-set woman greeted him as he stepped inside. She pushed a plate of cookies in front of him, offering, "I just got them out of the oven."

He took one as he asked for a room. She requested his identification and smiled. "Are you military?"

"Yes ma'am."

"I thought you were," she said, her smile widening to a full grin as she handed him his room key. "Go all the way up the stairs to your left. It's the only room on the third floor."

Trudging up the steep stairs with his duffle, he stepped onto the landing and retrieved the key she had given him. The door creaked as he pushed it open, and he was pleasantly surprised at the size of the …suite? To his right, was a nice sized kitchen area with a small dining table. To the left, a full living room with a double-sided fireplace and a door leading out to a balcony that spanned the full length of the building. To the right of the fireplace was a doorway that led to the bedroom with a king-size bed, and another door to the balcony. On the other side of the room was a pocket door that opened to a large bathroom equipped with an antique clawfoot tub and a walk-in shower.

He walked out onto the balcony for a moment and took in the view of the mountains in the distance and a stream below before returning inside and settling in. The down-filled comforter enveloped him as he sat on the bed. He set his alarm, kicked off his shoes, fluffed his pillow, laid back, and closed his eyes.

It seemed like only minutes later when the alarm sounded, and Owen rolled over to shut it off. His brain immediately kicked into gear. *It's now or never.*

Once he'd showered to wash off the muck from the trip, he searched through his bag and found a light gray, pearl snap shirt and a pair of pressed blue jeans.

He brushed his teeth, ran his fingers through his hair, spritzed on a shot of cologne, slid his sneakers on, then snatched his keys and phone from the nightstand and headed for the door. Taking the stairs at a jog, he swiped another cookie, gave the lady behind the desk a nod, and left.

Once outside, he pulled his phone from his pocket and typed in Cabin Creek High School. It was just up the street. He made a stop at the corner grocery store and picked up some flowers, figuring he'd try one more time.

The closer he got to the school, the faster his heart rate pounded. Thoughts raced through his head, creating different scenarios of how the day would go. He needed to remain calm.

As he turned into the school parking lot and shut the car off, he closed his eyes for a moment and took some deep breaths, then lifted a whispered prayer. "God help me." Glancing in the mirror, he removed his aviators, tucked them in his pocket, and pushed the door open.

The familiar scent of cleaning chemicals hit him as he entered the school and strolled toward the sign that said office. The door was locked, so he turned back to face the three hallways in front of him. He picked one at random and started down it but stopped when he noticed an older woman leaving one of the classrooms. She smiled, obviously noticing the flowers.

"Can you tell me where Miss Jackson's room is?"

"Oh yes." She motioned with her hand. "Go up this hallway and turn left. Her room is the last door on the left."

"Thank you." Owen nodded and smiled, then followed her directions. He made the turn and spied Bahn's room. Her door was open, and the light was on. An anxious breath escaped. *She's here.*

Perched on a ladder, she was reaching for a framed abstract mural hanging precariously from the ceiling. Below, holding the ladder, was a guy with salt and pepper hair. They were laughing.

He stepped back out of sight, trying to tamp down the irritation that had suddenly taken hold. A couple of days ago, he thought she was gay. Now he was wondering if there was something going on with them. This time, though, there would be no jumping to conclusions. No making stupid assumptions, no matter what kind of scenario the scene painted.

He waited as she loosened the frame and carefully brought the mural down. When he heard her say, "Thank you, I think that's everything," and heard the clank of the ladder, the knot in his gut loosened.

Moments later, the guy exited the room and jumped when he saw Owen standing just outside the door. He didn't say a word, just continued up the hallway.

Bahn was still facing away from him, moving the large mural to a safe spot. He stared at her. *Even in her grubby clothes, she is still so damn beautiful.* She turned with a quick jerk, like she'd heard his thoughts, and he froze.

"Owen?" Her heart dropped into her stomach. Was he really here? He stood silently, flowers clutched in his hand and a worried look carved into his handsome face. "What are you doing here?"

She hesitantly walked toward him, scared that if she made one wrong move, he'd evaporate into thin air. Her mind and emotions flipped into overdrive, and she immediately felt overwhelmed.

She didn't know if she should be happy he was standing in front of her, or mad.

Owen took a deep breath. "You, you didn't let me explain."

His timid demeanor broke her already shattered heart. She wanted to let him off the hook, let him have his time to explain, but his words had stabbed at a hurt that had nearly broken her spirit and had taken years to get past. She didn't want to rehash something that was so painful. Even if her heart felt like it was clawing at her chest to get to him.

Steadying herself, she did what she thought was best. "I told you I don't need an explanation, Owen."

Turning quickly, hoping he didn't see the conflict she knew was painted all over her face, she gathered a large box of items, pushed past him. and headed out the door and down the hall.

He followed with the flowers still in his hand. "I am not leaving until you hear me out."

Her unwillingness was obviously a battlefield for him. And by his actions, it was a fight he'd decided he wasn't willing to lose. And something about that had her even more conflicted.

Bahn turned and shot him a glare, and the tick of his jaw told her this was not going to be easy.

"I have never seen you run from anything in your life, Bahn. What are you afraid I am going to tell you?"

She whipped around and walked backward. "You just don't get it, do you?" she said, sarcasm seeping through every word. "I'm not running. I just choose not to listen to the same song and dance I've heard a hundred times before. It's really gotten old."

She pushed up against the bar on the door leading to the outside and walked over to her black SUV. Propping the box on her knee, she pushed the button to release the hatch.

"No Bahn, *you* don't get it. And I'll be damned if I'm going to let you shut me out."

The fire that had started in her gut turned into an inferno. The more she fought him, the harsher, more adamant his voice became. And it was obliterating her resolve. The box landed with a thud as she dropped it in the back and slammed the hatch, then turned to face him.

His teeth clenched. His jaw pulsed, and she saw the fury in his eyes. "You keep making these damn assumptions about what I'm going to say, but you're wrong. This has nothing to do with how you act, or how you look."

The gravel of his voice made her stop. He'd changed so much from the scared little boy she once knew. He stood with his shoulders squared, carrying an air of confidence and assertiveness, and she felt like she was losing her mind because it made her want him even more. She couldn't back down though.

But then his comment registered. If it wasn't about her looks or how she acted, what was it? '*I saw you*' repeated clearly in her mind, like he'd said it again, and a tinge of guilt started to whisper in the back of her head. Maybe there was more to his comment. She leveled her eyes with his, studying him as he crossed his arms, unwavering.

"I'm not willing to throw everything away because you're too damn stubborn to let me explain. If I have to follow you around the rest of the day talking to your back, you are going to hear me out."

His comment made the façade she was trying desperately to keep in place crumble. Her parents had told her a thousand times that she was stubborn, and a thousand times she'd proven them right. She pinched back a smile and did the one thing she told herself she wouldn't do. She gave in.

"Fine, Owen. You win." Yanking open the door, still trying to muster up the strength to accept what she'd just agreed to, she stalked back into the school, muttering, "Go ahead. Tell me what this is all about."

His confident demeanor suddenly deflated, as did the sound of his voice. Softer now, he started, "First off, I want to apologize. I should have told you from the beginning about that night, but I didn't know how."

She stopped and turned to face him, completely confused. "What night?"

His eyes darted around, and he motioned to the door. "Do you mind if we go back into your classroom?"

She realized they were standing in a hallway with several classrooms with ears.

"I have a better place." Tipping her head for him to follow her, she leaned against the bar, and pushed the double doors open again. The wind caught her untucked shirt, and it fluttered.

Owen's mouth kicked up to one side, and she caught his glance. "By the way, I got these for you. Peace offering?"

She reluctantly took the flowers and couldn't help but inhale when she saw the lavender. He must have remembered how much she loved the scent.

They walked around a large building, climbed into the bleachers on the other side, and sat down. Bahn straddled the stadium bench so she could look directly at him. "Okay, fire away." She still wanted to be angry, but now he had her curious as to what exactly he meant by 'that night.' What was it that he'd seen that made him fly all the way to Oregon?

CHAPTER 25

H e faced forward and stared out across the football field, not sure he could handle seeing her expression as he told her the story of that night. He knew his silence probably made her more suspicious, but he needed to gather his thoughts to make sure he didn't hurt her again.

"Do you remember me telling you how I helped my parents move over spring break between my junior and senior year of college?"

She tilted her head. "Yes."

"And do you remember telling me how you and your friends came down for spring break that same year and went to Dune Canyon to party? How funny would it have been if we ran into each other?"

Bahn's brows furrowed in obvious confusion. "I do."

"We kind of did."

"What do you mean, we kind of did?" Bahn questioned.

"While I was home, I went to Dune Canyon one night. I needed to get away. I had a bad break up with a girl from college, and I came home to lick my wounds. My parents had just moved back, so I—"

Bahn's hand flew up. "Hold the phone. You can't just gloss over the college breakup. What happened?"

"She cheated on me with my roommate. I'll get to that later, but

I need to tell you—"

"I'm sorry." Her voice had softened, and he glanced at her through his lashes. Her expression had gone from harsh anger to concern, and something about it made him unsettled. He didn't want her pity. That wasn't why he flew all the way to Oregon. He wanted more.

He waved her apology off. "It was a long time ago."

Returning his gaze to the landscape in front of him, he recalled the night. "Anyway, I went for a walk on the beach, and when I looked up, Dune Canyon was in front of me. There was smoke drifting above the berm. I was curious as to who found our secret spot, so I climbed the berm. I could hear voices as I hit the ridge and there was a huge bonfire, several tents and some ice chests. You guys had moved in."

"Yeah. I gotta admit, we had a sweet setup."

"I just don't know how you guys got all that stuff in there."

"It took quite a few trips for some of them. I knew what the trek would be, so Sarah and I were prepared."

"In my current state, I wanted to escape all the thoughts, all the memories, all the voices that were in the process of driving me crazy, and with the number of coolers I saw, you guys had just the beverages to do it. So, I headed down the berm and walked up to the first person I saw. The guy was wasted, and very friendly. He told me to help myself when I asked if I could join in.

"I asked where everyone was from, and the guy said Oregon. He said his friend Bahn used to live in Biloxi and had a great spot to go for spring break. When he mentioned your name, I knew it had to be you. So, I asked him where you were. He told me you were over on the other side of the rocks with someone named Sarah.

"With everything that had happened, all I could think about was seeing you. I knew, even though we hadn't talked in years, you would be able to talk me down from the ledge. But when I found you, you and some girl were making out. I don't know why it hurt so much, but the minute you looked up, I was just hit with a blinding rage.

"I walked away, grabbed a nearly full bottle of bourbon that was by the bonfire, and made my way up the berm. When I got back to my car, I polished off the bottle and passed out."

"Oh my god, Owen. I'm so sorry for …for…everything."

"You did nothing wrong. It's on me for assuming. For not being smart enough to talk to you about it. When you showed up Thursday, I kind of questioned it. I mean, it seemed like you were flirting some, but I wrote it off that we were friends. You said people made comments about your sexuality, but you never said if you were gay or straight. And when you said something about living with Sarah, I took it as confirmation that you were in a relationship. So, ultimately, it's my fault for making assumptions."

"Yes, we do live together... because we're teachers. We have no money. But I can definitely understand how you would have gotten the impression we were in a relationship." She began to giggle. "I really should have let you explain."

"You think? You still have that temper I remember."

She swatted him in the shoulder, and he fell over. "Thanks a lot," she laughed.

And just like that, it seemed the universe had righted itself.

She chewed on her lip for a moment. "I kind of let the ghosts of my past blow things out of proportion, didn't I?"

He raised one brow then chuckled. She wrinkled her nose and winced. They sat quietly for a few seconds before Owen slowly slid his hand in hers, lacing their fingers together, and said, "Let's just call it a misunderstanding on both of our parts."

"I still can't believe you were there." She paused, studying his face. "You know what's funny? I remember getting a glimpse of a guy staring at me. I can't believe I didn't recognize you."

"I had a beard at the time. But you probably wouldn't have recognized me anyway. I mean, we hadn't seen each other since we were twelve."

"How'd you know it was me?"

"Seriously? You said it yourself the other day. You're unique. The minute I laid eyes on you, even as a nine-year-old, I couldn't quit staring at you. You're mesmerizing. I knew the minute I saw your honey-colored curls; it was you."

"Kent said someone asked about me, but he couldn't remember the person's name."

"I don't know if I even told him."

"I can't believe it was *you*."

Owen nodded. "I had the same reaction when I realized you were there."

"How crazy is that?" She continued to ponder his story for a moment then her voice softened. "You need to tell me about this woman who broke your heart."

Owen took a deep breath. "It's not a big—"

"Owen!"

Her barking his name made him chuckle. He'd heard it hundreds of times when they were kids, and it always meant one thing. He had no choice.

Rolling his eyes, he huffed, "Fine. Her name was Melanie. I met her when I was working at the mailroom. She worked in the library. We'd crossed paths here and there, and I finally got the guts up to ask her to lunch after she showed up to drop off a package one day.

"We'd been dating for several months when my boss came into work unexpectedly the day before spring break. He said a shipment that had been delayed was coming in, and he needed to be there to sign for it and get it logged in and delivered.

"I was scheduled to be off in a couple of hours, and Melanie and I had plans, but he offered me four tickets to the basketball game he wasn't going to be able to go to that night. My roommate James was a huge basketball fan, so I figured, if he could find a date, we could all go together."

A smile broke out across Bahn's face. "Aw, did I make you a fan of basketball?"

"I wouldn't say I'm a fan. But I don't mind it."

"I'd call that a win."

He'd call it a win that his plan had worked, and she was actually listening to him.

When he didn't respond to her comment, she added, "I'm sorry. Please continue. I didn't mean to interrupt."

He tried to remember where he'd stopped. "Um, oh, so after he gave me the tickets, he let me go early because things were slow. The minute I was out the door, I tried calling Melanie and James and both of their phones went to voicemail."

"Oh crap." Bahn winced. "Yeah. Not a good sign."

"I didn't think anything of it. I was too excited about the tickets. I got to the apartment, unlocked the door, and there they were, on the sofa, in nothing but a blanket."

"Oh god." Owen again felt the stab from the betrayal, but the look of shared disgust on Bahn's face eased the hurt he couldn't seem to shake. "I will need their full names."

"Why?"

"So I can stalk them on social media and wreak havoc on their lives."

A smile crossed his face as he visualized her attack. And the more he thought about it, the more the laughter came as he released the pain he'd harbored.

"What?" Bahn asked when his laughter became contagious, and she joined him.

"Nothing," he said in between gasps. "Just picturing you going ballistic on them."

"It's going to happen."

"Oh, I don't doubt it a bit."

After they regained their composure, Bahn surprised him, wanting more of the depressing story. "So, what did you do after you walked in on them?"

"I slammed the door and headed back to my car. I was shaking, I was so mad. I don't know if I was madder at them for what they'd done, or myself for being so stupid. I mean, I should have known."

"No. Cheaters are sneaky, Owen. There is nothing wrong with trusting people."

"A few minutes went by, and I watched them leave in James's car. So, I gathered my stuff, loaded my car and headed home. I didn't know what I was going to do or where I was going to live. I just knew I couldn't live there anymore."

"So that was why you were home." All the fire that was in Bahn's voice earlier, had been extinguished.

"Yeah, and to help my parents get moved in. I stayed busy the first few days, so it didn't give me a lot of time to think. I told my parents the basics, and they didn't press me about it. But once we got everything unpacked and organized, I didn't have anything to occupy me, and my mind played that night over and over, tormenting me. I started turning everything around, blaming myself for her cheating."

"Why? There is no excuse for cheating. If you have a problem, you talk it out, not run to the nearest—" she closed her eyes and shook her head "—never mind."

"In the moment, my head wasn't screwed on straight. I felt so awkward around girls, and I kept thinking about what I could have done differently. So, I took a walk on the beach. I don't even know how long I was out there. I was about to turn around, and my phone chimed. It was Melanie. I started not to answer it, but the guilt had gotten to me.

"She begged me to forgive her and confessed that she and James had *gotten close* a few weeks earlier. She said she was lonely because our schedules never seemed to line up. James didn't work, nor did he want to, so he was always available. She kept apologizing and said she didn't want to lose me as a friend."

Residual anger still stole his breath, and he breathed deeply, shaking his head. "That hit me in the gut. Friends? Really? That's all I was to her? She wasn't asking to get back with me. She just didn't want to lose me as a *friend*.

"I couldn't stand to listen to her one more minute. After what she did, I couldn't trust the words coming out of her mouth, so I hung up. I know that was probably the wrong—"

"No. It was exactly the right thing to do." As Owen relived the painful events of the past, Bahn sat, never taking her eyes off him. "I, I don't know what to say. I am so sorry."

"It is what it is. It's a good thing I found out when I did, before things got really serious."

"I can't believe your girlfriend and roommate did that to you. How cruel. And then to call you and expect you to come crawling back?"

"Oh, and that's not all. I got a call from James the next morning about the rent. I don't know if I was still a little drunk or what, but I told him exactly what he could do with his rent issue. I suggested he move Melanie in and hung up. Luckily, there was a guy in one of my computer labs who had a big house and let me crash on a futon for the rest of the semester."

"Did you ever see them again?"

"Oh yeah. I had a class with James. Melanie cheated on him and got pregnant, then claimed it was his, so…" He got a sly grin on his face.

"Oh no. Looks like Karma came back to bite him in the ass, and you dodged a bullet."

"More like a heat seeking missile."

She giggled, and then looked straight at him. "You know flying up here just to clear this up was insane and had to be extremely expensive, but… I'm glad you did."

"Just returning the favor."

"So how long are you here?"

"I have a flight back tomorrow afternoon. I couldn't leave things the way they ended, but I still need to help Mom sort through all the paperwork."

"What were you going to do if I didn't let you explain?"

"I honestly didn't think that far. I guess, see what your town had to offer or drive back to Eugene."

"Where are you staying?"

"Just outside of town, at the Cottage Grove Inn."

"Oh, that place is nice. I stayed there when I went through orientation for the job."

"Yeah, it is. I have the whole third floor to myself. It's huge, and the view is amazing."

Bahn looked at her watch. "Oh, hey, I kind of need to get back. I have a meeting I need to go to at three. I'm sorry."

"Oh no, you do what you need to do."

She stood and picked up the flowers. "Can we get together later?

"Sure. I'm all yours until tomorrow afternoon."

Her fingers brushed against the petals of one of the flowers, then she glanced at him. "These are really beautiful." She buried her nose in them then returned her gaze to him. "Give me an hour."

"Just text me."

"We have a deli around the corner from my house. We can grab a bite and talk some more."

"Sounds great." He realized then he hadn't eaten since the sub sandwich at the airport the previous day.

Bahn gave him a quick hug and a peck on his cheek and scurried down the bleachers. Owen watched as she disappeared around the building and chuckled as he thought about how quickly her demeanor changed.

The bleachers clanged as he climbed down and wandered through the school complex, searching for his car. He was happy things had worked out and that he hadn't imagined her flirting. It made him want to pick up where that kiss left off. But he had to wait for the right time.

And what if things do go well? What then?

Owen's heart raced at the thought. All at once, he was excited again. And a little scared.

CHAPTER 26

◆

Driving through town, he stopped at a winery he'd passed as he was driving into town earlier. On the side of the building was a beautiful mural of Bengal tigers having their stripes painted by a rainbow of colors dripping down the wall. As he walked through the door, he was surprised by the size. Up front was a small gift shop with everything from wine stoppers and openers to stained glass and stationery. To one side, there was a small bar for tastings, and in the back were a dozen or so casks and several racks of bottles.

People were milling around, and after checking out the trinkets, he began reading the list of different wines to sample. Pulling a stool closer to the bar, he sat down and chose a flight of reds ranging from a full-bodied merlot to a lighter pinot noir blend. After spending several minutes on each, he decided on a cabernet with a nice buttery finish.

With his bottle in hand, he strolled back to the gift section. His eyes landed on a small, dark wood box, the words 'Love is a Treasure' inlaid in mother of pearl on its top. The same words as the bookmark in his dad's Bible. It was almost too perfect.

Staring at the items in his hand, he smirked as a plan came together on his way to the register. After handing the cashier his credit card, he asked, "What's the best place to get seafood?"

"Molly's," she said without hesitation.

"Thanks. I appreciate it." As he walked out of the winery, his phone chimed. Setting everything on the hood of the car, he fumbled for his phone, hoping to see her name light up the screen, and was disappointed when he didn't recognize the number.

Debating whether to answer it, he finally hit the button. "Hello?"

"Hello, Mr. Cramer?" He paused for a moment, thinking they were looking for his dad.

"Uh, this is Owen."

"This is Rebecca Wagner, from Radiant Homes Realty. I submitted your bid for Twenty-nine hundred Magnolia."

"Oh, yes."

"I was calling to let you know I spoke to the owner, and they have accepted your offer."

"They did? Seriously? Holy crap!" His throat tightened as his emotions bounced from excited to overwhelmed.

"Yes. I just hung up with them."

"Okay. Okay. Wow."

"We've submitted your loan information. You still need to do the inspection, but we can set that up for you. If everything checks out, we might be able to close by the end of June."

Owen leaned up against his car, rubbing the back of his neck, and a big grin spread across his face. "That, that sounds great."

"Okay, we'll move forward, and I'll be in touch."

"All right, thank you.

"You're welcome. Have a good day."

Owen stood and did a short happy dance. He dug for his keys and grabbed his packages as his phone chimed again. Bahn.

Crawling into the car, he set everything on the passenger seat. "Perfect timing."

"Would you mind meeting me back at my place? I'm a mess, and I need to at least change my clothes before we go anywhere."

"Sure. Give me your address."

"It's fourteen eighteen Parson's Place. Apartment two thirty-eight. From the inn go west—"

"I'll plug it into my phone. Hang on." He tapped in the address and the directions popped up. "Okay, got it. Be there in ten."

Her car was already there by the time he pulled into the complex. He knocked, and when she opened the door, her hair was wet, and she was wearing a fuzzy blue bathrobe. "Wow, you're quick. Can you give me a few minutes?"

He nodded.

"There's tea in the refrigerator if you'd like some."

"I'm good."

She turned to walk away but continued the conversation. "Did you want to go to the deli, or somewhere else?"

"I've got a place." Owen looked around and took a seat on a large sectional. The place was impeccably decorated, not overbearing, just the right balance of old and new.

Bahn came around the corner brushing her teeth and pulled the toothbrush away. "You do?" she asked around the foam in her mouth.

"Yeah, I asked around, and I was told Molly's is nice?"

"It's very nice, and very expensive. I've never been. You might need a reservation." She called back from around the corner.

"I already called. They said it should be fine since we're going early."

Owen stood and began to look at the artwork on the walls along with the old books stacked on the coffee table. "Your place is really nice," he hollered.

"Thanks," she hollered back.

Within a few minutes, Bahn appeared from around the corner in a long-sleeved, sapphire, peep-shoulder blouse, black corduroy leggings, and knee-high boots. Her hair was pulled up in a high ponytail with thick ringlets loose on one side, and large hoop earrings. No makeup except for a little mascara and some gloss on her lips. "Okay, this is about as good as it gets on short notice."

Owen worked to make his mouth move as he tried to tear his gaze away. "You look incredible."

"Aw, thank you." She smiled shyly.

Still unable to make his brain engage, Owen remained quiet, but just as things were becoming awkward, Bahn picked up the slack. "Do you want a tour of the place?"

"Sure." His eyes wandered. "Did you decorate it?"

"Pretty much. Sarah really isn't into the whole treasure hunting thing, or the decorating thing for that matter, so I did it little by little."

"Wait. Please tell me this stuff isn't from dumpster diving."

"Well…," she said in a singsong voice, "there are only a few pieces in here that are straight up bought new, and most of that is Sarah's stuff. Everything else is either from vintage stores, thrift shops, garage sales, and yes, there are also a few pieces I found in the trash. People throw away the best stuff." She pointed to a painting of a lighthouse on the edge of a raging sea. "That one, I found just sitting by the dumpster while I was still in college."

They walked around the living room as she pointed out her finds. "Okay, so my bedroom is not picked up. I kind of was flying through here when I got home."

Her bedroom was painted with royal blue and teal green colors. Her bed was neatly made with a soft watercolor comforter and several coordinating pillows. There were a few clothes strewn around the floor, but nothing like the way he left his room at his mom's.

"I never understood the whole fifteen pillow thing. I mean, it looks cool, but then every day you have to take them off when you go to bed and put them back when you make the bed."

"Leave it at, 'it looks cool.'"

Owen nodded and smiled.

"So that's about it. Sarah has the upstairs area."

"Bahn, seriously, this place looks like something out of a magazine. Well, aside from the clothes on the floor, of course."

She backhanded him in the arm. "I was in a hurry."

He chuckled. "But really, this place is impressive."

"Thanks. I took an interior decorating class and an art history design class in college as electives, and I absolutely loved them."

As they walked toward the door, Owen couldn't help but wonder out loud, "Why didn't you choose that instead of teaching?"

"Actually, I don't know."

The directions took them through town, then down a road with towering trees and a covered bridge. They turned up a dirt road that made Bahn wonder if the GPS was lost, but within minutes an old brick building with windows all around came into view. The porch area had large fire pits encircled with chairs. It was draped in strings of Edison bulbs hanging from a wooden pergola.

"This place looks amazing," Owen said as they parked.

Since it was barely five o'clock, they had their pick of places to sit, choosing a circular stone table with a mini-fire pit in the center. The burnished surface atop the stone pedestal reflected the flames, casting a warm glow on their little oasis. The waitress handed them menus and filled their glasses of water before walking away, giving them a few minutes to study the menu before returning.

"Would you like me to get you something from the bar or start you some appetizers?"

Owen looked at Bahn. "Do you like shrimp?" She nodded. "Can we get one shrimp cocktail and split it?" he asked the waitress.

"Yes, it's a good-sized portion."

"Okay, great." His eyes returned to Bahn. "Do you want a drink?"

"Nah, I'll stick with water."

He turned back to the waitress. "I think that will be it for right now."

When the waitress smiled and walked away, they started to peruse their menus. "What are you going to get?" she asked, hoping to get an inkling of how much to spend.

Owen chuckled and his eyes met Bahn's as he sighed. "I don't know. There are so many choices."

Bahn's lips pursed, and Owen snickered, then something passed over his face, and a zing of desire shot through her. God, he had the corner on sexy expressions.

"Thank God there's no bacon and eggs on the menu," she quipped, and he burst out laughing. "You gotta admit, that breakfast was much better than your standard bacon and eggs."

"Yes. But I think it had more to do with the company than the food," he confessed.

"I agree," Bahn replied quietly, feeling heat creep up her neck.

Hiding behind the menu for a minute, he cleared his throat and said, "I'm going to go for the salmon, but I can't decide which one. How about you?"

"The raspberry one sounds delicious."

"Okay. You get that one and I'll get the other. We can see which one's better."

"Deal."

The waitress returned and took their orders, and with a slight nod of her head she quietly disappeared. Admiring the fire in front of her, Bahn flipped through the questions she still had about the man sitting next to her. Their discussion at the school was cut short, and if she was being honest, she was still a bit shell-shocked that he was even there.

"So, what made you decide to come all the way out here?"

Owen squinted his eyes. "You wouldn't pick up the phone."

Bahn giggled. "I did do that, didn't I?"

"Then you left early."

"How did you know that?"

"Because I went to the hotel, flowers in hand, ready to grovel at eight thirty yesterday morning, and they said you had already checked out. So I did the logical thing and booked a flight across the country to ask for forgiveness. I couldn't leave it the way it was."

"What time did you get in?"

"Seven twenty-five this morning."

"Oh my gosh, you flew overnight? Have you slept?"

"I took a nap when I got to the hotel. I figured you'd be busy this morning, so I thought catching you this afternoon might be better."

"I'm still blown away that you're here. I'm really sorry about the whole misunderstanding. You were right to be confused."

The waitress brought out the appetizer and set it in the center of the table along with a couple of plates. They each grabbed a shrimp from the glass.

Owen wiped his mouth with his napkin after dripping sauce on his chin and sat back in his chair. Bahn leaned in and dabbed at a spot he'd missed on his cheek, then smiled and licked it off her finger. His eyes filled with fire as they locked with hers, sending swirls of desire through her. But the feelings were quickly extinguished when he looked away.

His throat bobbed as he asked, "Can I ask you a question?" still not making eye contact.

A little unnerved by his actions and the seriousness in his voice, she replied, "Okay?"

"What made you decide to kiss her?"

Letting out a relieved breath, she said, "Honestly, I think the main factor was alcohol, but there is also a bit of a back story that I'm not sure you want to hear."

"Uh…yeah," he said, tilting his head. "I flew all the way out here to hear it, remember?"

"Yeah, I guess you did, didn't you?" Bahn adjusted herself in her seat. She grabbed another shrimp, doused it in the sauce, and lingered momentarily as she gathered her thoughts.

"I think I told you I met Sarah my freshman year and we became friends. We were both in the athletics program and she was in a couple of my classes. We decided to become roommates our sophomore year. Up until then, I had no clue Sarah was gay. When she told me, I told her about how I had been bullied, and that I had been battling with a ton of identity issues.

"She shared what she'd gone through before and after she came out. It gave me a glimpse into her life. She said she'd dated boys early on, and then girls, and at one point I asked her if she noticed a difference between kissing boys and kissing girls. She said there was for her, and then said, 'Maybe one day I'll show you.' We kind of laughed it off and left it at that.

"Then we started partying. I think we both dove in over our heads, but at the time, I was overwhelmed with school and life in general and I was at the point of giving up. My grades crashed and burned, and I nearly lost my scholarship my junior year. I knew it going into spring break, and I wanted to get away.

"I came up with the idea of driving down to Biloxi with a few friends, and I mentioned it to a couple of other people. It quickly became much larger than I expected. It took two days to drive. I think there were eighteen of us in the caravan, all ready to party.

"Our last night there, we were all wasted and playing some crazy games. Kent came up behind me and kind of manhandled me into a hard, awkward kiss. Sarah scolded him, saying that wasn't what a kiss was supposed to be like, and she leaned in and kissed me softly. With the alcohol in our systems, things kind of spun out of control, and I think that's when you walked up."

"So how far—"

"That's as far as it went," she said nonchalantly, waving her hand. "Made out for a minute, then laughed about the whole thing."

The waitress dropped off their meals and asked if everything looked okay. They both nodded, and she refilled their drinks and walked away.

"She's much nicer than our other server," Bahn said with a snicker, then continued, "Anyway, it's just funny how society can make you question things, you know? There was a time when I really did contemplate whether I was gay. So many people were saying it to my face, and behind my back, and I didn't quite feel comfortable within my own skin because everybody told me I was different. I wasn't into the whole dating scene. I was too focused on school and sports. And I began to wonder if there was something wrong with me.

"Sarah asked me the next day what I thought of her kissing me, and if I was mad. I told her I wasn't and gave her higher marks than Kent. She said that wasn't saying much and laughed. Then I was honest with her, saying it was nice, but that was all. She said it was because she wasn't the one I was supposed to be with, and that I would know when I found that person.

"To be honest, there was never that deep, all-consuming desire. Not with Sarah, or with anyone I've dated."

Pausing to take a bite of her salmon, she was immediately distracted as the flavors hit her palette. "Oh my gosh, this is delicious. How's yours?"

"Same." Without saying a word, they both offered bites for each to try. "Oh wow. That raspberry glaze is surprising. I like the mix of flavors."

Bahn waved her hand in front of her mouth as she spoke. "Yours has some heat to it." She quickly took a sip of water. "But it tastes incredible."

"I know."

She wiped her mouth and continued. "Anyway, that night made me realize a lot about myself, and what I want."

"And what's that?"

Bahn studied him. The way he never let his eyes leave hers made her feel like she was the only thing that mattered to him. He'd always made her feel that way. "I don't know. I've never considered myself as a hopeless romantic—far from it, actually—but I kind of want what my parents have, what I've read about in books."

"And... that would be?" he said slowly.

Giggling at his continued curiosity, she tried to find the words. "That spark. That giddiness. All the butterflies everyone talks about. The contentment. My parents' marriage isn't perfect, but you can tell they adore each other. They're always touching each other, holding hands and sneaking kisses. And it's not only physical stuff. They build each other up and respect each other.

"I think it's important to have someone who validates you for who you are but is also willing to help you grow to who you want to be. That's love. Whether they're the opposite sex or same sex that's for you to decide and no one else. Ultimately, it's who you find that all-encompassing love with."

"I agree. If I'm being honest, I always felt like there was something missing with Melanie. Don't get me wrong, I enjoyed dating her. Well, until, you know. We got along fine. And I was hurt when I saw her with James, but it was more the feeling of betrayal of our friendship than our relationship."

CHAPTER 27

The waitress stopped by the table to refill their waters and leave the ticket. Owen gave her his card, and she smiled before walking away.

The words Bahn had spoken suddenly reminded him of what she'd said the night she left. *'I thought about trying to contact you at least a thousand times... I felt like you were honestly the only person on earth who knew the real me and understood. You never questioned any of my crazy ideas... No one, and I mean no one, ever made me feel seen the way you did... You made me feel like I had superpowers. Our bond was special. I never forgot that... And I never forgot you.'*

"What is going on in that enormous brain of yours?" Bahn asked, keying in on Owen's silence.

He looked at her out of the corner of his eye, trying to decide if he should broach the question, but ultimately chose not to. It wasn't the time. "Oh, nothing, I'm just really enjoying this." He smiled. "So, did you have any other relationships?"

Bahn snickered. "Well, I wouldn't call what happened between Sarah and I a relationship, more like a drunken one-night stand. But I did date one of the guys who went with us to Mississippi. His name was Troy. We ran in the same circle of friends, and we were in a class together.

"We started hanging out more after we came back from Biloxi and would eat lunch together quite a bit at the Student Union. One day he asked me to go with him to see Bruno Mars in concert. I wasn't going to pass that up. It was an awesome concert, and we had a great time. We dated for about four months. He was a good guy."

"Did you ever think about getting married?"

"We talked about marriage, as in the act, a couple of times. But I knew I wasn't ready. I was still trying to figure out my life, and he was still into the party scene. Things started falling apart after a little while and I finally broke it off. He was good with it. I think we both knew we weren't what either of us wanted or needed. We remained friends, so everything ended okay." Bahn looked up at Owen. "You must really like the sound of my voice because I feel like I've done all the talking."

"I'm just giving you a turn. I did all the talking earlier."

"True."

"At least you listened this time."

Bahn glared and threw her napkin at him, then smirked as she said, "I'm kind of glad I did. I got a yummy meal out of it."

Owen nodded in agreement.

Once again, the waitress appeared at their table. She asked if everything was okay, and they both responded with smiles. As she left the table with some of the dishes, Bahn giggled. "Yeah, she is much better than our other waitress. You should give her a big tip."

Owen looked at her and laughed, "You've mistaken me for someone who is rich."

"If you have the money to come here, you gotta have a stash somewhere."

"Maybe, or maybe I'm picky about how I spend my money, and who I spend it on."

With that, Bahn gave him a demure smile.

"Where to next?"

Bahn shrugged. "I don't know. There's not a whole lot to see in Cabin Creek. It's pretty small."

Owen lifted a mischievous brow and grinned. "Wanna go back to the inn?"

With a perplexed expression, she retorted, "I don't know. Should I?"

He rose from the table and motioned with his head, and they

made their way to the door.

As they drove through the center of town, he pointed out the mural on the side of the winery but didn't tell her he'd visited it. He made a stop at the grocery store where he'd gotten the flowers earlier, picked up some tiny cupcakes for dessert, then drove to the inn. The sun was just beginning to lower in the sky.

Bahn smiled as they parked.

"Are you okay with stopping here for a little bit?"

"Oh, yeah. I loved staying here. There was an older lady who worked the desk, and she always had fresh baked cookies."

"She's still here." He gave her the package of cupcakes as he grabbed the bag from behind the seat, and they headed for the door of the inn.

"What's in the bag?" she asked with a curious lilt in her voice.

"Just a little surprise."

Her eyebrows raised, begging him to elaborate, but he enjoyed the idea of making her wait.

The thud of their shoes rang through the house as they made their way up the wooden stairs, and Owen stopped before unlocking the door. With a playful grin he said, "Close your eyes."

Bahn hesitated, eyeing him suspiciously, but complied. She heard Owen unlock the door, then flinched when she felt his hand cover her eyes and pull her body into his.

"No peeking." His chest rumbled with his words, and the vibration sent goosebumps all over her body, making her shiver.

She'd done the same thing when he cradled her on the beach. At first, she thought it was from being wet, and although she hadn't wanted to give him the satisfaction of a win, he was right. The water was freezing. But even after she was warm, the goosebumps hadn't disappeared. The longer he'd held her, the more her body tingled. And now, breathing his scent in, feeling his hot breath against the delicate skin of her neck, the charge was so strong, it felt like every hair on her body was standing on end.

In a soft voice he said, "Okay, open your eyes."

He slowly removed his hand, and her eyes darted around the

room. The sunlight glinted off the windowpanes, and Owen looked at Bahn as she took in the view. He moved past her to the fireplace and switched on the gas logs. With a pop, the fireplace lit up. Bahn stared out the window, then caught Owen gazing at her. His coy expression made her smile.

"This is nice. My little room was cute, but nothing like this. And I definitely didn't have this view."

"I was surprised. The perks of being military I guess."

He walked over to the kitchen and grabbed a couple of glasses out of the cabinet, then the bag from the counter. "Would you like a glass of wine?"

"Sure."

"Is red okay?"

"Yes. I like both." Bahn opened the door to the balcony and walked out. She felt a tiny remnant of the cool spring air and wrapped her sleeves over her hands as she leaned her arms on the balcony rail and took in a deep breath. The purple clouds cascading across the sky warned of impending storms.

Her thoughts trailed off, recalling the events of the day. *Oh, the difference one conversation can make.*

She smiled as she heard Owen's footsteps behind her and turned her head. He handed her a glass and leaned against the rail next to her. The sun beams broke through the clouds and penetrated Owen's eyes, setting them ablaze. With his chiseled jaw, lightly tanned skin, and dark wavy hair, he truly was handsome.

She twirled her glass while staring off in the distance. "This is stunning. I could stay out here forever."

"Me too." He lifted his glass and gestured toward her. She held hers up, and they tapped them together before taking a drink.

Owen suddenly set his glass down and ran back inside, leaving the door open. When he returned, he had two tiny cupcakes in his hand. He held them out to Bahn, who took both, and grinned. Owen's mouth dropped open then shut in a pout. He slowly turned, evidently to grab a couple more, but she quickly handed one to him.

Pulling him next to her, she held her phone up, making sure she caught the beautiful background in the shot. Owen put his arm around her and snuggled her in tight as they held up their cupcakes. When she was done taking their picture, they popped the cupcakes into their mouths at the same time.

Bahn spun around, leaning against the railing again and took a sip of her wine. She closed her eyes for a moment and listened to the water as it rolled over the rocks below. Propping her chin in her hand, she looked at him and sighed as the corner of her lips lifted. "Did you ever think this past week would turn out like this?"

Owen's eyes widened. "No, can't say that even in my wildest dreams would I have come up with this scenario." He paused and his eyes met hers. "But I'm happy with how it's turned out so far. Except for the nightmare night in the middle. I could have done without that."

Bahn giggled. "Yeah, that was a bit unexpected. The food was good though."

"The food was excellent. But you nearly drowned, and what followed after caused that delicious meal to quickly become a distant memory."

Bahn stared at Owen as his face turned serious, and he suddenly became quiet.

She bumped her shoulder into his. "Hey?"

"What?"

"I don't know. You just got quiet."

Owen tipped his head and dragged his teeth over his lip like he was contemplating a question. "So that night," he paused, and Bahn rolled her eyes, not wanting to rehash how stupid she was for not letting him explain, "you said you had wanted to contact me over the years."

"Yeah. Especially after we moved to California, and then in college when everything started spiraling out of control. I tried looking you up on the internet after we came back from Biloxi, actually. I didn't figure I would find anything, since your dad had such a high security clearance, and I was right."

She looked down at the floor. "I know it sounds crazy. I know we were twelve, but just thinking about you somehow comforted me. You were...special to me. The day we moved away, I felt like I left a piece of myself behind."

"Yeah, you took a piece of me with you, too."

CHAPTER 28

14 years earlier

He sat up in the treehouse, his eyes riveted to the sliding glass door below, watching as people shuffled back and forth. For some reason, he felt like torturing himself even more.

Why now? Why did his best friend have to leave right now? She was the only person he wanted to be with on the bad days. She was the only person who could make him laugh, even when he felt his world was falling apart. She was the only person who truly understood who he was, or at least pretended she did. She was there for him for three years, and now she was leaving. Where would he turn now? His dad was gone. His mom seemed to be too busy for him. His siblings wanted nothing to do with him, and on that count, the feeling was mutual.

"Are you watching me again?" came a voice from below, and he jumped, startled back to reality. She climbed the ladder the two of them built from wood and rope they found on one of their treasure hunts a long time ago and pulled herself into the treehouse next to him. Drawing her legs against her chest, she slid her oversized sweatshirt over them to stay warm. "What are you doing up here? Aren't you cold?"

Still staring down into the house, he said, "You said it. I'm watching you. Or watching that." He motioned with his hand toward her house. "When do you leave?"

"Our flight is tomorrow morning sometime. Dad left Saturday with a bunch of stuff. He's going to get everything ready at the house, then pick us up at the airport tomorrow night, I think. He has to be at the base first thing Wednesday." She paused. "Isn't your mom driving us to the airport?"

"Oh. Yeah. I forgot." His eyes drifted to her. "How long will it take you to get there?"

"I'm not sure. I've never flown before. We've always driven when we moved. Most of our stuff isn't going to get there until next week."

"It's like you're going to a foreign country. You can't even get there if you drive."

"I know. Dad said Virginia is nice, lots of beaches and stuff. I think it'll be cool."

"You have beaches here. Why move?"

"It's not like I had a say in the matter. My dad got transferred to the base there, remember? It's the military. Anyway, what's the big deal? Ya gonna miss me?" She rolled her body into him to give him a playful nudge.

"Only when I don't have anyone to beat at video games."

"What do you mean beat? I happen to know that I have more wins."

"Oh, you wish."

"And I beat you in basketball too."

"That's only because you actually like the sport."

She stood and walked to the mini fridge, opened the door, and stared inside. Taking a Coke, she popped the top and took a drink. Her eyes darted to the photos on the bulletin board that held so many memories. Tilting her head, she seemed to study them. In the past few weeks, they'd hung up the photos from their treasure adventure. He especially loved the one of him with the bottle and treasure map, and another one of the two of them together when they'd gone to get ice cream after a baseball game. Owen noticed tears filling her eyes, but she discreetly wiped them away and applied a smile on her face as she turned back to him.

"So how long is your dad going to be gone?" she asked as she glanced back at the photos.

"He said eight months. Maybe longer. It depends."

"Depends on what?" She sat back down beside him.

"I don't know, I guess how the war goes. He didn't want to go."

"Really?"

"I heard him talking to mom. He was trying to reassure her that everything was going to be fine, but he said he didn't want to go."

Her gaze swung back to the photos, and she stood again. Traipsing back to the bulletin board, she began to remove some of them. "It will be. I don't think anyone really wants to go over there, but like my dad said, 'It's what they signed up for.' He went over there for a while and came back just fine."

Once she'd taken several that she obviously wanted, she walked over and sat on the beanbag chair.

Owen sat down beside her. He just wanted to be near her for as long as possible. "Did he ever talk about what he did while he was over there?"

"No. He showed me some photos, but that was about it. I got to talk to him at Christmas while he was there. I could barely hear him, and we didn't talk long. Maybe you'll be able to do that with your dad, too."

"Yeah, I hope so. When did your dad go to Afghanistan?"

"When I was like eight or nine. It was before you came here."

"Why didn't you ever tell me, especially when I told you my dad was leaving."

"I don't know, I guess you never asked." She held up the photos. "Can I have these?"

"Sure, I guess."

Sunlight broke through the window the next morning, and Owen was awakened by his mom tapping on his door. "If you want to go with me to take Vanessa and Bahn to the airport, you need to get up."

Owen rolled over and groaned. He didn't want this day to come. Maybe if he stayed in bed and went back to sleep, he could pretend it was all a bad dream. But then he would miss seeing Bahn for possibly the last time.

Slowly, he pushed himself up and shuffled to the kitchen. Dragging the milk from the refrigerator and a box of cereal from the pantry, he dumped them both in a bowl and started shoveling it into his mouth. It was tasteless. No zing of sugary sweetness. It was just mushy chunks sliding down his throat. He felt totally numb. His stomach clenched and the rest of his cereal wound up dumped down the sink.

Heading back to his bedroom, he dug through the pile of clothes on the floor to find a pair of pants and slid them on. After retrieving a clean shirt from the drawer, he went in search of his missing sneaker, finally locating it under the bed. It only managed to add to his anger. He grabbed some socks from his chest of drawers, made a stop in the bathroom to try to adjust his mop of hair, then plopped on the couch to put on his shoes.

Carissa appeared from around the corner. "Are you ready?"

"I guess."

She lifted her purse and keys from the counter and motioned for Owen to come along.

They backed out of the driveway and rounded the corner to the Jackson's house. Owen hopped out and knocked on the door. Bahn immediately jerked it open and rolled her bag out without saying a word. Her mom followed behind.

Bahn remained quiet for the entire ride. Owen didn't know if it was because she was leaving, scared of the flight, or just not awake. Regardless, he didn't feel like talking either.

He stared out the window, watching as the buildings and neighborhoods flew by. Every once in a while, he'd peek over at Bahn and catch her looking back. She would give him a slight smile that almost made things worse. He wanted to say something, but he was afraid that if he opened his mouth, he would cry, and he didn't want to cry in front of her. She was so strong. He'd only seen her cry a couple of times.

Open fields went by, and then Owen saw the tower and runways of the airport. His heart began to beat faster as dread set in, and he found it hard to swallow because of the lump growing in his throat.

They stopped under the sign for their designated airline, and Carissa and Vanessa hopped out and unloaded the luggage. Slowly, Owen and Bahn got out. Carissa hugged Vanessa, said something that Owen didn't hear clearly, and then hugged Bahn. Vanessa did the same with Owen. Bahn and Owen looked at each other, not knowing what to do.

Vanessa pulled her luggage up onto the curb. "Okay, Bahn, we gotta go. Give Owen a hug."

Bahn barely looked at Owen then gave him a halfhearted wave before stepping up onto the curb, hoisting her luggage with her, and walking off.

Owen stood at the back of the car and watched her leave. He shut the trunk and turned to get back into the car, all the while wishing he had the courage to give her a hug.

Looking up one last time, he saw Bahn looking back. Her luggage dropped from her hand, and she ran. Slamming into him, she wrapped him in a hug and squeezed him tight. Owen closed his eyes and wrapped his arms around her.

"I'm going to miss you," Bahn whispered, sniffling as she buried her head in his shoulder.

He tried to speak, but the words got caught in his throat. "…miss you too." Tears seeped from his eyes, and when Bahn pulled away, he could see she was crying too.

She turned quickly and ran back to her luggage, then gave him one last wave goodbye.

Owen waved again, opened the door, and got in.

His mom looked at him in the rearview mirror. "You okay?"

He couldn't answer, just stared out the window, feeling like part of his soul had been ripped out of him.

CHAPTER 29

Present Day

Owen stared into Bahn's eyes, noticing a sadness he also still felt whenever he thought about that painful day.

"It always seemed like you could read my mind. Like you knew what I wanted, even though I was too scared to admit it. I was so painfully shy as a kid, it seemed like everything terrified me. Most people ignored me, but you, you always challenged me to do more. You didn't let me get away with playing it safe, and with each new adventure we went on, I felt stronger. You made me brave. I don't know how you did it. You always knew how to live life with reckless abandon, and you had a way of giving me the courage to do things I would normally be totally petrified to do.

"Nothing seemed to scare you. Even when you got hurt, you just bounced back and went at it with full force again. I envied you, because of the way you lived." His teeth grazed his lip as he confessed, "I was terrified when I enlisted, but I remembered all of our adventures, and knew I could do it."

"Oh no, don't put that on me…." Her voice trailed off, and in her silence, she studied him, making him curious about what she was thinking.

An uneasiness filled her eyes as she lifted them to his. The crooked smile that had been imprinted on her face suddenly disappeared as her brows drew down in increasing distress. "Didn't you say you joined the military when you were home for spring break?"

Owen looked at her, confused.

"You did," she rushed out. "You said you decided to join the military when you came home to help your parents move." Her voice began to quake, and he could see in her expression as the realization set in. "You joined because of me. Didn't you? Because of that night at Dune Canyon."

He looked away so she wouldn't see the truth, but he obviously wasn't fast enough.

"Oh God." She stepped back. "You did."

His eyes closed to avoid the anguish etching her pretty face. Trying to dispel her growing hysteria, he said, "Bahn, hold on—"

"It's true, isn't it?"

Owen pinched the bridge of his nose, and his mind raced through what he could say to make it better.

"Answer me, damn it." Tears now filled her eyes.

Recognizing he had missed his chance, because she had already jumped into the deep end, he dove in. "I had thought about it for a while. Like I said, I felt lost. My brother and sister both had jobs and had gotten married. I just wanted to have that life with a family, and the whole Melanie thing went south, and—"

"But I was the last straw, wasn't I?" Her lips pursed and a tear spilled down her cheek.

"Bahn, I—"

"You, you nearly died, Owen." She covered her mouth, like the words made her physically sick, and turned away.

He reached over, pulling her into him, and wrapped his arms around her. She buried her face in his shoulder and sobbed. "Bahn," he said in a near whispered voice, "no matter what had happened that weekend, it probably wouldn't have changed the outcome."

It was a lie, but one he had to tell. The minute he knew she was there, his mind had conjured up a scenario of seeing her again and how it would change everything. But when he saw her in the embrace of someone else, his dream fell apart. In his fragile state, knowing his best friend was so close, yet unreachable, shattered him. But he couldn't let her know that.

"It was my decision to join. I needed to prove to myself I was strong enough. I knew what I was getting into. And honestly, with how things have turned out, I'm glad I did it."

Her body convulsed against him as she tried to breathe through the sobs. He should have known she would see through his lie. He never could get anything past her. She always knew.

He rubbed his hand up and down her back, trying to soothe her. His eyes closed as his heart broke for her. But he knew how she felt. He couldn't imagine a world without Bahn. Whether she was in his life or not, just knowing she was living somewhere, still lighting up the world, made his heart sing. But having her in his arms in that moment was almost too much.

"Shh, come on now," he said, continuing to caress her, "we're supposed to be having fun."

His face buried into her hair; he breathed deep. Her scent was spicy and intoxicating, and he couldn't stop himself from pressing kiss after kiss into her hair.

As her sobs lessened, she gradually lifted her head until her eyes met his. Tears and mascara streamed down her face. "I don't know what I would do if I found out you had—"

Seeing the fear spark in her eyes, he knew what she was about to say. "But I didn't, Bahn. I'm fine. I'm here. And we're together. How cool is that?" He was hoping for a glimmer of a smile, but the sadness on her face persisted.

He lifted his hand to her face and wiped the tears from her cheeks. The cool air gave them a light pink tint. Gently pecking her forehead with a few brushes of his lips, he gazed into her eyes again. Tears glistened in the corners, and their translucent gleam made it seem like they could see deep inside him. She stirred up something in him that was quickly taking over.

His fingers caressed the nape of her neck, and he tenderly lifted her mouth to his and leaned in. She sighed, and his lips brushed gently against hers. When he paused, a timid smile tugged at the corner of her mouth. He tightened his hold and leaned in again. Her body softened against his as he stole one kiss, then another. Her lips were delicate and soft, and her mouth tasted of vanilla icing.

Pulling away just long enough to tilt his head, he leaned in again, deepening the kiss, hungry to taste her again. She opened for him, and his tongue swept in, tasting her fully. Savoring her. Flavors of sweet vanilla and wine danced on his senses.

Putting his back against the rail, he pressed her against him, continuing the fevered onslaught. He couldn't get enough. His hand slid to her cheek, and he backed away.

The vulnerability in her expression took his breath away. The confident girl he knew had disappeared.

He lifted his hand to her cheek once more. "Your cheeks are cold. Do you want to go inside?"

Bahn smiled, pulled her sleeves down over her hands and nodded. "Yeah, it is a little bit chilly."

He grabbed their empty glasses, placed his hand on the small of her back, and escorted her back into the room. "A bit different from Biloxi."

"Just a little bit."

"Would you like another glass of wine?"

She nodded, and as he set the glasses on the counter to fill them, she grabbed one of the cupcakes, popping it into her mouth as she sat on the couch. Unzipping her boots, she pulled them off and set them aside before tucking her legs under her.

As Owen poured the wine, he tried to calm the voices that were firing off in his head. Though he'd fantasized about a romantic evening with Bahn, his nerves were getting the best of him, and he suddenly felt like the shy little twelve-year-old boy not quite knowing what to say. He hoped the wine would kick in soon and help him relax.

Pulling his phone from his pocket, he switched on his playlist and handed Bahn the glass of wine. "Is this okay?" he asked, sitting down next to her.

She nodded and snuggled into him, grabbing his hand.

"Geez, your hands are like ice. I'm so sorry. You should have told me you were cold." He leaned forward, slid the powder blue Afghan from the chair beside them, wrapped it around her shoulders, then sat back.

Clouds had taken what was left of the sunlight, and the room was now lit by the flames from the fireplace. Bahn snuggled into him, and he put his arm around her as she laid her head on his shoulder. They were quiet for several moments as they watched the fire send sparks up the chimney.

Taking a sip from his glass, he said, "I feel horrible. We should have come in sooner." The fireplace crackled as Owen began to gently rub Bahn's arm. "I'm just not that experienced with the whole dating thing."

Bahn turned to Owen with a look of surprise. "You seemed to do just fine with that kiss outside."

A slight grin crossed his face. "Oh really?" Owen thought back to their conversation earlier. "How did I rate?"

Bahn laughed, tapping her lip with her finger, and coyly responded, "Hmmm…it's been too long, I think I need a redo."

Owen tugged her legs over his until he had her cradled in his lap, then leaned in, gently brushing his lips to hers. She smiled, and he captured one lip and then the other, his tongue barely touching each before he slowly tilted his head, taking the kiss deeper, letting his tongue slide against hers, dragging a whimper from deep within her.

Need began to swirl within him. Brushing his lips over her jaw and down her neck, he ached to taste more of her. His fingers threaded through her curls as he tilted her head so he could continue his exploration.

Their kisses quickly grew hungrier, and Bahn sat up, moving to straddle Owen's lap. His heart raced and his body lit on fire. Her hand stroked the stubble on his cheek, and a smile slowly lifted the corner of her mouth. His breath caught in his throat as he gazed into her eyes. She was so beautiful when she smiled. Her lips were a dusty rose, with a perfect cupid's bow, and knowing what they felt like, and what she tasted like, he suddenly wanted more. Cupping her cheek, he brought her lips to his, kissing her slowly, passionately.

In that moment, his heart took over, silencing all the negative voices. Everything fell away, and he was finally able to convey how he felt. His hands skimmed down her back, resting on her bottom.

Bahn pulled away, trying to catch her breath, and grinned. "Oh, I'd say that's a ten." Her hand connected with his chest, and her eyes jerked up to his. "Your heart is pounding."

"I know. I can feel it."

"Do I make you nervous?" she asked with a slight chuckle.

Owen lowered his head and slowly raised his eyes to her, wondering if he should lie, then realized it was probably useless. She would see right through him. "A little."

"Why?"

"Not you, this." His hand volleyed back and forth between them. "Like I said, I'm not really experienced."

Bahn giggled then paused. Her brows lifted and her mouth dropped open. "How inexperienced?"

Owen leaned his head back on the sofa, and looked away, feeling like things were quickly becoming very awkward. He wished he'd never said anything. Would answering the glaring question staring him in the face bring their wonderful evening to a screeching halt?

"Look at me." Bahn wrapped her hand around his cheek and brought his eyes back to hers. "Are you trying to tell me you've never been with anyone?"

Heat filled his cheeks, and he dropped his focus to the fuzz on the Afghan. She leaned down, trying to make eye contact again, but he resisted.

"It's okay," she said softly, but moved from his lap to sit beside him.

His heart stumbled, figuring she was just being nice. "Are you sure?"

"Yeah," she said softly with half a smile.

"That wasn't convincing at all," Owen joked, but humiliation coursed through his body.

She turned to face him. "I just wish I would have known, so I wouldn't have attacked you and scared you," she said with a smirk.

"I think you might have that backward. I believe I attacked you."

Her hand fanned her face. "Yeah, you did. And it warmed me right up. I definitely don't need that Afghan anymore."

The comment managed to relieve some of the embarrassment, and he laughed as he picked up another cupcake. Peeling the wrapper off, he dangled it in front of her. She opened her mouth like a little bird and wrapped her lips around the whole thing in slow motion, managing to send every bit of blood in Owen's body south. He chuckled and shook his head, then reached for another one and shoved it in his mouth.

"Can I ask you something?" she questioned, still chewing on the cupcake.

"Sure. Now that you know my big secret, I'm pretty much an open book."

"Are you saving yourself for marriage?"

Letting out a sigh, he shook his head. "No, not really."

"Oh…" Bahn tipped her head, and in that moment, he saw a gleam in her eye that appeared only when something piqued her interest. He swallowed hard, knowing what was coming. "Why then?"

And there it was. She was like a toddler when she latched onto a subject she needed to understand, drilling down with question after question until she was satisfied.

He continued to slowly chew his cupcake, not really wanting to own up to the truth. But somehow Bahn worked her magic again. Regardless of the voices in his head, he knew she wouldn't judge him. Even though they'd been apart for years, he still felt like they were connected.

Giving up on ever coming back from the humiliation, he cleared his throat. "I was too shy. I've always felt awkward, especially around women. I wasn't lying in the treehouse. They scare me. Plus, Dad put the fear of God in me about getting a girl pregnant and taking responsibility. And the best way to make sure you don't get someone pregnant is, don't have sex. So, if I ever chose to have sex with someone, I wanted it to be someone I was willing to take that risk with. Someone who meant something to me. Someone who was more than just a good time.

"Melanie and I kissed and fooled around a little. It was fun, don't get me wrong, but I don't know, it was just that. Fun. Sex to me means more. Since I never felt like we got past the point of just having fun, I never felt the need to take it further." His eyes turned to meet hers. "Does that make sense?"

"Yeah."

"When was your first time?"

"College. Unfortunately, I made a dumb decision due to too much partying. So, my first time was kind of a blur."

The thought of another man having his hands on her sent a sudden stab of jealousy through him, but he couldn't help being curious, even though he figured it was going to make him even angrier.

Noticing her deflated expression, he stroked her arm and tried to keep his feelings to himself. "Did you enjoy it?"

"What I can remember of it, it was okay. It kind of hurt. And it didn't take very long, if you know what I mean."

Her underwhelming response had a smile pulling at his lips, but then his mind got stuck on her words, '*what I can remember…*' and anger immediately filled his blood with fire. "He didn't force—"

"No. He didn't take advantage of me, if that's what you're asking? It was consensual. We even kind of laughed about it later. Like I said, I kind of lost who I was, and I didn't know what I wanted. We'd met in one of the classes we had together. He was studying to be a coach too. One night, we wound up at the same party. He was decent looking, had always been nice when we talked, and that night he said all the right things to make me feel special. We'd both been drinking a little too much, and it just happened."

"Was it awkward?"

"A little. But you just kind of go with what feels right. Looking back, it kind of stings that it was a meaningless one-night stand. I know I wasted something special. And having sex with a guy didn't really help with my identity crisis, because it wasn't like there was anything really between us other than too much alcohol and lust."

Bahn shifted, pressing her back into Owen's side. Drawing her knee up, she rested her elbow on it and dug her fingers in her curls. Staring at the fire, she grew quiet.

Owen waited for her to continue, but her words never came. As the silence continued, he became worried that Bahn had ventured back into some bad memories, or worse, was rehashing their argument.

"Everything okay?" he asked hesitantly.

Bahn took a deep breath, and Owen's heart dropped into his stomach when she hesitated before she spoke. "Do you..." she paused, her voice barely above a whisper, and the timidness in it made him even more worried. "Do you... feel anything...for me?"

CHAPTER 30

O wen slowly turned Bahn to face him. He rolled his eyes, relief washing over him as he chuckled and said, "What do you think?"

"I, I don't—"

"Bahn. You have been my best friend for seventeen years. You know me better than anyone, and I mean anyone. The only other person who knew the real me was my dad, and he's not here anymore."

"Yeah, but best friends aren't—"

"Do you think I would have kissed you if I didn't feel—"

"You kissed Melanie."

"True. But I damn sure wouldn't fly across the country just to set the record straight with her. But the question I have is, do you?"

"Uh. If you remember correctly, I kissed you first."

His mind raced to the kiss on the beach, and his body deflated. "I'm so sorry, Bahn."

"No." She searched his eyes. "Don't be sorry. I didn't say it to make you feel bad. You were right to be confused."

Snickering, he said, "After that kiss, I definitely was." Grasping her hand, he began brushing his thumb against her soft skin, contemplating what everything meant. "So…, where do we go from here?"

"What do you say we pick up where we left off?"

He immediately pulled her back into his lap as a flash of light streaked across the room.

Bahn jerked her focus to the window as a low rumble echoed from outside.

Owen looked over his shoulder and then back at Bahn. She scraped her lip with her teeth and looked at him through her lashes. His hand wrapped around the back of her neck, and she responded, leaning in. Caressing her cheek with his lips, he worked his way to her mouth, capturing it, tasting her again. With his arms tightened around her, he stretched out his legs, then moved from under her, laying her on the sofa next to him.

Staring into her eyes, he studied her features, searching for any reservations she might have. They had been best friends, but was she really ready to take it further?

Her hooded gaze dipped to his lips, and he had his answer.

Kissing her softly, he moved from her lips to her neck, while his hands skimmed her body, exploring every curve. He'd never experienced the bone deep, all-consuming need that suddenly filled him.

As kids, they were each other's alter ego, balancing one another. She drew him out of his shell, and he reined her in as she sought out her next adrenaline rush.

When he was leaving the funeral, it was like her soul called to him. Even before he saw her blonde curls, he sensed it was her. His mind didn't believe it, but his heart knew.

Every time she spoke, with that little bit of humor that laced her sultry voice, his chest tightened to the point he fought to breathe. And her touch sent a charge through him, like an impending lightning strike.

There was definitely something more there than just their friendship.

Bahn's breaths quickened as his lips brushed against her neck. The feel of her body against his set him on fire. She moved him under her, straddling him again, fanning the raging flames threatening to devour him.

Grabbing hold of his shirt, she popped the snaps and flung it open. His bare chest exposed; she would be able to see the scars of war up close for the first time. He wondered how she would react and fought the need to cover them.

Tenderly running her fingers over each spot, she paused momentarily, then, leaning down, she kissed the wounds one by one. The way her lips brushed against the hardened skin had him sucking in a ragged breath, trying to stave off the overwhelming emotion taking hold.

As she worked her way from his neck to his chest, then to his stomach, Owen's eyes followed her. Her soft lips against his bare skin made him tremble as his desire ramped up. His teeth clenched and he tried to hang on to the last shred of his self-control, but as her breath fanned out across his heated skin, and her fingers danced along his waistband, he was quickly losing the battle, and a strained groan rumbled from his chest.

Concern flooded Bahn's face. "Is this okay?"

Owen sat up slightly, which didn't help his current situation. "I...I—"

"We can stop if you want," she said quickly, and started to move off of him, but Owen grasped her thighs, stopping her.

"No...I...don't want...I just ..." a sheepish grin pulled at his lips, and he slammed his eyes shut. "I need a moment, or this is going to end very quickly and very embarrassingly."

"Oh. Okay." She leaned forward slightly, giving him a bit of relief. "Is this better?"

His eyes met hers as her fingers rubbed circles in his short hair. "I..." he panted, his hands wrapping around her hips and pressing her to him. Her head dropped to the bend in his neck. "I..."

He felt her smile against his skin, and her hips jerked as her teeth tugged on the lobe of his ear before brushing soft kisses across his cheek.

Crashing his lips into hers, his last thread of control snapping, he slid his hand into her hair and let out a low moan.

Pure primal need took over and he raised up, pressing hard kisses along her pulse point and down to the sensitive hollow of her shoulder as he brought his hand up under her shirt, letting his thumbs skim the tender skin of her breasts.

The room closed in, and all he could see was her beautiful face. He wrapped one hand under her chin and brought her mouth to his, immediately taking her mouth hostage, plunging in, seeking to satisfy the intense hunger. Needing to have her skin against his, he pushed her shirt up, and with one last kiss, he backed away before lifting her shirt over her head, then dove back in. She felt so right in his arms.

Her hands reached inside his shirt and began stroking the bare skin of his back, making his muscles twitch.

His lips trailed down her golden skin along her neck. With the rise and fall of her chest, Owen placed light kisses to her delicate mounds. Dragging down the lacy material covering her breasts, he took a nipple in his mouth.

His eyes lifted to see Bahn staring at him, chewing on her bottom lip. The vulnerability in her expression nearly did him in.

Backing away for a moment, he could see so much history there, so much need to know she was desired. He leaned in, capturing her mouth again, gently wrapping his hand around her cheek, then backed away, letting their eyes connect again.

"God, Bahn. You're so perfect."

A slight smile lifted at the corner of her mouth.

Pushing up from the sofa, he stood, lifting Bahn with him, holding her against him while her legs wrapped his waist. Curls fell into her face, and she reached back and freed the rest, shaking her head then smiling. He looked at the bedroom and paused, "Are we…" then looked into Bahn's eyes and tipped his head. She smiled back at him and nodded, and he carried her through the doorway.

The lit fireplace warmed the room as reflections of the flames danced off the walls. Music quietly played. Bahn dropped her feet to the floor, placed her hands on his muscular chest, and followed the ripples down his belly.

He stroked her hair and leaned in, kissing her as he reached around her back to unclasp her bra. When he couldn't quite get it to release, Bahn reached back to help.

"Gonna have to work on that," he said with a sheepish grin, pulling her in again, kissing her neck and letting his hands slip down to her butt.

Her fingers grazed his well-defined arms while she removed his shirt, sending tingles through him, making him shudder as he tried to contain the desperate urge to take her right then and there.

Smoothing his hands against her heated skin, he slid inside her leggings and panties.

Bahn backed away. "These can be tricky."

Owen tipped his head, wondering what she meant, then broke out in a fit of laughter when she nearly fell over after getting her foot caught in them.

She slipped between the sheets, and Owen took in the scene. She looked like a Grecian sculpture with the soft fabric swirled around her. She was breathtaking. Moving slightly, the sheet dipped down just enough to expose one of her breasts and his entire body shuddered as he bit down on his lip. Pure primal need coursed through him. He needed to taste her, touch her…claim her.

Her eyes dipped to his waist, and he snickered from her obvious enjoyment of him unbuckling his belt, so he snuck in a few flexes as he finished undressing.

Placing a small foil package, he'd retrieved from his wallet, on the nightstand, he slid into the sheets beside her and rose up on his forearm, pulling her to him. Her face was softly lit with the glow of the flames from the fireplace, and her translucent eyes captured his, studying him. She was exquisite.

The back of his fingers ran along her jawline, and his thumb traced her bottom lip before he captured her mouth again.

Her fingers dug into his back, pressing her silky skin against his. His hand grazed the soft skin of her side as the carnal need overwhelmed him. Moving down her neck, he nipped and sucked, feasting on her, his need continuing to climb as her cries intensified. He had to have her now.

Grabbing the packet from the nightstand, he quickly secured the condom. Then, wrapping his hand around her hip, he pulled her beneath him and broke the kiss to take in the moment their bodies became one, pushing in slowly.

She let out a whimper and he stilled for a moment, closing his eyes, trying to calm the sensation that would end their night far too quickly. When he opened them again, he found Bahn staring at him with a bright smile. He leaned down and brushed his nose against hers as his hips began to move. His mouth moved to her lips then her neck and breast, and she closed her eyes and softly moaned when he took her nipple in his mouth again.

A growl rumbled from deep in his chest as his need intensified and his pace increased. "Is this okay?"

Her breaths came in short gasps with the movement of their bodies together. She nodded as soft whimpers escaped her, and it drove his need into a frenzy.

Her hands stroked his body, traveling to the small of his back and around to his hips, sending sparks through him and bringing him ever closer to his climax. Pieces of hair drifted into her face, and he gently moved them away and continued his feverish kisses. Her mouth moved slowly down his jaw, across his neck and down to his chest as her breaths became harder and her whimpers turned into moans.

The tingling started deep in his spine, and he knew he wasn't going to be able to hold out much longer but there was nothing he could do about it. It felt too damn good. He captured her mouth again in a hungry kiss. "Bahn," he whispered, then let his teeth graze the sensitive skin of her neck.

She stilled for a moment, then gasped before letting out a guttural cry. Her fingertips dug in. Panting and trembling, his name escaped her lips. "O-, Owen." Her cries intensified as her body began to let go and he raised up and watched her come apart in his arms. It was the most beautiful thing he'd ever experienced. His body was engulfed in a surge of electricity as she wrapped around him with her climax, and his body exploded.

CHAPTER 31

◆

She had lost all control of her body. Deep moans turned into shuddering cries as Owen coaxed wave after wave of absolute ecstasy from her. She struggled to open her eyes, but as she did, she found Owen staring back at her. His jaw pulsed and his body jerked as a deep, strained groan reverberated through him, mixing with the noises she couldn't seem to control. If she wasn't already at a loss of oxygen, the look on his face would have completely stolen her breath.

As he relaxed, he moved off her and Bahn laid with her head resting on Owen's chest, running her fingers up and down his torso. His heart was still thundering in his chest. Probably the same as hers, she suspected.

Her mind was trying to process everything that had happened. It was overwhelming. She hardly ever cried, but she couldn't hold back the tears she felt spilling from the corners of her eyes. She had never experienced anything like it.

Owen flinched, and he moved to face her, obviously hearing her sniffle.

"Hey," he said softly. "You okay?" His voice sounded gravelly in the darkness. "I didn't hurt you, did I?"

She snuggled into him, wiping away another tear. "No. God no. I've just never… that was—"

"Was it okay?"

She giggled as she nodded. "I can't even—"

He kissed the top of her head, and she thought about how incredible it would be to just stay snuggled in his arms and fall asleep. The thunder rolled in the distance, reminding her that she was going to have to get out in the mess. She had work tomorrow, and she couldn't wear what she had with her to finish cleaning her room.

But a few more minutes wouldn't hurt. She closed her eyes and enjoyed the moment.

"Are you asleep?" She heard him ask in a barely audible voice a few minutes later.

"No."

He rolled over to face her and whispered, "Stay with me tonight."

"I want to, but I can't."

"Why?" he whined.

"I have a meeting first thing tomorrow, then I have to finish cleaning, and I can't wear what I have here."

He propped himself up on his arm. "I'll set the alarm so we can get back to your place in time for you to change. Please, Bahn. Stay."

The thought of how early they'd have to set the alarm made her cringe. She normally waited until the very last minute to get up. But their time was limited. Owen would be leaving.

Realization set in, sending more tears to her eyes. She didn't want to waste one minute away from him. "We would have to be up around five forty-five."

"Done. I'm used to getting up early. Another perk, compliments of Uncle Sam."

Her eyes locked with his for a long minute. "Okay. I'll text Sarah and let her know."

Owen threw off the covers and wandered into the bathroom. And although she hated the thought of having to get up early, as she watched him traipse into the bathroom completely naked, she smiled and stretched. Under her breath she whispered, "Worth it."

Crawling out of bed, she dug for her phone in her pants pocket. As she started her text, she suddenly remembered Sarah had no clue what had happened during the day.

Bahn: **Won't be home tonight.**

Sarah responded quickly.

Sarah: **...Okay?**
Bahn: **Long story, tell you later, don't worry.**

She chucked her phone onto her pile of clothes and walked into the bathroom. With no door on the shower, Bahn leaned against the wall and watched as Owen let the lather from his hair and face sluice down his body. She could see the muscles in his legs and arms flex with each movement and she scraped her teeth across her bottom lip and sighed.

As he wiped the soap from his eyes, he noticed her staring at him. "What?" he quipped while the water dripped across his face.

"Nothing, I'm just taking in the view."

"Do you like what you see?"

"Uh huh."

He chuckled and shut the water off, then shook his head like a puppy after a bath. Bahn giggled. He reached for a towel to wipe his face and stole a kiss.

As he dried off, Bahn looked into his eyes. "So... how was it for you?" She had taken notice that he never said anything earlier, and she was curious since it was his first time.

A big grin crossed his face. He obviously knew what she was referring to. "Eh," he shrugged, "it was fine." Tossing the towel at her, he added, "It's all yours," and jogged out without turning around.

Bahn's eyes narrowed as she smirked and pulled the towel from her head, setting it back on the hook. She pulled her hair up in a messy bun and turned on the water. Hot droplets stung as they hit her skin, sending tingles down her back. She quickly lathered her body and rinsed off.

When she emerged from the shower, she noticed a graphic T-shirt sitting on the vanity. It made her grin. She threw it over her head and pattered out to the bed.

Lifting the covers, she crawled in and giggled as Owen tugged her to his side and kissed her on the forehead. "It was amazing." He grinned and snuggled down beside her, kissing her softly on the lips. The day obviously caught up to him as she watched his eyes become heavy.

Running the back of her hand along his scruff, she wondered how she could have gotten so lucky. He pulled her close, and she closed her eyes, and within a few minutes she was asleep.

A loud clap of thunder pierced the silence of the room and Bahn stirred awake. Peering through half-opened eyes, she looked around the room, momentarily forgetting where she was. But then she remembered and smiled, closing her eyes again.

Just as she began to drift off, she could feel Owen moving, and he moaned, then whimpered. His body jerked and his breathing became erratic. She rolled over and gently tapped him, but there was no response. "Owen, wake up," she called out as she nudged him some more, still to no avail.

Becoming more alarmed as he began to thrash around, she sat up in the bed and started stroking his arm and calling to him. "Owen? Owen, wake up. You're having a nightmare." She shook his shoulder as his whimpers became cries, breaking her heart. "Owen, please, wake up."

His eyes popped open, and he sat up. His chest heaved with deep, gulping breaths. His gaze was distant, and from the fear in his eyes, Bahn still wasn't sure if he was awake.

"Owen, are you okay?"

He swallowed hard, and his breathing was still labored. His body was rigid and trembled violently as sweat shimmered on his skin.

Bahn stroked his face carefully. "Owen, can you hear me?" Tears pooled in her eyes. "Come on. Talk to me."

Breaking free, tears began streaming down her face as she started to panic. She grabbed his face with both of her hands. "Wake up, Owen. It isn't real. Come back to me."

His eyes fluttered and he sucked in an audible gasp. Turning to face her, she could still see the terror in his watery eyes. She wrapped her arms around him and held him tightly as tears continued to stream down her face. His body continued to shake, and his breathing was still jagged. She stroked his back for a while until he pulled away and looked directly at her, the tears still glistening on his face.

"Did I hurt you?"

Confused, Bahn shook her head and responded, "What? No. You just had a bad nightmare, and you were having a hard time waking up."

Owen pinched his nose and fell against the pillow.

"It's okay. It was just a nightmare."

"It was a little more than a nightmare, Bahn." His hands rubbed his face.

"What do you mean?"

His eyes closed and he let out a sigh. "I have PTSD. I thought I was doing better. I hadn't had an episode like that, or a panic attack, in quite a while."

Bahn could hear the frustration in his voice. "What triggers them?"

"I have no idea. The panic attacks would hit at random times. The night terrors happened more often when I was recovering and then lessened with time." Owen flung the covers off and wandered to the restroom, shutting the door behind him.

Bahn heard the water running and waited for him to return. He was back within minutes and silently crawled back into bed with her.

"So how do they treat it?"

"Well, I have to take this lovely pill, which I just did, and I have to call my therapist and let her know. I was having weekly sessions until I took leave for Dad's funeral. They seemed to be helping. I just hate taking the pills."

"What are they for?"

"Anxiety."

Bahn paused, trying to decide if she should broach the next question. She figured there was no easy way to ask. "Why did you ask me if you hurt me?"

Owen's jaw clenched and he looked down at the covers. "Because you were crying. And sometimes, when the nightmares hit, some soldiers have been known to lash out at the people they're with."

"Oh," Bahn said softly.

Owen looked at Bahn with sadness in his eyes. "I'm so sorry, Bahn. I know I should have said something, but I still feel strange talking about it."

"Must have been all the excitement," Bahn joked, but even though she got a chuckle out of him, she could see the worry in his expression. "Owen, there is nothing to apologize for. You have been through hell. Do you think all the excitement and stress over the past few weeks got to be too much?"

Another loud clap of thunder hit, and they both jumped.

He tilted his head toward the window and said, "That doesn't help." Looking at her with remorseful eyes, he pulled her in close. "I'm sorry, though, that I woke you up."

"You didn't. It was the thunder. But it did scare me a little when you were having the nightmare."

"I bet."

"I couldn't wake you, and you were shaking so bad and moaning and you were obviously in distress… I kept yelling your name, but it was like you were in a trance."

"Well, just be glad it wasn't like my worst one." A smirk pulled at his lips, and he gave Bahn a side glance.

She picked up on his smile. "Why?"

Pinching his lips together, he confessed, "I kind of wet the bed."

Bahn burst out laughing. "I'm sorry, I know it isn't funny…but…"

Owen's mouth tipped up on one side, and he tucked his chin. "Nah, it's alright. I was still in the rehab facility when it happened and was pretty doped up. It wasn't funny when it happened, but now it kind of is." Owen looked at the clock and she followed his gaze. Three fifteen. "We better try to get a little more sleep."

"Yeah." Bahn snuggled down in Owen's arms again. Soon she could feel his breaths fall into a rhythm.

She tried desperately to get comfortable, but her body wouldn't settle down. Thoughts of the night raced through her brain. He stoked an undeniable fire in her, but she couldn't help but feel a little anxious about the new revelation. *Could he really hurt me?* She closed her eyes and sighed, trying to put it out of her mind.

CHAPTER 32

Slowly raising up on her elbow, she blinked several times to focus her eyes and checked the clock. Five fifteen. Her inclination was to snuggle back down in the covers, but she knew she would never be able to go back to sleep.

The rain continued to patter on the roof, and she waited for the next clap of thunder. A streak of lightning lit the room, and on cue, the thunder rumbled.

In the flicker of the flames from the fireplace, she could see Owen's profile. He was sleeping peacefully. Taking in the outline of his body under the covers, she watched as the muscles in his back expanded with each breath.

Butterflies filled her stomach thinking about their night together. It was incredible, but there was a lot to think about. She softly kissed his neck and shoulder. His body stirred. Her lips again glanced across his shoulder and down his back as her fingers lightly outlined the muscles on his chest.

He slowly rolled over, pulling her in close and kissing the top of her head. "I like your way of waking me up better than the alarm clock. Did you sleep okay?"

No. Not exactly. "Eh, sleep is overrated. Are you ready to get up and get moving?"

"Yeah, I guess we better."

Bahn leaned over and gave Owen a kiss before she hopped up, grabbed her clothes, and ran to the bathroom.

When she came out, Owen was standing outside the door with coffee. "Are you ready to go?"

"Yeah, I guess, if we have to."

As they made their way through the inn, they grabbed bagels and slathered some cream cheese on them before heading out. The lady who checked Owen in was at the front desk and waved sweetly.

The door creaked when Owen opened it, and as they stood on the porch, Bahn noticed the rain had lightened up but was still a gentle shower. Owen grabbed Bahn's hand, and they jogged to the car, quickly getting in and shutting the doors.

The streets were dark, the bustling little town not yet coming alive. It seemed a bit desolate.

"The town seems to be asleep." Owen echoed her thoughts, sounding a bit sleepy himself as he spoke.

"It's still too early."

"I didn't get to look around much yesterday. What kind of stores and shops do they have other than the ones on Main?"

"There isn't a whole lot to Cabin Creek. If you want to go shopping or do anything of substance, you have to go to Eugene," she said as they pulled up to her apartment.

Though the rain had nearly stopped, the air remained heavy. The sky had gone from black to dark blue with the parting of the clouds and the sunrise breaking through.

Bahn's keys jingled as she unlocked the door. "I hope I don't wake up Sarah." She was happily surprised to see lights on inside already. "Make yourself comfortable. I'll make some coffee."

She watched as Owen smiled, taking in the different design elements Bahn had strategically placed around the room. He leaned into a self-portrait she'd done of her sitting in an overstuffed chair staring out at the ocean with her feet propped up. She liked it enough to actually hang it, and to have Owen staring at it with an appreciative smile on his face made her proud. With the coffee brewing, she ducked around the corner to her room.

Owen said something but she couldn't quite understand him, so she returned to the kitchen. "I what?" she asked as she grabbed a couple of mugs from the cabinet and poured them some coffee then handed one off to Owen.

"You really are talented with your art and decorating."

"Thank you. I could play in the shops all day long."

They walked back into Bahn's room, and Owen sat down on her bed as she continued to get ready. "Then why didn't you choose it for your career?"

Bahn stopped and thought. "Honestly? I don't know." She began digging through her drawer and pulling items out. "All my life I've tried to fit into a mold of what my parents wanted me to be. I was their miracle baby. They'd tried several times to get pregnant and had lost a couple early on. Then I came along. I think they had my life planned out before I was a year old."

She continued to move about the room getting ready as she thought back to her childhood. "I love them both, and it's not so much them as it is me. I wanted to be the perfect child. They both were into sports, so I thought I needed to be into sports. I did soccer and T-ball and finally basketball," she bemoaned.

"But I thought you loved basketball."

"I do," she said half-heartedly.

Owen smirked and she knew her words weren't convincing.

"That's the thing. I do love basketball, but I feel like I spent my life falling in love with stuff others wanted me to fall in love with. When I was younger, I did what made my parents happy. When I got into college, I did what all my friends wanted me to do. It seemed like the only one who didn't know what would make me happy, was me."

"So, if you had it to do over…"

Bahn turned and looked at Owen. Crossing her arms, she took a deep breath. "I think I would have liked to have at least tried my hand at design."

"Well, why don't you do it?"

"Because I went to college to be a teacher and coach. All that money would be wasted. Plus, that entails starting my own business, and that takes money. Money I don't have."

"Start it on the side."

Bahn could see a spark of excitement in Owen's eyes, and she wanted to believe it could happen, but there were so many obstacles. "Teaching takes up all of my time."

"Stop making excuses, Bahn. I've never known you to let anything stand in your way if you wanted it bad enough. Start doing things for you."

She left the room and Owen followed. Retrieving a large thermos from the dishwasher, she rinsed it out and started pouring coffee in it. "I did. I flew across the country to see you."

Owen chuckled. "Well, that was a good start."

From the corner of her eye, she glanced at him and smirked, but then thought about what Owen said about making excuses.

As she retrieved items from the pantry, Sarah appeared from around the corner. "Oh. Hi," Sarah said awkwardly, looking surprised at the early morning guest.

"Hey, Sarah. This is Owen." Bahn nonchalantly nodded at Owen while she searched the freezer.

"Owen? As in *the* Owen from Mississippi?"

Bahn smiled at Sarah. "Yes. *The* Owen. It's a long story, and I promise to tell you all about it later, but before you go running off at the mouth, we got everything worked out."

Sarah turned to Owen. "Not sure I know what got worked out, but... I guess it's safe to shake your hand. I'm happy to finally meet you."

Owen held his hand out to Sarah. "You too. Bahn has told me a lot about you." Sarah gave Bahn a raised brow, and Owen jumped in. "It's all good."

"Okay. Wow," Bahn said, her head still in the freezer. "Where did you guys go last night? And remind me to thank Jean for the leftovers. Is that beef and broccoli?" She held up a container, unsure of its contents.

"Yeah. We went to the new Chinese food restaurant. It was amazing. And as you can see, they want to make sure you don't leave hungry. She took the orange chicken. It was good too."

"What would we do without leftovers?"

"You guys have quite a system there," Owen remarked as he watched Bahn load up thermoses and containers for their lunch.

"Teacher budget." Bahn let out an exasperated sigh. "Another reason."

"Hey, I'm telling you, start it as a side gig. You don't need anything except maybe business cards and some photos of this place. You could start posting on social media and see where it goes."

Bahn rolled her eyes at him.

"What business are you starting?" Sarah chimed in.

"I told Bahn she should go into business decorating homes. This place looks amazing."

Sarah's eyes cut to Bahn. "See? Now do you believe me?" She turned to Owen. "I've been telling her the same thing since we were in college."

Bahn stared at them. "And I told you both, I don't have the time nor the money."

Owen walked into the living room, sat down on the sofa and began to look around the room again, then a smile spread across his face. "I can be your first customer."

"What?" Bahn heard every word but was confused.

"I completely forgot to tell you. I got the house! The lady called from the real estate office while I was at the winery. She said if everything goes well, I can move in at the end of June. I'm going to need your expertise to decorate it."

"You may be limited with what the landlord will let you do."

"That won't be a problem since I'm the landlord."

"Wait. You bought the house?"

"Yep. I started calculating what it would cost for rent as opposed to a mortgage, and I'm actually going to be paying quite a bit less a month."

"Have you saved enough for a down payment?"

"Dad left us each some money that I'm using."

"Lucky. And I would love to help you decorate, but I used up all of my money with the last trip."

"I'll fly you in."

"I can't. I have the coaches' conference at the end of June."

"What about the first of July?"

"Teachers' conference first week of July."

A look of frustration grew across Owen's face.

Sarah looked at Owen. "How far is Mobile from Biloxi?" she questioned.

"Not that far, maybe an hour."

"Perfect." She turned to Bahn. "We get out of the coaches' conference on Wednesday at noon. Why don't you drive over? That would at least give you Thursday, Friday, and Saturday before you had to be back. Our flight doesn't leave until Sunday at two."

Owen gave Bahn a pleading look. "Please? I will take any help I can get. I can come get you."

Not wanting to argue the point anymore, and secretly glad Sarah suggested it, she relented. "Fine. I'll come help you decorate."

She tried to act like she just gave in to them ganging up on her, but a smile skirted across her face. Owen noticed and winked. The thought of having free rein on a project was a dream she'd had for a long time. Although she got to decorate their apartment, it still had some of Sarah's touches.

Sarah gave him a high five. "I'm reserving my opinion about you until I talk to Bahn later, but that was a good move."

"Why, thank you. It was an act of desperation, honestly. I have no furniture and zero decorating skills. If it were up to me, I'd probably have a card table, folding chairs, and a blow-up bed in the house."

Bahn looked between them both and smiled. Her two best friends. "I need to finish getting ready. You good here?" she asked Owen.

"I'm fine."

CHAPTER 33

◆

A s Bahn disappeared into her room, Sarah walked over to a dark wood bookcase, pulled out a book, handed it to Owen, then left without saying a word.

The small, shimmery, blue book had a square, silver frame on the front outlining the words 'Treasured Adventures' written in white. He began to flip through the pages filled with his and Bahn's photos through the years they had together. Photos of the treehouse and their junking outings spilled onto the pages along with those from the beach. The last photo in the book was the one they shared together, eating ice cream. Owen sat silently reliving the memories. In a strange way it made him happy yet unsettled.

Bahn wandered into the kitchen, grabbing up items quickly. "I'm late. I need to be at school in fifteen minutes for my meeting." She headed to the door with her arms loaded.

Owen jumped up from the sofa and grabbed some things from Bahn and followed her out the door.

"I'll get some breakfast, check out of my room, and come by around ten to help, if that's okay."

"Sounds great."

He set everything in his arms in Bahn's backseat, then shut the door and watched as Bahn slid behind the wheel. After giving her a quick kiss goodbye, he watched her back out of the parking space and drive away. He was surprised at the ache in his chest that simple interaction caused.

As he was walking to his car, he saw Sarah leaving the house with her arms full, so he ran to help. Taking several items from her, he walked with her to her car.

"It was really nice meeting you," Owen offered.

"You too. After what she said yesterday morning, I was wondering if I'd ever get to meet you."

"We kind of had a misunderstanding."

"I kind of gathered that." As she opened her car door she said, "You know, she's talked about you since we were in college together. Filled me in on all the crazy things you guys did… Sorry to hear about your dad, by the way.

"Thanks."

"Bahn told me a little about him. Sounds like he was a really good man."

"He was."

"You want to fill me in on this misunderstanding?"

"Long story short, I showed up one night during spring break when you guys were partying on the beach. I witnessed the kiss you had, made an assumption I shouldn't have, then proceeded—"

"Ah. Got it. You assumed she played for the other team and told her so."

"Yeah," he said with a sigh. "She'd told me a little bit about you, how you met in college and that you guys lived together now, so seeing you guys together at the party, then her telling me you guys were living together, I just… Well, let's just say I've learned to ask more questions before making assumptions."

"Good idea. But it shows how much she means to you if you flew all the way here to straighten things out. Kind of crazy…and expensive…but I like that you care about my friend so much that you'd do that. And I'm glad you guys worked it out. You're very special to her."

Owen nodded. "She's very special to me too." He handed her the items as she loaded the car, then she started walking back to the condo.

"Would you mind if I took that photo album with me?"

"No. Go ahead and grab it."

Owen ran inside as Sarah waited to lock the door. "Don't let Bahn know I have it."

As Owen gathered his belongings, he looked around the room, thinking about how things had changed in the past twenty-four hours. His T-shirt, that Bahn wore, lay crumpled on the bathroom floor, and it made him smile. He picked it up, inhaled her scent, then added it to the pile in his duffle and walked through the living room.

The half-eaten container of cupcakes still sat on the coffee table, the wine bottle on the counter. The bag the wine came in sat next to it. He picked it up to throw it away, but realized something was still inside. The treasure box from the winery. He'd meant to give it to Bahn the night before.

An idea formed along with a mischievous smile, and he stuffed the wooden box into his luggage.

Once he'd walked through the room one more time, he picked up the soft gray hoodie he'd left out and stepped into the hallway. With one last look, he smiled and closed the door.

Throwing the hoodie on, he headed downstairs to eat breakfast and check out. Traveling back up the main road, he noticed that the town was now full of life. The clouds had finally given way to traces of sunlight.

His mind drifted to the thought of leaving Bahn behind. Where do they go from here? So much had happened, and his feelings were all over the map. It wasn't just because of their intimate night, there was something more there. He knew now, Bahn had felt it too. But could it all be just stemming from the childhood memories and the bond they'd formed so long ago? So many questions fought to take over his mind.

He pulled into the school parking lot and headed in, retracing the path he'd taken the previous day. He found her class easily but realized as he approached that her door was closed. Bahn's voice, along with that of someone else, reached his ears, and after a few minutes, an older woman opened the door.

Her body jerked, not realizing he was there, and she let out a yelp as she stepped out of the room and hurried away.

Bahn was sitting at her desk with an annoyed look on her face.

Knocking softly on her door, he stepped inside, and she looked up.

"Hey." Her expression immediately brightened as she stood and quickly closed the distance between them. The way she carried herself told him she was needing some comfort, so he wrapped his arms around her. That was a good start. Her hands reached inside his unzipped hoodie and squeezed, sending tingles up his spine.

Kissing her forehead, he backed up. "I got here a few minutes ago, but you were still in the meeting. How did it go?"

The deep crease of irritation returned between her brows. "Not good. The board voted to reduce the athletic budget," she said sarcastically. "Which means reducing my pay...again. I keep myself on a pretty tight budget, so I'm still okay, but if anything were to happen, car breaks down, medical bills, or something catastrophic, I'm screwed. I have nothing to save now."

"Damn."

"This is the second year they've done that to me... and to Sarah too. It just makes me feel unappreciated. I mean, I get it. The athletic department is partially funded by ticket sales, and if you don't have the ticket sales, you don't have the money coming in. Unfortunately, some of our teams haven't done so well the past few years, which affects us all. But this cut has now dropped us below the salary Sarah and I were hired at."

"Seriously?"

"Yeah. And you would think, because I've had winning seasons since I was hired, my salary would go up. No, we haven't won the championship yet, but our record has improved by a large percentage. However, since it hasn't brought in the ticket sales to compensate for the losses, my hard work means nothing."

Bahn's frustration fueled the anger within him. "So, even though you're a great coach, it means nothing? That's so unfair."

"Yeah. But it's the job I chose, so..."

"Have you thought about looking for a different job?"

"Oh yeah. But then I think about the girls and their excitement when they win, and I feel like I'd be bailing on them."

"I get it. But Bahn, remember our conversation earlier about doing things that make everyone else happy? At some point you have to choose—"

"I know. I know."

Owen took a deep breath trying to tamp down his frustration. It wasn't Bahn's fault. She was doing her job. Doing it well, even. But she was sacrificing her own comfort for it. Everything about it was wrong, but there was nothing he could do to change it, and continuing to rehash it would only make her more upset.

He looked around, choosing to move on. "Well, is there anything I can help you with while I'm here? I won't be able to hang out long, but I'll help with whatever while I can."

She sighed, and Owen could see the frustration written all over her beautiful face. "Yeah, that would be great. I have two heavy book boxes that need to go down to the storage room. Do you mind? I can get the custodian to bring me a dolly to move them if not."

"I don't mind a bit, but you're going to have to show me where the storage room is." He walked over to pick up the first box. "Damn girl. You weren't lying when you said heavy."

Bahn snickered and he shot her a playful glare as he hoisted them up and she led the way. They meandered through the halls in silence and dumped both boxes off. Owen couldn't help but feel some animosity now as he scrutinized the building after what Bahn shared.

Heading back to her room, he checked the time and sighed as he quickly calculated the very last minute he'd be able to stay before having to leave for the airport. "Do you want me to go pick up something for lunch?"

"No, I brought mine from home."

"Oh, right. Well, that will give me a little more time to hang out." They entered the classroom, and Owen began to look around. "What other heavy items do you need my help with?" he said flexing his muscles.

Bahn snickered. "I got nothing. All I have left to do is a little cleaning, then I'm going home."

"I wish my flight was later." He leaned up against her desk and rubbed the back of his neck. "I really don't want to leave."

Tugging Bahn into him, he brought his arms around her and laced his fingers together at the small of her back. She really did fit perfectly in his arms.

"I don't want you to leave either, but I'm glad you wouldn't take no for an answer and decided to come." Owen scooted back to sit on the desk feeling the sting of what leaving meant. "What are you thinking?"

"About us. Just trying to figure out what to do." He could see in Bahn's expression she knew what he was talking about. "I'll be damned if I'm going to lose you again. But this is kind of an expensive trek across the country."

"I know. It's been on my mind too, especially with the latest information I received." She slid her hands down his arms. "But I'm coming down in a few weeks for the conference. I'll get you all that information. Let's just focus on that for right now."

"Yeah. Text me where you're staying, and when you're done with the conference, and then we can start treasure hunting." Just the thought of the new adventure had him fighting the grin spreading across his face.

"You're going to have to send me photos of your new place so I can get an idea of what to do."

"No. It has to be a surprise. You'll see it when you get into town."

Bahn rolled her eyes. "You and your surprises. Okay, fine. Can you at least send me a floor plan, and maybe some photos of stuff you like?"

"I like your place." Her fingers threaded through his hair, and he closed his eyes letting the sensation calm his anxious spirit.

"Oh geez, Okay. *I* will send you photos of stuff *I* like, and you can tell me if you like it or not. I'll start looking into shops around your area."

"Just remember I'm on a fairly tight budget."

"Oh, don't worry, I'm the queen of budgets. I told you, I don't shop new usually. What big items do you need?"

His eyes opened. "Everything. I'm in a furnished apartment on base right now."

Owen noticed Bahn's somewhat solemn expression fade.

"Okay. I'm really getting excited now. This is going to be fun."

Pulling out his phone, he asked, "What day is that Wednesday?"

"I think it's the twenty-fifth, maybe?"

"And you get out at noon, Sarah said?"

"Yeah. We have a working lunch then we're free to go. And the conference is in the hotel where we're staying, so we can leave from there."

He typed all the information in. "What hotel is it?"

"I'm not sure. I'll text that information to you later."

"Oh, right." As he clicked out of the screen, he saw the time. "I better get going. I don't know what the traffic is going to be like, and I forgot I still have to turn in the rental." His hands patted her butt as she stepped back.

He stood up from the desk and dropped a gentle kiss on her lips. Grabbing her hand, they strolled out of the school without saying a word. As he approached the car, he searched his pocket for his keys.

"Owen?"

He looked at her. The sun was again reflecting perfectly in her beautiful sea-green eyes. He would never get tired of staring into them. "Yeah?"

"I'm really going to miss you."

At that moment, that twelve-year-old girl's voice rang in his head. His mind replayed the memory, and he felt that horrible ache in his heart. His throat threatened to close up and he swallowed back the pain. *No. I'm not letting her go this time.*

He took a step forward and wrapped his arms around her. "I'm going to miss you, too." His voice broke and he had to finish with a whisper, but he didn't care. He pulled her chin up and leaned in. As their lips met, he kissed her with everything he couldn't put into words and hoped she felt it.

Backing away, he ran his thumb across her lip and let his forehead rest against hers for a moment, hoping beyond hope he could figure something out. The last thing he wanted to do was leave her. But he was determined to find a way for them to be together.

With one last peck on the cheek, he stepped back. "I'll see you in a few weeks."

She swallowed hard and blinked away tears.

"We'll figure it out. Let's just take it one day at a time for now." She nodded.

He opened the car door and climbed in, keeping his gaze squarely on her until he pulled away. He'd figure something out. He had to.

CHAPTER 34

◆

Though people filled the lines and corridors of the airport, they might as well have been ghosts to him. Visions of the past few days played in his head. *How could so much change in such a short time.* He sat his bag down and pulled out his phone.

Owen: **I made it to the airport.**

Within minutes, his phone buzzed. He clicked to find a photo of a bucket of suds, a spray bottle of disinfectant, and a soapy sponge with the caption,

Bahn: **Wish I was at the beach.**

He chuckled but also felt a twinge of pain, remembering the conversation they had.

Owen: **One month.**

Fumbling with his bag, he went to pull out his laptop but found the photo album instead. Carefully opening it, he began to look through the photos. Memories flashed through his mind as he turned the pages filled with photos that captured their childhood.

His memory dissolved into thoughts of the past few days, the time he spent with her. No one made him feel the swirl of emotions that she did; the excitement and contentment all at once. He continued to stare at the photos, and as he got to the last one with the ice cream, he noticed how close he was to her. His arm was wrapped around her. He knew even then.

Owen: **Hey, can you send me the photos you took this week?**
Bahn: **Sure.**
Owen: **Send them to ocramer@foxmail.com.**
Bahn: **Okay. What are you going to do with them?**
Owen: **Just a little project.**
Bahn: **Let me guess. It's a surprise.**
Owen: **You're catching on.**

"Flight thirty-three twenty-four to Seattle will be boarding momentarily," he heard over the intercom.

Owen: **We're boarding, so I'll let you know when I get home.**
Bahn: **Okay. Be safe.**

He closed the photo album and zipped up his bag. Within moments, the intercom announced the boarding process. His heart sank as he walked forward and boarded the plane. He didn't want to leave, but was anxious to get back home and get settled in.

Sunlight drifted through the small window on the airplane as Owen sat down. A feeling of déjà vu hit him, and suddenly he remembered his dad's project. It would keep him occupied on the flight home. He wanted to crack the code and figure it out. This flight was going to be short, so there was no use trying to get any work done until the second leg. And with the early morning already catching up to him, he leaned up against the window, adjusted the hoodie, and closed his eyes.

It seemed like only minutes when the familiar ding went off, and the captain came over the intercom announcing their final descent.

As Owen stepped off the plane into the airport, he reached in his pocket and flipped on his phone, hoping he had a message. There it was. His heart skipped and he stifled a smile.

Bahn: **I miss you.**

He walked quickly to his next gate and clicked on the message as he sat down. A photo of a calendar counting down the days popped up.

Owen: **What have I done to you? Where is the snarky Bahn I had breakfast with last week?**

Bahn: **Still cleaning her damn classroom and wishing she was having breakfast with you again.**

Owen: **One month.**

His mind suddenly drifted to the things he had to get done in that time period and the reality of how busy he was going to be hit him hard. At least it would make the time go quicker. Checking off the different tasks in his brain, he decided it would be best to get everything written down before he forgot.

He brought up his notes on his phone and began jotting down the things he needed to accomplish in the coming weeks. There was just so much of it. "Crap. What if the house thing falls through?" His eyes lifted from his phone. "God, please let everything go smoothly," he said under his breath.

"It will," came a small voice next to him.

He turned to see a frail older lady with white hair and kind eyes. Gazing at her face, etched with years of wisdom, something settled in his soul. He believed her.

"Where are you headed?"

"Biloxi. You?"

"Dallas. I'm going to my great grandson's birthday."

"Well. I'm sure he'll be excited to see you. How old is he?"

"He's turning three. He's my youngest. I have eight ranging from twenty-two down to three." Her face brightened. "And I'm waiting on number nine."

"Wow!"

"And they are all the brightest, kindest, and most handsome and beautiful children you'll ever meet." As she spoke her eyes twinkled.

Owen knew she meant every word, and he couldn't help but smile.

"How about you? Do you have any children?"

"No, not yet." His thoughts drifted to his niece and nephew, and he wondered if he'd ever have a child of his own. "One day, maybe."

"Oh, I'm sure you will." She again sounded like she was stating a fact of what was to come in Owen's life.

"I gotta get married first." The vision of Bahn wrapped up in his sheets flashed in his mind, and another smile formed on his face.

"I know that smile. Your day is coming sooner than later."

Owen's eyes popped open. Was she psychic? What did this lady know? He suddenly felt a warm rush of blood to his face. "I think I'm going to get me a snack. Would you like something?"

"A bottle of water would be nice."

"Sure. I'll be right back."

He hoisted his bag on his shoulder and wandered up the

concourse. A deli not far from his gate was exactly what he was looking for. He bought a sandwich and a couple of bottles of water, then returned to his gate. After unscrewing the lid, he handed off the water to the lady, then dropped his bag on the ground and sat down in his seat. "My name is Owen, by the way."

"Nice to meet you, Owen." She held out her boney hand and Owen gently shook it. "I'm Bernice. You're military?"

Owen stared at her in amazement. He seriously was beginning to wonder about the woman being psychic, then realized she had seen his duffle. "Yes ma'am, for another few weeks, then I'm done."

"My husband was too." She looked away but patted his hand. "Thank you for protecting us."

He didn't quite know what to say, so he just nodded.

"Alright ladies and gentlemen, flight twenty-six forty-three, heading to Dallas, will be boarding in just a few minutes…..," the voice announced over the intercom.

"Well, it looks like we're on our way," Bernice said sweetly.

Owen stood and held his arm out in case she needed help.

She graciously took it. "Thank you. It was very nice talking to you, Owen."

"You too, Bernice. Have fun at the birthday party."

"I will. You can't help but have fun with little ones that age."

"Oh, I'm sure you're right about that."

She tipped her head to Owen as he helped her find her spot in line. "You will learn that very soon, young man. I think everything is going to work out just fine." Her comment sent goosebumps all over Owen's skin. His brows shot up and she winked at him, then finished their encounter with, "Have a safe trip."

Swallowing hard, he responded hoarsely, "You too."

He watched as Bernice walked up to the attendant and held her ticket out, then disappeared down the jetway while he stood and waited for his group to be called. His mind drifted to their conversation, and he chuckled. Minutes later when he boarded, he glanced down to see his new friend. Their eyes connected and they smiled at each other.

As he searched for a seat, he replayed their conversation, continuing to wonder if she could somehow see the future. Things did seem to be heading in the right direction for once.

He stowed his bag and sat back, waiting for the plane to ascend into the clouds. The ground quickly disappeared, and within minutes he heard the familiar ding. He pulled out his computer and stuffed his bag back under the seat, opened his father's project and got to work. He had to figure out the puzzle.

As he stared at the pages of code, detailed instructions, and the intricate designs, the hours ticked by, and he became more and more frustrated. Everything was running together, and he closed his tired eyes and leaned his head back trying to understand the data that he'd almost memorized by now. That's when it hit him.

He looked back down at one of the equations buried deep in the program. He'd thought it looked off earlier, and he was right. His dad hadn't finished it. It was almost like his dad was right there with him and they were figuring it out together.

With renewed optimism, he started to dig in again just as the flight attendant announced that they would be landing in Dallas momentarily and he had to stow his computer.

He knew he was going to have to race to make the connecting flight to Gulfport, so he grabbed up his bag as the plane touched down on the tarmac, and as soon as he exited the plane, he ran down the jetway to the concourse where the information board displayed the flights with their corresponding gates. His gut bottomed out when he realized he was at terminal D and his gate was at terminal A.

Running down the stairs, he raced up the breezeway to the train station, catching one just about to leave. The minute he stepped on, the doors closed, and the train lurched as it took off. One stop turned into four, then six, and Owen glanced at his watch for the second time. He had ten minutes before the flight was supposed to take off. "Gate B fifteen through twenty," the train's intercom boomed, and they stopped... again.

"Dammit, I'm not going to make it."

The train pulled out and flew up the tracks. "Gate A one through six," came the announcement. As soon as the door opened, he jumped out and ran up the stairs to the concourse, finally finding his gate only to see no one in the area except the desk attendant.

"Owen Cramer," he yelled as he approached the desk. She pointed to an attendant by the gate who motioned him over. He scanned Owen's ticket and opened the door. He made it. Barely.

Once they were in the air again, he dug under the seat and

retrieved the computer along with the papers. His pulse ticked up as he scrutinized the material, going back and forth between what was written on the paper and what was on the screen. Little by little, things began to line up. As he tapped away on the computer, he began to calculate measurements on the designs, add in coding to the programs, and adjust the intricate equations. "Yeah, Dad, I get what you're doing." A chuckle escaped, garnering a glance from his new seatmate.

With each keystroke, it became more evident what needed to be changed and added, and also what an enormous asset to military security it would be once it was implemented. If he took it to them when he got back to the base in Florida, it would mean they would have full rights to it since he was still part of the military. But if he waited, patented it and presented it as a civilian… he chuckled under his breath, and this time his buddy in the next seat chuckled too.

Finding a stopping place, he shut his computer, slid it back into his bag, and returned it under the seat, then sat back and sighed, knowing exactly what he should do.

It was late by the time he was headed home, but with the time difference he was hoping Bahn would be up. All the lights were off in the house as he walked in, so he tried to be quiet.

Owen: **Made it home.**

He went to his bedroom and kicked his shoes off, preparing to catch up on his sleep. Pulling back the covers, he crawled in but couldn't seem to get comfortable. He missed having Bahn snuggled against him.

Owen: **My bed doesn't feel as comfy as the one at the Inn.**
Bahn: **Check your inbox.**

He opened his email and clicked. The page flooded with photos. Glancing through them, he realized she'd taken many more photos than what he'd thought. There were some at breakfast then on the beach looking for seashells. There was one in her sunglasses and then one when they were trying to find the treasure. He noticed a funny one she'd taken over her shoulder at the beach—him in the background wading into the water with a scowl on his face, and her giggling in the foreground. It made him laugh. The last one was them with their cupcakes.

Owen: **These are amazing. Thanks.**
Bahn: **I didn't realize I took so many.**

Owen: **Neither did I. I think you took a few without me knowing.**

Bahn: **Maybe just a few. So, what did you say you needed them for?**

Owen: **I didn't. I said it was a surprise.**

Bahn: **Dang it.**

Owen: **What are you doing tomorrow?**

Bahn: **Getting ready for basketball camp.**

Owen: **I've got to go with mom to the banks and a few other places to get paperwork transferred, so it may be later before I can call you, but I will.**

Bahn: **Okay.**

Owen: **I better get some sleep. I will talk to you soon.**

He set his phone on the table, pulled the covers up, and flipped the light off. Somehow, simply texting with her had relaxed him, and it wasn't long before sleep engulfed him.

CHAPTER 35

The next couple of days were spent just as he'd expected, helping his mom finish his dad's estate business. She wasn't ready to do anything about his personal items, so once the business side was handled, Owen was free to work on the next project.

He enjoyed the time he spent with his mom getting everything settled. She was eager to hear about his trip and smiled as he told her how things were going with Bahn. He shared briefly about finding a place to live and remembered to send Bahn the floorplan that he'd quickly drawn on his computer. Many of the houses in that neighborhood had similar floorplans, so he hoped she wouldn't catch on to exactly which house it was. It didn't take long for her to begin sending him ideas for furniture.

Late Friday afternoon, he ventured out to Keesler Air Force Base and met with Colonel Blaisdale and several others he would be working with. They spoke highly of his dad and offered their condolences. His new boss was an older gentleman who knew his dad well and seemed eager to bring Owen on board. They discussed the job and when he would be able to start, deciding after he completed his required military service, he would do some training in the position and start after he'd finished moving.

He was given a short tour before filling out the necessary

paperwork. After his visit, he had some time, so he decided to stop by the lawyer's office. He showed him the information he had on the project and asked what needed to be done to get a patent for it. Mr. Sherman walked him through the process and explained what he'd done with the previous patents of his dad's.

Owen left with his head swimming from the information, and even more on his plate. As Saturday arrived, it was time for him to load up and head back to Patrick Air Force Base to finish out his time there.

His mom gave him a big hug, and he set out on his drive back. When he arrived at his apartment, he looked around, trying to gauge how long it would take him to pack and load all his stuff, and realized just how much he didn't have. Most of the furniture came with the apartment. Other than some linens, kitchen items, an old desktop computer, and his small TV, there was nothing else. Bahn had her work cut out for her.

Work was a formality. He did what was required, but his head wasn't in it. His thoughts were a thousand miles away, in a small town in Oregon, wondering where he stood with the girl who had wrapped herself around his heart.

They talked and texted daily, and sometimes even video chatted. Their conversations always flowed easily, and their banter and jabs made him laugh. As the days went by, he became more confident of his feelings and more anxious about hers.

His mind drifted back to the airport, sitting at the gate and looking through the photo album of them as kids. He saw the photo of the two of them with their ice cream, how happy they seemed, and then remembered the day she left, and the sadness in her eyes. Could they really have been meant for each other back then, and life had finally been set right when she showed up in the treehouse?

Regardless of his feelings, there were glaring obstacles they would have to overcome for them to have a chance. The distance between them was the big one, but also his PTSD. The old negative voices ticked off reason after reason they were destined to fail, and the pit of his stomach churned.

He visited with his therapist, and she gave him some suggestions on combating the nightmares. She also set him up with someone new in Biloxi, but would that be enough?

Mid-June finally arrived, and Owen finalized his paperwork for his transfer. Once again, his life had taken a turn, and as he walked out of the office, he wondered what the future held. With one last look around, he hopped in his truck, already loaded with his belongings, and started the drive back. An hour into his trip his phone chimed.

"Mr. Cramer?" He again wondered if they were calling for his dad.

"This is Owen."

"Yes, this is Wendy from First Title. Do you have a minute?"

Owen's stomach clenched. All his plans hinged on him getting into the house. He had no plan B—well, except staying with his mom, and he'd rather that not happen.

"Yes Ma'am."

"We have completed the inspection on the house on Magnolia."

"Okay?"

"Well..." Her hesitation had him letting out a defeated sigh. He steeled himself, preparing for the bomb she was going to drop. "It's very rare that this happens..."

His jaw clenched, and if he could close his eyes he would. It would be great if she would just spit it out.

"It usually takes a good six weeks to close on a house, but it looks like you're ready to go. The inspection didn't reveal any major issues, and we have everything we need except your salary agreement. If you can get that to us, I would like to set up a time for closing."

He had to play back her words in his head, just to make sure he heard her correctly. "Seriously? I'm on my way back to Biloxi now. I should be there later this evening, and I can email you the salary agreement then. Can we set it up for Thursday or Friday?"

"Let me check the calendar."

Owen threaded his fingers through his hair, trying to settle his heart rate as he waited.

"Can you come in at ten o'clock Friday?"

"Yeah. Yeah, that works for me."

"Okay. I've got you down. I'll send you an e-mail with all the information you'll need and the address once we have the salary agreement."

"Thank you."

As he disconnected the phone, a huge grin spread across his face. "Hell yeah!" He banged his hands on the steering wheel. "I just bought a house!"

Ribbons of road were before him, but somehow, they seemed to pass quickly. He called Bahn to give her the good news.

"I got the house! It's official!"

"Yay!"

"I close on Friday."

"That's crazy! So, what are you going to do for furniture until I get there?"

"I'll make do. Probably get me a blow-up bed and a bean bag chair. I have a TV, so that's really all I need."

"At least buy a bed, please. You don't need me there to help you do that. You don't have to get a headboard or anything, just the mattress, box spring, and a frame. It's not hard."

"Okay. I'll take mom and she can help me."

"Geez, Owen. Do you need someone to hold your hand for everything?" Her playful jab held no heat.

"Hey!" he bit back. "I make a lot of my own decisions… just not ones on furniture."

"It's a bed, for crying out loud. Lay down on it. If your eyes get heavy, buy it."

He grinned at the phone. "Yes ma'am."

"Hey, I'm sorry, I gotta get back to basketball practice, but call me back this evening. Okay?"

"I will. I'll let you know when I get to Biloxi."

"I'm so excited for you."

"Me too."

Dusk had taken over the sky as he pulled into Biloxi. As the sun began to set, the clouds were lit with a beautiful backdrop of pinks and oranges and yellows. He knocked on the door at his mom's house, then let himself in. A wonderful smell attacked his senses and made his stomach growl. He realized he hadn't eaten since he left that morning.

His mom peeked around the corner from the kitchen. "Are you hungry? I was getting ready to put everything away."

"Yes. Please tell me it isn't a casserole."

"No. It's roast with potatoes and carrots."

"Great. Load me up." He dropped his bag in his room and kicked his shoes off before returning to the kitchen and draping his arm around his mom for a hug.

"Guess what?" he said, smiling from ear to ear.

She eyed him briefly before continuing to spoon gravy on his potatoes. "What?" A smile lifted the corner of her mouth.

"I am officially a homeowner."

Her eyes widened and she took a step back. "Homeowner?"

"I close on Friday." He put his hand on his chest trying to steady his breath.

"Seriously? Where is it?" She leaned in for another hug.

With everything that had happened, he'd completely forgotten to tell his mom he'd even submitted a bid on their old house. "It's the house on Magnolia."

Carissa's mouth dropped open with her gasp. "No." Owen nodded, still grinning. "Really? I mean, I knew you had found a place, but I thought you were going to rent..." Tears welled in her eyes as her hand pressed against her chest. "But... you're buying our old house? How?" She handed the plate of food to Owen.

"The money Dad left, and a VA loan. The house sat on the market for a while I guess, and I think it was about to go into foreclosure. The realtor said the owners were motivated to sell because they'd already moved away." He set his plate on the table and his mom sat while he returned to the kitchen to get some tea. "I made an offer—probably less than it was worth, but all I could afford—and submitted a letter saying it was my old house, and it had sentimental value. And the owner accepted it. The great thing is my payments are going to be less than the rent of any of the places Bahn and I found." He sat down and filled his fork. The flavors had him closing his eyes, savoring the bite.

"I can't believe it. You know I have so many great memories at that house." She paused, and then a smile emerged. "I have something I need to show you that I found while you were gone. I think it will be perfect for your new place."

"What is it?" he questioned, not even trying to hide his curiosity.

"I'm not saying." She paused again. "It's a surprise," she said, holding back a smile.

It was nice to see her smiling again. She'd always been strong, and even through his dad's death, she'd remained stoic. But he'd been there right after it happened. He'd heard her crying in her room. He knew how much they loved each other. It was obvious. And he hoped, one day, he'd find that kind of love.

The smile that had grown into a wide grin had Owen chuckling, and he realized where he'd gotten his love for surprises. Shoveling another forkful into his mouth, he was completely consumed with trying to figure out what his mom was hiding.

"Mom, can you at least give me a hint?"

"Nope. But I know you'll be very surprised."

Although the roast was quite tasty, Owen barely noticed. He was too curious. He finished the food at breakneck speed and practically threw his plate in the sink.

"Okay, now will you let me in on your little surprise?"

"Follow me." Carissa wandered outside to the shed in the backyard. She yanked open the rusty door and flipped on the light.

Inside, Owen saw his dad's lawn supplies, a few things to clean the car, and a couple of old bicycles.

"I came out here and started snooping around, kind of looking through some boxes and stuff, trying to figure out what I might need to get rid of." Carissa pushed past the bicycles and came to a shelf. She pulled something from the shadows and handed it to Owen.

"What is it?"

"Unroll it." She motioned with her hand.

As he unrolled it, his heart felt like it was going to completely stop. Outlines of shapes began to appear. It was the mural of the world he and Bahn had found all those years before.

"Oh my gosh, Mom!" His throat tightened and his eyes landed on her, just as she reached for something else.

She pulled out the two wooden folding chairs, then, leaning down, she lifted the old bulletin board and the two framed pictures. The table was flipped upside down on the top shelf, and the starfish bowl sat on the second shelf behind some old speakers. Owen couldn't stop smiling.

"Your dad was a pack rat. He kept everything," she said looking around. "We had to trash a few things—the bean bag chair got a hole, and we kept the mini fridge in the garage until it died a few years ago—but I had forgotten all about this stuff until I found it the other day."

Owen sat in a daze, staring at the treasure his mom had presented him. He couldn't wait to dig it all out and get it cleaned up. He already knew exactly what he wanted to do with it.

CHAPTER 36

No amount of research would have prepared him for the pile of paperwork he had to sign at the closing. His mom had offered to go with him, but he made the decision to handle it on his own. The droning of the middle-aged heavyset lady explaining the documents made his head hurt. All he knew was he felt like he was signing his life away with every "initial here" and "sign there."

But nothing made him feel more like he'd finally arrived as an adult than being handed the keys to *his* house. With keys in hand, he left the closing and immediately swung by his mom's house, picked her up, and let her watch him unlock the door. She was camera ready, and he didn't even have to paste on his usual fake smile. It was completely real, and it showed no signs of disappearing any time soon.

The door creaked as he pushed it open, and the musty smell hit them in the face. As they stepped inside, he began to point out the changes that had been made and some ideas he had. He headed into the kitchen and was greeted by a nice surprise. "Oh, cool. I didn't notice before, but they left the refrigerator." It wasn't the nicest he had seen, but if it worked, it was one less item he had to purchase.

Continuing to point out items, he stopped, suddenly realizing his mom wasn't responding. When he turned, he saw tears streaming down her face. She chuckled as she wiped them away, and he wrapped his arm around her and gave her a squeeze. She smiled as she wiped away more tears. "I have so many great memories here."

"Me too."

After they finished the tour, he drove them to a discount store to pick out a bed and was surprised when they could deliver it that evening.

Once they arrived back at his mom's house, he began loading his truck with the items his mom had found in the storage shed. Carissa insisted on returning with him to help him clean, and she followed him back in his old car to get it out of her driveway. She tackled the house while he tried to mow the foot high grass in the yard.

As the sun started to set, they sat on the floor in the living room, laughing and reminiscing about the great times they'd spent in the house, and he couldn't help but wonder what new memories would be made.

They had made a good dent in the cleaning, and the house smelled of lemon and bleach. The yard was mowed and edged, and it actually looked like it hadn't been abandoned anymore, which he was sure the neighbors appreciated.

The doorbell rang and startled them both. Two men stood at the door holding a box spring. "Come on in," Owen said, pushing the door open wide and directing them to the bedroom.

"Do you have any queen-size sheets?" Carissa asked, following Owen to the bedroom.

"Actually, no, I don't."

"When you take me back to the house, remind me to give you some. I have plenty."

"Perfect."

By the time he was headed back from his mom's house, it was late, and he was exhausted. His brain was tired from all the monotonous paperwork, and his body was tired from working at the house. All he wanted to do was go to bed. After getting the sheets on the bed, he sent Bahn a short text saying, "I'll call tomorrow"—and crashed.

Beams of light showered the bedroom, and Owen squeezed his eyes tighter. *I definitely need some curtains.* Giving up on the idea of trying to go back to sleep, his feet hit the floor, and he sat on the edge of the bed with his eyes partially opened. Scanning the barren space, he snickered. "This is mine."

And what the hell was I thinking? I am tapped out on money. How am I going to fill this place up?

Standing slowly, he stretched, then padded up the hall into the kitchen. He glanced at the empty countertops and frustration began to set in. There were some things he already missed about staying with his mom. One was having coffee when he woke up.

He retrieved his phone and started a list for the day. First thing on the list, go to Mom's for breakfast. Next, buy a coffee maker. His eyes scanned the area around him. A few boxes dotted the floor, and not much else. He let out a loud sigh, realizing just how big of a task was ahead of him…and Bahn. That's what he needed, the expert.

"Dear god, what time is it?" Her gravelly voice made him chuckle.

"It's seven thirty, you should be up."

He heard her moving around, but she stayed silent. Then, letting out a loud sigh, she groaned. "One, It's Saturday, the weekend. It's treated like vacation. I don't get up before nine. We've been over this. And two, you obviously forget I am not in your time zone, because the birds aren't even up yet."

"Oh shit. Sorry. Yeah, that fact kind of slipped my mind. I'll let you—"

"Oh no. You aren't getting off that easy. I'm awake now. You have to deal with the grumpy me now. What the hell is so important that you must call me in the dead of night?"

"Well, first, I wanted to tell you I'm sorry I didn't call last night. I was up late cleaning."

"Cleaning?"

He searched his photos and sent her one his mom took of him putting the key in the lock of the door. It didn't show much else, so he figured it wouldn't give his surprise away.

"Oh my gosh, Owen! You're in your house?"

"Spent my first night last night."

"Let me guess, in a sleeping bag on the floor."

He ran into his bedroom and snapped a photo of the unmade bed and sent it to her.

"Yay! Good job. I am so proud of you."

"But I literally have nothing else. I'm about to go to the store to at least get a coffee maker before you get here. Mom gave me some pots and pans and basics, but I started a list of things we're going to have to get while you're here. We're going to be busy, and I doubt we'll get everything done."

"Oh ye of little faith. You obviously haven't seen me shop."

"As a matter of fact, I haven't. Should I be scared?"

"What you went through in basic training has nothing on my marathon shopping."

Owen chuckled.

"You think I'm exaggerating. I'm not."

"Well, to spare me some of the pain, start shooting ideas at me for things I'll need. Maybe I can pick up a few of the mundane items that I won't need your help with."

"Take me for a tour first, so I can get an idea of what's needed."

"Nice try, but no. It's got to be a surprise."

"Fine!" He heard her take a noisy breath then there was more rustling. He imagined her in an oversized graphic T-shirt and soft cotton shorts, stretching as she tried to wake up. She yawned and said, "Let me wake up a little, and I'll go through my place and text you what I have."

"Sounds good," he said, pacing.

"Give me a bit."

He knew what that meant as he disconnected the call. She was going back to sleep. He didn't blame her. Five thirty was too early. He was surprised she was even coherent.

Shaking his head, he smiled and continued to look around the house and jot down things he might need. Even basic furniture seemed like it would be a substantial expense. As he wandered back through the living room, his eyes drifted out the front window and he caught sight of his old blue Honda sitting in the driveway.

"Bingo."

He called his mom to make sure she'd be able to help him. Sliding the keys in his pocket, he checked some addresses in his phone and set out on a quest to put some cash in the palm of his hand.

Two hours later, he'd shaken hands with a gentleman at a local dealership and walked away with a check for seven thousand dollars. He was hoping for a little more but felt like that was plenty to get some furniture in his house, especially with Bahn's decorating skills.

His mom picked him up and they stopped at a nearby restaurant for a late breakfast. As they were just finishing up and getting ready to leave, Owen's phone chimed.

"Do you have a desk?"

Owen smirked. "Yeah, there's actually a nice built-in next to the fridge. I just need a chair."

"Oh, great! How about a washer and dryer?"

Something else he'd neglected to add to the list, and they weren't cheap. Although, that didn't seem like an immediate need. He reasoned he could always take his laundry to his mom's when he went over to visit.

"No. But I do have a refrigerator, stove, and a dishwasher." Lowering himself into his mom's car, he whispered, "Coffee maker."

Nodding, she threw the car in drive, and they headed to the store.

"Okay, I'll research some of the appliance places. I'm going to email you the list of some places we can go. Hit me up with some colors you might like for the walls. This is getting fun."

Owen could picture Bahn sitting on her sofa, her hair pulled up on top of her head and her laptop propped on her legs. It made him smile.

He continued his conversation with her as he walked into the local electronics store. Bahn gave him the name of the coffee maker she had, stating it was lightning fast at making coffee. *That's exactly what he needed.* Once he'd found it, his mom insisted on buying a few other items before they left the store.

Back at the house after his mom dropped him off, he started removing the items from the bags and laying them out, trying to figure out where everything would go. It took him several minutes to decide which counter he should put the coffee maker on. *God, I am horrible at this.*

The next day, he took the new sheets and towels to his mom's to wash. *Yeah, this is going to get old quick.* Even though he didn't have much he needed to wash currently, he knew that wouldn't always be the case. He didn't like doing laundry, and the thought of having to lug it anywhere quickly lost any appeal. And although he knew his mom didn't care, and it would give him a reason to stop by, it just felt like an inconvenience.

He let out a breath at the thought of how much of the budget a washer and dryer would eat up. It wouldn't leave much for everything else. His excitement about buying the house was waning quickly.

Five fifteen came early Monday morning, and it made him feel all the more guilty for his early call to Bahn. With his new job starting soon, he figured it was time to get into a routine. He'd only known military time for the past several years, so this was going to be a new experience.

He threw on a pair of shorts and a T-shirt and headed out the door. Fog had settled in over the area and brought a thickness to the air. Standing on the porch, he stretched his legs and thought about which way he wanted to go. He felt like he should know the area, but it had been so long. He finally decided to stay close. It had been a while since he ran, so he didn't want to get too far away in case he needed to turn around.

Heading up the street past Bahn's old house, he noticed the house was still vacant. His mind immediately began to replay the memories. Why did she have such a hold on his life? Every time he talked to her, he felt like a different person. She made him feel like he could accomplish anything.

As the memories flashed through his mind, he let them take him away. Time passed quickly, and while he was stopped at a light, he found himself at his and Bahn's old stomping ground—the Ocean Shores apartments.

Curiosity got the best of him, and he ran around the side of the complex. Like the gates of heaven, he found the ones securing the dumpsters wide open. Even in the early morning darkness, he could see they were loaded down with possible treasures. He smiled, thinking Bahn would have a field day in there, and made a mental note to return with his truck later.

When he got home, he spied the items he and Bahn had confiscated on their first treasure run sitting in the corner. He chewed on his lip and decided Bahn was going to get more than one surprise when she came back to Biloxi.

CHAPTER 37

Setting her suitcase on the chair next to the bed, she stared at the items scattered in piles across her covers. Her stomach fluttered with the thought of the trip. She was so conflicted. Excited by the fact that she was going to see Owen again, and help him get his house set up, but worried she was just setting herself up for heartbreak.

She let out a breath and sat down on the bed, feeling overwhelmed. Picking up her notebook, she flipped through what she had written down. Everything from possible paint colors to approximate room dimensions to places to check out and things to buy filled the pages.

"You've been staring at that notebook for fifteen minutes. When are you going to start packing?"

She glanced at the piles of clothes on the bed. "I'm just not sure what to take."

"Uh huh. Looks like you have it figured out. It just hasn't made it into the suitcase."

She knew once she got started it wouldn't take her long to actually pack. Sarah was right. All she needed to do was move it to the suitcase. But in that moment, it seemed like a daunting task.

"And what about last night, when I asked about what time we should head to the airport, and you gave me some nonsense about ordering dinner?"

"I'm sorry. I just—"

"This doesn't have to do with a certain man with decorating issues, does it?"

She never could hide anything from Sarah. Turning to face her, she rubbed her forehead with both hands. "I don't know what to do."

"About what?"

"Him."

"Oh, I think you know exactly what to do about him."

"Sarah. He's across the freaking country. As much as I would love it, there is no way things can work out for us. He just started his life there, and I have my life here. I don't know why I agreed to help him. It's just going to make it harder when I have to leave."

"But in a perfect world, you would like something to work out with him, right?"

"I don't know what I want. I'm so overwhelmed. It's been so long. We barely know each other now. Yes, I loved spending time with him, but, honestly, I don't know what was going on between us—"

"Yes or no. Don't think, just answer."

"Yes. But it's not that easy."

"The best things in life usually aren't easy. You have to work for them. And I've never known you to shy away from a challenge."

"You both keep telling me that. But this is my heart I'm risking."

"Then I guess you have to decide whether he's worth the risk. And my impression is, he is."

"How do you know? You've barely spoken to him."

"And you know this...how?"

"Wait. Did you talk to him?"

"We may or may not have talked when you weren't around. But I don't have to know him to know what he does to you. I've never seen you so upset when you came home after that fight, or so happy when he flew out here to work things out with you."

"I'm just scared things will go wrong, and I'll lose the chance at even being friends. I just got him back."

"And what if it could work out perfectly but you were too damn scared to take the leap? You have no idea what might be in store."

"It could be a disaster."

"And if you continue with that attitude, it will be." Sarah shoved some clothes out of the way and sat on the bed. "Look, all I know is, he's very important to you. Even when you hadn't heard from him in years, you still talked about him. And when you reunited, I saw a whole different person than the one I got to know in college. It's kind of funny. You were so much softer and gentler when he was around. A little more vulnerable. I'm not used to seeing you like that, and that in itself says something."

"Yeah, and that's what scares the hell out of me. He's always been able to do that to me. I don't like being vulnerable."

"You need someone in your life you can be vulnerable with. Someone who makes you comfortable enough to let your guard down, so you can feel everything. Trust me, you won't know true happiness, true freedom to be yourself, until you find that person you can do that with. And I think you might have found him."

Bahn thought about when she first reunited with him in Biloxi. How easy it was to talk to him. Her mom didn't even know some of the stuff she shared with him. But it had always been that way between the two of them. She always tried to act tough and confident, and when she first got to Biloxi, she still had that mindset. But there was something about Owen that made it okay for her to let down her guard. Sarah was right. She never felt more herself than when she was with him. She was still scared though.

"Even so—"

"And look at the opportunity he's giving you. You get to do what you're passionate about, while exploring the possibilities of your relationship. Just try to go into it without any preconceived notions, holding nothing back, and see where it takes you."

"Are you trying to get rid of me?"

"No. I just think you're letting your fear of rejection dictate how you're going into this, and I think you should give him a chance."

"I would love to be able to do that, but I have a life here. I've spent years establishing my career, and I love coaching my girls."

"I know you do, and you're damn good at your job. But be honest, are you as excited to go back in a few weeks as you were when Owen asked you to decorate his house?"

That answer was easy. "Not after the pay cut they just gave us."

"I rest my case."

Bahn's eyes darted around the room. Backpacks and suitcases sat against the living room wall. At least she was able to get most of her stuff packed. She still felt like she was forgetting something. Nothing new. She probably was.

It would be really great if she could untie the knot that currently took up residence in her stomach. Even after her talk with Sarah, she still couldn't get the nerves to calm down. It wasn't the flight, although she wasn't a fan of flying. It was… everything.

Even though she'd never really thought a lot about her feelings for Owen past being childhood best friends, it was obvious there was something there once they were reunited. Something more. And although she didn't go into detail of what happened when she was in Biloxi, or when he came to plead his case to her, Sarah had very aptly pointed out the writing on the wall. There was no use in making light of the situation or trying to lie about it. Sarah knew her too well.

Since he'd left, she'd had so many fantasies of what might happen while she was staying with him. How they'd create a perfect space for him, together. But then her mind would do a deep dive into the darkness of what could go wrong, and the thought of him never speaking to her again would suck the breath right out of her. She hated the yoyo of emotions her head was putting her heart through.

Finding the laptop she was searching for; she sat down at the table and flipped it open. Taking a deep breath, she tried to clear her head of the chaos and scanned her 3D mockup of his floorplan she'd created in the app she downloaded. She would have to ask Owen if the previous owners had done any kind of remodeling as it might affect her design ideas. Not that he would tell her, since he insisted that it remain a surprise.

Like he'd heard her thoughts, her phone buzzed with a text from him.

Owen: **Are you all packed and ready for your trip?**

And with that one simple text, she suddenly felt calmer. Just picturing him sitting there waiting for her to text back made her smile.

Bahn: **As ready as I'll ever be. I know I'm forgetting**

something though.

Owen: **Why do you say that?**

Bahn: **I always do. Never fails. I got to last year's conference and completely forgot my sneakers, which doesn't sound bad until you consider that at coaches' conferences we work on drills and plays, and you can't do that in sandals or street shoes. Luckily Sarah had an extra pair.**

Owen: **Sarah to the rescue.**

Bahn: **Trust me, she's saved my ass more times than I care to remember. I nearly left my computer bag behind in a hotel room once.**

She could picture Owen laughing at her. He'd had to save her ass too many times to count when they were growing up.

Owen: **Sounds like you haven't changed.**

Bahn: **Shut up.**

Owen: **Do you have any food requests? I'm about to make a grocery store run.**

Bahn: **Cookie dough ice cream.**

Owen: **Already had that on the list. What else?**

Bahn: **Cokes?**

Owen: **Already in the fridge. Try again. Oh, and I already have steaks and potatoes.**

Bahn: **Sounds like you got all my favorites covered.**

Owen: **Awesome. Anything special you need for the bathroom? Shampoos? Soaps?**

Bahn: **Nah. I'll bring my shampoo and stuff, and any soap is fine with me. You know me, I'm not too fancy.**

Owen: **Well, I knew you at twelve. I'm hoping your tastes have changed some.**

Bahn: **Not much, actually.**

Owen: **Just know, I'm not feeding you SpaghettiOs no matter how much you beg.**

Bahn giggled at the comment. She definitely had an obsession with SpaghettiOs when she was little. There was a time when she ate little else. But she hadn't had any in years.

Bahn: **Oh, I never beg. But no SpaghettiOs? Maybe I should rethink this trip. It's been a busy summer. It might be nice to just have a few days to rest up before heading home.**

Owen: **Wait. I might be willing to negotiate.**

Bahn: **I don't know. You said no SpaghettiOs.**

Owen: **What would it take for you to reconsider?**

Bahn: **What was that about begging?**

Owen: **God. You're still crazy.**

Bahn: **Annnddd…That surprises you?**

Owen: **Not at all. But let me know, Miss Crazy, if you think of anything else.**

Bahn: **I do have a question. I know all the houses around that area are similar in style, meaning white walls, hardwood, and Formica. I'm trying to get some ideas of ways to make the biggest impact in the least amount of time. I need to know if the house has had any renovations done.**

Owen: **Fishing for hints?**

Bahn: **I just want to be prepared. We won't have that much time, and I want to get as much done as we can before I have to leave.**

Owen: **No real upgrades that I can think of besides the ensuite bathroom off the main bedroom. Other than that, they painted. It's up to you if you want to change the colors.**

Bahn: **It's not up to me. It's your house. If you don't like the colors, we can paint. I made sure to pick up some paint samples I thought you might like. And I stuck my work clothes in my suitcase.**

Owen: **Work clothes? As in those cute overalls you had on when you were cleaning your classroom?**

Bahn: **You thought those were cute? They're ripped and covered in paint and God knows what else.**

Owen: **I wasn't really focused on what the overalls looked like, if you know what I mean.**

His obvious flirting had a smirk tugging at her lips. He was so different from the shy, sensitive little boy she used to know, but she still saw glimpses of him from time to time. The sadness she saw in his eyes when she drove away on the beach that day was the same look he had in the hospital after she was hit by a car—complete devastation.

He'd blamed himself for her getting hurt because his basketball hit the rim and shot off into the street. But it was her fault for blindly running out into the street without looking. There was a connection between them, even then.

Bahn: **Well, lucky you. They're packed and ready to go.**
Owen: **Are you sure? You might want to check.**
Bahn: **I hate you.**
Owen: **No, you don't. You love me and you know it.**

All the calm he'd instilled in her evaporated with that one comment. Why did it unnerve her so badly?

The conference was an absolute waste of money. Thank God most of the cost wasn't hers. Not that it wasn't informative, it probably was. She just didn't retain anything from any of the sessions she attended. Her mind was a million miles away.

Or more like sixty.

She tried to engage and make it seem like she was at least somewhat interested, but after the second day of Sarah trying to discuss the sessions, and Bahn having no clue what she was talking about, she gave up. Sarah laughed at her obvious inability to focus. She couldn't even be mad at her for doing it either. It was pathetic. She'd never felt so distracted.

"Go ahead. Say it," Bahn groused, noticing the smirk on Sarah's face as she cut into her Belgian waffle. "What part of the conversation did I miss?"

"None of it, I don't think."

"Okay. What did I forget in the conference center?"

"I think you got back to the room with everything."

"Well, apparently there is something you aren't sharing. You're smirking hard core."

"I was just wondering when you were going to notice that your shirt was on inside out."

"I…" She looked down as the words processed in her head. Yep. Sure enough, her red, sleeveless, V-neck top was inside out. For heaven's sake, was she going to need Sarah to dress her now? "Thanks for not letting me walk around like this all day."

"No problem. I got you." Sarah sipped her coffee and set it back on the table. "I know you're in your head about the whole Owen thing."

"You think? Geez, I can't concentrate. I haven't retained

anything. I hope you took good notes."

"I was supposed to be taking notes?"

A surge of panic made her heart jump. "You had a notebook. I thought—"

"Good lord, woman, get a grip. Of course I took notes. You act like we just met."

"Sorry."

"No need for apologies. I just hate that you're so anxious. You should be excited."

"I am. But I need to be realistic."

"You're still stuck on the whole stupid long-distance issue?"

"It's not stupid, Sarah. He lives on the east coast and I'm on the west. If we were a couple of hours from each other, it would be different, but it's like he's on a different continent. It's a thousand dollars every time I want to see him. I don't have that kind of money to spare, especially now."

"I get that. But you're here right now, and I think you should focus on that. Let go of the what ifs. See where things go. If it's meant to be, things will work out. Look what Jean and I went through. I never in a million years thought we'd be together. She was in a committed relationship with Gary."

"Gary was a tool and a cheater."

"Doesn't matter who did what or how it happened, it happened. That's all that matters. You have an opportunity at love, and you're about to throw it all away because you can't see how it would work out."

"I don't know if it's love. I—"

Sarah chuckled and patted Bahn's hand. "Oh, my sweet clueless Bahn. You have been in love with him since I've known you. Whether you recognize it or not, your heart knows."

"He was my best friend."

"That's the best kind of relationship."

"We spent a lot of time together, Sarah. That doesn't mean we're in love with each other. It just means we have history, and we care about each other."

"Yeah. Keep telling yourself that and you're going to ruin your best chance at happiness."

"Okay fine. I'm in love with him." The words felt right with how she felt, but it only made her realize her true fear. "But what if he doesn't feel the same for me?"

"Trust me on this one. That man loves you. He wouldn't have traveled across the country just to clear his conscience."

"You don't know him. He is just that type of person. He hates making people mad. He would have done it for anyone he considered a friend."

"Wrong. I don't doubt he would do just about anything for a friend, because you're right, he does seem like that type of person. But I saw how he looked at you. He didn't just fly across the country to clear things up."

"But what if you're wrong? I don't think my heart could take losing him again."

"And that right there tells me you love him. But like I said before, that is where the decision comes in. Is he worth taking a chance on? I think you know the answer to that."

CHAPTER 38

O wen pulled up to the hotel with five minutes to spare. Digging in his pocket, he shot off a quick text.

Owen: **I'm here.**

Opening the door, he leaned out and pushed up the umbrella. The rain pattered on the material as he jogged to the entrance. Closing the umbrella and leaning it against the wall, he smoothed his shirt and raked his fingers through his damp hair before stepping through the sliding doors. The place was desolate.

He ventured further into the lobby, removing his glasses and cleaning off the droplets. The quietness set his nerves on edge. He wondered if he somehow got the wrong time—or even the wrong place—but then his phone buzzed.

Bahn: **On my way.**

He could feel his heart tick up, and suddenly he couldn't keep a smile from splaying itself across his face. *How does she do this to me?* He shook his hands as his nerves bordered on causing a full-on panic attack. It seemed like this day took forever to come.

The elevator bell chimed, and he heard her voice before their eyes found each other. Pin pricks spread through his body. God, she seemed even more beautiful than before. Her hair was pulled back with her crazy sunglasses, and the red, sleeveless, V-neck T-shirt she wore showed off her toned arms. A glance below her skinny jeans brought a smirk to his face. Flip-flops.

A smile scrolled across her face, and she wrinkled her nose as she quickly made her way to him. He wrapped his arms around her, and she squealed as he lifted her off her feet and spun her around.

"I missed your face," she said in a squeaky voice, then she ran her fingers through his hair, which had grown out considerably. "And I love the glasses. You look so smart."

"Why, thank you. I missed you too." He set her down but continued to hold her. "I don't know about being smart though. I forgot to reorder my contacts."

"Okay, this is awkward. I think I'll just leave you two alone," came a voice behind Bahn.

Owen looked up to see Sarah. He released Bahn from his grip and reached his arm out to give her a friendly hug. "Hey, Sarah. How was your week?"

"Besides this awkward moment, it went pretty well. I managed to keep her alive for you, which wasn't an easy feat."

They all laughed as he said, "I appreciate that."

Bahn gave Sarah a hug. "I will meet you at the airport on Sunday."

"Sounds like a plan. You guys be careful." Sarah released Bahn and headed for the door.

Owen grasped the handle of Bahn's luggage. "Are you ready?"

"I think so."

He leaned the bag against his hip to open the umbrella and held it over Bahn's head as they jogged to the truck. As Owen climbed into the driver's seat, he noticed she had picked up a black piece of material he'd left lying on the console.

She held it up to him. "What's this?"

He gave her a crafty grin. "It's your blindfold. I'll tell you when you need to put it on."

"You're seriously going to make me put on a blindfold?"

"Yep. I told you. It's a surprise."

"Dear god, you're taking this surprise thing to a new level," she said, shaking her head.

The miles flew by as they discussed a game plan for the next few days. Bahn went through her list of places they needed to go and things they needed to buy. She showed him photos of items she'd found, and they both chattered excitedly about how great the finished product would be.

As Owen hit the last few miles of highway, he instructed Bahn to put on the blindfold and she begrudgingly obliged. A few minutes later, the truck lurched to a stop and Owen hopped out. He opened the umbrella and ran to Bahn's side to help her out.

"I should have worn tennis shoes. The wet grass is making my flip-flops slimy."

"Sorry, it's been raining for days, and I haven't been able to mow." Owen held her hand and directed her to a designated spot, then let go and quickly moved away as he pulled his phone from his pocket. "Okay, you can take the blindfold off."

She took the edge and slid it up and immediately began jumping up and down. "Oh my God, Owen, It's your house!"

He snapped photo after photo of her elation then promptly dropped the phone when she ditched the umbrella and ran to him, wrapping her arms around his neck and continuing to bounce. He knew there was no way to contain her excitement, so he joined in.

"I can't believe it."

"Good surprise?"

"The best."

Once she'd settled down some, Owen locked eyes on hers that still held an excited sparkle. "Ready to go in? I've got so much to show you."

"Yes."

After getting her bag, he picked his phone up, checked it for damage, then wiped it off as they made their way to the porch and inside the house.

"So how did you do it?"

"I used the money Dad left me. I think they were desperate to sell. I wrote a short note with my offer telling them it was my house growing up, and they accepted the offer. The great thing is, my house notes are about five hundred dollars cheaper than anything we looked at for rent."

"Are you kidding me? And you got a bigger place. And it's still close to the beach. This is awesome." She walked into the kitchen and ran her hand along the counter then along the back of a gray office chair pushed up under the built-in desk.

"Yeah, there's a pretty large crack in the Formica. I'll need to get a new countertop at some point, but it'll work for now."

Her eyes continued to dart around the room. "The tile floor is new."

"Yeah. It's in both baths too. I love it, because it's that Terrazzo floor like you guys had in your house."

They walked back into the living room and Bahn unzipped her bag, pulling out her computer along with a spiral notebook. She opened it and walked into the kitchen. Her eyes scanned the rooms, then she leaned over the bar and started spouting furniture layout ideas to Owen, but he had a hard time concentrating.

The V-neck shirt she had tied at the waist made his head spin, and when she leaned over, he felt like he was going to pass clean out. Bahn had no idea. He could tell she was in her element and happy as a clam. She kept making suggestions for placement of this and angle of that, and Owen finally couldn't take it anymore. "Bahn...take a breath."

She cocked her head and looked out of the corner of her eye. His willpower melted into a puddle on the floor.

He grabbed her wrist and dragged her to him, draping it around his neck as he lifted her up onto the counter. Their lips met and sent an electric charge throughout his body as her fingers dug into his hair.

With his mouth still pressed to hers, he said, "I have wanted to do that since I laid eyes on you today."

She smiled, but something was off. That telltale mischievousness wasn't there. Bringing his hand up to her face, he searched her eyes. Maybe it was just nerves. He rubbed his thumb over her soft cheek and moved his fingers to the back of her neck, into her hair. Her soft curls tickled as they threaded through his fingers.

Tugging her in again, he softly pressed his lips to hers before sinking deeper. He moved in closer to her to get a better angle, but she brought her hands to his chest and slowly backed away.

This wasn't how he'd envisioned this going at all.

Lowering her head, she gently leaned her forehead to his. This wasn't good. His heart pinched with her rejection, and he tried to look at her, but she avoided his attempt. Licking her lips, she finally made eye contact for a moment then looked away again.

"I can't do this, Owen," she said softly.

Stepping back, Owen tried to get her to look at him again. "Why? What did I do?"

"You did nothing wrong," she said quietly as she slid off the counter.

"Then what can't you do? Is it about us?" He motioned between the two of them.

She nodded slowly. "After you left, I couldn't stop thinking about everything that happened. Every moment of our lives together was replaying over and over. I couldn't sleep. I couldn't concentrate. I had a thousand thoughts rolling inside my head about... us. What was *us*, exactly? Was it just everything that had happened with your dad, with reuniting, and reliving the excitement of our youth, and the fight. Did it just have our emotions somehow boiling over? Or was it more? I was so confused.

"It's not that I don't feel a connection to you. You've been my best friend for seventeen years. Even when we were apart, you still weren't far from my thoughts. And now that I have you back in my life, I don't want to ever lose you again. But as far as being more than friends, we're on opposite coasts, and I don't know how to make it work.

"Sitting on the plane on the way here, I had so much on my mind. I continued to try to figure out a plan so we could see each other. But even if we did work something out, it would be expensive. And how often could we do it with our schedules? I'm busy with games on the weekends during the school year." She pushed past him. "I can't just see you every six months. That's not a relationship. Long distance relationships usually fall apart, even when people live just a couple of hours away."

"I get it, but..."

She slid down the wall onto the hardwood floor and pulled her knees up to her chest. "I'm on a teacher's budget, Owen. A slim one at that. I'm barely able to pay my bills and still have food to eat. As much as I want something more, I don't have the money to fly across the country."

There was nothing she said that Owen hadn't already thought of himself. He sat crossed legged on the floor across from her, staring intently at her while she vented. He could see the hurt in her eyes as she continued to pour herself out to him, and it rocked him.

"I know but—" he tried to break in, but she wouldn't have it.

"Owen, there are no buts. However much I would love there to be an 'us,' we have to face the fact that our lives have taken separate paths that are a continent apart. Trust me, I think I have been through every scenario in the book, and in the end, I had nothing." She paused and stared up at the ceiling. "I wish the long-distance thing could work, but honestly, I can't risk losing you again in the event that it doesn't. So, I would rather keep you in my life as a friend, calling and texting and hoping to see each other when we can."

Owen stared at the floor, silently drawing circles with his finger, digesting everything Bahn had said. He wanted more. He wanted everything. But she had a point. What if it didn't work? Now that they'd been reunited, could he live with not having her in his life at all? But the bigger question was, could he live with not knowing if they could have made it work? Was she just scared, or was there something she wasn't telling him? Some other reason she didn't want more than friendship.

There was one thing that scared him. Continuing to focus on the floor, he chewed on his cheek, unsure if he was ready for the answer to his question. "Can I ask you something?"

"Sure."

"Are you scared of me?"

"What? Why would I—"

"I saw it in your eyes, Bahn. After I told you what could happen with the nightmares."

"To be honest, I was scared, but not of you. I was scared I somehow triggered your nightmare. I was more scared for you from what I saw you going through. Would your PTSD be a factor if we were in a relationship? Yes. To the point that I would want you to get the best care possible. But that's not why I think we should just be friends. I just don't see how we could make a relationship work."

After a moment, he looked up and took a deep breath. "As far as triggering the nightmare, let me assure you, you had nothing to do with it. They come and go. Hopefully after some time they will stay gone.

"I've gotten set up with a therapist here. I'm supposed to meet up with him tomorrow afternoon. He said he has something for me. I'd like you to go with me. He'll be able to explain more about why I have the panic attacks and nightmares." He looked deep into her eyes, hoping she would agree to come, and she nodded.

"And Bahn, I get it. I have run every possible scenario through my head more than once. I know it would be hard if we tried the long-distance thing. This last month has been hell, and I can't imagine what it would be like if we were apart longer. Talking to you on the phone and video chatting is great and all, but it's not like having you with me. So, I get what you're saying.

"But when I left you in Oregon, we agreed we would take this one day at a time. I know it seems like an impossible situation, and I won't push you into anything you don't want, but for right now, can we stick to that? Not make any decisions for right now. I will do whatever you feel comfortable with, and if you don't want to stay, I will take you back to your hotel. But I'm kind of hoping you'll stay."

CHAPTER 39

H e tried to steady his breaths, tried to remain calm, even though inside he could feel the panic surging to the surface. He knew how scared and confused she was. It wasn't like he didn't feel it too. But he was sticking to their plan and wasn't quite ready to give up on them yet. Time would tell.

She studied him. "No. I wouldn't have had you pick me up if I didn't want to stay and get you set up."

Owen let out a silent breath and tried to school his face in a satisfied expression, hoping she wouldn't notice how excited he really was. He knew what they were up against, and he wasn't sure if things would work out. But having her agree to stay at least gave him time to convince her they were worth fighting for. He needed to take his cues from her though. Needed to follow her lead. Which meant playing it cool.

"Awesome. I'm really glad you said that, because I honestly didn't want to have my mom help me furnish this beast." They both laughed. "No offense, but after shopping for a bed with her, I realized how different our tastes are."

"So, you did take her with you?"

"Only because she wanted to buy some other things for the house."

"Speaking of buying stuff, let's get on to the business at hand."

In typical Bahn fashion, she switched gears on him, scanning the room and moving on to the notes she had. "So, you have four bedrooms. What do you want to do with them?"

"I put my weights in my old bedroom, so that one will be my workout room."

"Okay. That takes care of one room. And the main bedroom will be your room, but what about the other two?"

"Well, since I have a nice little area in the kitchen for an office, I guess the other two will be guest rooms."

Bahn took off up the hallway with Owen close behind her. He knew the minute her eyes landed on the painting hanging on the dark, navy-blue wall of his old bedroom that she would have questions. "Where'd you get that?"

Owen's mouth tipped up in a crooked smile at her reaction to the painting of two iridescent angry waves made up of small circles and squares of different colors. Just enough of a beachy feel, but still masculine. "I went treasure hunting."

Her brows dipped. "Without me?"

"I couldn't pass it up. It wasn't going to be there long."

"Where?"

Owen chewed on his lip trying to hide his smile.

Bahn narrowed her eyes, studying him, and her mouth dropped open as realization set in. "You didn't."

The smile was winning no matter how much he tried to fight it.

"Owen Cramer, how could you?" Her hands pushed against his chest. "You went to Ocean Shores without me? I feel betrayed," she said, feigning heartbreak.

"Oh, trust me. If you want to go dumpster diving, there is plenty of stuff over there to find. This painting was sitting next to one of the dumpsters on top of the desk chair you saw earlier."

She stepped closer, examining it. "I love it. Did you find anything else?"

"Yeah. I'll show you my best find when we get to *my bedroom*," he said, wiggling his eyebrows.

"Oh lord, I can't wait," Bahn responded sarcastically, backhanding him in the chest. "If it has to do with leather whips, I think I'll pass."

"Actually, leather plays a big part in it."

"Oh, now you have me really curious. But let's figure out what to do with these other rooms first."

She peeked her head into each of the empty rooms and turned back to Owen. "If you still like to play video games, you can set one up as a game room with a couple of nice chairs and a big screen TV with a console. Kind of a mixed game and mini theater room."

"That would be cool. We could have a mini fridge and small bar set up."

"Yeah."

"Let's use the bedroom across from the weight room for that and leave this other one as a guest room."

"I think that would work well." She opened her notebook. "Okay. We'll need a bed for in there. I would suggest at least full size. That way you can still have two guests sleep in there. As for your old room, we'll call that a flex room. Since the weights don't take up the entire room, we can utilize it for something else too, if we need to. Plus, *flex* room. Weightlifting...get it?"

"Ha!" he said sarcastically and she playfully backhanded him again.

"What time is it?"

He pulled out his phone. "Nearly three."

"Okay. Let me get this all into my laptop and then we can tackle the guest room first. I don't want to sleep on the floor."

A twinge of disappointment hit him. "Oh, okay."

Her eyes met his. "I hope you—"

"No. I learned my lesson about making assumptions. I bought a blow-up bed."

Bahn giggled. "Thanks," the sarcasm spread thick in that single word.

"I didn't know—"

"I'm just playing. But that bed should be new, and one of the first things we buy. Do you have any discount department stores that carry furniture?"

"Yeah. There's one just up the street that mom and I went to. They deliver, but it looks like it's stopped raining. We could probably just cart the bed back in the truck."

"Okay, let's go. And maybe we can get some inspiration while we're there."

"You sure you don't want to see *my bedroom*?" He had to give her one last playful jab. Even though she'd put a damper on a possible relationship, he still couldn't help but be excited about her being there and hadn't completely abandoned the idea of them being together either.

She rolled her eyes. "Surprise me later."

He gave her his best sorrowful puppy eyes, batting his lashes like he was about to cry.

Shaking her head, she took a noisy breath. "Fine. Let's see this den of sin."

"Is that how you have it labeled in your notes?"

"No. But I'm wondering if I should."

Owen smirked, and waggled his eyebrows again, garnering a giggle and a shake of her head. After a moment he playfully whined, "I wanted you to see my excellent find."

"I'm still mad you went without me."

They wandered up the short hallway and he opened the door. As she walked into his room, he could tell she was imagining what the room could look like. She pursed her lips at the unmade bed with a white islet comforter, white sheets, and two small pillows. "This needs to change," she said as she twirled her hand over the bed. "I mean, I'm good with the wall color if you are, but can I ask why you put it on this wall and not the purple accent wall? It's in between the windows, so, for one, you can't see out the windows, and two, if you get a headboard it won't fit."

"And that's why I asked you to come," he said with a grin. "All of this can change. My mom just gave me some of her bedding to get me by. I actually like the wall color, and since we don't have that much time, let's focus on getting the place furnished."

As she peeked her head in the master bath, he moved over to the dumpster find he was so proud of and removed the dirty clothes that were tossed on it.

"Oh, this is nice." Her voice echoed from within the bathroom.

"Yeah, the previous owners completely redid it." When her attention turned back to him, he motioned like Vanna White to a sea blue leather chair.

"No, you didn't."

"I did." He nodded slowly, grinning from ear to ear.

Bahn quickly ate up the space between them, her eyes fixed on the chair. "Seriously?"

"It was sitting right next to the desk chair and painting. I'm thinking there was a divorce involved. Had to have been. I mean, why else? There is nothing wrong with any of the stuff. I got some saddle soap and wiped it and the desk chair down, and they're like brand new."

"Yeah. It looks new. In all my dumpster dives, I've never found anything like this. She ran her hand along the chair. "I can definitely work with this. Was there anything else?"

"Oh, hell yeah. There was a bunch of stuff beside the dumpsters, and they were full. Honestly, I didn't go digging. I was on a run and went by. Snooped around for old times' sake, then came back with my truck."

"Well, we will be making a stop there while I'm here. But right now, let's go find me a bed."

"Sounds like a plan."

Heading out of the room, he high fived her, then went in search of his keys while Bahn dug some sneakers out of her bag. On the way to the truck, Bahn continued to share some ideas and Owen couldn't help but smile at how excited she was. He helped her into the truck and hurried around to the other side. The minute he was behind the wheel, Bahn grabbed his hand and smiled.

"Let the adventure begin."

At the store, Bahn became laser focused. It was obvious how passionate she was, and Owen couldn't help but smile. After they agreed on the mattress and box springs, Bahn picked out bedding and curtains for his room. He had to admit he questioned the choice immediately, but kept his mouth shut because he had no desire to do the decorating himself. By the time she'd gotten bedding for the guest room, and rugs and mats for the bedrooms and baths, Owen was completely lost in trying to picture what she was envisioning.

Once their purchases were made, they tied down the mattress and box springs for the guest room in the bed of the truck and headed back to the house. By six, Bahn had the curtains hung, the beds made, the mats and rugs down, and the towels put away. She called Owen to come check out her work.

Owen stood in his bedroom, amazed at the transformation that had already taken place. Within a couple of hours, Bahn had added a warmth to his room that hadn't been there before. The rug she'd found sat at an angle under the foot of his bed. A light teal blanket lay at the end of his bed on top of the off-white comforter. The gray pillow shams had tiny purple and teal diamonds that pulled everything together. It had just the right mix of colors to make it beachy and comfortable and still masculine. "I can't believe how different this already looks."

"Do you like it? Be honest."

"It's perfect. It looks clean and comfortable."

"And now with the bed turned up against this wall, you can see outside. And the sun won't be so bright in the mornings."

Owen nodded in agreement.

"I really just wanted to make this a place for you to chill."

They wandered to the guest bedroom. Bahn had added throw pillows and an afghan with pops of coral colors to a printed navy and white comforter, and it immediately brightened up the room. "I figured you didn't want to fight with the throw pillows, so I didn't get any for your room, but I wanted them in here."

"Good call."

"I think we can add a lamp and nightstands, maybe a couple of pictures, and be done for now in here. I don't think it needs a chest or dresser since it's just a guest room.

"I agree. I've got other big items the money needs to go to right now. Maybe later, if my situation changes, we can add the other furniture."

"Yeah." A flash of something crossed Bahn's face, but it was gone just as fast. "Speaking of big items, we need to make our first stop tomorrow at the appliance store to get that out of the way. Then we can go play."

"What time do you want to start?"

"No later than nine."

"Nine? Don't you think that's a little early?" he taunted. "I mean, you're technically on vacation."

Without lifting her head from the paper she was marking up; she gave him a playful glare from beneath her lashes. "I'm working."

He glanced down at the notes she'd made. Lists of tables, chairs, bookcases, and lamps littered the page. Everything down to the plants were listed.

He pulled her notebook out of her hand and looked through the pages. She'd taken his rough drawing of the layout and done a fully furnished drawing, complete with couches, chairs, tables, and the rest.

"Wow, Bahn! This is incredible."

"Thank You. Hang on and I'll pull up the mockup on my laptop. It looks more realistic. Of course, I don't know if all the stuff I have on there will fit. Oh, do you have a tape measure? I have the rough measurements you sent me, but I need to make sure it's accurate now."

"Yeah, I do."

Owen stood and went to the coat closet and pulled a large gray box down. He grabbed the tape measure and handed it off to Bahn. She began measuring the walls in the living room then moved on throughout the house, penciling in each measurement on the layout.

Owen watched her from a distance for a bit, then left her to do her thing while he continued with other things around the house. He found her standing in his bedroom a few minutes later as she wrote in her last figure. "Are sandwiches okay for dinner?"

Bahn made a pouty face. "I was hoping for steak and potatoes."

"I haven't gotten the grill yet. Add it to the list," he stated.

"It's okay. I was just—"

"No, I'm serious, add it to the list. I planned on getting one, but I ran out of time," he said with his mouth cocked to one side.

"Okay, then. But sandwiches are fine as long as you have Cheetos."

That was another thing he would never forget about Bahn. She had a love-hate relationship with food. There were certain foods she was obsessed with and others she would physically gag over. "What else would you serve with a turkey sandwich?"

They strolled to the dining room. Where the table would eventually sit, Owen had laid out a quilt with everything set out nice and neat on the floor, including two tapered candles. On Bahn's plate there was a heaping pile of Cheetos.

As she sat on the floor, her mouth tipped up in a smile. "Aw. This is nice."

"Hopefully we can find a dining table and some chairs tomorrow," Owen commented.

After dinner, they sat on the floor, discussing her ideas on the layout, making sure he was happy with her suggestions. Owen finally broached a question that had been bothering him since their earlier discussion. "Are you sure you're good with staying here? I can get you a hotel room if—"

"No. The guest room is fine. We can get an earlier start that way."

A slight smile tugged at his lips. *At least she was under the same roof.*

CHAPTER 40

Owen's alarm buzzed. He rolled over, picked his phone up off the floor to shut it off, and was startled when he looked around, forgetting where he was for a moment. He still hadn't gotten used to his new place, and with the new stuff Bahn had added, it was like waking up in a hotel room.

Throwing the covers off, he sat on the edge of the bed and ran his fingers through his hair before padding up the hall to get some coffee. It was nice to have it waiting for him.

He figured Bahn wouldn't be up for a while, so he would go for a run. After dressing, he set out everything she would need for her coffee, in case she woke up before he got back.

The door creaked as he quietly shut it behind him and turned up the street on a path that would take him along the beach. He hoped the sound and smell of the surf would help him clear his head.

Bahn's reservations were valid, but he still wasn't sure they were all based on the distance. His insecurities were getting the best of him. He knew how he felt about her, and he didn't think it was simply a factor of their recent reunion, or a result of the emotional upheaval from his dad's death. But was it the same for her? Was he enough for her? Melanie's betrayal stabbed at his insecurities.

They needed to talk. The problem was, he didn't know what to say. He had a plan, but he needed to figure out where her head was before he could set it in motion.

Continuing down the beach, he watched as the sun turned the water from plum to gold. By the time he rounded the last corner, the sky was filled with a beautiful mix of pinks and purples and blues. He loved sunrises.

The apartment complex came into view, and he jogged around the back to see if there might be any treasures he and Bahn could take off their hands. Just as he suspected, the dumpsters were filled to the brim and overflowing. This would be fun. He took off up the street with a wide grin on his face.

Bounding up the steps, he pulled his shirt off as he quietly pushed the door open. Wadding it up, he wiped his chest, then grabbed a glass from the cabinet and filled it with ice water. The hallway door squeaked, and Bahn came around the corner in a pair of yellow cotton shorts and a soft gray sleeveless tank. Her hair was everywhere, and Owen was already in trouble. His eyes locked on her body, and he felt his hair electrify. She was adorable.

"Coffee?" he croaked, trying to get his breath under control.

She glanced up, noticed him, and jerked. "What time is it?" she said, rubbing her eyes.

"It's almost eight." He poured her a cup and handed it to her. "I set the cream and sugar out. I was just about to hop in the shower. Do you need anything?"

She added a couple of scoops of sugar and a splash of cream and stared at him without saying a word. Long enough to make him wonder if she was really awake.

Finally, she responded, "No. Go ahead."

Stretching his arms over his head as he walked off to his bedroom, he caught her out of his periphery, leaning forward, still gaping at him. *Oh. Interesting.* A plan started forming and he smiled as he shut the door. *Oh yeah, Bahn. My little plan might be just what's needed to find out where your head is.*

Damn it. Why couldn't he have aged badly? That would have made this so much easier. But no. Just my luck he has to look like he stepped out of a Calvin Klein ad. From the way his body rippled

when he was squeezing his shirt and stretching, his muscles looked like they had muscles, and each one was perfectly placed for my viewing pleasure. And worst of all, he doesn't even know how gorgeous he is. He's still the sweet, thoughtful Owen I remember. Although, he isn't quite as shy. And that new confidence just adds to my problem. Ugh. What did I do to deserve this torture? It's so unfair.

If life was fair, they'd have found out they were living only a few miles from each other when they reunited, and she'd be climbing Owen Cramer like a tree by now and never looking back. But life was cruel, and the truth was, she had three days with him and then it was back to reality. And as much as she would love to dive right back in where things left off in Oregon, she didn't think her heart could take it. So, she had to keep her feelings in check. Try to focus on the job at hand, and not the hard body that was currently showering.

She squinted her eyes at the visual her mind suddenly chose to display. Maybe she should have gotten a hotel.

Bahn searched the pantry for something to eat. Although she normally ate fairly healthy, today was all about finding pleasure in the situation. Sugar-filled marshmallow cereal should do the trick. And damn it if it didn't remind her of when they were kids.

Wallowing in the memories, she took a few bites then dumped it out. Keeping her head screwed on straight was turning out to be impossible. And on top of it were Sarah's words playing in the background. 'Let go of the preconceived notions. Let go of the what ifs.' She would love to do that and see what the future held, but she couldn't.

Traipsing back to the bedroom, she closed the door and laid across the bed with her arm draped across her stinging eyes. She wanted to help him. She promised him she would. Plus, like Sarah said, this was her chance to do what she'd always wanted to do.

Decorating her place was fun, but she knew her taste and had been roommates with Sarah long enough to know she couldn't care less what she did. This was different. This was figuring out what someone else's likes and dislikes were and creating a comfortable space around them.

Her job as a coach was rewarding in the beginning, and in some ways it still was. She enjoyed getting a chance to mold kids into productive adults, and there had been many times when students had told her how much she'd taught them. But the downside was the administration. The school district didn't seem to care about their employees or how many hours they put in. She knew the district was struggling, but that didn't mean they shouldn't treat their employees with some respect.

Owen's suggestion about starting her decorating business as a side job sounded amazing but was never going to happen. Between teaching and coaching, not to mention the hours spent grading papers and going to games, she didn't have time. Heck, she barely had time to sleep.

At least, just this once, Owen had given her an opportunity to play. And she wasn't going to let her feelings get in the way of that. She could do this.

After her little pep talk, she dug through her suitcase for some clothes then opened the door. The scent of whiskey and cedar hit her nose, and she knew he was close by. She raced for the bathroom with her necessities in hand and shut the door.

Once she'd showered, her emotions felt a bit more under control. She dusted a little pink shimmer on her cheeks, applied some mascara and ChapStick, threw her hair in a high ponytail, and called it good.

When she opened the door, he was there, leaning in the doorway in a pair of navy shorts and a thin white tank covered by a blue and red checked button-up that was left open. The sleeves were rolled, displaying his corded forearms. His eyes crinkled as a crooked smile filled his face, and it made her skin sizzle.

Crap. So much for control.

She swallowed and watched as he did the same. There was so much charge in the air, and it seemed like neither of them knew how to handle it. They just stared at each other.

Finally, Owen cleared his throat. "I, I was wondering if you wanted to get some breakfast before we get started."

"I had a bite of cereal. I'm good. I'm not that hungry, but if you are, we can stop."

"Nah. We can get something later."

He paused, and his eyes skimmed her body, which had Bahn taking a deep cleansing breath. *I can do this.*

"Are you ready?"

"Sure." Bahn followed him into the living room where she retrieved her notebook. "I've got several places we can check out. What time is your appointment with the therapist?"

"It's at one. I figure we can hit a few places this morning, break for lunch, stop by his office, and then maybe come home, change, and go dumpster diving."

Home. That sounded so...nice. She loved her condo, but it never felt quite like home. Even after decorating it, she never felt settled. She'd figured she would at some point, but she never did. She'd just have to settle for making Owen's place his home.

Out of all the places she'd lived, Biloxi had always felt like home to her. And now Owen had made it his. Something about that sent a twinge of jealousy through her.

"Bahn?" His soothing voice called her back from her thoughts and her eyes slowly focused on his. His brows drew together in concern, then he replaced it with a plastic smile that told her he knew she had zoned out. "Does that sound okay?"

She cleared her throat. "Yeah. Great. Let's get moving. We have a lot to accomplish in three days. The quicker we get started, the more we can get done."

Three days. In some ways she wanted it to go by fast, and in others, she hoped something would happen, like a freak storm, that would strand her there indefinitely.

Between the appliance store, where Owen had gotten a great buy on a washer and dryer, the vintage store where Bahn knew she'd hit the jackpot on furniture, and the consignment shop they hit for some odds and ends, Owen's truck was loaded down with furniture and they had just enough time to drop everything off, stop for lunch, and make the therapist appointment.

Stopped at Burger Hill for lunch, Bahn sat down at the picnic table out front and took in the place that had always been a favorite of theirs. It was almost exactly as she remembered it. There were a few changes, probably caused by the hurricane, but for the most part, everything around her made her feel like she'd stepped back in time. And the memories took hold.

Most of them included the little boy with the glasses and dark wavy hair. She was almost certain she was sitting at the exact table she and Owen sat at when they took their last photo sharing the ice cream. She smiled remembering it, but it was the strangest feeling, because her heart ached from it too.

Owen returned with their food and Bahn squirted a healthy amount of ketchup into her basket of salty shoestring fries. "The big M has nothing on these fries."

"I know. I normally make this my first stop when I come into town. Now that I'm going to live here, I have a feeling I'm going to have to add a couple of extra miles on my morning runs to counterbalance my visits to this place."

Dipping a long plastic spoon into her malt, she slid a heaping spoonful of the vanilla goodness into her mouth and moaned. "I think the last time I had a malt, it was from here."

Her eyes lifted to Owen's as she spoke. He was staring, his wide eyes rounded, his lips slightly parted. He slammed his mouth shut, his jaw ticking as he swallowed, before jerking his gaze away and clearing his throat.

Bahn held in a giggle. She liked the fact that she could do that to him. In fact, she kind of loved it. He made her feel wanted, and it wasn't on purpose. She always enjoyed taking him out of his comfort zone, but this was on a whole different level.

Something about the challenge of making Owen crave her sent a zing through her, her logic for keeping her distance suddenly lost. She knew the teasing would come back to bite her in the ass, because the last thing she needed to do was poke the bear, but she loved seeing that hunger in his eyes.

Filling the spoon again, she pretended not to notice as his eyes locked on her mouth. She slid the thick dessert against her tongue and let a little of it remain on her lip so she could lick it off. And just to add the cherry on top, she moaned again.

Owen hopped up, jostling the table, and ran his hand through his hair as he mumbled, "Going to go to the bathroom."

"Okay," Bahn said with a giggle.

Owen tipped his head with one eyebrow nearly hitting his hairline, but then, shaking his head, he quickly walked away.

Continuing to eat her lunch, she started getting worried when Owen didn't come back. His expression popped into her head again, and she couldn't hold back her laughter as she dipped a few fries in the ketchup.

When he finally returned, he didn't say anything, just avoided eye contact and dug back into his food.

"You okay?" she asked, breaking the silence.

"Yeah," he returned, but didn't add anything else.

"You were gone for a while."

Still not lifting his gaze to her he shot back, "Long line."

She knew he was lying. There weren't that many people at the restaurant. But she didn't want to push her luck, so she let it go.

He checked his phone and blurted, "It's twelve thirty. We probably should be heading out."

"How far away is it?"

"Not far. Just off the base."

He picked up the last bite of his burger and shoved it in his mouth. Bahn did the same and sucked down the last of her malt. She had to admit, she was feeling much better than she did earlier.

Maybe Sarah was right. She was overthinking things. And doing that was going to ruin the whole entire trip. She needed to take things one day at a time, just like Owen said.

CHAPTER 41

S lowly rolling to a stop in front of a huge barn out in the middle of the country, Owen was completely confused. Which was a state he was getting used to since Bahn had shown up. She'd told him they needed to stay in the friend zone, and he was trying his best…sort of. But the way she let her malt linger on her lips, and the way she moaned when she licked it off, had him running for the bathroom just to get away so he didn't leap across the table and take her right out there in broad daylight. There was only so much he could take, and he was already on the edge with the outfit she had on.

She had to have been toying with him. There was no way she was that oblivious to what it was doing to him. But if she wanted to play games, he'd take that challenge and raise the ante. Right now though, he needed to figure out why his therapist wanted to meet him out here. He'd called to give him the location just as they were leaving the restaurant.

Trifecta Training was on the door and that was the only clue he got as the door opened and Gordon Nickson, a stocky Black man with a bit of silver in his hair and narrow silver-rimmed glasses, gave him a kind smile and then let his eyes settle on Bahn. "I see you brought reinforcements."

"Hey, Gordon. This is Siobahn Jackson." His fingers lightly

grazed her back, and she flinched. "She's a friend of mine."

He turned to Bahn, and the side of his mouth tucked in when he noticed how rattled she seemed. "This is Gordon Nickson."

Bahn held her hand out and Gordon shook it, then escorted them down a hallway and into a large room with a sofa, a couple of chairs, and a desk. Owen took a seat on the sofa and Bahn sat next to him. Gordon opened a laptop, scanned it for a moment, then picked up a notepad and a file from the desk, and sat in one of the chairs across from them.

"How've you been since our last visit? Any issues?"

"No. Not really. I've been busy training for the new position, and then finalizing everything with the house, so I've had some anxiety, but nothing extreme. No nightmares."

"Good to hear. And have you been sleeping soundly?"

"It's getting better. Not quite sleeping through the night consistently but having more good nights than bad."

"And you said no nightmares."

"No. And that's why I asked Bahn to come with me. She witnessed my last one and was scared she'd somehow triggered it."

Gordon's eyes moved to Bahn's, and Owen could tell all the playfulness she'd had just a short time before had vanished. Her fingers were laced, and her thumbs were moving back and forth over her skin as she tried to soothe herself. The one thing Bahn despised when they were growing up was being vulnerable. She was great at putting on a strong front for everyone, even when she was hurting, but he knew the truth.

He moved his hand in between hers, threaded their fingers together, and her body stilled.

"The truth is, young lady, anything can cause episodes." Gordon picked up the file folder and opened it. "Owen, I'm guessing you're okay with me discussing your case in front of her."

"Yes."

"All right." He paused for a moment. "You said your last episode occurred on a trip to Oregon. Correct?"

"Yes. I haven't had any issues since."

"And you hadn't had any problems for a while prior to that, correct?"

"Yes. No nightmares for a while, although I did have what I would call a panic attack when I got the call about my father. I discussed that with my other therapist."

"Yes. I have that in your file."

"And your father died during a tour of duty?"

"Yes. In March."

"So, recently." Gordon sat back in his chair and scribbled something on his pad of paper.

Owen had touched on the nightmare with Gordon before, but they'd mainly been getting acquainted. He was happy they were revisiting it so Bahn could understand better what it's like. "So would you say you were in a high stress situation when you had the nightmare?"

"Somewhat. We had my dad's funeral the week before. Bahn came down for that. We've known each other since we were kids but hadn't seen each other in years. We had an argument and that's why I flew to Oregon. The nightmare happened the night I got there."

"So, why don't you tell us what you remember about the dream."

Sucking in a breath, he stared at the dingy tile, trying to call up the memory. "A couple of my buddies and I were putting together some equipment. I remember Rob made some comment and we were all laughing. It was a normal day. Quiet. I heard a loud pop, and the guy next to me fell into me and took me down. More pops, and I headed for cover carrying the guy. Rowdy was next to me, but he wasn't the one who got hit. Smoke was everywhere. I could see Robbie was still out in the open. I made eye contact, and I knew he was a sitting duck unless we got to him. I could smell the stench of the burn pits, and my stomach turned."

Owen closed his eyes, trying to call up the visual. "I remember making a run with my gun firing, and I heard someone calling my name, but I had to get to Robbie. When I got there, though, it wasn't him. It was an Afghan soldier, and he shot me." Bahn's hand squeezed his, tight. "I kept hearing voices calling my name, but everything was numb. I couldn't move."

"And when you woke?"

"I was sitting up in bed. Bahn was calling my name. She was crying, so I was scared I hurt her."

"He hadn't," Bahn said emphatically. "He hadn't touched me. He was thrashing and jerking, but he never touched me. And then it was like he was in a trance. I was just scared because he wouldn't wake up, and he was screaming and upset."

"Sometimes it can be hard to wake them from the nightmare, especially if they hadn't slept well before."

"Which I hadn't."

Gordon tipped his head. "So, you woke to him screaming?"

"No. I woke up from a loud clap of thunder and lightning. And as I was trying to go back to sleep, he started moaning."

Gordon smiled. "Okay." He leaned forward and put his elbows on his knees and his focus landed on Bahn. "From what I'm hearing there are several factors that could have led to the nightmare. It was a high stress period with the funeral and the trip. He was in a new location, which is another factor. It's hard for service members to trust their surroundings. The enemy was always hiding. He said he hadn't slept well before. That's a huge factor in nightmares and panic attacks.

"But the one thing that I think might have played a major factor in this, is the weather. If he was sleeping well and was in a dream state, and the noise of a thunderclap hit his subconscious, it might have triggered the nightmare. Again, it's hard to know for sure, because it sounds like there are several factors that could have played a part, but you, young lady, aren't one of them."

Owen couldn't help but smile when Bahn's face softened with a wave of relief. He squeezed her hand. "See, I told you."

"Now, Owen, you said you asked her if you hurt her."

"Yeah. I know PTSD can trigger violent nightmares that can cause a person to act out. And..." he took a deep breath and eyed Bahn, wondering if she would be okay with what he was about to share. Heat filled his cheeks.

Like she read his mind, she said, "It's okay. I have a feeling he already knows."

He cleared his throat. "I have never had anyone sleeping with me when I had a nightmare."

"Well, it is true, unfortunately, that partners or spouses have been injured from a person having nightmares."

Owen closed his eyes not wanting to see Bahn's expression. He recalled perfectly the fear in her eyes when he asked if he'd hurt her.

"It can happen to anyone, though, whether they've been in the military or not. It happens more with people who are prone to sleepwalking or sleep talking. They tend to act out their dreams.

Usually, the partner gets kicked or hit with a flailing arm. Very seldom are the injuries serious."

"What about the stories of someone being choked or punched?" Owen questioned.

"Although those cases are out there, they're very rare."

Now it was Owen's turn to feel a wave of relief.

"Do you have anything else you would like to discuss?" Gordon's eyes bounced from Owen to Bahn, but neither spoke. "Okay. Well, I have something I wanted to talk to you about. I'm sure you're wondering why I asked you to come here."

"Yeah."

"This is a training facility primarily used for service dogs."

A lump immediately planted itself in his throat. He'd thought about what it would be like to have a dog. There were several dogs he'd befriended while he was on his tours. His family never had a dog because of their constant moving. The closest they came to a pet was an old cat named Tigger who belonged to one of the neighbors but spent more time at their house. He'd befriended Owen when they lived in Maryland and came by when he saw him outside.

"You think a service dog would help me?" he asked, trying not to let his emotions show.

"I do. From what I've read in your file, I think you'd do well with a service dog. I have one I want you to meet, if you're okay with that?"

"Okay. Yeah."

"Good." Gordon stood. "Sit tight. Let me go get him." He exited the room and Owen let out a loud gust of air.

Bahn unlinked their hands and put her hand on his back and lightly scratched. "You okay?"

"Yeah. I am. Everything is just…" He couldn't even complete the sentence because he couldn't describe how he felt. So many things had happened. Good things. He was truly happy for the first time in a long time, but he was worried that at any moment the other shoe would drop, and shit would go sideways again.

He let his eyes rest on Bahn for a long minute. "I'm really glad you're here."

"Really? Why?"

"It's helped me. These meetings are unnerving. It's hard for me to feel comfortable. And I hope it didn't make you uncomfortable talking about that—"

"Oh, you mean basically telling Gordon we slept together?" She giggled.

"Yeah, that." He could feel his cheeks heating again.

"You're so red right now, you know that?" That mischievous smirk that never failed to make him smile filled her face, then softened. "But no. It didn't bother me. Again, I figured he made that connection early on when you said I was there when you had the nightmare. And I'm glad we discussed it. I hate that you have those terrifying dreams, though. My nightmares usually consist of getting lost somewhere and not being able to find my way out. And I don't dare take any sleeping medication because they give me those dreams where you feel like you're falling."

"Oh, I hate those."

Owen continued to play the night over in his head. The panic and sadness in Bahn's eyes still felt fresh. Gordon's explanation sounded logical, but it didn't make him feel any better about scaring Bahn. And the bad part about it was, it could happen again.

Lost in his thoughts, he barely heard Bahn when she broke the silence. "What do you think about the dog?"

"I've always wanted a dog. We asked for one when we were kids, but every time it seemed like we might be able to get one, we moved."

"Yeah. I've always wanted one too. Can't have one in our condo though."

Gordon came through the door with a shaggy red-haired dog. The dog immediately went to Owen and Bahn and smelled them both before making it around the room, sniffing everything. "This is Max. He was surrendered to the shelter a week ago. The vet believes he's less than a year old. One of Trifecta's points of action is saving and rehabilitating dogs who've been turned over to the shelter."

Max came back to Owen to sniff him some more, and Owen held his hand out. He immediately stepped closer, so Owen rubbed the soft fur on his head.

"He has to stay in quarantine for six weeks to monitor his health, and wait out the allotted time for him to possibly be reconnected with family if he's been lost. But the shelter believes he might have been part of a puppy dump. He was recovered with two other dogs."

"So, is there anything I need to do during that time?"

"They suggest you come to the training facility as often as you can to see if you guys will be a good match. They'll be working with him on commands. Once the quarantine period is up, if you choose to adopt him, you'll both be required to go through training for the service aspect."

"How much does it cost?"

"The adoption and service training classes are taken care of through an organization called Freedom Friends. After training is completed, you'll be responsible for his care. But as a member of the organization, you get discounts on vet fees. And if you buy your food out here, you'll pay a discounted price."

"Wow!" Owen watched Max wandering the room and patted his leg to see if he'd come. He did, and Owen gave him a good head scratch. "Yeah. I'm definitely interested."

"Okay. There's papers you'll need to fill out so Max can be put on hold. That way no one else can claim him unless his actual owners show up."

Owen kneeled and stared into the eyes of the friendly dog as he scratched him under his chin. His fur was so soft, and he could already picture him running around the backyard and playing with him on the beach. Max took that moment to lick his face.

"One question. Do I need to keep the name?"

"No. It's just one they gave him when he was brought in. Do you have something else you want them to call him?"

He swallowed hard "Yeah. Cooper."

"Cooper?" Gordon responded.

"Yeah. For my buddy who didn't make it home."

CHAPTER 42

A fter touring the facility, filling out the necessary paperwork, and spending a little more time with Cooper, Owen and Bahn strolled out to his truck. Bahn was overwhelmed with everything that had occurred, and she couldn't imagine what Owen was feeling. Her heart hurt for him, for what he was currently going through, and what he was forced to deal with from his time in the military. She had been through some tough times in her life, but nothing even came close to what he had to deal with. Thank God he had Gordon.

"Gordon seems pretty cool."

"Yeah. He's much more laid back than my previous therapist."

"Oh?"

"She was way more clinical. Everything was by the book. I didn't even know her first name. Gordon, on the other hand, asked me to call him by his first name at our initial visit. He told me about his military experience, and his failed marriage because of it."

"Aw. That makes me sad. He seems like a nice guy."

"He is. He said he came back a very different person than when he went in, and his wife couldn't handle the change. When he came back from his last tour, PTSD wasn't widely recognized as a disorder, so treatment for it wasn't available. He said he knew something was wrong, but his doctors didn't know what to do with him.

"Finally, one of his commanding officers got him in touch with a psychologist who diagnosed him, and he was the reason he went back to school and got his license."

Bahn reached up and rubbed his shoulder. "I know it can't be easy being that vulnerable."

"I'm just glad I had help when I got home. I can't imagine what Gordon went through. Trust me, I was not in a good place when I came back to the States."

They got in the truck and Owen continued. "I really don't mind my appointments with him. He doesn't treat me like I'm his patient. It's more like talking to a friend. And it helps that he's been through it and come out on the other side. It's still hard to talk about it, but he gets it. He knows what it's like."

"That's great. It's good that you have him there for you. I'm sure it's not easy to find someone you're comfortable with." She knew. She'd never had anyone she was that comfortable with besides Owen and maybe Sarah.

Owen moved his hand and laced his fingers with hers. "It's not. But I'm lucky. I have you now, too."

Bahn couldn't help but smile. "I guess we're both lucky then."

He surprised her by pulling her hand to his lips and kissing her knuckles. And she let him.

Absorbing the comfort, she allowed herself to fall back into the focus of the day. "So, what's next? I've got a couple of thrift stores left to explore. We still need to find you some living room stuff. How's the money holding out?"

"With your shopping expertise, I'm doing pretty well. I was thinking of going back to All The Things, since we really didn't look at their sofas."

"You sure you don't want to check the dumpsters first?"

Chuckling, he said, "As tempting as that sounds, since I'm way ahead of where I thought I'd be at this stage—moneywise, anyway—I want to check out some new stuff."

"Lead the way, then. But let me say, this is the last new item you're allowed to purchase."

"Yes ma'am."

God, why did that sweet boyish tone in his voice make her want to lean over and kiss him? She knew it would just wind up in a broken heart, but he was becoming harder and harder to resist.

When he'd pushed his hand in between hers at the appointment, it calmed her immediately. And it didn't get past her that it was his appointment, and yet, he was comforting her. He could read her so well. She glanced over at him. He was so handsome. So unassuming. And for the first time in a while, he looked relaxed. At home.

Pushing her fears away, she leaned up and placed a chaste kiss on his cheek.

His mouth tipped up in that panty-melting smile. "What was that for?"

"For letting me be a part of your world."

"You've been a part of my world, Bahn, since we were nine, whether you've been there physically with me or not. And you always will be, regardless of what happens in the next couple of days. Just remember that."

He threw the truck into drive, and as they eased onto the road, his words played over in her head. She knew what he said was true. Regardless of what happened in the next couple of days, he would always have her heart. Just like he had when they parted fourteen years earlier. And just like back then, she didn't want to think about what would happen when she left in the next couple of days.

As they drove through town, she noticed how nice it felt just to be with him in the quietness. With everything going on, she still felt relaxed, content even.

Owen eyed her more than once. She wanted so badly to ignore the voices in her head and give in to her heart. To take Sarah's advice and see if their relationship might work. And regardless of how hard she was trying to stay away from him, it seemed her heart kept drawing closer to him with every minute that passed.

"What's going on in that head of yours? You sure you're okay?"

Her eyes shifted to him. "Yeah. I am." *One day at a time.*

They parked at the store, and she gave him her best teacher glare. "Sofa. That's all. Nothing else."

Owen smiled. "Yes ma'am." That was quickly becoming her favorite words from his mouth.

Entering the store, she had to admit, it truly lived up to its name. They wandered back to the furniture, and one piece immediately caught her eye. It was a soft gray sofa with an ottoman. The closer she got, the more she liked it. It was a retro style with a tweed material that had multi-colored specks woven together. She even saw some flecks of purple. Her mind whirled, picturing ways to arrange the room. She turned to find Owen with his arms crossed, staring at the same sofa. "What do you think?"

Owen sat down on the sofa and patted the arms. "I think this is it." He propped his feet on the ottoman, testing it out. "It's comfortable. You should test it out. See what you think."

"It's your stuff. It really doesn't matter what I think."

"Yes, it does."

His tone caught her off guard. If she didn't know better, she'd think she'd made him mad. Not wanting to test that theory, she sat. It really was comfortable, and the material was much softer than she thought it would be. It felt almost velvety. "I really like this."

Off the arm of the sofa, she saw a round, slatted, wooden stool that appeared to be similar in color to the TV console they'd found at the consignment shop earlier. She wondered what else she'd missed in the store the first time they shopped there. She had been so focused on her mission of finding a bed for his guest room, she'd completely bypassed everything else.

Heading back to the front of the store, she snagged a cart and started down the first aisle. Every time she added something, Owen whispered in her ear that he was told he could only purchase the sofa. About the fifth time of having him in her ear, she backhanded his chest, and he flinched then chuckled.

"I rescind my instructions, okay?"

By the time they had loaded the sofa, and everything else she'd found, the bed of the truck was full. Again.

"We better get this back to the house before the rain hits. It's clouding up."

"Oh, you're right. I didn't even notice. It's getting late anyway. I'm getting kind of hungry. What are you craving?"

Owen's mouth twitched, and he chewed on his cheek.

Bahn knew exactly where his mind went. Hers did too, and she couldn't help but push his buttons a little more. Staring out the window, but keeping him in her periphery, she slowly ran her tongue along her bottom lip while her hands rubbed her bare thighs.

His fingers gripped the steering wheel tighter, and he shifted in his seat. When the truck jerked to a stop in the driveway, Owen bailed out, slamming the door behind him. Bahn slowly stepped out of the truck and shut the door, and he was there. He grabbed her wrist and held it tight, practically dragging her behind him as he ran up the steps.

The minute they were inside, he pressed her against the door and captured her mouth. His arms snaked around her waist and held her tight against him. "Tease," he said, smiling against her lips.

She pulled back and winced. "Owen." Her voice came out strained.

Owen leaned his head against hers, his expression suddenly solemn. "Bahn, I understand your reservations. I do. But please, right now, just don't think. Go with your heart. Don't pull away. Remember what you said in Oregon? You told me to do what feels right. This. Feels. Right."

His eyes begged for her just as his words did. This was not the moment to play with his heart. "I was just going to say that the doorknob..." She turned, and his eyes glanced down to see it digging into her back.

Latching onto her wrist again, he pulled her into the bedroom. His hand wrapped around the back of her neck, and his mouth crashed against hers in a fit of desperation. Her little moves to tempt him had unleashed a wild animal, and with every move he made, she realized she would have never been able to deny him. No matter how much she tried to tell herself it was only going to hurt more if she gave into him, she wanted him. She needed him. She was as desperate as he was.

He let his lips drift down her neck as he pushed the straps of her tank top and bra off her shoulders. His hand slid up the back of her top and unhooked her bra. A lazy smile formed on his lips at his victory. Then he ripped everything over her head and his mouth found her nipple. His tongue circled one before his lips closed around it, then he did the same to the other.

Bahn couldn't breathe. Her hands slid beneath his shirts, and her nails dug into his back with every swirl of his tongue. Letting her fingers slide along the waistband of his shorts, she came to the button and worked it undone, along with the zipper.

"Tell me you want this, Bahn. Don't do this just for me."

Her hand slid along the elastic of his boxers, and she gently kissed him. "I want this, Owen." And she did. She'd never felt anything remotely close to their night in Oregon. From the moment he let his inhibitions fall away, she knew nothing would ever be the same. It wasn't just sex, something to satisfy their animalistic need, it was deeper. Every time their eyes connected; it was like he was somehow seeing her from within. And the way he worshiped every inch of her body proved to be a healing balm to her battered soul.

No matter how hard it was going to be to say goodbye to him, she realized she'd rather have him completely for a few days than not have him at all. Because she loved him. Sarah was right…again.

He picked her up and laid her gently on the bed, then yanked her shorts off. And when he placed a condom on his new nightstand as he undressed, Bahn shook her head. "You don't need that."

His head lifted and eyes filled with confusion at her words. "What?"

"I'm on the pill. You don't need it."

Owen stared at her, his question coming slowly. "Are you sure?"

"If you don't feel comfortable, it's—"

"No. Trust me, I'd rather have nothing between us."

"Then don't use it."

His lip caught in his teeth, and she took a deep breath and watched as he moved closer. Starting at her toes, he began brushing kisses to her hot skin. Inch by inch, he made his way up her body, and with every touch of his lips, he drew her in more and more. She bucked her hips when his mouth caressed her inner thigh. His eyes lifted to hers, and he gave her a crooked smile.

His hot breath hit her stomach followed by the tips of his fingers grazing along her ribs, and she could feel prickles erupt. A whimper escaped, and she lifted her knees on either side of him as her hands glided down his back. His thumb brushed against her nipple, and he blew on the other, bringing it to a peak before his mouth covered it.

She shuddered and breathed, "Owen."

Lightly biting into the hollow of her neck, he said nothing, just continued to feed on her. Raising up, he licked his lips and gave her another one of his sexy smiles, then brought his mouth to hers, letting his tongue explore.

Her fingers strummed against his muscular back, running along every ridge and valley. She loved the way his skin felt beneath her hands. Moving them lower, she planted her palms against his butt and pressed him into her more.

Letting out a low growl, his hand cupped her chin as his lips trailed down her cheek. When he raised up and their eyes met, she could see the hunger his gaze conveyed. She'd never felt so wanted and desired.

Slowly, he slid into her, and she sucked in a trembling breath as her body melded with his.

His eyes closed as he said, "Mmm, so good," in a low growl.

Giving in to the feel of him filling her, she let her eyes drift shut. He was perfect in every way. She wrapped her legs around him as he took control and began to move. Her fingers continued their ministration against his skin. With every motion, she could feel his muscles contract against her fingers.

Every touch, every kiss was perfectly timed, perfectly placed to bring her closer to her release, like he had every part of her memorized. Her breaths were coming in gasps, and she let out a moan as he moved in and out of her in a slow, languid motion. He was in no hurry.

She threaded her fingers into his hair and tugged. His eyes opened and his body began to tremble as his rhythm increased. She could tell he was close, and she wanted to watch as he found his release.

Sweat glistened on his skin, as his movements became more frenetic, and his fingers gripped her body. "Bahn," he grunted.

Shifting, he plunged deeper into her core, detonating a charge that rocked her body, sending waves of electric pulses firing through her. She let out a guttural cry as her body began to move on its own accord, chasing the waves of pleasure.

Forcing her eyes open, she met his piercing blue eyes, locked on her. His jaw ticked and his lips thinned around his gritted teeth, and with a low, strained groan, his muscles tightened, and his body jerked as he followed her over the edge.

With his body pressed heavy against hers, they rode out their orgasms. She combed her fingers through his now damp hair and brushed her lips to his neck. His breaths were still labored as he raised up and moved off her, delivering a soft kiss to her lips. Thunder rolled and they both jerked their heads to the windows.

"Shit. The furniture."

After throwing their clothes on, they raced out the door. Owen pulled the truck to the front door to make unloading easier. They brought all the smaller items inside, dumping them wherever they could find an empty spot but making sure they had a clear pathway for the sofa. "I felt a drop," Bahn announced as she unloaded a set of folding TV trays.

"We only have a couple of other things before we get to the sofa. Shit. I just felt one too." Owen filled his arms and raced into the house, nearly bumping into Bahn heading back out. "Be there in just a second to help with the sofa and ottoman."

Bahn lifted her side of the sofa as Owen exited the house. He hopped into the back of the truck and picked up his end. They moved in sync, without saying a word, tipping the sofa the same direction to get it through the door. After setting it down, they went back for the ottoman.

Once it was all unloaded, Owen and Bahn dropped onto the new sofa and watched the rain sluice down the window. They beat the storm, barely, and had laughed the entire time they were hauling items from the truck.

Bahn let her eyes roam the room. She was happy with how things were coming together. *I bought more than I thought.* There was still so much to do. TVs to be hung, pieces to be put together, bookcases to be filled, and everything still needed to be put in its place. And there were still some things they needed to find. But she could already see the warmth coming through.

"What next?"

"I say we pick up where we left off before we were so rudely interrupted," Owen said, waggling his brows.

Bahn let out a belly laugh at his expression, then leaned in for a kiss. "I think I've created a monster."

CHAPTER 43

A s Owen's body came to life, something tickled his nose. He went to move his hand and felt the satiny skin that was currently pressed to him. Moving Bahn's curls away from his nose, he inhaled deeply before placing his hand against her toned stomach. She stirred and he kissed her bare shoulder.

Raising up, he checked the clock on the nightstand. Six thirty.

As he settled back against his pillow, he longed to continue what they'd been doing late into the night, but he knew Bahn liked her sleep. He didn't want to disturb her right now. Maybe later though. A smile tugged at his lips. It had definitely been a nice way to end the day. Now more than ever, he was sure what he had planned would work.

He slid out of bed and kicked something hard on the floor. Pain shot up his leg, and he groaned. Who knew what it was. Things were scattered everywhere. He took deep breaths as he held his foot, trying to will the pain away. It would have been a good idea to get things put away, but at the time, they had better things to do.

Limping into the bathroom, he shut the door and turned the light on. Wincing from the glare, he stood in front of the mirror, trying to remember why he was there. Oh, yeah, to change clothes... that he forgot to grab.

Shutting the light off, he shuffled back into the bedroom and retrieved some running shorts and socks from a basket of clothes.

After starting the coffee maker, he slipped on his sneakers, shoved his phone and keys in his pocket, stepped out on the porch, and quietly shut the door. He never liked running as a kid, but after years of military training, he'd learned how to mentally push past the pain. Now, running was his way to decompress and think through his problems.

He took his normal path down to the beach and breathed deep the salty ocean air as he hit the sand. His mind played through the last few weeks. The pain that seemed so overwhelming had subsided, and as he stared at the practically empty beach, he was surprised at how content he felt.

For the first time in a long while, he found it hard to come up with anything that was troubling him. Life was good. Bahn had set aside her reservations about their relationship and dove in, and he couldn't be happier. He knew it might be short lived, but he would take what he could get for now and deal with the fallout later. They had two days, and he didn't plan to waste them worrying about how things might or might not work out.

He turned the corner, and the familiar apartment complex came into view. He wondered what treasures they would be able to rescue. It was still dark out, but a well-placed streetlight gave him just enough light to see what others had thrown out. He slowed his pace and jogged into the disposal area.

By the dumpster, where he found his chairs and painting, he noticed a few more pieces that might make it to his house. *She must still be cleaning out his stuff.* He started chuckling at the fact that he had created this whole scenario around the furniture he'd found, ever more amused that he kind of felt sorry for this imaginary dude losing all his stuff. He had some high-quality items, in perfect condition. It was definitely worth saving from the dump.

Once Bahn was awake, they could put on their grubbies and start collecting their treasures. A quick scan of the rest of the dumpsters suggested they'd be spending several hours combing through everything. It would be fun. He chuckled again realizing he would have never thought dumpster diving would be fun when he was a kid. Oh, how Bahn Jackson had opened his eyes to an entirely different world than he lived in.

The heat of the day had already settled in, and he could almost feel the steam pouring off him as he glanced up to see his house coming into view. A cold shower would feel good. Maybe he could talk Bahn into joining him.

His thoughts revisited their night together, and his heart fluttered. No matter how many hours they spent exploring each other's bodies, he couldn't get enough of her and knew that would never change. He would never get enough of how her satiny skin felt, or the flavor of her, or how sweetly she sounded when she came apart.

His heart pinched with the fleeting thought that she might choose to return to being friends at the end of their days together. And he would have to honor it. But that wasn't what he wanted, and he was fairly sure that wasn't what she wanted either.

Bounding up the steps, he pushed open the door and the smell of coffee still lingered in the air. The house was quiet, but when he peeked into his bedroom, Bahn wasn't there. He checked out the back door to see if she was sitting on the porch, but it was also empty. A cup sat next to the coffee pot with a sip of coffee left. Where was she?

"Bahn?"

He checked back in his bathroom, then the guest bath. As he came out, he heard a noise and continued down the hallway. When he opened the door to his old bedroom, every bit of air escaped his lungs.

In a pair of black spandex shorts and a matching sports bra, Bahn stood with her back to him. Her body covered in droplets of sweat, a free weight in each hand, she dropped down to one knee.

The corner of his mouth tucked in when her head started bobbing and she started to sing the lyrics to a popular song, missing many of the words. He leaned against the door jam and smiled as a few more memories flooded in. She'd never been a strong singer. Taking in the scene, he picturing what their life could be like. He wanted every bit of it.

As she dropped the weights, she startled, finally noticing him. "Geez, you scared the daylights out of me," she said, gasping for breath and yanking her earbuds from her ears. "How long have you been standing there?"

"Long enough to hear your rendition of Swifty's "I Knew You Were Trouble.""

"I was singing it about you."

Owen's mouth dropped open. "I'm not trouble," he protested playfully.

Her hand pushed against his bare chest. "Oh, you are lots of trouble."

Latching his hand around her wrist, he yanked her to him. "Trouble you can't get enough of." He smiled and brushed his lips against hers. "Want to get a shower with me?"

She whimpered. "See. Trouble."

"Is that a yes?"

"As much as I'd love to say yes, I think I'm just going to rinse off since we're dumpster diving."

"Oh. Good point. And speaking of which, I went by the apartments on my run." He chuckled. "It looks like she's still throwing his stuff out."

"What'd you find?"

"I didn't look too closely, but there were two barrel-shaped chairs that looked pretty cool."

"Okay. We'll go get cleaned up and then head over there.

"Did you get something to eat for breakfast?"

"Oh, right. Breakfast. No. I'm good with some toast though."

"Go get cleaned up. I'll make us some toast then run through the shower."

She gave him a thumbs up and started to move past him, but he snagged the strap of her sports bra and dragged her into a heated kiss. When she backed away, she licked her lips. He searched for any hesitation in her eyes, but there was none. Good.

Bahn reached around Owen, who was slathering a spoonful of strawberry jelly on the toast and stole a slice. "You about ready?" she asked, munching on her toast.

Owen turned to see Bahn dressed in her torn-up overalls with one side unhooked, and a V-neck T-shirt underneath. Her hair was a mess of curls on top of her head. She was positively edible.

"We aren't on a schedule. Sit. Eat."

"But we might miss out on the good stuff."

"Nah. Doubt that. It doesn't look like anyone has picked up on our little treasure secret. Some of the stuff I saw earlier is still there."

"Still," she whined, tilting her head and giving him her best puppy dog eyes.

Owen laughed. She was irresistible when she was excited. He wrapped his arms around her and leaned against the counter.

"The dumpsters are stuffed full, and it's going to take us some time to go through them. We might wind up missing lunch. So, eat. And anyway, I was wondering if you wanted to visit the thrift stores you had on your list first, before we get dirty."

"No. We can see what else we need after we get everything organized then hit those places."

"Okay. If you're sure." He motioned for her to eat.

She lifted her slice in front of him and took a bite. "I am," she argued around a mouthful of toast. "But this is finger food. I can take it with me."

"Fine. I have a feeling arguing with you about this is futile. Let me run through the shower or you aren't going to want to be in the same county with me, and then we can go."

CHAPTER 44

B acking into the area with the dumpsters, Owen couldn't stop smiling. Bahn was vibrating with excitement. Her bright white grin was plastered on her face, and it had been there since she climbed into the truck. When he finally put the truck in park, she made a quick exit, leaving him in her dust. He killed the engine and got out to find her already inspecting the red, faux leather chairs he told her about.

"Oh my gosh. They would be perfect in the game room. They even swivel."

"Oh, I didn't even notice that."

After loading the chairs, Bahn took one side of the dumpsters and Owen took the other, just as they had when they were kids. He still wasn't as excited about digging through them as Bahn. "I can't believe people throw this stuff out. Can you imagine how many houses could be furnished?"

"I know. Most of it will wind up in the dump." She turned to him and squinted her eyes. "Do you think—"

"We aren't going to the dump, Bahn. Get that out of your head right now."

She laughed as she made her way to the next dumpster, pushing away what looked like some old curtains, then squealed, "Look at this."

Owen strolled over to see what she'd found. A three-tiered glass, wood, and metal TV console was pushed against one of the dumpsters.

"This would work in the game room. It's not exactly what I was picturing, but I think it would fit." She put her hand on the top shelf and pushed it back and forth. "It seems pretty sturdy. Your TV would hang above it, and if you get a sound system, the tall speakers can go on either side. Games would go in the cabinet, controllers and systems on the shelves… What do you think?"

"Yeah. I think that would look cool."

After moving the console to the back of the truck, they continued to pick through the discarded items. Owen climbed on a step stool they brought and peered into the dumpster where they found the chairs. "Hey, I got something." Lifting the rolled-up item out of the dumpster, he laid it on the ground. "This thing is brand new. It still has the tag on it."

Bahn helped him unroll it. "Hell yeah!" The large rug was purple with a multicolored tornado-type swirl down the middle of it. "This is perfect for the game room."

Behind another dumpster was a large, round piece of blue tinted glass, and that was all Bahn needed to take a header into the dumpster. After digging under three garbage bags, Owen heard a loud echoey 'yes.' He stepped on the step stool and saw Bahn trying to drag a chunk of wood to the side.

"You're going to have to come down here and help me. It's heavy."

He climbed down in the container and quickly realized Bahn was not wrong. The base for the glass was solid. Owen had no idea how they were going to get it out of the dumpster, but he knew Bahn would figure it out. And she did.

After loading the coffee table and a few other small items, Owen raised the tailgate. "I wonder if I should strap it all down. I bet dad has some cables in the truck somewhere."

Bahn's face lit up, and she held up one finger, asking him for a minute. She jogged off and disappeared over the side of one of the dumpsters. Within minutes, she returned with several strands of string.

"Where did you get that?"

"The venetian blinds in the dumpster."

Owen couldn't hold back the bark of laughter.

When everything was unloaded, Owen glanced around the room, then his eyes moved to Bahn. "Okay. Do your thing." He motioned to the piles of stuff currently crowding the living room. "Tell me what you need me to do."

Bahn giggled and stood, inspecting her surroundings, then moved to each room not saying a word. Owen could practically see the wheels turning in her head. Finally, she pointed to the rug they'd found. Owen hoisted it over his shoulder and carried it up the hallway.

Piece by piece, the clutter in the living room disappeared and each room was slowly transformed. Pictures covered the walls. Books filled the bookcases. Knickknacks decorated the shelves.

Owen's phone chimed. "Hello?"

"Hey sweetheart. How's everything going?"

"Hey, Mom. We're nearly done. The washer and dryer should be delivered today. And I think we've found just about everything we need. The place looks amazing. Bahn has definitely worked her magic."

"Well, since you guys have been so busy, I thought maybe I could treat you to lunch tomorrow."

"Why don't you come over for lunch. I'll grill some steaks, and you can see the place. You won't believe it."

"Are you sure? You guys must be exhausted. I thought about stopping by today, but I didn't want to interrupt."

"We haven't been home long. We went dumpster diving."

"You didn't."

"We sure did. And we found some great stuff."

Hearing his mom's laugh through the phone made him smile.

"You guys and your treasure hunts."

"Just like old times." The thought of their treasure hunts made his smile spread into a full grin. "So, what about coming by around noon tomorrow? Would that work?"

"That sounds perfect. Do I need to bring anything?"

"No. I think we have everything we need." He walked out the

back door onto the patio. "And, Mom," he peered back through the window at Bahn, who was still shifting things around. "Don't say anything about the treehouse stuff. I'm going to surprise Bahn. Okay?"

"Gotcha. My lips are sealed."

"Love you, Mom."

"Love you too, sweetheart."

He disconnected the call and gazed out at the treehouse then back through the window to Bahn. Wiping his hand across his mouth, he thought about the past, then let his mind move to the present, and then to what the future could hold. It was time for him to decide. His hands started shaking and his heart felt like it was going to jump right out of his chest as he stepped back into the house.

"Hey. I invited Mom for lunch tomorrow so she can see the place. I need to go pick up some steaks and stuff to grill."

"Okay." Bahn turned. "Let me get my shoes."

"You're busy doing your thing, I don't want to drag you away. And, anyway, I need you to stay here in case they drop off the washer and dryer."

Bahn's brows dipped. "Are you sure?"

"Yeah. You're in the zone, don't want to distract you."

She ate up the distance between them and wrapped her arms around him. "I don't know if I've told you but thank you for letting me do this. I have had so much fun."

"I think you have that backward. I should be thanking you. I can't imagine what this place would look like if I tried to decorate it."

She smirked then dropped a light kiss to his lips. "You sure you don't want me to go with you?"

Owen tried to school his face into a blasé expression so she wouldn't get suspicious. "Nah. I'm just going to pick up a few things from the store, and I might drop by the training facility to check on Cooper."

Bahn stared at him for a long moment. "Are you okay? You seem kind of quiet since you talked to your mom."

Of course, she would see right through him. "I'm fine. It just hit me when I invited mom to come over, that we're almost done."

Bahn pinched her lips together, and he could see the sadness shadow her pretty face. "Yeah."

"Don't. Don't go there. We've got one more day. Let's enjoy it."

He picked up his keys. "I'll be back. You continue to play."

He brushed a kiss across her rose-colored lips and quickly left. It was time to set his plan in motion.

He slid his phone from his pocket as he opened the door to his truck. "Hey, Mom. Sorry, one last thing. Do you have the number for the Jacksons?"

CHAPTER 45

━━━━━━━━━━◆━━━━━━━━━

Bahn couldn't focus. She stood in the middle of Owen's bedroom, her eyes glued to the rumpled sheets where they'd spent a sleepless night making love. For the first time in her life, she felt whole. She felt accepted as the person she truly was. Owen had ravished her body over and over again, unable to get enough, unwilling to let one moment be wasted. She knew the feeling well, because she knew their time together would end soon.

Owen's expression as he said 'we're almost done' stabbed at her heart. She knew what he meant, but she couldn't help but wonder if *they* were almost done. Would she see him after she went back to Oregon? Would they stay in contact with each other? Or would they wind up getting caught up in their jobs and drift apart, not speaking for another fourteen years.

Her memories flipped back to that day at the airport. She could still remember the sadness in his eyes. Still feel how tightly he'd held her. Still hear the pain in his voice. And she could still remember how much she'd cried for him in the days that had followed. And she knew it was about to happen all over again.

How on earth had her world been flipped upside down so quickly. The past two days had awakened something within her that she hadn't felt in a long time. She felt so alive and excited. She'd been forced to give it up back then when her family moved. This time it was her decision, but there was a mountain of obstacles in the way, and she didn't know how to get past them.

She'd accepted her life, grown comfortable with it even, but the past few weeks had shown her how she'd lost herself within it trying to please others. And that only made her sadder that she was going to be returning to it. The only good thing she could find about it now was getting to mentor the young girls and hanging out with Sarah. But with the way Sarah's relationship had been going recently, she'd spent more time alone than with her, and she'd probably be gone soon also. Just the thought of what might be in store for her had Bahn sucking in a jagged breath as tears welled in her eyes.

She never considered that seeing what it would be like to have her dreams come true would be so painful. Realizing it was a fleeting moment in time, and not something she would be able to sustain in real life, sent a feeling of dread through her.

Memories of the past couple of days flooded her mind as the tears spilled down her cheeks and the pain exploded in her chest. It was so unfair. Sitting on the edge of the bed, she let her world cave in, and she slowly fell back, feeling crushed by the realization of what she was going to be left with.

Owen had said not to think about it, but now, with the day looming, that was all she could think about. They were going to be thousands of miles apart. She wanted him. Needed him. She loved him. She always had. And the cruel truth was, she couldn't have him. He was ripped away from her once before and all she'd been left with were their memories together. And as much as she wanted to try the long-distance thing, she couldn't reconcile the idea that if it didn't work out, she would lose him forever. She would much rather have an occasional phone call or silly text message from her 'friend' than not hear from him ever again.

As hard as it was going to be, she needed to steel herself for her impending departure. But she would never forget these past few days, because she knew they would be counted as some of the best days of her life.

Brushing the tears from her cheeks, she sat up, taking in the room again. Grabbing the dusting rag, she wiped down the new furniture then filled Owen's new chest with the clothes he had folded in the basket in his closet. The last thing she did was make the bed. Tugging the comforter up, she choked back a sob picturing the two of them, arms and legs entwined. She draped the teal-colored blanket on the end, smoothing it with her hand. When she was done, she took one last look at the room, flipped the light off, and shut the door.

After getting everything in its place and chit-chatting with the appliance delivery guys once they'd installed Owen's washer and dryer, she poured herself some tea. Glancing at the clock on the oven, she wondered where Owen was. He'd been gone for almost three hours. She shot off a text to make sure he was okay, but figured he just lost track of time playing with Cooper.

Since the weather had cooled from the rain the previous day, she decided to sit out on the porch and wait for him. Setting her tea down on the colorful mosaic top of the table they found, she dropped onto one of the brightly colored metal chairs next to it and stared out at the dark green grass and the massive trees that wrapped around the treehouse. This really was a nice place. She could picture kids playing in the treehouse, only they wouldn't be theirs. A lump lodged in her throat.

Memories of them in the treehouse flashed through her thoughts, each one a testament of how lucky she was to have had such a great childhood and such a great friend in Owen. She finally rose from her chair and trekked across the yard, keeping the treehouse in her sight. Needing to see it one last time. Feel its walls wrap around her. Hear the laughter that it held in the wood.

As her foot hit the first rung, the memory of seeing Owen for the first time after so many years came to mind. The tears in his eyes nearly ripped her heart from her chest.

"Bahn!" Owen called from the porch.

Her head jerked in his direction.

"What are you doing?"

Seeing him standing there with his hands in his pockets, and that sexy smirk on his face, she dropped her foot from the rung and ran back to him. "I finished everything, and I thought I would sit out on the porch since it's such a nice day, and the treehouse started calling to me."

"It kind of does that, doesn't it?"

"God. I have so many memories."

"Great memories." Owen wrapped his arms over her shoulders in a hug. "Maybe we can go later, but right now, I need your help. I kind of went nuts at the grocery store."

"I was kind of getting worried. You were gone for quite a while. The appliance guys dropped off your washer and dryer."

"Oh good. I'm sorry I made you worry. I went out to check on Cooper and got to talking to one of the trainers. And then, like I said, I kind of bought out the store."

"It's okay. I figured you were hanging out with Cooper."

"He remembered me. Came right up to me."

"That's great." She was happy for him but a bit jealous that Cooper was going to get to live his life with Owen and not her.

"Well, lead the way, captain. Those groceries aren't going to unload themselves."

CHAPTER 46

It was everything she could do to keep the tears at bay. This was going to be their last real day to spend together. Tomorrow would be spent driving to Gulfport and flying back to her real life. This trip would be remembered in the photos she'd taken, tucked away in one of her albums. But it was so much more than that.

Last night they'd made love, then held each other while they fell asleep. But sleep had eluded Bahn. She wanted so much to wake with the morning sun and have a solution to the distance that separated them. But it never came.

The tightness in her chest, and the thought of the flight home had her near panic. The more she thought about it, the more she didn't want to go. But she had to. She'd already signed her teaching contract.

She tried to act as normal as possible, but the dark cloud looming made it difficult.

Owen seemed to be trying to make the best of it. He kept telling her how much he loved what she'd done, walking from room to room with a big goofy grin on his face.

She'd felt like they needed to talk about her leaving and tried to bring it up a couple of times, but Owen kept changing the subject. Like he didn't want to face what was about to happen. It bugged her, but she didn't want to get into an argument before his mom showed up.

The doorbell rang and Owen chuckled. "I have a doorbell."

He jogged to the door and hugged his mom as she stepped inside. Her eyes widened and her mouth fell open. "Oh my gosh, this place looks like something out of a magazine."

"Right? Bahn has skills."

"It wasn't all me. You found stuff too."

"Yeah, but you put it all together to make it look like this."

"You wouldn't have time to do mine before you leave, would you?" Carissa asked playfully.

Bahn wished Carissa was being serious and she had more time to spend living out her dream. But she didn't. "Unfortunately, probably not since we'll be heading out first thing in the morning."

"Well, maybe next time."

The words hit Bahn right in the chest. And she wondered when the next time would be.

"Give me a minute to turn the steaks and I can give you the full tour."

As Owen headed out the door, Carissa turned to Bahn. "I've never seen Owen so happy. I can't tell you how much I appreciate you coming for Phillip's funeral, and I know it meant the world to Owen. And just so you know, I'm serious. I want you to come back and decorate my place."

"I would love to, but once school starts, I'm not going to have a lot of time on my hands between teaching and coaching. I have no idea when I'll be able to make it back."

"That's not a problem. It's going to be a while before I can let go of Phillip's stuff. But please let me know when you are coming back for a visit."

"I will."

Owen returned and escorted his mom through the house while Bahn worked on the sides for the steaks in the kitchen. She'd set the table with the new dishes they'd found at the thrift store that morning, made a pitcher of tea, and just removed the apple cobbler they'd made—with the ten pounds of apples Owen got on sale—from the oven, when Carissa and Owen returned to the kitchen.

"I'm truly in awe, Bahn. This place is absolutely stunning."

"Thank you. But again, Owen had a big hand in it. He knows

what he likes and wasn't scared to tell me. Although there were a few times I had to override him."

"There were a few times I won," Owen scoffed playfully.

Bahn tried to set aside the pain and live in the moment. Owen was so happy, so she tried to play off his feelings. "You did. And we have those things hidden well."

Owen narrowed his eyes and swatted her on the butt with his oven mitt as he passed. "I've got to go get the steaks. Are we ready?"

"Yep."

"What can I help with?" Carissa asked, coming up beside Bahn.

"The table is all set, so pick your spot and start loading your plate."

Owen brought the steaks in, and after everyone got what they wanted, they sat down at the table and settled into a comfortable afternoon of conversation. Bahn talked about the conference she'd attended and what was planned for the year. Owen discussed his plans to patent the project his dad had started, and he was working on, and then sell it to the military.

After the apple cobbler was served—a la mode, of course—Carissa pitched in to help clean. "I just can't get over how amazing this place looks." She stood in the living room continuing to take everything in, then picked up her purse.

Owen draped his arm over Carissa's shoulder. "You don't have to rush off, do you?"

"Actually, I made plans to play cards with a group of ladies this evening. But thank you so much for inviting me to come see your new place. And Bahn, I meant what I said. When you come back, you have to help me decorate my place."

Bahn pasted on a smile. "I promise. I will."

Carissa wrapped her arms around her and gave her a squeeze. "Please come back soon."

"She will, Mom," Owen reassured her.

Bahn stiffened at his words as Carissa released her. Inside she was hanging on by a thread, and she knew it was about to snap.

When his mom drove away, Bahn couldn't take it anymore. "Why did you say that to her?" She could already feel the tears starting to pool on her lashes.

"Say what?"

"That I would be back soon. I have no idea when I'm going to be able to come back."

"I was just making conversation, Bahn." He reached out his arms, but she stepped away. She needed the distance so she could start putting the walls up. Their time was over. Everything was done. She needed to start facing reality, and so did Owen.

"But you're letting her assume I'm coming back."

"Well, I'm hoping you will. You want to, right?"

"Yes, but as much as I would love to, I don't have the time or money to fly across the country. I told you that when I got here. We've been living this fairytale life for the past three days, but it's coming to an end, and I have to face the fact that I have to get on that plane tomorrow and go back to the life I left. And you need to face that fact too."

"Bahn." He took a step toward her and ran his finger along the side of her face, moving a wayward curl away, then wrapped his arms around her. "I think if it's meant to be, we'll figure something out."

She wanted to stay in his embrace. It felt like home. But she pushed away. "There isn't anything to figure out, Owen. You live here. I live there. We're twenty-five hundred miles away from each other. Don't you get that? And I'm broke. More than broke. I was only able to come this time because it was on the school's dime."

"But once I get the patent for this project, I'll have some money. I can fly you in."

"And how long will that take?"

"I don't know."

"If it's anything like copyrights, it's not a quick process. It can take years."

"It doesn't matter."

"But it does. Don't you see. Neither of us have money right now."

Owen crossed his arms over his chest and the smile that had resided on his face nearly the entire day was gone. "Is that all it is, Bahn? The money? Or is there another reason?"

"What do you mean?"

"I just need to know why you're so quick to write us off. It's like you have no faith in us lasting if we did try to make this work, so you don't want to even try. Every time I try to come up with a solution, you're quick to shoot it down. Are you trying to find an excuse to end what we have because you really don't want to be with me?" Owen's jaw pulsed and Bahn could see the storm brewing in his eyes. "Am I not enough for you?"

Bahn's stomach dropped. In the blink of an eye, the timid little boy had reappeared in front of her. "What? Owen, no. I've loved being here, and I would stay here with you if I could. But I can't. My life is in Oregon."

"Okay then," he said in an even tone. His eyes shone with tears of resolve and something she couldn't quite read. It sucked the air out of her.

He chewed on his lip, then said quietly, "But before we have to go back to our lives, I have one last surprise I want to give you."

Bahn's brow raised in confusion. "What is it?"

A tiny hint of a smile returned. "Did you not hear me? I said it was a surprise."

She could tell he was trying his best to put up a strong front. His boyish grin was making a comeback, and she had to admit, it was lightening her mood.

"You aren't going to make me wear a blindfold, are you?"

"No. No blindfold. Stay here for five minutes, then come out to the treehouse."

"The treehouse?" Now she was curious and confused. "What did you do to it?"

"You'll see." He waggled his eyebrows and donned a Cheshire cat grin, then turned and took off in a jog through the backyard, and she watched as he crawled into the treehouse.

CHAPTER 47

◆

All the memories clouded her brain at once as she stared out through the backyard. A light suddenly shone through the seams around the closed windows.

What is he doing out there?

She stuck to his instructions, and the second the five minutes were up, she began her trek across the yard. As she reached the ladder, she hollered, "Are you ready?"

"Yeah. Come on up."

With each rung she climbed, her pulse sped up with anticipation. When she finally reached the top, she pushed open the door. Flipping it back with the rug, she pulled herself up as a wave of déjà vu hit her. Her breath instantly caught in her throat as she took in her surroundings and was transported back in time.

Tears filled her eyes. The treehouse was almost identical to what she remembered when she was a kid. The mural was hung in the same spot, as well as the flamingo pictures. The table and chairs were in the same place, and the bulletin board was filled with their photos. The plastic plant and the wicker basket were back in their original place, and the Christmas lights were draped just as they were before.

Covering her mouth with a trembling hand, she looked around and smiled, tears streaming down her face. "How? Where did you find—"

Her eyes landed on Owen, who was kicked back in a bright red bean bag.

"Dad kept it all. Mom found it in the back of the shed."

She smiled as she choked out, "That's not the same bean bag."

"No." He patted the bag. "The other one died. The fridge is new, too."

She continued to take it all in. "The rug even looks good."

"I spent an entire weekend cleaning it. Everything needed a good scrubbing."

She leaned in and looked at all the photos. "How did you get these? I thought I took them when I left?"

"You did. I asked Sarah if I could borrow the album," he said as he held it up.

She crossed her arms and continued to study the photos as she wiped away more tears.

"Bahn, I know tonight is our last night, and I understand your reservations. I have heard everything you've said, and trust me, I thought about the fact that maybe we're just wanting to relive our past. I mean look at those photos. We had an awesome childhood. At least the time we were together. No one went on the number of adventures we did. And I also considered the fact that maybe we were just caught up in the moment. That our emotions were high because of being reunited. But that's—"

Bahn let out a sob. "Owen, maybe I'm a coward, but I don't think I can handle not having you in my life again. I'm so scared that something will happen if we try to do the long-distance thing. That we'll become frustrated, and it will ultimately drive us apart. And I just—"

"Will you hang on a second? Let me finish."

Taking her eyes off the photos, she let them rest on Owen, not quite sure where he was going with his comment. But hearing the demand in his voice, she nodded.

"I was going to say, I think the emotion of us being reunited, and us trying to relive our past, were only part of what brought us together. I think there was something we didn't understand when we were younger. And because of that, I've added something new to the treasures in the treehouse."

Bahn darted her eyes around and began to search the area, but nothing seemed different. When she looked back at Owen, he was holding a treasure chest in his hands. When he held it out for her, she hesitantly took it, then met his eyes. He nodded and she opened the box.

Photo after photo of them from their recent times together, along with the seashells, glass, and items from their treasure hunt filled the wooden box. Tears she thought she'd gained control of began to fall again, but she didn't say a word.

"The inscription on the top says, 'Your Love is a Treasure.' It was on a bookmark in my dad's Bible marking a verse that said, 'She is more precious than rubies. Nothing you desire can compare to her.'"

Bahn stared at him, trying to understand what he was saying. "Owen, I…,"

"When I was about to leave to go to Oregon, my mom told me, 'Sometimes you know something is right from the very beginning.' She said we were 'kindred spirits.' And the more I thought about it, the more I knew she was right. Bahn, you coming into my life a month ago really just confirmed something I didn't quite understand fourteen years ago. I'm pretty sure I loved you the day you walked away from me at the airport, and I never stopped. I just didn't understand it. It took seeing you again to realize what it was, and I really don't want you to leave me again."

Bahn knew he was right because she'd felt it too, but it still didn't change the fact that they lived so far away from each other. It only made the heartbreak worse. "But what about—"

"I know you said you went through all of the scenarios for a long-distance relationship and came up with nothing. But I think you forgot about one."

She looked at him, still not understanding what he was alluding to. She was sure she had thought of everything, but her body broke out in goosebumps with the possibility that they had a chance.

"Hand me the treasure chest." He took it and leaned forward, rolling off the bean bag onto one knee, and began to play with it. "Now most people don't know that treasure chests usually have hidden compartments. This one is no exception."

He pushed a button on the back and a small drawer lined with red velvet popped out. A beautiful princess cut ruby and diamond ring sat in the middle of it. She stared at it, not sure she was believing what she was seeing.

Her hands began to shake, and it spread throughout her body. She lifted her head to see Owen grinning from ear to ear. "Bahn, you're the most amazing person I have ever met. You're smart, funny, drop-dead gorgeous, and maybe a little bit of a drama queen, but that's okay. I think I can handle it. God, Bahn, my life is so much better with you in it. I am a different person when I'm around you. A better person. A person I like because you make me feel strong and brave. And because of that, I want to ask you something."

He took the ring from the secret compartment and pinched it between his fingers. "Siobahn Jackson, will you marry me?"

A gasp escaped, and she fell to her knees as her hand covered her mouth. Her eyes searched his. Was he serious? Was this really happening? Every reservation, every scenario she'd conjured up, swarmed her thoughts, but his voice rang through it all repeating his words. 'I'm pretty sure I loved you the day you walked away from me at the airport. And I never stopped.'

She wanted to answer, but nothing came out, so she resorted to nodding her head and held out her hand.

"I'm taking that as, yes?"

She nodded again, and he pushed the ring onto her finger. Perfect fit.

She held her hand up, admiring the beautiful ring. The ruby sat flush with a ring of diamonds that extended down the band. So unique. So, her.

"Holy shit, Owen," she finally said, her voice barely audible through the sobs.

He looked into her eyes and smirked. "So. We're getting married?"

She leaned forward to hug his neck and it pushed him off balance, tumbling them both onto the bean bag.

"Yes," she choked out between laughter and a few happy sobs.

Wedging herself next to him, she held up the ring, tilting it back and forth, watching it sparkle, then turned to him. "I love you so much. I have wanted to say that for so long, but I couldn't. Acknowledging it would have made leaving you hurt worse."

She began kissing him all over his face and then down his neck, finally laying her head on his chest. "So how long have you been planning this?"

He looked down at her. "Well, honestly, I knew I had to figure something out when I left the school parking lot."

She giggled. "Me, too."

"Then I met this lady named Bernice while I was waiting on my flight to Dallas. She asked if I was married, and it made me think about what I wanted. And I just knew. Then, when Mom found all the stuff in the shed, a plan started coming together."

"If you had been planning on proposing this whole time, why didn't you when I told you we couldn't do the long-distance relationship?"

"I had planned to, but you threw me off when you said you wanted to just be friends. I needed to make sure you felt as sure as I did about what we have before I popped the question. And I honestly wasn't, until yesterday. I called your parents on the way to the grocery store and asked if it would be okay."

"And what'd they say?"

"I think they knew we were meant to be together. They were excited."

"I was wondering what took you so long to get the groceries."

"Sorry, I had a lot to do. I talked to your parents, and once they gave me their blessing, I went by the jewelers to see if they still had the ring I wanted. I panicked because it wasn't in the display case where I found it. But they'd set it back for me. I guess they knew we were meant to be together too. Then I went to visit Cooper. And after that, I went to get groceries."

Bahn took in a deep breath trying to wrap her head around what was happening, then realized there was still the looming problem. "Okay. But what do I do now? I mean, I'm supposed to fly home tomorrow."

"Actually, I've been thinking about that."

"Shocker."

"What if I fly home with you? We can pack your stuff. You can resign from your job, and we can drive back?"

"That would be great, but I already signed my contract. If I break the contract, they might withhold my license, and possibly even charge me a penalty."

"And what if they do?"

"I might not be able to get another job."

"Teaching," he said with a hint of sarcasm in his voice.

"What are you getting at?"

"Is that what you really want to do?"

Her brain was so overwhelmed with everything that was happening, she had to repeat his question. "Is that what I want to do?"

"Yeah. You don't *have* to teach. You don't even have to work if you don't want to."

And she was back to having to repeat what he said, but this time in her head. *I don't have to teach.* She mulled that over and couldn't keep the smile from curling the corners of her mouth.

"But wait. What about your job? You just started. They aren't going to let you just leave."

"I've been training for the past two weeks. When I got the house, I talked to them about getting moved in and asked for these two weeks off before I officially started the job."

"But what if I'd said no?"

"Then I guess I would just start my job early. I don't know. I didn't really think about that."

"You were that sure?"

"No. Again, it hit me hard when you said you thought we should just be friends. But there was one thing I was sure of, and that was that I loved you and that was all that mattered. I was hoping you felt the same way and that I could change your mind about being friends."

"But, if I'm not teaching, what am I supposed to do once I get here?"

"How about starting your business? I mean, you already have my mom on the hook. And she has friends who I'm sure, once they see your work, will want to use your expertise also. Oh, and don't forget the other job you're going to have to start working on."

She flipped her hair and gave him a confused look. "What's that?"

He looked at her and nodded at the ring, then lifted her hand for a kiss. "Our wedding?"

A grin crossed her face again, and he smiled. She knew he could see the wheels already turning in her head.

She leaned in and began kissing his face all over and then down his neck. He pulled her down on top of him and she ran her hands under his shirt. His body stiffened under her touch, and she knew she would never get enough of that response; like he was fighting to control himself. Her mouth found his, and she kissed him slowly, hoping to convey that she was finally his forever.

The kiss quickly became feverish, and she backed away breathless. Her eyes met his and a smirk passed across his face before he bit his lip and lifted one brow as he growled, "Ever had sex in a treehouse?"

EPILOGUE

O wen stood on the beach, the music softly playing mixing with the sounds of the surf washing ashore behind him. The wind lightly whipped the sheer watercolor material attached to the pergola Owen stood next to, catching his attention for a moment. Greenery and flowers, along with fairy lights mixed in with the material, gave a serene effect to the scene.

A hand clasped his shoulder, and a voice rang in his ear. "You ready?"

"I've been waiting for this for years," Owen pitched back to Rowdy, his friend from his military days who'd come in from Colorado to be his best man. His brother Beau had also made the trip to stand with him. Cooper sat dutifully at Owen's feet with his tongue lolling out of the side of his mouth. Owen leaned down and rubbed his head just to settle his nerves a bit.

Looking back at the rocks that wrapped around the secluded beach, Owen was still amazed at what Bahn had accomplished. White curtains were draped on stands along the rocks. Waitstaff dressed in beach attire stood behind tables holding covered serving dishes.

Round tables, covered in pastel cloth and decorated with flowers, dotted the sand and were surrounded by wooden chairs. More sheer water colored fabric was strategically tied to certain chairs and draped with flowers, making a beautiful pathway to the pergola.

Guests were told to dress in casual beach attire, the setting classy but also comfortable.

In the months since she'd moved down, Bahn had stayed busy. Owen was right. Once his mom put the word out, Bahn had more work than she could handle, and she was in the process of putting together a business plan. She'd also been asked to help coach the youth basketball league, which she'd quickly accepted.

They'd had to push off their wedding a couple of times just because she couldn't fit it into her schedule. But May was the perfect month for their wedding. It was the month they met all those years ago, and it was the month they were reunited.

The music swelled and their guests stood, just as a pair of curtains in the back parted. There she was, on the arm of her dad. Her bright beautiful smile rivaled the sun's glow. And she took his breath away.

Her dress was simple—white with wide straps of lace wrapping a satin bodice that draped loosely at her breast. The gown hugged her body just enough that when she moved up the aisle, he could make out her form beneath it, and he had to close his eyes for a moment just to compose himself. The closer she got, the bigger her smile grew. And so did his, even though his eyes were filling with tears.

Suddenly, scenes were flashing through his mind of all the moments they'd spent together as kids, stopping on the day they were reunited. He thought about his dad and wished he could have been there to see this happy moment. He looked at the woman he was marrying walking toward him and remembered the moment she appeared in the treehouse. The moment he was at his lowest. The moment…he said a prayer. A prayer for better days. And he couldn't help but laugh.

ABOUT THE AUTHOR

DeDe Ramey is a multi-award-winning author. Her vivid imagination and love for people watching gave her a passion to write romance novels filled with swoon worthy heroes, smart, sassy heroines, unexpected nail-biting suspense and a good helping of steamy, heart melting romance.

Growing up in the beautiful historic town of Georgetown, Texas, her crazy life experiences with family and friends helped develop her rich colorful imagination.

She is mom to two grown kids and Nina to one grandson.

When she is not reading or writing, she enjoys going to concerts, exploring the national forests and parks, or search for adventures in new cities with her husband Keith, her very own hero of over forty years.

FIND HER
https://linktr.ee/dederameybooks

www.ingramcontent.com/pod-product-compliance
Lightning Source LLC
Chambersburg PA
CBHW070544260626
47161CB00002B/498